BACK ROADS

This Large Print Book carries the
Seal of Approval of N.A.V.H.

BACK ROADS

SUSAN CRANDALL

WHEELER
PUBLISHING

Published in 2003 by arrangement with Warner Books, Inc.

Wheeler Large Print Hardcover.

The text of this Large Print edition is unabridged.
Other aspects of the book may vary from the original edition.

Set in 16 pt. Plantin by Myrna S. Raven.

Printed in the United States on permanent paper.

Library of Congress Cataloging-in-Publication Data

Crandall, Susan.
 Back roads / Susan Crandall.
  p. cm.
  ISBN 1-58724-560-4 (lg. print : hc : alk. paper)
  1. Policewomen — Fiction. 2. Sheriffs — Fiction.
 3. Indiana — Fiction. 4. Large type books. I. Title.
 PS3603.R375B33 2003
 813'.6—dc22   2003062128

For Bill, my partner in all things.

As the Founder/CEO of NAVH, the only national health agency solely devoted to those who, although not totally blind, have an eye disease which could lead to serious visual impairment, I am pleased to recognize Thorndike Press* as one of the leading publishers in the large print field.

Founded in 1954 in San Francisco to prepare large print textbooks for partially seeing children, NAVH became the pioneer and standard setting agency in the preparation of large type.

Today, those publishers who meet our standards carry the prestigious "Seal of Approval" indicating high quality large print. We are delighted that Thorndike Press is one of the publishers whose titles meet these standards. We are also pleased to recognize the significant contribution Thorndike Press is making in this important and growing field.

Lorraine H. Marchi, L.H.D.
Founder/CEO
NAVH

* Thorndike Press encompasses the following imprints: Thorndike, Wheeler, Walker and Large Pr int Press.

Acknowledgments

Although writing is a solitary endeavor, it isn't done alone. I owe much to many. First of all, thanks to my sister, Sally Hoffman, for setting my feet on this path initially. Thanks to my mother, Marge Zinn, for her unflagging faith.

My critique partners, each in their own unique way, have helped shape this book into its final form. I have the most fabulous critiquers a writer could ever wish for, the ladies of WITTS (Women Inspired to Tell Stories): Garthia Anderson, Vicky Harden, Brenda Hiatt, Esther Hodges, Pam Jones, Alicia Rasley, Laurie Sparks and Betty Ward, and my on-line critique partner, Karen White.

I'd also like to thank police Chief and ex-county sheriff, Dick Russell, for his time and patience in answering all of my logistic and procedural questions regarding sheriffs' departments in Indiana. Also, my appreciation goes to the boys at Randall and Roberts for insight on how a sheriff can be removed from office, and to firefighter Craig Orum for his description of battling wildfires.

I am forever grateful for the guidance and support of my editor, Karen Kosztolnyik, and the enthusiasm and backing of Beth de Guzman at Warner Books. And a huge thank-you to my agent, Linda Kruger; I'd probably still be spinning my wheels if not for you.

Prologue

If you stand in one place long enough, your shadow will move on without you. As the sun and moon arc overhead, the dark silhouette of your body slips silently across the ground, anchored only by the soles of your feet. Leigh Mitchell had seen herself thus, standing stock-still on the courthouse square of the southern Indiana town where she'd been born, as her shadow, and her life, slid slowly and unremarkably by.

She'd been county sheriff for two years, elected against all odds, she felt, because of her brother's lifelong popularity in their community. Not that she wasn't qualified; she was. But there was a certain pecking order in law enforcement. She'd bucked the system and won. Still, the tedium of drunken teenagers, games of mailbox baseball, speed traps, and old man Grissom's constant calls about UFOs hovering over his corn field were wearing unbearably thin.

Her thirtieth birthday had settled on the horizon, hunched like a stone gargoyle, dismally staring her in the face. In everything around her she saw the quiet accusation: you are wasting time. A sense of near panic took root in her belly as the blossoms of spring gave way to the rustling green leaves of summer. By the Fourth of July, the fruit of that seed sent tendrils of dread squeezing her windpipe.

Her restlessness occasionally threatened to take over her good sense entirely. But it was nearly autumn before she gave in to it, driven by the certainty that if her life didn't change, she'd end up as withered and dusty as the parched ground under her feet.

Still, had she known the crosswinds from that malcontented summer were going to blow in the fall from hell, she'd have gladly remained dusty and boring.

Chapter 1

The diesel cloud enveloped Will as the truck driver pulled away from the intersection. He stood on the side of a dark two-lane highway with all of his earthly possessions crammed into a road-worn backpack, deciding which direction to take. Heart warred with head, his good sense telling him not to venture down this road. It had been paved with good times on his previous visit; why take a chance on ruining it? But he'd been pulled across the miles by the innocent and secure memories engraved during the one carefree summer of his youth. How he longed for the simple comfort of familiar surroundings, of childhood dreams yet to be born, and to be, even for the briefest time, away from the ugliness that stained his adult world.

The shroud of exhaust cleared, and there before him was the sign: GLENS CROSSING 4 MI. Will looked at the red taillights of the truck receding into the night, then in the direction of the town.

He'd just walk a little closer, camp nearby, then decide in the morning. Tonight, painful thoughts of his current situation made it far too easy to crawl back into the past. The darkness had a way of distorting both past and present, making them more hideous and more marvelous than they actually were. In the light, he could see things more clearly — the horror of the last months less pronounced, the delights of the one wonderful summer less remarkable.

He walked a good part of the way toward the town. His aching feet told him he'd covered over two miles, when it caught his eye. There, across the wide open expanse of a bean field, rose the lighted spokes of a Ferris wheel. A harvest moon, so large and low in the sky that it appeared to be painted on the black of night, sat on the horizon, seemingly side by side with the carnival ride. A filmy haze sent three gray fingers across the enormous golden disk. One of those fingers appeared crooked and beckoning.

Well, hell. A sign? The hairs on the back of his neck prickled and rose as the skin at the base of his skull tightened. Had he been thirty minutes later, that moon would have been up in the sky where it belonged, away from the thin clouds, the inviting golden light brightened to cold blue-white.

Instead of being calmed by the thought of divine intervention, he sighed heavily with the weight of too many miles, too many memories. He closed his eyes briefly and told himself, once again, to wait.

Tomorrow. A word which had for the past four months become his mantra.

He glanced around, looking for a good place to bed down for the night, and heard the steady thrum of a sub-woofer pounding ever nearer. A

12

long minute passed before he saw the head-lights of the car.

It sped past him, the reverberation from the speakers battering him in the chest. He watched it pass, wondering how the hearing of the car's occupant could ever recover. Immediately, the brake lights brightened and the car slowed. The driver slammed it into reverse before the tires stopped rolling forward, adding a squeal to the bass and the smell of burnt rubber to the air.

The car stopped in front of him, nearly rolling over his toes. The tinted window came down and a girl in her late teens leaned across the passenger seat. For a moment his heart skipped a beat. If he didn't know she was dead, he'd have sworn he was looking at his sister, Jenny — same shoulder-length brown hair, same tilt to the green eyes.

Then the girl smiled and the eerie similarity disappeared, the smile too wide, the lips too full.

"Need a ride?"

He started to tell her no, when she added, "I'm just going to the carnival, but I can give you a lift that far."

The carnival. The Ferris wheel. Well, damn, he didn't have to be hit over the head to get the picture. He was *destined* to walk the streets of Glens Crossing once again.

A peculiar sense of security radiated from the

garish lights that flashed against the pitch black sky. Blue, red and green bare bulbs, strung like gypsy baubles, broke the darkness overhead, washing out the stars. Leigh Mitchell watched the brightly lit spokes of the Ferris wheel revolve, feeling once again that life in Henderson County hadn't changed much since she was five years old.

This year the dust puffed a bit higher underfoot and the flat, dry odor of dead grass was stronger because of the drought. But the carnival, as most every other social landmark, remained essentially unaltered from season to season, year to year, decade to decade. It was the last fling of summer; the boisterous, colorful boundary between seasons. Trampled grass beneath her tennis shoes, the tempting aroma of grilling sausage and green peppers, sticky cotton candy on smiling cherub faces, hard-won stuffed animals wrapped in teenagers' arms — all the same as last year, and the year before, and the year before that.

Glens Crossing was a town where respectable widows remained widows. Where your lot was pretty much cast when your birth certificate registered the north or south side of the tracks that bisected town. Where expectations were strong and habitually met. Here, your secrets were never your own.

She guessed that, in a nutshell, could be pegged as the crux of her discontent. Her place in this town had been carved long before adulthood. She'd been "the Mitchell girl" — the responsible one, the one who had to grow up early because her parents were gone, the one teachers could count on to follow the rules and go above and beyond in the classroom, the one adults smiled at when passing on the street, the one invisible to her classmates. No one ever looked her way when mischief had been done — wouldn't even consider the possibility that Leigh Mitchell had strayed outside the realm of good behavior.

Nothing had changed in the past twenty-three years.

A pack of giggling teenage girls bumped her as they hurried by, calling a quick and insincere apology over their shoulders. Leigh shook her head to rid herself of maudlin thoughts and moved on through the crowd.

She nodded as she passed Mr. Grissom of local UFO fame. Beside him, his tiny, mouse-like wife clutched a bag of saltwater taffy close to her bosom, as if she feared someone would wrench it from her grasp. The woman spent so much time isolated on their farm, pinned under her spouse's heavy thumb that she hardly seemed capable of human interaction. On the rare occasions that Leigh had seen and spoken to her, Mrs. Grissom's tongue had been quickly shackled by a stern look from her husband.

Mr. Grissom tipped his hat to Leigh, while his wife lowered her eyes and tightened her grip on the taffy.

It was time to inspect the perimeters. Although Leigh was off-duty and the carnival actually fell into the city police's jurisdiction, she felt a sense of obligation to serve and protect. Besides, there were only six full-time officers on the local force. She always helped out where she could.

The darkness edged close to the back of the vendors' trailers and the rides. Not much real mischief likely around here, but Leigh's perimeter walks had probably saved more than one set of parents from being made grandparents before their time. She grinned at the memory of embarrassed faces and muttered explanations. Even though she rarely wore a uniform, opting for a sheriff's department knit shirt and a non-regulation .38 in a fanny holster when on duty, the kids all knew who she was. Tonight she was weaponless.

A whooping alarm sounded at the duck shoot. Youthful voices rose in a cheer as the hawker hailed another winner. In spite of his jovial announcement, the man didn't look the least bit pleased to hand over a huge Pink Panther to the marksman.

Leigh neared the end of the midway and stopped in her tracks. Standing in the dim lighting at the entrance to the semi-trailer that served as a traveling Tunnel of Love, Brittany Wilson was talking to a man Leigh didn't recognize. She slowly worked her way in their direction.

Brittany was a constant source of gossip and speculation — the town's wild child. She was the daughter of Leigh's brother's partner, and a spirit much too lively to be contained by their rural community. Leigh admired such vivacity, so unlike her own plodding responsibility. Even though most of the girl's escapades had so far been harmless (forking yards, sliding down the dam, swimming in the quarry, toilet papering the courthouse square), Leigh took extra care to watch over her, just in case her adventurous nature took her down a path of no return.

Leigh strolled closer, keeping an ear open for some indication of their conversation. Before she could get close enough to hear, Brittany turned and saw her. The girl waved Leigh closer.

"Hey, Leigh." Brittany turned her gaze back to the stranger. "This is . . ." She giggled. "What did you say your name was again?"

"Will Scott." The man stepped forward and extended his hand to Leigh. A wedge of bright light from the ride entrance crossed his face. His smile was relaxed, but a restlessness played about his eyes. Eyes of the brightest blue shot a bolt of lightning straight to her core. It was a reaction totally visceral, immediate and intense. She hadn't been this overcome by pure sexual temptation since Bobby Thompson in the seventh grade. Man, that kid took her breath away. Of course, she reminded herself, that didn't work out too well. Bobby never even knew she existed.

"Leigh Mitchell." She liked the feel of his handshake, firm and dry, not loose and floppy like so many men when they shake hands with a female.

A crowd of teenagers called to Brittany. The girl didn't hesitate to abandon them. "Gotta go! See you around, Will."

"Thanks for the ride," he called after her.

Leigh tucked her chin and eyed the man from under drawn brows. "Ride?"

"Brittany saw me hoofing it down the road and gave me a ride into town."

Leigh muttered, "I'm going to kill that girl."

He grinned. "I gave her the standard 'never pick up hitchhikers' lecture, but it was a little lame coming from someone taking advantage. But" — he nearly looked ashamed — "I really was grateful for the lift." He raised a foot out in front of him. "New shoes. Blisters." Then he added, as if he were trying to pull the girl from hot water, "She did promise never to do it again."

"I'll bet."

Brittany lived several miles outside of Glens Crossing, in a house nestled on a hundred acres of ravined woodland. She had to travel four country roads and the main highway every time she came into town. The girl couldn't resist strays — familiar or foreign, canine or human.

Leigh looked at Will more closely. He didn't appear to be a homeless vagrant. His hair and clothes were neat and clean. An engaging intelligence showed in his features and his diction spoke of a decent education. Yet, there was something that said "bad boy" about him. Deep down, Leigh had always wanted to have a fling with a bad boy. "Visiting someone in Glens Crossing?"

He shook his head, but didn't offer more. He looked down the length of the midway.

"Just passing through, then?"

He shrugged and answered in a distracted tone, "Probably."

She continued to study him, allowing herself to assess him more fully. She prided herself on nailing a person's true nature on something just short of first sight. It was a gift that she'd fostered, knowing that in her line of work quick assessment could keep a dicey situation from going completely bad.

Will's gaze was fastened on the Ferris wheel, a childlike gleam in his eye. He appeared totally relaxed, not at all like a person with ulterior motives or something to hide.

Just as she started to excuse herself, he said, in a nostalgic tone, "I saw the lights of the Ferris wheel from the highway. I couldn't resist. It's been such a long time. . . ." Then he looked her in the eye. "Ride with me?"

"Well, I really have —"

"Please."

There was such boyishness in his smile, such spark in his eyes she couldn't refuse. After all, she was off-duty. *Let it go.* It was time to do something she wanted to do, simply because she wanted to do it. And, she realized as she looked at him, she did want to spend more time with Will Scott. The mere thought of passing the evening with a total stranger, especially one this attractive, seemed to be the first step in the right direction to break out of her mold — something that a truly cautious and responsible Leigh just wouldn't do.

She decided then and there, this year it was just too bad for those parents whose teenagers were swept away on a tide of hormones. Every morning for the past week as she looked into the mirror she had recited: *I am not responsible for every action of every person I know.* She was still trying to make herself live the pledge.

"Okay." The very utterance of the word was liberating. Good-bye old Leigh, hello new.

He took her hand — the contact of an excited child to a parent, not man to woman — and moved so quickly she stumbled along behind. Of course, she had to overcome her initial reaction and *allow* herself to be dragged — all part of being New Leigh.

Steve Clyde, one of her deputies, and his wife passed by. His lingering surprised look as he said good evening tickled Leigh right to her toes. *Maybe I'm not so predictable, huh fella?*

Being an independent woman — there was only so much reinventing a person could do in one night — she stepped up to the ticket booth

20

first and purchased her own ticket. Behind her, Will protested that since she sacrificed her time to go with him, he intended to pay.

She just smiled. There was nothing sacrificial about her decision. In fact, it was rather selfish. She liked him; he piqued her curiosity. Although he had the look of a bad boy, he openly showed childish joy at a simple small-town carnival — something most men had outgrown, or buried beneath a veneer of masculine indifference. Leigh liked simple things. It was nice to meet someone who could share and understand.

Once at the top of the Ferris wheel's rotation, Leigh gripped the lap bar with one hand and, with gentle movements that wouldn't rock their seat, pointed out the little downtown. It was built around the brick and limestone courthouse whose lighted clock tower stood above all else. As she looked at it, she realized with a pang of regret, that clock tower represented the absolute center of her universe. Suddenly the future rolled out in an endless desert of sameness and that sense of suffocating panic rose once again.

Was she going to be an old woman whose days had to be filled with listening to others recount the excitement of youth, the adventures of life, simply because she hadn't experienced any of her own? The very thought made her shudder.

The wheel started to turn again and they

were slowly lowered below the tree tops. "Where are you from, Will?"

He shrugged, rocking the seat slightly. "Nowhere, really."

"Come on. Everybody's from somewhere. Birthplace, high school, there has to be someplace to anchor you."

"Been on the move so long, I can't remember living in one place long enough to call it home." There was a hint of some emotion in his voice that Leigh couldn't quite put her finger on, intense — yet somehow wistful.

She looked at him and saw a momentary trace of bitterness in his eyes. But he smiled and quickly disguised the emotion. Then he looked away and said, under his breath, "Nope, no home for me."

The seat jolted as the wheel jerked into motion once again. Leigh quickly grabbed the bar with both hands.

He touched her arm. "Okay?"

"Yeah." She looked away, hating to admit weakness. Over the years she'd perfected an image of strong competence. Only her brother Brian saw anything else. "Just not crazy about this ride. Got stuck on one when I was eight. Took an hour for them to get the damned thing started again."

His head jerked around to look fully at her. "Really? Here in Glens Crossing?"

She still didn't meet his gaze, but nodded. "Scared the living daylights out of me."

After a minute he said, with apology in his tone, "You really didn't have to come."

"Gotta do some things that scare you, or you might as well curl up in a closet and wait to die." She didn't elaborate that this was her *new* motto, not the basis of her entire life up to this point.

"Amen to that."

She gave him a sideward glance. "A risk taker, are you?"

"The bane and boon of my existence." He offered a slight smile, but his voice certainly held no hint of amusement. In fact, he sounded a little sad.

They stopped at the bottom and the attendant swung the bar away from their laps. Will stepped out and offered Leigh a hand. He didn't let go when they walked down the midway. It felt like a gesture of friendship, nothing more. It felt — comforting.

"I haven't been to a carnival like this in years," he said. "I think I was eleven the last time . . ."

"And where was — ?"

"Hey, elephant ears!" He pointed to a vending trailer and quickened his pace. "Want one?" Without waiting for an answer he held up two fingers to the concession worker. Then he fished a wad of bills from his pocket and paid the woman.

No wallet?

As he waited for the butter and cinnamon

sugar to be slathered on the huge pastries, Leigh took in his full appearance. At first she'd assumed, with those gas-jet blue eyes, that his longish hair was brown. But now that he was standing in bright light, she saw it was raven black. He was dressed in well-worn jeans, molded over time to the contours of his body. She'd bet those babies still looked like he was in them long after he'd taken them off.

Shame on me, she thought, and jerked her gaze away from his firm little posterior.

He wore a black T-shirt, a battered backpack carelessly slung over one shoulder, and definitely new athletic shoes. Except for the shoes, which should have been scuffed motorcycle boots for this image, he looked like a James Dean movie character; a bad-boy drifter, breaking hearts in every county as he moved aimlessly from place to place. He wasn't devastatingly handsome, yet the strength in his face was commanding. And those eyes . . . intense enough to nail you to the wall with a glance and keep you pinned there, heartbeat hammering in your ears. He moved with unconscious confidence, a man fully content with who he was.

She realized he was speaking. Leigh forcibly cleared her head, hoping she hadn't missed anything important while she was dallying in her lusty thoughts.

"Eat it before it gets cold." He shoved a waxed paper holding the hot elephant ear into her hand and they walked on.

As she took the first bite, she considered the extra miles she'd have to run in the morning. Penance for sins against the body. But the buttery sweetness carried all unpleasant thoughts away and she enjoyed every morsel of it, until the last sticky finger had been licked.

They'd made a complete circuit of the carnival grounds by the time Leigh had finished eating. Their conversation had remained limited to comical observations and common chit-chat, talking of carnivals and small towns. She still could gain no sense of his origins. When he'd refer to a specific location, she'd question if that's where he'd grown up, or gone to school, or some similar leading question. He'd always shake his head and say, no, it was just someplace he'd passed through. He had no accent to give her a hint of where he'd come from. But he did have a very appealing sense of humor. Which quickly made her forget he was a virtual stranger.

"So," Leigh asked, "are you staying in town?"

"Tonight, at least."

"Then where?"

"Why all the questions?" He snapped his fingers and looked sharply at her. "You're the reporter for the local gossip column." The words were delivered with a teasing smile.

"Something like that." Now *she* was being evasive.

"Lived here long?"

"All my life."

"Let's see." He closed his eyes and made a motion with his fingers near his temple, as if summoning great powers of concentration. "Graduated in the top ten percent of your class." He took a veiled peek at her, then closed his eyes again. "I'd say college, in-state of course. Degree in journalism and relentless interrogation." He grinned at the jab, but didn't open his eyes. "Then you came back to work for the local paper. Hmm, let's see, oh, yes, student council. Homecoming queen?"

She laughed as he opened his eyes and focused their powerful beam on her. Her cheeks warmed under his scrutiny. "Hardly. That was my sister-in-law." She didn't tell him he'd hit the nail on the head about everything else — well, except she'd led him to think she worked for the paper.

"Sister-in-law. Married, then?" His gaze flicked to her left hand, as if truly worried. "I didn't see a ring. . . ."

"No, no. Kate is my brother Brian's wife."

"Good." Before she could ask him what he meant by that, he sighed and said, "It must be something to have all of your life concentrated in one spot — past, present, future. The memories have to hover so much closer to the surface." His eyes temporarily seemed to lose focus. "High school . . ." He shook his head, as if to jiggle the memories into their proper place. Then, suddenly, he held up a finger, asking her to wait, and strode off.

She watched him walk away, her interest amplified by every one of his ambiguous answers. Which themselves might go unnoticed by most people, simply because he was so good at delivering them. But Leigh's job was to hear what people *didn't* say, to be accurate in her first assessment of a person's nature. She found Will Scott warm and interesting, yet with a carefully maintained distance. She sensed a soul colored by painful shadows, not stained with malicious and devious character. A challenge to decipher — and Leigh could never resist a challenge.

He returned shortly with a couple of tickets in hand. He took her by the elbow and guided her toward the entrance of the Tunnel of Love.

"I never got to do this with a date in high school," he said as he herded her into line. "Always wanted to."

"Oh, I don't know . . ." Her feet dragged in the direction of the ride.

"I've got the tickets. You wouldn't make me go alone, would you?" Then he eyed her with an air of dramatic suspicion. "Or are you afraid of the dark, too?"

"Of course not! But . . ." An excuse was ready to spill from her mouth when she reminded herself that this reticence to follow her desires was exactly the thing she was beginning to hate most about herself. She bit the refusal back. "I'll go."

As she looked at him standing next to her,

something deep in her belly thrilled at the prospect of being in the dark with him. Forbidden fruit.

So as she climbed into the "boat" next to a man she didn't know, her body hummed with possibilities. The tinny pod clanked along on a chain pulley in three inches of slimy green water.

"Since we're traveling down memory lane," Leigh said, "fulfilling lost wishes, I assume when we're done here, you'll go straight to the basketball shoot and win me one of those big stuffed dogs." She paused and lowered her eyes and her voice. "I always wanted one of those." Her sister-in-law Kate had enough to fill a large room by the time they'd graduated high school. And not all of them had been provided by Brian, Henderson County's star quarterback. Kate had had quite a following. Leigh used to call them her male harem. And she'd had a hard time keeping the envy out of her voice when she did.

Will flashed her a brilliant grin, just as they passed into the tunnel. Then it was black as pitch. That's when it struck her that she sat wrapped in darkness with a stranger, who, for all she knew, could be the new millennium's Jack the Ripper. And although every cell in her being said it wasn't so, she knew her attraction was speaking, no, shouting, over her good sense. Living recklessly might just have a price. Did she really want to pay it?

She reassured herself with a few simple facts. First, she knew how to defend herself. Second, they were in a public place. And lastly, if he were going to attack someone, it would have been Brittany out on a deserted road. Not such a risky situation at all.

He made no move to touch her and she felt a little foolish about her earlier apprehension.

After a few seconds, he said, "I'll see what I can do — about the dog. My aim is better at the duck shoot though."

Smiling, she relaxed fully and enjoyed the ride.

As they floated along, black lights occasionally illuminating hearts and flowers, a bad recording of *Dr. Zhivago*'s "Lara's Theme" reverberating in the confined space, all Leigh could think about was senior year homecoming. By then Brian was away at college and no longer there to strong-arm one of his buddies into taking her to important school functions. He always said the guys were just intimidated by her because she was so smart. What a joke. Once he was gone she reverted to the female equivalent of a nerd. So, in order to keep her mind off the dance she was missing, she'd spent the evening scrubbing Aunt Belinda's floor. Then, of course, there were all the carnivals spent with girlfriends, not dates. To hell with it. She was going to take a leap of faith — not a blind leap, but a leap just the same. The prospect both thrilled and terrified her.

Good.

She absorbed the comforting heat from the man beside her and waved a hand in the air; it flashed in jerky motion in the strobe lights. "Duck shoot, ring toss, basketball — no matter. I just want that damn dog."

Chapter 2

Brittany leaned over the side of the Ferris wheel seat as it crested its rotation. There, down below, she saw Leigh walking beside that hitchhiker dude — looking like they'd hooked up.

No way. Leigh was, like . . . the sheriff.

And Will was totally hot.

She watched closely. It was hard to believe, but the way he put his hand on Leigh's back as they moved through a bunch of people watching the basketball shoot, it sure looked like they were together. Brittany watched with growing curiosity, stiffening as the boy beside her tried to pull her closer.

As if, she thought. Stupid jock. Just because she'd broken up with Jared, every jerk-wad in school seemed to think she was *interested.* Wasn't gonna happen, buddy. She was beyond this high school crap. She scooted away from him and gave him her bitch-queen look, then turned back to watch Leigh.

Oh geez, Leigh was carrying one of those stupid stuffed animals. How lame. She almost felt sorry for her. That had to be why Will was hanging out with her — pity. Couldn't bring himself to dump her when she latched onto him on the midway. Why else would he be with her?

Losing sight of them as her seat dipped below the crowd, it appeared they were leaving the fairgrounds. Man, Brian was gonna love this.

Leigh settled the four-foot-tall mass of fake fur and wadded stuffing into the booth next to her. She had insisted they walk to the Crossing House Tavern, less than a mile away, not wanting to ruin the evening by revealing she wasn't a reporter, but the county sheriff. She'd made her mind up on the way to the bar — opportunity knocked and she was going to answer the door. She really liked this guy and didn't want her daring escapade to be inhibited in any way. A woman with a badge had a way of dousing a man's interest. Tonight she was free. She could do as she pleased, follow her desires, then Will would travel on. An experiment in adventure, so to speak. And since she couldn't take the stuffed animal to her county-owned SUV without the emblem on the door and SHERIFF written in eight-inch letters across the back gate giving her away, the huge pup accompanied them.

Benny Boudreau, owner of the Crossing House, had looked up as she struggled through the door with the stuffed dog. The man had a full head of silver hair, but his heavy eyebrows remained coal black, making them look like a cartoonist had drawn them with a bold marker.

He raised them over narrowed eyes, staring at her as she settled in the well-worn booth opposite Will. She rolled her gaze to the ceiling, put her forefinger on her chin and bounced slightly, as she always did, to remind Benny of the broken spring he kept promising to fix. He shook his head, gave her a slight smile and a single wave, then returned to his inventory sheet.

Leigh was glad he was a soft-spoken man, preferring quiet gossip to boisterous chatter, therefore not inclined to call "Hi, Sheriff" across the room. She had to admit, she'd be disappointed if she ever slid into this booth and the spring failed to poke her in the backside. It was a private, wordless communication be- tween her and Benny — something she would truly miss.

Benny's eyes kept drifting from his paper- work to the booth across the bar. Luckily, or maybe not so luckily, Leigh was so wrapped up in conversation with the guy across from her that she didn't notice.

Wasn't like her to show up with a date. And what was up with that dog?

In his years behind the bar, Benny had seen couples come and go, infatuation overcome in- telligence, love spark wildfires and then die into embers. The way this guy looked at Leigh made Benny's gut tighten. Leigh just wasn't used to guys trying to pick her up. Once or twice she had come in with somebody, but those were lo-

cals. Benny had never laid eyes on this guy —
and that made him even more suspicious.
Somebody passing through might not understand where they drew the line here in Glens
Crossing.

Sure, Leigh was the sheriff and it might
sound stupid to worry. But Henderson County
wasn't like the rest of the world.

Maybe he'd just drop by their table in a bit,
say hi, see what was what.

Leigh was still, and would always be, the
Little Mitchell Girl to Benny — all skinny legs,
bony elbows and wild brown hair. He had
known her all her life and there was just something about her that made him go soft inside —
had since she was a kid. Maybe it was the way
she had always peered at him with serious eyes,
or the fact that she'd moved through life like an
adult since she was seven. After her parents
were killed, he liked to think of himself as a
guardian of sorts. It just seemed somebody
ought to look out for her. Her brother did a
pretty good job of it, but it didn't hurt to have
another pair of eyes and ears tuned to the
goings-on around here.

Yep, that guy she was with would take some
watching. He forced himself to return to the
damn inventory sheet. Pretty soon the place
would be jumpin' and he wouldn't have time to
take a leak, let alone count bottles.

Leigh looked around. The bar was still nearly

34

empty. Too early for the regulars, she guessed, and the dinner crowd must have been drawn to the carnival. She and Will placed their order with a waitress she hadn't seen before, a woman who looked to be into the last stretch of a very long forty years.

Once the waitress left, casting a caustic eye toward the stuffed dog, Leigh petted the animal's head. "What kind of a dog do you think Eliot is?"

"Eliot?"

"He definitely looks like an Eliot to me — you know, like Ness. But I can't tell the breed. What's your guess?"

Will delayed his answer while the waitress clinked two bottles of Bud Light and two frosted mugs between them on the dull black Formica table, then moved on.

"Let's see." He screwed up his face and tilted his head, peering into the plastic eyes of the beast. "I'd say a Great Pugmatian."

Leigh sputtered in her beer. "Pugmatian?"

"He's white with black spots, like a Dalmatian, but has a square face like a prize fighter — a pug face. Pugmatian." He seemed quite satisfied with his decree as he leaned back in the corner of the booth, stretched one leg across the seat and took a long swallow of beer from the bottle, ignoring the glass.

"Pugmatian it is. Do you suppose there's really a breed that looks like this?" She crinkled her nose.

"Nah, looks like a mutant of some sort. Poor bastard." He lifted his beer to the dog in salute, then tipped his head back and drained the bottle.

Leigh watched the muscles of his throat work as he downed the beer, mesmerized by the sheer maleness of it. She realized she was staring when a loud thud drew her attention to the bar. Blinking and flinching at the same time, she turned to look at Benny.

He was eyeing Will speculatively. Was this supposed to be something like a father clearing his throat in disapproval? The flashing of the porch light before the kiss at the end of the date?

The bartender wiped his hands on the white — well, Leigh was sure it had been white at one time, perhaps when she'd been a kindergartner — apron wrapped around his substantial middle. He then locked gazes with Leigh and she had no doubt that he was readying pertinent questions at a rate that would put her desktop computer to shame. She could see the wheels turning, summing up the situation, processing the facts, and sprinkling in a large amount of imagination.

Instead of the town busybody being an old woman with little to occupy her time, that station in Glens Crossing was served by a man with a finger on the true pulse of the community. No bad blood between relatives, no hint of scandal, escaped the eyes and ears of Benny

36

Boudreau. He wasn't malicious about it, he just seemed to feel it his civic duty to keep everyone quietly informed. Perhaps it was a form of self-preservation, since his own wife had taken off and left Benny and their three kids.

What rumors about Leigh and the stranger would circulate by morning? Wouldn't matter. Leigh would slip back into her old safe self and Will would be well on his way to — wherever.

Someone started the jukebox. A sultry tune, with lots of plaintive guitar solos and a faintly Latin beat enveloped the dimly lit bar.

"Dance?"

Leigh turned her startled gaze back to Will. "Are you serious?" There was no dance floor, just a four-by-five space of peeling gold linoleum in front of the jukebox.

He nodded, stood and held out a hand.

Might as well really give Benny something to talk about. Rising, she slipped her hand into his.

Once in front of the jukebox Will stopped and faced her, raising his hands palm out in front of his chest. His gaze held hers as she hesitantly placed her hands palm to palm with his. They lingered that way for a moment, her cool fingers against his warmth, while his eyes seemed to draw her closer. She could no more have stopped the tiny step she took forward than she could have made rain pour from the heavens. His lips parted slightly as he laced his fingers with hers.

Then he began to lead her. Slow, simple steps at first. As she grew accustomed to the rhythm and his movements, he added a few turns. It quickly became obvious he was no hack; the guy really knew how to dance.

The music mixed with the beer; Leigh began to loosen up and let herself flow. Will spun her under his arm, keeping their fingers locked. She found her back molded to his chest, her arms crossed over her front. Their entwined hands rested on her waist. She had no choice but to move her hips with his as he slowly undulated with the music.

His breath brushed her ear and Leigh's temperature started to rise as goosebumps ran down her arms. Her body felt liquid against his. His movements became her own. She closed her eyes and let herself be consumed by her senses: the beat and sway of the music, the heat of him against her back, the scent of fresh air and male that emanated from him, the scratch of his day's stubble when he leaned down and pressed his cheek against hers, the delicious ripple that his closeness stirred deep in her belly.

Suddenly, he took all that away by spinning her around to face him again. The movement took Leigh off guard, or she might have fought to remain where she was, wrapped in a cocoon of pure sensation. But as she found herself staring directly into those commanding blue eyes, she realized the sensuality had just begun.

One of his hands nearly burned through her jeans where it settled on her hip and pulled her against him. She followed, mesmerized, as he took them through the final steps of a Latin dance she didn't know, but would always remember.

The song ended. Neither of them moved out of their dancer's embrace. Leigh could see his pulse, rapid and strong, in his neck. She leaned back slightly and looked into his face.

He smiled, but didn't let her go. That thrill in her belly exploded, sending glittering sparks to the far reaches of her body. Suddenly she wanted to taste those smiling lips. He moved his head slightly in her direction and she moistened her mouth in anticipation. But he didn't kiss her.

After a moment, Leigh searched for the right words, slightly embarrassed that she'd let herself get so carried away. "You dance pretty well for a guy with blistered feet," she finally managed.

"Proper motivation." He said it softly, with much more feeling than the simple words conveyed.

Leigh stepped away from him and drew in a deep breath. "Well . . ." Her hands dangled at her sides, as if they'd lost their purpose when he let her go. She quickly tucked one of them into her jeans pocket. "Thanks for the sacrifice."

He didn't move. "Anytime."

She went back to their table and slid in next to Eliot, noticing a trace of censure in his shoe-button eyes.

"Mind your own business," she muttered.

On his way to the booth, Will signaled the waitress for another round. The woman stood near the bar, slack-mouthed after watching them dance. Leigh thought she looked as if she'd just witnessed an exotic tribal ritual, captivating, yet completely unfamiliar to her culture. Leigh felt her cheeks warm a degree further when she realized that just about summed up her own feelings. She'd never experienced anything quite so erotic in her life, although Will hadn't even touched her in any way that could be construed as sexual. For a moment, she almost believed she was beautiful.

With feral hunger in her eyes, the waitress stared at Will until he slid into the booth across from Leigh.

Leigh glanced around the room. There were two women seated at the bar with similar looks on their faces.

"Well," she said, "seems you've made quite an impression."

He looked around, confusion on his face. "I hope I didn't embarrass you."

She could hardly believe it; he appeared to be totally unaware of the animal magnetism he radiated and its effect on all females within a hundred yards.

The waitress dropped off the beers. Completely ignoring the fact that Leigh was even present, she handed Will a folded scrap of paper, flipped her hip as she turned, and left, casting a suggestive smile over her shoulder.

He rolled the note up and dropped it into his empty beer bottle without reading it. He then lifted his fresh beer to Leigh and glanced at Eliot. "To remedying missed opportunities."

"Tunnels of Love and stuffed dogs." She clinked her mug against the neck of his bottle and they both drank. When Leigh set down her mug she was tempted to shake that paper out of the empty bottle and see what it said. She had a pretty good idea. It gave her a small sense of womanly victory to know that he hadn't bothered to read it.

"Where did you learn to dance like that?" she asked.

"Spent some time in Miami, the Keys, south of the border. It was too hot to do much more than dance and drink beer."

Leigh wondered how anyone could dance like that in the heat. She was near fainting from her own internal fires by the time the song had finished.

"What did you do down there?"

He concentrated on wiping down the condensation on his beer bottle with his thumb and index finger. "This and that. I'm not much of a career man."

Leigh studied him for a moment. He lifted his clear gaze to hers. She could detect no sign of duplicity. "So, where are you headed?"

"Nowhere" — he lifted a shoulder, a rueful look on his face — "everywhere. Let's just say I'm on a journey of self-discovery."

"That's pretty ambiguous."

"But true. I'm seeing the country, work enough to eat and rent a bed, then move on. I wouldn't have stopped here if it hadn't been for that Ferris wheel."

"So, you're going tomorrow?" Her intelligence fought against her emotions. She wanted the answer to be yes, then no, then yes again, then . . . Oh, hell. She closed her eyes and demanded a halt to the mental argument. What she wanted didn't matter one bit.

"Can't let the grass grow . . ." His eyes held a distant light for a moment, then he seemed to snap back. "Want to dance again?"

Leigh chuckled dryly. "Don't think my reputation would stand it." She pointed to the string of people coming in the door. The bar was filling up. She put ten dollars on the table and stood. "I'd better get going."

He pushed the money back toward her. "My treat."

"Hoosier hospitality." She left the money on the table. "We don't let our guests pay." Picking up the stuffed dog, she headed toward the door with a grin on her face.

Then she added under her breath, "And, believe me, the treat was all mine."

As the door of the bar closed behind her,

42

Leigh thought with disgust, some wild adventure. She really had cut loose — two beers and a dance. Hold the presses! Sheriff Mitchell nearly had a spontaneous experience.

Well, so much for New Leigh.

Stopping in mid-step, she almost turned around and went back inside.

Almost.

Benny had been ready to vault over the bar and grab that guy dancing with Leigh by his long black hair and toss him out on his ass. It looked damned near like they were going to do it right there in front of the jukebox. This was a decent establishment, for Chrissake. Just when he'd shaken off his shock enough to move, the song ended and they returned to their booth.

If that guy slid in on Leigh's side, that was going to be it. He was going to have to do something.

Relief and disappointment fought for the front seat as they took the same seats they'd vacated — across from one another, Leigh next to that big stuffed mutt.

Well, if she looked like she was walking out of here with him, Benny'd just have to think of a way to stop her. No way was he going to let Leigh disappear into the night with Don Juan there. Brian would want him to do something.

When the moment finally came, Benny didn't have to invent a distraction. Leigh picked up the stuffed animal and walked out the door by herself.

His shoulders relaxed slightly. Good. At least she hadn't lost her senses entirely.

Will smiled and leaned back in the booth. He knew Leigh hadn't intended for him to hear her last comment. As he'd watched her wrestle that ridiculous dog out the bar-room door, he had to disagree; the pleasure had been his. There was something so fresh, so honest about Leigh Mitchell, and yet, so, so — reserved. Not his usual type at all — the party girl, one who wore her emotions lightly, one who never asked for more than today.

Leigh's quiet personality screamed in contradiction to her long, lean, sensual looks. Full lips. Whiskey-colored eyes. And that wild, curly hair around her shoulders. Oh, she'd liked the dance all right. But he sensed her turmoil. He knew the moment her resistant feet stepped across her normal boundaries and *allowed* herself to like it.

The irony of her choice of names for that dog struck him. Eliot Ness. Could she have sensed his true reason for staying on the move? Nah, that was ridiculous.

However, he did almost give himself away in that instant on the Ferris wheel, when she had mentioned she'd been stuck for an hour as a child. His own memory of that night had come crashing back so furiously he didn't have time to raise his guard. He could hardly believe he'd come this close to full circle.

That had been an incredible hour for him, perched like a bird on a wire, looking down at the lights, the people, the town, with the stars in the sky seemingly within reach. He'd never experienced such freedom. He also remembered the little girl with the curly ponytail that sat in the seat directly in front of him. She'd spent the entire time trying to calm the frightened younger child riding with her, pointing out the sights, making light of the situation. Who could have told that all of her bravado had been feigned, that she'd been so shaken that twenty years later she still didn't want to ride a Ferris wheel?

Would she remember him? That would certainly complicate things. Surely not. Their two seats had been at the top, hers slightly lower than his. He'd spent plenty of time studying her, but couldn't recall her turning around and looking at him.

He shook his head and returned to his beer. He'd made a huge mistake, breaking the rules he'd set for himself when he'd hit the road. He never should have indulged in that dance. His survival depended on remaining inconspicuous, a wallflower, a nondescript face in the crowd — in a word, beige. He knew better than to attract ttention like that. Jesus, the look on the waitss's face told him he'd gone too far. And the tender had looked ready to rip his heart out.

But as he recalled the passion burning in Leigh's eyes and thought of the feel of her body pressed against his, he was anything but sorry.

Little matter. Tomorrow morning he'd move on, unnoticed and unattached. The town might buzz for a few hours about the dirty little dance the newspaper lady had with the stranger in the bar, but soon other things would take precedence. He would be forgotten. But, the question chimed in his mind, could he forget? How long could he continue leaving everything behind the minute he began to feel the slightest hint of attachment? That feeling had come astoundingly quick here in Glens Crossing.

Yet, tomorrow this town would be just another shadow in his murky past. One more fragment added to the amorphous life he'd created.

Today he'd been reckless, self-indulgent. He couldn't afford to be so again.

Chapter 3

It was a long walk back to Leigh's Blazer at the fairgrounds. A walk filled with temptation to turn around, retrace her steps and spend the rest of the night talking to, and dancing with, Will Scott. She'd forgotten how it felt to be treated like an attractive woman — not the sheriff. It felt good. Really good.

Her inquisitive mind nagged, demanding she unearth the missing pieces of the puzzling man who'd made her smolder with a simple dance. But it was more than animal instincts, more than sexual attraction, even though he had sent plenty of hormones ricocheting around in her body. She *liked* him — too much. Feeling this strongly made her very uncomfortable — totally against her plan.

So she resisted. Decidedly, baby steps were the path for her. Tonight marked the beginning of her new outlook on life. She hadn't been as daring as she'd hoped, but it was a start. Maybe reinventing oneself took a little warm-up. Maybe she'd be like the software companies and New Leigh would go through several updates and revisions. Today was New Leigh version 1.0, the slightly bold, yet not-off-the-wall Leigh.

With a chuckle, she strapped the stuffed dog

— her new symbol of delayed adolescence — in the passenger seat, then headed home. She glanced at the dog's plastic eyes staring dully at the road ahead. Maybe she'd start a collection. Who knew, by the time she reached forty she might have numbers to rival Kate's. For some childish reason, that thought brought warm satisfaction rising in her chest.

Flipping on the radio, vaguely hoping for a tune similar to the one she and Will had danced to, she discovered it was time for the news. She listened with half an ear as the newscaster announced that the trial of the leader of a major South American drug cartel had been slated for late next month. Somewhere in the mix of reliving her evening at the carnival and the sultry dance replaying in her memory, she thanked God that her quiet neck of the woods remained largely untouched by the rampant drug problem troubling most of the world. Sure there was the occasional marijuana find. For the most part it wasn't the kids but their parents who were the culprits. The teen population of Henderson County thrived in the shadow of a bygone era. She only hoped they wouldn't be overwhelmed when they ventured out into the real world of college life.

She settled back in her seat, warmed by the closeness and safety of her surroundings. Maybe she was a fool for her earlier discontent.

Approaching the bridge near the Crossing House Tavern where she'd left Will, a flash of light down on the creek bank caught her eye. She slowed and looked more carefully.

Probably just a night fisherman.

But the light didn't travel downstream to where the water deepened enough to fish. It remained stationary, there where the water was ankle deep at best. The drought had severely limited the fishing holes in Henderson County. The ones that remained, outside of the reservoir, were usually so crowded with anglers no one could catch much of anything.

She backed up and parked on the side of the road. Grabbing her flashlight from the glove box, she chided herself for being so anal. There were a million innocent reasons for someone to be down there. Why couldn't she just let the logical explanation suffice? Why was she driven to delve into each and every question that crossed her path in a day?

She left her light off and made her way down to the creek as silently as she could. There was a fairly well-worn path, so her footfalls didn't create much noise. She'd just take a peek, assure herself everything was aboveboard, then slink back to her car. No reason to embarrass herself and disturb whoever was down here.

As she got closer, she saw a flashlight propped on a rock, but no one around. A pair of sneakers with socks stuffed inside sat near the water. Stopping, she listened and peered intently into the darkness near the light. Still, no one —

The force that landed on her back knocked the wind out of her and drove her facedown on the ground. Her chin hit hard, slamming her teeth together with a loud *clack*. Stunned and gasping for air, she could do no more than dig her fingers into the dirt and wait for her brain to regain control of lung and limb. The body on her back was large, solid. Silent.

Her arms were wrenched behind her and the man flipped her over, still straddling her hips. She didn't even see the knife blade before he pressed it to her neck.

Wide-eyed, she continued to wheeze laboriously, certain she'd asphyxiate before the knife could do the job.

Hair fell over her attacker's face, obscuring his identity. He had effectively pinned her to the ground, his knees keeping her arms useless under her back. He didn't even seem to be breathing hard from the exertion.

She waited, vision blurring as her eyes watered. What next? Rape? Murder?

"Jesus Christ! What the hell are you doing here?" Still on top of her, Will Scott straightened and pushed the hair out of his eyes. Then he sheathed the knife under his belt.

He lifted himself off her and sat on his knees. She rolled to her side, lungs still heaving to draw in a full breath.

As her desperate struggle for air diminished, she finally became aware of other parts of her body once again. One of Will's hands rested on the back of her neck, the other rubbed the small of her back.

"That's it," he said, "relax and breathe."

When she could draw an unobstructed breath, she rolled onto her back and blinked her eyes until the stars winking through the trees were no longer blurred.

Will leaned over her, blocking her view of the heavens. His eyes caught the light of the creek-side flashlight; they outshone any star she'd ever seen. "Why are you following me?"

She slowly scooted to a sitting position. "I wasn't following you!" Her rasping croak made him cringe, then he seemed to become more agitated.

"What are you doing here then? Night fishing?"

She didn't like his acerbic tone. "No." She coughed. "I saw a light —"

"You traipse around alone in the woods investigating every light you see? You could get into some serious trouble."

"Here, in Glens Crossing?" She had to chuckle, which set off a burning in her lungs again. Even the law enforcers in Henderson County were in little danger of more than an angry diatribe from pissed-off parents who were sure *their* offspring would never do whatever they'd been caught red-handed doing.

"Now you sound like Brittany," he said, with something bordering on animosity. "The place you think safest usually harbors the greatest danger. You folks should take that to heart around here."

One of Leigh's college professors had drilled the same point home. Most crimes happened when and where people felt there was no threat, places where victims made themselves easy pickings. Maybe she had been lulled by their sleepy little community as much as Brittany. But she could never admit that to Will.

She snapped a sarcastic little salute. "Yes, sir!"

The strain left his face and he laughed, a soft deep rumble as intimate as a caress from the night breeze.

Flustered, she went on the offensive. "How come I'm getting the lecture here? You're the one who attacked me with a knife! Wanna explain that?"

He glanced down, apparently unwilling to hold her gaze. "Too many years on the road. I learned the hard way to always be on my toes, never take safety for granted."

"Geez, you'd think you'd spent time in special forces training. I didn't even hear you before you knocked me down."

His gaze turned flinty and moved to the woods on their left. "Glad to know I've kept my edge."

"Kept it? From when? And what are you doing down here, anyway?"

He held up one muddy foot. "Soaking my blisters in the creek."

She gave him a look of mock sympathy, then sharpened her tone. "You didn't answer my other question."

"I've decided to limit you to one per session. Even a reporter has to learn her boundaries. You're enough to wear a man out with all those whats, whens and whys." He got to his feet and looked down at her. "You okay?"

"You just knocked the wind out of me. I'll recover." She rubbed her fingers across her throat where he'd held the knife but felt no injury. "Guess I don't need to tell you it's against the law to slit someone's throat just because she surprises you?"

The change flowed over him like someone poured it from a bucket. "If I'd intended you harm" — his voice sounded as hard as his face looked — "you'd be carrying your head now."

Without another word, he walked rigidly to the creek and sat on the bank.

Leigh stared at his back as she heard his feet plunk one at a time into the water. She now knew, although he held it tightly in check, something lethal lurked within Will Scott. Something he'd nearly unleashed on her.

She got up, straightened her clothes and picked up the flashlight she'd dropped at the edge of the pathway when Will attacked her. There certainly didn't seem to be anything more to say. After a moment's hesitation, she turned and started back toward her Blazer, wishing she'd never come down this path. If she'd just driven on home, she would've been able to hold on to the fantasy that she'd stepped outside herself and nothing bad had resulted. She could've kept the memory of Will as he'd been when they danced, not the coiled spring that jumped her and held a knife to her throat. She would have been able to remember the heat in his blue eyes, not the icy detachment she'd seen just before he returned to the creek.

Just as she started up the incline to the road, something snapped behind her. She spun around quickly, the flashlight held like a club.

Will's hand clamped around her wrist before she could swing. Her knee was halfway to his crotch when his gentle voice stopped her in mid-thrust. "I just wanted to say, I'm sorry."

She was still trying to rein in her galloping heart. Too ashamed to say anything, she remained silent. Twice tonight she'd put herself in the position of an easy victim. She *was* getting soft with the relative calm of life here.

The moon had just begun to wane, casting enough light to show his eyes. Caring eyes once again, not the eyes of a criminal. Just looking into them flipped all of the switches that had been turned on during that dance in the bar.

The space between them seemed to be decreasing. The wrist he held slipped easily behind her back. Again, the fresh outdoorsy smell of him wrapped around her. And those eyes . . . she was quickly lost in them. He kept a light hold and applied the slightest pressure, making her take a half-step closer. They stood nearly chest to chest for a moment before he kissed her.

The gentle brush of his lips against hers popped circuit breakers she didn't know existed. He no longer pressed her against him, she did that all on her own. Nerve endings buzzed with heightened anticipation of his touch, but he made no further move for a long moment.

His hand came to rest on the side of her neck, his thumb laying across her windpipe. A chill danced from his fingers, down her neck, across her breasts; she wanted more. That realization shocked Leigh into regaining some of her senses. Even though she knew his touch to be a caress, it brought home just how easily he could harm her if he'd wanted to. She jerked her lips from his and shook her head.

And she thought Brittany was the one in danger of doing something foolish!

Taking a step backward, she slapped him soundly. "That's for scaring the piss out of me!"

He didn't say anything, just stood with his hands at his sides.

She stalked toward her truck, trying to ignore the little voice that scolded for striking out at Will because *she'd* been careless. But dammit, she didn't like the vulnerability he brought out in her.

God, she hoped her truck wasn't close enough that he could see the emblem on it. Then he'd know she was an officer of the law and not a reporter. What kind of bumbling sheriff would he think she was? Barney Fife came quickly to mind.

As she got in her truck, she thanked God she'd never have to look Will Scott in the eye again.

Watching Leigh's curly hair bounce as she stomped up the path that inclined toward the road, Will ignored the sting in his cheek. He only felt the twist of regret that he'd never lay eyes on the woman again. He wanted to once again feel his lips against that hair, draw in the herbal scent of it, as he had when he held her while they danced. Foolish wantings. He thought he'd cured himself of them.

He knew she'd been scared. He'd scared himself. The close call in Tulsa had spooked him more than he'd realized. Since the deaths of the two marshals, he'd been on heightened alert — but, Christ, he'd just pulled a knife on an innocent woman. Another confirmation that he'd taken too big a risk. Any social interaction was too much. The stark terror in her eyes had emblazoned itself on his mind, just one more horrific memory to add to the stockpile he'd accumulated over the years.

Returning to the creek, he sat down and buried his face in his hands. All he'd wanted was a single good memory to counterbalance the others. Was it too much to ask, one carefree night?

The carnival had acted as a salve to his soul, a dose of childish delight to heal wounds that festered more with each passing day. For a moment, walking beside Leigh along the midway, he'd almost forgotten who he'd become; he could believe in himself once again. Then, in a split second he'd ruined it, taken sandpaper to the fragile scab that had only begun to form.

This town, these people, they were a link to a past he could never reclaim. He'd only spent a few weeks here, but that handful of days had marked him for life. Something extraordinary had seeped into his soul. A belief in quiet, steadfast goodness. There was nothing noteworthy about his activities in Glens Crossing — the carnival, shopping at the dime store on the square, going to the drive-in to see the latest James Bond movie in his great aunt's roomy old convertible; he even joined in a couple of baseball games at the park. Regular stuff. And maybe that was the magic of it. He didn't have to fight his way in, have to prove himself. Even though he was an outsider, he felt like he belonged. People liked his aunt, so they liked him. Acceptance had been that simple.

If only he could say that today. This town might be the same, but his great aunt was long dead, as was the boy he used to be. He had changed. There was no denying it, he wasn't fit to live among decent people.

As he spread his bedroll by the creek and stretched out under the stars, he tried to summon only pleasant recollections of this town. If he focused carefully, concentrated hard, maybe he could erase the smear of ugliness he'd created tonight. This place could forever be that one perfect spot, clean and unspoiled, the one he could draw upon to sustain him as he waded through what was left of his life.

Chapter 4

Even though Leigh's night's sleep had been interrupted by a forty-five-minute call from her deputy, who wasn't quite up to solo handling of a single car accident out on Quarry Road, she forced herself out of bed at the 5:30 alarm. As her feet hit the floor, she asked herself again why she'd hired Calvin in the first place. But she knew the answer: he wanted to be a deputy more than anything in his sheltered life. She knew the feeling; it had been what propelled her into a degree in criminal justice at Indiana University. And she knew he could be a good officer, if only she could instill a little self-confidence in him. Most of the time his fear of doing the wrong thing kept him from doing anything at all.

The morning haze was still thick as she did her usual three-mile run. The sun was just beginning to burn through when she added another mile. Her penalty for last night's elephant ear.

On her way back home, she passed her brother's house, an impressive two-and-a-half-story limestone Tudor with leaded glass windows and a huge arched oak door. The large yard held a detached carriage house and a swimming pool. It had been built in the thirties by the owner of the stone quarry, the big money in Glens Crossing at the time.

She saw Brian in the driveway, loading something into the trunk of his dark blue Mercedes, and decided to stop.

"Going camping?" she called breathlessly as she neared.

Brian jerked up so abruptly, he hit his head on the trunk lid. "Dammit, Leigh! Don't sneak up on me like that!" He rubbed the back of his skull, rumpling his straight blond hair.

"I'm breathing like a racehorse, my tennis shoes were flapping on the street out in front — I'd hardly call it sneaking." She reached up and felt his injury. "No blood. I think you'll live."

He managed a smile. "Want coffee? Made it myself. Kate left for Cancun yesterday."

She held up a hand. "Noooo way am I drinking *your* coffee. What's Kate doing in Cancun?"

"A week at a spa. She needed a break."

Leigh nodded and swallowed her words. A break from what? Her sister-in-law had a cleaning lady, a gardener, a pool man, no job, no kids, and no hobbies that Leigh could tell. Kate needed a get away about as much as fish need glasses.

Brian retrieved another box from the garage and put it in the trunk.

"So, planning on a little communing with nature while she's gone?" She pointed to the trunk full of camping gear. Brian used to love to camp, back in the days before he went into the real estate business.

He slammed the lid closed. "Nope. Bought that lakeside cottage we've been looking at instead. Kate's idea of roughing it." He chuckled, but without much humor. "Giving the gear to Goodwill."

"Hmm, too bad. I hoped when you had kids you'd take them, like you used to take me."

They'd been orphaned when Leigh was seven. Brian was only two years older. Still, he always took his role as older brother very seriously; keeping the bullies away, taking her to the father/daughter dance in junior high, helping her with algebra — whose textbooks may as well have been written in a foreign language as far as Leigh was concerned — campaigning for her when she ran for student council. She knew, although he always denied it, most of her dates in high school were secretly arranged by Brian. Everybody loved Brian. But Leigh was beginning to wonder if there was a single exception to that rule — his wife.

Brian smiled, but still looked sad. "Not looking very likely."

She knew about the growing rift between her brother and Kate over having children. Brian had been ready for years, but Kate always felt they needed something else before the time would be right — a new car, a cruise, a bigger house, and now the congressional run. Leigh suspected Kate wanted Brian to have the seat in Congress more than Brian himself did. Was Brian trying to hold his marriage together by taking this giant political leap? It seemed he was skipping a couple of vital steps in "the plan." He'd worked out a strategy for a Mitchell political dynasty, starting with him and her, followed by their children.

However, it was beginning to look like neither of them were going to produce offspring. Her life's course had been set, she was out of the running. And now she saw the defeat in his eyes. He had given up hope of ever being a father. For him it was more than the plan though, he wanted to build a family with lots of children to support one another. A family, safe and strong. The family they had lost as children.

She put a hand on his arm and gave a reassuring squeeze. "If I were you, I'd hang onto that camping stuff a little longer. Kate's not thirty yet." Leigh only wished she felt as confident as she sounded.

He pulled a lock of hair at Leigh's temple that had spiraled loose from her ponytail. "I'll think about it." He opened the driver's door and got in.

Leigh stepped out of the way as she watched him back out of the drive, her heart swollen with impotent sympathy.

Hank Brown wiped his hands on a red shop

rag as he walked out to meet Leigh in front of the service station.

"Mornin', Sheriff. What can I do for you?"

"Just an oil change, Brownie. I know you're hard pressed since Skeeter broke his leg, but can you do it within the hour? I have to go over to the courthouse to pick up a warrant."

Brownie grinned. "Well, it just so happens, you're in luck. Hired myself a new guy today." He called over his shoulder to the open garage door, "Hey, buddy, come meet our sheriff."

With the difference between bright sunshine and the dimness inside the garage, Leigh hadn't seen the man with his head stuck under the hood of a car until he straightened and moved closer to the doorway.

She raised the bill of her baseball cap with the sheriff's star embroidered on it to get a better view of the new man. He turned his back to her as he set his tools down. A brick landed in her stomach when she saw the sunlight glint off coal black hair.

"This here's my new man, Will Scott." Brownie hooked his thumb over his shoulder at the man coming into full light. "I could only talk him into hiring on temporarily. A sorry thing, too. He's a real good worker. Already done more this mornin' than Skeeter'n a full day."

Will wiped his palms on the gray coveralls with Brown's Auto Repair stitched in red on the front. Then he extended a work-stained hand.

63

"The *sheriff*" — Will looked pointedly at Leigh — "and I have met." He offered her a slow, sly smile.

Leigh closed her eyes for a second, swallowed dryly and met her worst humiliation head on. "Yes, we have, Brownie — yesterday." She looked unsmilingly at Will and shook his hand, trying not to think of the way that hand felt on her hip last night. God, he looked as sexy in coveralls as he did in tight jeans. "Didn't expect to see you again."

"I know." Accusation colored his tone and shone in his eyes.

For a moment no one said anything else. Then Brownie broke into a wide, knowing grin. "Hey! You the fella everyone's talkin' about? From the Crossing House?"

"Afraid so," Will said, his gaze still on Leigh.

Brownie slapped Will on the back, a gesture of masculine congratulations. "I'll be damned." He looked at Leigh. "Sorry, ma'am." She nodded, but didn't think he looked a bit sorry. "The whole town's buzzin' about this guy and I went and hired him without even knowin'."

Flames of embarrassment licked Leigh's cheeks but she refused to be cowed. She held Will's gaze, her eyes narrowed. "How did you come to hire Mr. Scott?"

"Damndest thing. I was drivin' in this mornin', stewin' over how I'm gonna get all these customers taken care of with Skeeter laid up, and I seen Will here with his head under the hood of Miz White's old pick-up. Before I could stop and offer a hand, he had the thing goin' again and ol' Miz White nearly ran me over pullin' back on the road. That woman's always in such a dang hurry!"

"Well, Brownie, looks like this was your lucky day." *Just not mine,* she thought. She nodded to Will and began to walk away. "I'll be back to pick up the Blazer in an hour."

"We'll have it ready, *Sheriff.*" Will's mocking tone went through her like a javelin hurled by an Olympian, but she didn't turn back around.

Will watched her go. He'd almost turned Brownie down when he offered the job, but he was down to his last ten dollars. He would have been flat broke had Leigh not picked up the tab for the beers last night. Weighing the facts, he'd decided to stay. Might as well be here as anywhere. He'd managed to spend as long as two weeks in one place with no problem. A week should do it. Then he'd have enough cash to drift a little farther and choose the next stop carefully, without the distracting emotions that had brought him to Glens Crossing — and were now keeping him here.

He told himself that spending a week around the lady sheriff didn't factor into the equation. But he knew the truth, no matter how he tried to drown it out with logic; he'd do anything to erase that look of fear that dominated his memory of her. Maybe he could replace it with something more . . . appealing. But, he swore to himself, he wouldn't complicate her life, no matter how tempting the thought. He knew, although his time in this cozy town would be limited to days, it might be all he'd ever get of the calm life he so craved.

Brian called Leigh at her office in the late afternoon to see if she wanted to go out to dinner, since he was "bach'ing it." However, her little adventure with Will was having a profound effect on the town. After the surreptitious looks, thinly veiled innuendo, and gossiping whispers she'd endured all day, she was in no mood for any more public exposure. She didn't want to go into the gory details so she just told Brian she was tired and wanted to go home.

He snickered knowingly. "Too much partying last night?"

"Not you, too! I knew I should have taken that job with the FBI. How could I have let you talk me into coming back to this fishbowl?" She tried to sound truly peeved, but the humor of the situation was finally seeping in. The image of Mildred, one of the waitresses at the Dew Drop where Leigh had lunch, leaning close and talking to a booth full of blue-haired ladies whose eyes immediately turned to Leigh with expressions that bordered on horror, popped to the forefront of her mind. She had to bite her tongue to keep from laughing. She wouldn't give Brian the satisfaction.

"I hear your boyfriend got himself a job right here in River City." He was going in for the kill.

"I'm going to ignore your classification of *Mister* Scott," she said with the haughty detachment she reserved for Brian when his teasing hit too close to the mark. "Yes, he is working for Brownie."

"You're a bit too testy, I'd say." His chuckle faded as her silence stretched. "Better be careful, little sister. You've got no idea where this guy's been." Seriousness had crept into his voice.

"You make him sound like a dirty penny. 'Don't put that in your mouth; you don't know where it's been.' "

"Exactly," he said gravely.

"I'm a big girl."

"Now there's a mature adult statement."

She sighed. She knew Brian was just looking out for her — as he always had. "Well, he wasn't supposed to still be here."

"You sound disappointed." There was more accusation than question in his statement. She didn't like the father-with-the-shotgun tone in his voice.

"Disinterested. And this subject is completely worn out."

"Right. I'm just saying —"

Ooooh, Brian, the all perceptive. "Enjoy your dinner — *all by yourself.*"

"Ouch —"

She hung up the phone before he could get in another lick.

With a throbbing headache, she locked up her office and headed home.

Several people actually pointed at her as she drove through town. Dear God, would this ever pass? Only in Glens Crossing would one stupid dance be the subject of such widespread attention. She thanked her lucky stars that no one knew about the fiasco by the creek. No one but Will Scott, that is. If she played her cards right, she could avoid him completely until he left town.

As she turned into her driveway she said a little prayer that Skeeter's leg would heal with uncommon swiftness.

After making herself a salad, she poured a well-deserved glass of wine and headed to her front porch to eat. On her way through the living room she turned Brian's picture, the only framed snapshot in the house, to the wall as punishment for his torment. Even the eyes in his photo could see right through her. No one knew her like he did.

Another pair of knowing eyes flashed in her mind. Had she imagined it, or did Will Scott possess that same irritating insight into her soul?

Enough of him. She dropped fish flakes into her aquarium, picked up her glass of wine and went to the porch. Brian said it was unnatural to have pets without fur. But she found that a fish's complete lack of demands suited her just fine. You didn't get so attached that when the time came to flush one you suffered for days.

Bye-bye fishie, and it was done.

She settled in a wicker chair and set her wine on the porch rail. Her bungalow sat on a wooded acre just outside of town. It was far enough off the road that she could enjoy complete privacy, at least until the leaves fell from the trees. She'd never had a day when she'd been so thankful for the cover.

A horn honked on the road, followed by teenage howls and the loud revving of an engine with a leaky exhaust. The foliage completely blocked the road. She doubted the kids were sending her a hello, so she wondered what they were honking at. She didn't have to wonder long. A second later Will Scott walked up her driveway.

Would her humiliation never end? This should teach her not to try to change the color of her spots.

Swallowing a bite of salad without chewing, she watched him come closer. The gravel crunching under his feet seemed abnormally loud. She didn't stand up.

"What brings you out here, Mr. Scott?" she called as he stepped onto the grass of her front yard.

"Just needed a walk to unwind at the end of the day." Stopping at the base of the porch steps, he gave her an easy smile. Freshly showered with his hair still damp, he looked cool and slightly dangerous in the early evening light.

"How did you know where I live?" She crossed her arms over her chest.

"Mighty suspicious tone there, Sheriff." He nodded back toward the road. "Didn't. Just happened by. Name's on the mailbox."

"Oh." Maybe she was imagining the *dangerous* part. But he definitely looked cool — a real contrast to her own heated response to his presence. She had enjoyed relaxed conversation with this man last night. Why then did her mouth suddenly feel full of feet?

"What happened to that Hoosier hospitality?"

"Sorry, please have a seat."

He had to walk past her to get to the only other seat on the porch — the swing. She concentrated on his hands. His nails were pink and white, with no trace of the grime of earlier in the day. He smelled like Dial soap.

The wicker swing creaked under his weight as he sat down. "Real homey place you've got here." He rubbed his hand along the arm of the swing.

"I like it. Actually" — she didn't know why she felt compelled to set the record straight — "my brother owns it. I rent. Can I offer you something? Wine, a Coke?"

"No, thanks. I just *dined* at the Dew Drop Inn."

In spite of herself, she felt a disrespectful smile twitch the corners of her mouth at his loose use of the word. She tightened her lips and cleared her throat. "Where are you staying, now that you've found a job here?" She hadn't meant to sound so accusing. More feet.

"Hey, I was on my way out of town. The *job* found *me*," he corrected. "Who am I to turn down work? A man's got to eat." He paused and looked at his hand on the swing chain. "Brownie offered me his spare bedroom as part of the 'employment package.'"

"Meals not included?"

"Have you seen what that man eats?"

Leigh couldn't suppress a laugh. "You mean the three building blocks of nutrition: fried, fried and deep fried?"

"I see you've broken bread with the man. Course, the Inn has much greater variety: *gravied,* fried and deep fried."

Her self-consciousness melted away with their laughter. They were back on even ground once again.

Once she relaxed, he looked at her and said, "I guess I should thank you for not carting me off to jail last night."

She held his gaze. If she hadn't been so mortified over her own foolish behavior, she might actually have considered it. "I probably should have. I'm giving you the benefit of the doubt. But be warned; if I hear of another stunt like that, your ass'll be in jail before you know what hit you."

"Point taken." He raised a hand as if swearing in for testimony. "You'll get no trouble from me, Sheriff."

Leigh doubted that. She might not have any legal trouble, but on a personal level she sensed a tidal wave headed her way. And she wasn't sure how to brace herself for it. She'd come to know him only through her desire to break away from her old self. And, he'd seemed the perfect choice for implementing her plan. A man with no intention of passing more than a single evening with her. A safe trial. She wasn't looking for attachments, no lasting repercussions. But the more time she spent with Will, the more she liked him. She found herself far too comfy in his presence, too curious about him. And far too interested in the fact that he viewed her in a way no one else in town did — as a woman.

It would have been so much better if he'd left town.

She looked at him. For a moment, he eyed her with frank curiosity. "I know you have a brother. Any other family around here?"

She shook her head, glad for the change in topic. "Our parents were killed when we were in grade school. Aunt Belinda and Uncle Worth took us in. She died two years ago, and he followed shortly thereafter. How about you? Siblings? Parents?"

"One and two. My sister died a few years ago. Both my folks are gone."

This was an amazing breakthrough — an actual fact about Will Scott.

Just as she was about to question further, his expression changed and he turned the tables on her once again. "No cousins here in town?"

"Uncle Worth and Aunt Belinda were our only relatives and had no children of their own."

"Your aunt and uncle must have been good people. Two half-grown children are a lot for a childless couple to take on. Must have been quite an adjustment for them."

Bitterness rolled around in the back of her throat. She swallowed it. "They did the best they knew how." And, she realized, that was the painful truth. Aunt Belinda had been like a child herself, even in her prime. It was Brian they'd wanted; unfortunately for them, he'd refused to be separated from his sister. So as a package deal, they'd had to accept Leigh. They *had* given her food and shelter, attended to her physical needs. It was the complete lack of emotional support that scarred. Leigh knew Brian sensed it, tried his best to make up for their shortcomings. She had to admit, there was no malicious intent in the pain her aunt and uncle inflicted upon a grieving young girl. But that still didn't make it go away.

When she glanced at Will, he was staring at her, studying her. "What?"

"There's a whole mouthful you're not telling me."

"It was a long time ago." She dismissed his

concern with a lift of a shoulder. "Doesn't matter now."

Stark naked pain pulsed in his eyes. His hand gripped the swing's chain until his knuckles whitened. "Don't discount the past. It has a way of sneaking up on you in the middle of the night."

"Does yours?" she asked, fully aware this was *not* the direction he intended this conversation to take.

He licked his lips, then pressed them tightly together. A muscle twitched in his cheek. Whatever memories haunted his nights, they weren't good ones. Finally he said, in a grave tone, "Yes."

That look she'd seen when he walked away from her at the creek once again hardened his features. He closed her off. She had to admit, it frightened her a bit. The pragmatist in her demanded she keep both eyes open when it came to this stranger. In this moment there was nothing of the man with the perfect rhythm and sensuous movements that had tempted her beyond reason.

He glowered at the grove of trees separating her house from the road for several minutes. Gradually, the twitch in his cheek ceased, the tension ebbed from his body and the color returned to his fingers. When he turned to face her again, the strain disappeared so completely that Leigh nearly questioned if she had seen it at all.

Nearly, but what her trained eye had seen deep in his gaze spoke of a road-weary spirit who had left plenty behind him in the dust. Just what that happened to be, she was determined to find out. There was a hard-edged vigilance that seemed a nearly steady undercurrent to his easygoing manner. He masked it well, like someone who has had a lot of practice.

"I'd like that glass of wine, if you don't mind," he said.

She got up to get it, knowing the window on his soul had closed. He was once again in complete control.

Will sat staring at the purpling sky after the screen door closed behind Leigh. He'd forced his body to relax, but there was a thrumming ball of tension in his very core. What was it about this woman that made him crack open doors that he'd nailed shut and sealed with concrete? Doors that he knew if he opened would result in a total meltdown. He'd managed to survive knowing that the past was done, irrevocably, irretrievably over. Leave it and focus energy on things in his control, things he *could* do.

But in a matter of hours, Leigh had him poking around, picking up the pieces and examining things better left alone. Yes, he had things that snuck up on him in the night, bit him right in the ass — things that seeped into his dreams. But that's where he kept them. Once awake, he banished them back into the darkness where he could pretend they didn't exist.

It was apparent that Leigh had things hiding in the dark of her past too. Things she'd locked away. Like that night years ago when they were stranded on the Ferris wheel. The difference was, she was facing her demons. She got right on that carnival ride without an outward flicker of fear. Damn he admired that.

He searched his memory, looking for another glint of shared past. He certainly hadn't recognized her on sight. It was her admission of being stuck on the Ferris wheel that made him realize their paths had crossed before.

His mind skipped along snippets of that summer, jumping rapidly from one to another. Each one burst forth for only a millisecond before moving on to the next, like a radio flipping quickly from station to station, producing only a few notes, just enough to recognize the song as familiar, then bouncing to the next number on the radio dial.

He didn't find Leigh there, but his mind paused long enough on one incident for him to grab hold and stop the flickering images.

His first weekend in Glens Crossing. He and his aunt were headed to the go-cart track, where she was to work in the concession stand run by the hospital auxiliary. She had chattered all Saturday morning about how much fun he would have, how many new people he would meet. He'd smiled and acted like he was looking as forward to the afternoon as she was, but inside his gut knotted and his muscles buzzed with tension.

For as long as he could remember, everywhere he'd gone, he'd had to carve out a place for himself in an established social pecking order. He'd moved around so much, city to city, school to school, that he'd developed a tough attitude and a hard-edged shell, something he'd thought he could leave behind while visiting kindly Aunt Salma in her tiny Indiana town. He hadn't imagined his two-week stay would involve planting himself in a new group of kids.

The racetrack was just outside of town. As they parked in the gravel parking area, he was surprised by the number of cars, trucks and trailers. It seemed every male in Glens Crossing between the ages of eight and eighty had a home-built go-cart.

At first Will had stuck by his aunt's side, helping take Coke bottles out of the big ice chest and prying the tops off as people ordered. But Aunt Salma quickly shooed him out of the stand to go watch the carts, insisting that this was his vacation, he should just have fun.

He didn't hesitate long. As much as he wanted to avoid dealing with other kids, the high whine of the little engines had been beckoning him since they'd arrived. Being a city boy, he'd never been around a local dirt track. There was a single set of old, worn bleachers about six rows high, the little shanty that was the concession stand, an outhouse, and the open field with a dusty oval carved out of the weeds. Not much as tracks go, but it seemed like heaven to Will. For a while he hung near the guys who were working on their carts, itching to get his hands greasy. Fathers and sons had their heads bent together, changing spark plugs, tuning carburetors. It was a scene both foreign and inviting. He could never imagine he and his dad . . .

He was just beginning to feel the sting of being an outsider when a guy right behind him yelled, "Somebody give me a hand here." Will looked over his shoulder and saw a tall, skinny guy who looked to be about a senior in high school working on a bright yellow cart.

Will fell to his knees next to the boy who had both hands on the engine. "What do you need?"

"That spring over there" — he nodded toward his tool box — "right in the top compartment, the little one."

Will flipped the tool box open, noting the name stenciled on top: Brownie.

How could he have forgotten this? It was a turning point, one that made Glens Crossing the place he kept locked deep in his heart. Brownie not only let Will help fix the engine, he introduced him to several other guys and let him drive the cart in a few practice laps. Will loved the speed, the noise and vibration of the engine at his back, the bump and spray of dust on the track, passing the other carts like they were standing still. Brownie had the fastest cart in town. Will had been so covered with dust that his aunt actually took a whisk broom to him before she let him in her car. She'd laughed and told him he even had mud in his teeth.

Will didn't see Brownie after that — not until yesterday. But a couple of the younger boys had invited him to play baseball, included him without challenge or ridicule.

An ache rose in Will's chest as he rocked in Leigh's swing. My God, he'd been working so hard to keep his past buried, that he'd nearly obliterated the good with the bad.

When Leigh returned with his wine, she sensed a marked change in Will's disposition. A calm seemed to have come over him. When she handed him the glass, his blue eyes locked on hers with a warm attentiveness that reached deep and left its mark.

He held her gaze and said, "I really love it here."

Unsure if he meant here with her, or here on her porch, or here in Glens Crossing, she hesitated and smiled. "Yes. Me too."

The moment passed and she sat back down across from him. As they drank their wine, their conversation took on the same innocuous quality it had last night. They chatted until the crickets started to chirp. When he got up to leave, Leigh realized they had talked only about her and Glens Crossing. He had managed to avoid revealing anything beyond the superficial about himself.

An awkwardness rose with their parting, as if neither of them quite knew how to end the evening.

The words "I'm sorry" always came hard to her. She stood in front of him, looked into his eyes and offered her own brand of apology. "Thank you for not chastising me about misleading you last night. It's just —"

He put a hand on the side of her face. "Far be it from me to cast stones. I'm quite familiar with the need to be someone else."

His touch was cool and dry against the warmth of her cheek. And it sent tiny electric shocks straight to her core. For a moment she thought he was going to kiss her. She even parted her lips slightly in anticipation. But he dropped his hand to his side.

Disappointment tugged at her stomach as she watched him go down the steps and across the lawn. She wondered about his last statement until he turned onto the road and the trees blocked him from view.

His visit left her restless in a way totally new to her. For a few minutes she paced the porch. Although Will certainly managed to shake up the doldrums of her life, something, like an itch just beneath the skin, plagued her. She wanted a fling, she wanted an adventure outside her normal parameters. And he could certainly provide both. With a simple caress of the cheek he had managed to ignite a smoldering desire she had no idea resided deep inside her. A desire that left her restive and wanting.

But Will was just passing through and would soon be leaving.

She stopped in mid-pace.

Isn't that exactly what she wanted? A diversion? Unfettered pleasure?

Of course it was. Unlike most women of child-bearing age, she had no delusions of a blissful marriage and a house full of children. Her brother's experience had told her the unvarnished truth about happily-ever-after. That was *not* the path for her. She was going to concentrate on making herself the best person she could be, embracing the possibilities of each day as they came — there just wasn't enough assurance that the partner she would choose would do the same. As she saw it, time had a way of tearing things apart. No, for her career would come first. But that didn't preclude a short waltz with romance now and again. She'd just take a couple of turns around the dance floor with Will Scott, before he disappeared from town like the spring rains.

She took her plate to the kitchen, threw away most of the salad and poured a second glass of wine. Then she returned to the porch. Sitting in the same spot on the swing he'd vacated, Leigh imagined she could still feel the warmth of his body. Thoughts of him swirled and churned her emotions into a fine mess. Thinking only made her restlessness worse. She tried to block out thought, concentrate on the night sounds. But the next moment she'd realize Will once again had crept back into her mind. Against her resolve, memory of a gesture, a phrase, a look in his eye would simply be there.

Twilight moved into full darkness before she registered the passage of time. The old owl that lived in a nearby tree hooted, drawing Leigh back to the here and now. With a sigh, she went in the house, leaving the door unlocked, as she did every night.

Just before bed, she glanced at the unlocked front door again. Remembering Will's comments about false feelings of safety, she walked over and flipped the deadbolt. It took a bit of muscle; she couldn't remember the last time she'd used it. She stood looking at the thumb-turn for a few seconds. This was ridiculous. No one in Glens Crossing had ever felt the need to lock out their neighbors. She wasn't going to start now, just because some stranger drifted into town with a heart full of distrust and a sackful of bad memories. Besides, the lock was as old as the house — nothing a twelve-year-old with a butter knife and an ounce of luck couldn't overcome.

She unlocked the door again and went to bed.

Chapter 5

Leigh stopped to grab a cup of coffee-to-go at the Dew Drop on the way to her office. She ran into her deputy, Steve Clyde, at the counter. Thirtyish, he was a small man, made entirely of muscle and brains — obviously mixed with a healthy dose of testosterone, since he and his wife of ten years had six kids and another due at Christmas.

"Morning, Steve."

He nodded in greeting. "Thought you liked to make your own coffee in the morning." There was a glint in his eye that she didn't particularly like.

"Opened the can this morning and didn't have enough to make a pot." Partially true. She left out the fact that there was a new, unopened can in her pantry.

"I see." He looked pointedly over his shoulder to the far end of the counter where Will Scott sat with his nose buried in a newspaper and his hand wrapped around a coffee mug.

My God, was she that transparent? As she glanced around the room, she realized there was uncommon interest in the air. People usually smiled and said hello. But today they all looked as if they'd been caught with their hands in the cookie jar, gazes shrinking with a mixture of guilt and unbending curiosity. Apparently, Steve wasn't alone in his notion that Leigh had stopped for reasons other than coffee.

Mildred, the reigning senior waitress at the Drop, set down a paper cup in front of Leigh, then looked over her half-glasses toward the far end of the counter. She leaned closer to Leigh and whispered, "It's okay, honey. You just go on and ask him out."

"Good grief!" Leigh muttered, and left with her coffee in hand.

A fling might be harder to manage than she'd originally thought. With all of the public attention, if she'd said as much as good morning to the man, there would have been an article about it in the *Glens Crossing Recorder*.

Seemed like people could not just mind their own damn business.

Will sat quietly, with his eyes fastened on the paper, giving the impression that he had no idea what was going on around him. In fact, nothing could be further from the truth. He was a man constantly in tune with his surroundings, listening to conversations, watching body language, testing the very atmosphere. Although he sat with his back to the door, he knew immediately when Leigh had entered the café.

He'd already heard enough quiet speculation floating around the room that he knew better than to acknowledge her presence. If she wanted to initiate contact, that was one thing. After all, she was the one with the reputation to protect.

As far as he could tell, the people of this county respected her. But he knew firsthand what a rough road women had in law enforcement. They were either considered creampuffs, unable to handle difficult situations, or dykes with something to prove. He knew both positions were dead wrong.

He'd worked alongside a few women over the years. And in every case, they were more reliable, more courageous and more clever than their male counterparts. Maybe it was the lack of testosterone getting in the way of the work. Being a male himself, he hated to admit it, but clashing masculine egos could create quite a toxic reaction — misdirect the focus, poison the work.

However, Will knew his opinion of policewomen was deep in the minority. And outside law enforcement, in the public sector, the attitude was often worse. Female officers were held to much higher moral and professional standards than male officers. Once an accusation was cast toward a woman in law — or politics, as Leigh had a foot in both — forgive and forget was never as forthcoming as for a man. The fact that Leigh held an elected position said she had the confidence of the majority. But man, that minority population could make things a living hell for her, given the proper inspiration. Glens Crossing was a small town. Will was *not* going to be that spark to ignite public recrimination.

Still, when she left without saying anything to him, he couldn't shake his disappointment.

Well, what did you want, a big good-morning kiss?

He cringed when he realized that was exactly what would have made him happiest. He had no right to even fantasize about such things. There would never be a home, a woman, a family to fill his life. It simply could not be. The last four months had convinced him of that. The decision had been made. The cards had been dealt. The ship had forever left its mooring. He had been cast upon the sea of solitary living, and there he would remain, forever alone, bobbing from island to island, depending upon the currents that carried him.

He'd come to Glens Crossing to visit the only place from his past where he could remain anonymous. It was a small nugget he'd given himself and it would fast melt away. He had to savor it enough to last a lifetime.

He folded his paper and left money on the counter for the coffee and tip. The weight of speculative eyes made the hairs on the back of his neck prickle, shriveling any hopes he'd had of spending more time with the local sheriff before he left town. Leigh couldn't afford the gossip and he certainly couldn't afford the attention.

Alma Lynn White snagged Leigh's arm as she passed her just outside the door to the café, slopping the coffee through the opening in the lid of Leigh's cup.

"Oh, my! I'm so sorry." She waved a flighty hand in the air. "I just wanted to tell you about yesterday morning. I swan, I thought men like that had gone the way of the dinosaurs. I tell you, it gives a body hope for the human race." The words had tumbled out in the woman's customary rush.

Leigh blinked. "What does?" Mrs. White was from Tennessee, therefore a bit more southern than Hoosier, and wanted everyone to remember it. She drove a pickup truck held together with more wire and duct tape than sheet metal and bolts, but she spoke like a southern belle on a speedball.

"Why the way that man" — she craned her neck around Leigh and pointed inside, toward Will — "saved me from being stranded. Who knows what would have befallen me if he hadn't come along."

Leigh hid the smile that threatened to insult the dear woman. Alma Lynn White was seventy if she was a day, smoked cigars when no one was looking, and was mean as a snake if you crossed her. Southern belle veneer or no, helpless she was not. Everyone in Glens Crossing knew it and steered clear. "I see."

"Such a gentleman." Mrs. White fluttered away, disappearing inside the café as quickly as she had materialized from the street.

Leigh shook her head and moved on. She climbed into her Blazer that was angle-parked at the curb. *So that's who I have to thank for Will's remaining in my fair city,* she thought. The pure serendipity of it made her wonder if she had any control over her life at all. If she hadn't been so bummed about her birthday, she never would have gone to a bar with a stranger. Will Scott would have remained no more than a face passing in the crowd. If she had just driven past that light by the creek, she would have had no insight to the dangerous possibilities of her own folly. If Alma Lynn's truck hadn't broken down when and where it did, Will would have traveled on and been no more than a memory to warm Leigh on lonely nights.

Reviewing this fall of events as she drove to her office made her wonder what lay around the next corner. Certainly nothing she could foresee. Apparently, soothsaying was not in her genes.

Leigh's morning slid by without a ripple in her usual routine. The only surprise came from her own subconscious, when she was taken unaware by thoughts of piercing blue eyes and hot, provocative dance movements. Which was exactly what she had wanted, something slightly wicked to covet and relive in private moments. All was going according to plan. Except for the fact that those eyes and that body were just blocks away instead of evaporated somewhere into the big, wide world, never to incite temptation again. And she *was* tempted — in ways she hadn't dreamed possible.

With effort, she managed to corral her attention back to business. Then came the afternoon.

There was no getting away from her own conflicted thoughts. Will Scott had been in town less than forty-eight hours and had already raised the heads of speculation. Leigh heard theories all afternoon as she made her county rounds. Some were told directly to her. Others she picked up by shamelessly eavesdropping.

Late in the day, she'd heard Francine, the dispatcher, talking to her sister-in-law on the telephone. Obviously the opinions were flying fast and furious at Hildie's Day Spa and Salon. Hildie's used to be a beauty shop, but Francine's sister-in-law had dragged Glens Crossing another step closer to cosmopolitan when she took down the old white sign with the lavender silhouette of a ponytailed, pert-nosed debutante and replaced it with a classy script-only gold on black, forever changing the name — at least in print. Leigh had yet to hear anyone announce they had an appointment at the "Day Spa."

According to what Leigh gathered from

Francine's side of the conversation, there was a considerable consensus among Hildie's patrons that Will Scott was the older man Brittany Wilson had taken up with. In addition to his riding into town in the girl's car, he'd been seen talking to her by at least *four* different people.

Leigh silently scoffed at this. The *unsubstantiated* rumor that Brittany had a secret "older" boyfriend had been floating around town for a couple of weeks. Will had arrived only the day before yesterday. Besides, Leigh doubted the older man theory altogether, suspecting Brittany had started it herself, just trying to get her father riled up.

Another, albeit less popular, theory had Will as a dot-commer whose company had gone bust in the Nasdaq crash. Speculation had it that he was looking for a place to start over.

"Is he as good-looking as everyone says?" Francine asked.

Apparently Hildie herself had gotten a look.

"Hmm. Well if he's looking for single women, he's come to the wrong town!" She gave a little gasp of revelation and lowered her voice. "Maybe he *is* here for the Wilson girl." There was a long pause. "Well, sure he danced with her — but she's the *sheriff* for crying out loud."

Francine was just starting on a third possibility when she happened to notice Leigh standing at the filing cabinet.

"Gotta go. I'll talk to you after work." She turned toward Leigh. "Can I help you find something, Sheriff?"

Leigh pulled the first file she laid her hands on and waved it in the air. "Nope, got it." She felt Francine's stare as she returned to her office.

Wrong town for single women, huh? Even her own kind didn't see Leigh as a female. It was worse than she thought.

Leigh spent the next couple of hours in her office trying to look busy. Her hands moved over the keyboard and dialed the telephone, but her mind wouldn't let go of that single statement — "but she's the *sheriff*." It had sounded like Will had been consorting with a toothless octogenarian.

Finally she gave up. Her feminine ego had been sullied and she couldn't rest until she proved herself worthy of a uterus. She'd just stop by Brownie's garage and ask Will out. If he turned her down, that would be that — and she could count herself as the law enforcement equivalent of a nun — married to the badge. She'd just have to cash in her idea of New Leigh and spend her days predictable, dependable — and celibate.

"I'm leaving, Francine. Have to stop by the courthouse on my way home. See you tomorrow."

"Okay, then. Have a good evening."

As Leigh walked out the door, she wondered just what kind of evening Francine imagined a "good evening" would be for an asexual being such as herself. Doing something *responsible,* no doubt. Bundling newspapers for recycling or picking up litter on county roads. No more had the thought crossed her mind, than she flushed with shame. Francine, and everyone else in her office, had always been respectful and kind. She'd let that single offhand remark, which she had to admit had not been intended for her ears, to get way too deep under her skin.

Still, it stung — mostly because it rang so true.

Rounding the corner by Brownie's garage, her heart sank when she saw Will Scott standing outside with Brittany Wilson beside the girl's Camaro. Bad timing.

Will noticed her coming down the street and smiled, waving as she passed. Brittany looked over her shoulder and gave a half-wave before she put her hand on Will's arm to reclaim his attention.

Leigh half-wished she did have business at the courthouse, then she could have a reason to double back by here. But since she'd been seen heading in the direction of her house at what was very close to the end of the work day, it would seem just too obvious to circle around the block like a vulture until Brittany left.

She sighed and felt very, very dull.

Perhaps tomorrow an opportunity would avail itself.

Until then, she was going home to eat some serious chocolate.

★ ★ ★

When Brittany had pulled her red Camaro up in front of the open overhead garage door, Will had glanced up, waved, then buried his nose back under the hood of the Ford Probe he was working on. Only when she came up and stood silently behind him did he realize she'd come to see him. That realization hit with a one-two punch. While he'd already sensed the girl was trouble just waiting to happen — and he had plenty of that on his hands already — the possibility of helping her was completely irresistible.

He straightened and looked her in the eye. She stood close enough that he was bathed in the scent of her perfume. A slight, slow smile spread across her face; he imagined she'd be at home practicing in the mirror to get just the right amount of sultry sexiness mixed with little-girl charm. She had no idea how dangerous such a combination could be. Or maybe she did, which only led him to forge ahead rather than send her away as any sane adult male who wanted to stay out of jail would do.

"What brings you here?" he asked, crossing his arms over his chest and taking a tiny step away from her. He wanted her to understand, while he was willing to lend an ear, he in no way wanted anything to do with her romantically.

The smile grew. "Heard you were still in town. Just wanted to see how you're getting along."

Will moved out of the shadows of the garage, into broad daylight where everyone could see he was behaving himself. He stopped beside the fender of the Camaro. "I'm doing just fine, thanks. Did you enjoy the carnival?"

She moved in closer to him, lifted a shoulder and watched her own hand as it slid along the fender of her car. "I guess. It's pretty stupid, actually. But there's not much going on around here."

"You're sounding restless." Will couldn't help but think of his sister. Had she been feeling restless too? In such a hurry to get out there in the world that she'd fallen into a carefully crafted trap?

Again, the shoulder rose and fell. "Sounds like you had a good time that night, though." She raised her gaze to meet his and a new cattiness flashed there. "Surprised me. A bunch of guys at school thought the sheriff was gay."

Will couldn't suppress the bark of laughter. Leigh Mitchell might be many unusual things, but lacking in interest for the opposite sex wasn't one of them. Jesus, the woman nearly burst into flames with a single dance.

Brittany quickly added, "*I* didn't think it — some of the jocks do, er, did until the other night." She paused and fingered the buttons on her white shirt. "Guess you like to dance?"

Seeing the trap being laid before him, Will

moved cautiously ahead. "When the mood is right."

"Maybe —"

"Listen, let's get this straight right now. I like you, but I'm not about to travel down that road. If you want to talk, I'm a good listener. But I don't date teenagers."

Just then, Leigh's Blazer passed on the street. Will cursed the timing. He really wanted to talk to her again, but not in front of Brittany. There were enough rumors flying around town without hyper-imaginative teen gossip adding to them. He watched the Blazer slide by with an unfamiliar knot in his chest. He raised a hand to wave, while what he wanted to do was flail his arms in the air, flag her down and climb in the truck beside her.

He realized he was staring at the receding vehicle when Brittany touched him on the arm.

"Whatever. Don't get your shorts in a bunch. I'm not asking you out, for God's sake. I'm just making conversation."

Will cast one last look at Leigh's Blazer, then turned back to Brittany. "Good, 'cause I like talking to you. Just so we understand one another."

She raised a palm in the air. "No problem. You're old enough to be my dad."

She spoke the right words, but the look in her eye shouted contradiction. He'd have to move carefully.

What was it about this town that made him

go completely against what he *knew* to be good for him? As much as he wanted to shake some sense into Brittany's tart little attitude, or better yet, turn his back and never cast another thought toward her problems, his heart bled at the blatant starvation for attention that shone in her eyes. From what he could gather, it wasn't that she didn't get attention — on the contrary. But somehow, Will sensed that any amount of attention, at this point in her life, would still fall far short of *enough*.

"So," he said, "how are things going at home?" In their conversation on the way to the fairgrounds the other night, Brittany had boiled over about her dad. She'd just finished a telephone conversation with him that left her mad as a hornet. Seems Dad was making what she felt were unrealistic demands — setting curfews and the like.

Shrugging she said, "Like he's got room to talk about *responsible behavior*. I ignore him. I live with Mom, anyhow."

"You know if he didn't care about you, he wouldn't bother."

"You're just like everybody else, taking his side. He wants to be the boss. No doubt that's why he married Lauren; she's young enough to push around. It just makes me sick." As she finished this statement, Brittany got in the flashy car her father thought would fill the void he'd left. She slammed the door hard enough to make Will flinch.

And there's the crux of the problem, he thought, as he watched her pull away. Daddy left her and went to live with another girl — one that competed more with her than with her mother.

That thought brought something he hadn't considered into sharp focus. Had Jenny considered his absence an abandonment as well? He'd never considered how it looked from her point of view. Had she thought him a deserter? She was his little sister; he had assumed that she would always be safe and good. Had his leaving made a crack in her security that had to be filled?

The memory of the day he told her he was leaving rose as fresh and painful as if it were yesterday.

Of course, Jenny didn't know the truth of what he did. She thought he worked with an engineering firm that specialized in international projects. She knew he traveled frequently to remote parts of the world — places where communication was difficult. It was a cover that had always worked with few complications. But this time he'd explained to her that he was going to be gone for a much longer period of time. She wasn't taking it well.

Their father had died when Jenny was very young. Will had stepped in and filled the role. He was much older than his sister, but not old enough to achieve the perspective of what his leaving would mean to her. He was totally unprepared for her reaction.

At first there had been anger and rage — lots of name-calling. Will had been stunned by her broad and brassy vocabulary. That should have been a clue to him right there. But he'd attributed it to hurt feelings, not to keeping bad company.

The next few days she shifted to crying and pleading, spouting fears of disaster should he leave.

He'd been moved by both the anger and the tears, but so sure of the rightness of his course that he didn't falter.

When the day arrived for him to leave, he'd been uncertain if she'd go to the airport. Half of him selfishly wished she wouldn't. He needed to work on shifting mental gears, readying himself for the task ahead. Dealing with a scene on the concourse was the last thing he wanted.

But she'd come. And she'd behaved herself. Which only gave him the mistaken impression that she'd accepted his departure, understood that things were going to be all right without him. She held herself together, even smiled as she kissed him good-bye. But as he headed down the jetway to get on the plane, he looked back over his shoulder to wave one last time and his heart shifted in his chest. She'd buried her face on their mother's shoulder, sobbing. For one brief instant, fear shot through him — and a certainty that her dire predictions were right; something was going to go very wrong.

It had been too late. The wheels were already in motion. There was no turning back. He'd comforted himself with the fact that it would be him in trouble. He could handle it. It was all part of the job. Not once did it cross his mind that Jenny would be the one.

God, he'd never been so wrong.

It was just supposed to be a few months. Then the months evolved into years. He had walked away from life as he knew it, naively thinking that once his work was done, he'd be able to slide right back into it.

His work still was not done. And life as he knew it resided beneath a granite headstone that he would never see.

Leigh had just torn open the ribbon-wrapped gold package of Godiva she'd been saving for an evening such as this — one where her life appeared as an unending spiral into insipid sameness — when the phone rang. She picked it up, absently stuffing a square of chocolate into her mouth at the same time. Her salivary glands had been working overtime since the mere thought of chocolate had entered her mind. She couldn't wait any longer.

"Hello."

"Hey, little sister. Sounds like I'm interrupting your dinner."

"Worse. Godiva. You know better than to get between me and my chocolate."

"Oooh, bad day?"

It had been Brian who had hooked Leigh on solace-through-chocolate. In those first months after their parents had been killed, Brian had become finely tuned to Leigh's moods. She had been a quiet kid, made more quiet by circumstance. It seemed senseless to tell anyone she was sad — how could she possibly be anything else? But Brian managed to sense degrees of her sadness and frustration. Just when she'd felt like she couldn't take any more, he would come home with a silent offering of chocolate. Of course, it had been Hershey bars and, on rare occasions, Fanny Farmer from the drugstore back then, not expensive Godiva and Ghirardelli. Leigh didn't know if it was the chocolate or the heartbreakingly sweet way he gave it to her that made the difference. But it lifted her every time.

For a moment she pondered his question. Bad day? Not really. She said, "Odd day."

"I'd imagine so — considering." He let the last word hang, knowing from years of experience that she'd bite.

"Considering what?" Leigh's jaw tightened. She'd heard the rumors, suffered the glances. And after she had showed up at the Drop for coffee, there could only be more ridiculous speculation.

"Well, for one, Benny's just about worn out my ear, worried that you're gonna run off with this drifter. Said he saw what he called, 'a connection.' Said you were 'different.' He just wouldn't shut up. I finally had to pay and leave. But the guy followed me to the front door. Swears he's seen enough to know when there's something between two people."

"That's ridiculous."

"Is it? Leigh, Benny knows you. And from what he's telling me, there was a whole *new* you in that bar the other night."

She remained silent. How could she tell her brother that's exactly what she wanted — a whole new her? He'd never understand.

Brian's tone fell into lecturing mode. "I'd bet my bottom dollar I'm not the only one he's been harping to about it, either. This isn't good, Leigh. You should steer clear."

"Benny exaggerates. I danced with Will. No big deal. I might dance with a lot of people — if they'd only ask." She popped another chunk of chocolate into her mouth to dilute the lie. She did dance with Will — and it *had* been a big deal. An earth-moving, skyrocket-lighting, breath-stopping big deal.

Brian sighed. "Listen, I know it's hard for you, here in this town. But this is just temporary. The first step. One of these days you'll be in a much bigger arena, playing on a whole new level. Things will be different then. You've gotta be patient. Keep in mind everything you do now affects how things shake out later."

"I'm sick of everybody in this stinking town

making such a big flippin' deal out of a stupid dance!"

"It's not just the dance and you know it. It's your reputation, the trust people put in you. I'm just saying, don't tear down all we've worked to build over some ass-shaking gigolo who blows through town. Don't give your enemies any ammunition."

Ass-shaking, she couldn't dispute, and a fine ass it was. But gigolo! Nothing could be further from the truth. Leigh closed her eyes and bit her tongue. She'd heard this lecture in various forms a thousand times before she ran for sheriff, and a thousand times since. As a female in a traditionally male job, she was an easy target, fair game for all the shit-slingers and rednecks. And as much as she knew Brian was right, she still wanted to sock him in the face.

"All right. You've made your point." She hung up the phone before he could continue his sermon. Given the chance, Brian could beat a dead horse into the next kingdom and beyond. Sometimes, like now, she hated the fact that a political agenda sometimes supplanted the simple brother-sister friendship that had pulled Leigh through the darkest days of her life.

She sighed, recognizing self-pity when she wallowed in it. She guessed it was time to grow up and face the fact that those days were long gone. Brian wanted a career in public service. She should be adult enough to stand on her own two feet and give back just a little of what he'd given her. It was her turn to play the supporting role.

This gave her a whole new perspective on her New Leigh program. If a single dance and a wave in passing caused this kind of stir, what would happen if she really did cut loose?

Chapter 6

Although Brian had made his point, one thing hadn't changed — Leigh desperately needed to bolster her feminine ego. Francine's words had echoed in her head as she'd drifted to sleep. Leigh had dreamed she was at Brian's congressional ball, dressed in the ugly sheriff's uniform complete with breast-flattening flack jacket, drawing disdainful stares from the elegant men and women around her.

In her desperation to blend in, she searched the ballroom and, as it happens only in the illogical evolution of dreams, found a hidden boutique behind a tall potted palm. She grabbed like a madwoman, adding frills and accessories — a necklace, a flowing scarf, a beaded handbag, rhinestones in her hair, four-inch stiletto heels — trying to soften and femininize a brown and tan polyester uniform clearly made for a man. In the end, she looked like the result of a horrible accident between Barney Fife and Phyllis Diller.

But she'd gathered her courage and asked a handsome man — who looked decidedly like Will Scott in a classy tuxedo — to dance. A young beauty in a sparkling red dress sidled up to him and latched onto his arm. His blue eyes fastened on Leigh for a moment, as if making a decision. Then he politely excused himself. Leigh stood, feet rooted in mortification, the heat of shame blooming on her cheeks, watching the ultra-feminine curves press against the black tuxedo jacket.

The next time Leigh saw Will, he was engaged on the dance floor with Ms. Red Dress, moving easily from a tango to a much more intimate dance where he caressed and twirled the woman as the entire assembly watched and applauded.

When Leigh awakened, she'd been in a sweat with an ache in her chest the size of the Milky Way. The entire thing was stupid beyond belief. Leigh never even wore that dreadful uniform, unless she was in court. Yet she couldn't shake the horror and panic that rose in her. The cool shower she took after she pried herself out of her sweat-dampened sheets did little to ease that ache. She had to do something or she was going to slide down a long gravelly embankment toward complete isolation from the opposite sex. Once at the bottom, she didn't think there would be enough substance to that bank for her to scale once again.

A date. She needed a date.

It took all of thirty seconds to go through the list of possibilities at her disposal. The lawyer she'd gone out with once was too kinky to consider. Besides, Leigh heard he was seeing someone from Bloomington on a relatively steady basis — there was food for thought.

That left the few unmarrieds from high school and Randy Thompson who'd recently gotten out of alcohol rehab — a place Leigh had personally had a large hand in sending him to. Hardly an advantageous precursor to a date. In the end, there were only two eligible men of her acquaintance that she could consider spending an entire evening with. Recently divorced Mike Nichols and Will Scott.

Of course, Will was off-limits.

Leigh picked up the phonebook and looked up Mike's number.

Should she invent some pretense for the call, or just ask him outright for a date? Past experience told her if *she* didn't do the asking, it just wouldn't be happening. She could do all the leading, leave a thousand openings, and still the guys just couldn't get the hint — or maybe they couldn't get past the badge. It was much like the way some men couldn't get past a woman making more money than themselves. A woman in power was a being to be reckoned with, not romanced and wooed into bed.

Mike was a large animal veterinarian. They'd been friends since they were twelve. Somehow it felt strange crossing that line and asking him out. On the other hand, he should be a fairly safe prospect. His divorce had been final only for a couple of months. No way would he be looking for something serious and permanent. In fact, he was probably toying with the idea of a New Mike.

She should still be able to catch him before he left for work. Feeling ridiculously nervous, Leigh dialed the number.

What if he said no? Would they ever be able to recover their status as friends? And it certainly wouldn't do anything to alleviate her growing insecurity as a woman.

That was silly. She was an adult — attractive enough for the casual date. And they had known each other forever. Of course he'd go.

Unless . . .

He wouldn't be cruel about it. He'd make up some lame excuse, then things would be awkward every time Leigh passed him on the street. Maybe he'd even take to hiding from her, crossing that street to avoid passing close enough to speak. She shuddered at the image of Mike ducking behind parked cars and walking in a crouch until she was out of sight.

Leigh hung up with her ears burning before he answered.

God, she hoped he didn't have caller ID.

As she stood there staring at the phone as if it were a coiled viper, the worst happened. It rang.

For a second she thought about ignoring it. That made her feel even more childish. What was the matter with her?

"Hello." She waited for the response, hoping that by some stroke of luck it wasn't Mike.

"Hi, Leigh. Did you just try to call me? I was in the shower and didn't catch it."

Hmm, Mike in the shower. She tried to picture it. The thought left her cold. Now, Will Scott in the shower . . .

She realized he was waiting for an answer. "Oh, yeah. It wasn't anything important. Just wanted to see how you're doing." *Nice recovery.*

"I'm good. Getting used to flying solo again."

There it was, her opportunity to ask. She swallowed hard. "I've got an idea; why don't we go out to dinner tonight?" God, how stupid she sounded.

"That'd be great. I could use some friendly conversation. How about I meet you at the Crossing House at seven?"

Stupid and sexless. "All right. See you then." Leigh hung up, feeling a bigger fool than when she dialed in the first place. Meet her at the Crossing House. She mentally kicked herself for not at least mentioning Easton's, the "nice restaurant" in Glens Crossing, the one people went to for birthdays and anniversaries. Once again, a male missed the point entirely. There was no getting around it, she was a hermaphrodite, like an earthworm.

She wanted a date.

What she got was a beer and onion rings with a buddy.

She sighed and left the house — dressed in men's clothes, baseball cap on her head, riding in her masculine vehicle, a cold black revolver tucked at the small of her back. Little wonder no man would give her a second glance. She drove into town more depressed and desperate than she had been when she'd awakened from that horrible dream.

Leigh almost skipped lunch. When she walked into the Dew Drop, she immediately wished she had.

Seated in a booth right at the front, so there was no way to pretend she didn't see them, were Brittany Wilson and Will Scott. He faced the front, while Brittany's back was to Leigh. At nearly the same instant that Leigh set foot across the threshold, Will looked up and smiled at her.

Disappointment fell like a brick on her chest. So much for her excellent people-reading skills, her quick and accurate assessment of a person's character. At the carnival, she had decided he was a decent guy; since then he'd pulled a knife on her and now here he sat having lunch with a high schooler. Men had gone to prison for less.

Brittany spun in her seat to look at Leigh with a frown on her face.

Leigh forced herself to step closer and said, "Hi, you two."

Will scooted over. "Have a seat; join us."

A little ménage à trois? She caught the thought just before it made its way out of her mouth. Her mind had settled firmly in a sexual track this morning and there seemed no redeeming it. "Thanks, I'm just getting a sandwich and taking it back to the office." Hadn't planned on it, but that seemed the only thing to do now.

She looked at Brittany, who appeared ecstatic with Leigh's declining of the invitation. The drastic comparison between the teenager's navel-revealing shimmery tank top and Leigh's sturdy-knit golf shirt with the department logo on the chest made Leigh feel exactly as she had in her dream. She couldn't keep the acidic tone out of her voice when she asked, "Shouldn't you be in school?"

Brittany laughed. "You *are* getting old and forgetful! Today's Saturday."

Shit. So it was. Lately, all of Leigh's days, except Sunday, blended together. She guessed that's what happened when you had no personal life.

Will said, "When you get to be our age" — nodding toward Leigh — "you're lucky to remember your own name."

Leigh forced a smile and gave them a wave of dismissal as she headed toward the counter. Will's attempt at gallantry would have been noteworthy, had he not been sitting here lunching with a girl who was eighteen-going-on-thirty. Up until this moment, Leigh had admired Brittany's edgy personality. Now it just seemed foolish, risky — and not a little tacky.

While she waited for her sandwich, Leigh made certain to keep Mildred engaged in conversation. It was everything she could do to keep from turning around and watching every exchange between Will and Brittany. He had

110

seemed so darkly sensitive and decent — and, she hated to add, interested in her as a woman.

How could she have been so wrong?

When her order was ready, she paid for it, walked out the door and dumped it in the first trash container she passed. Her appetite had completely disappeared.

Even if Will insisted Brittany was off-limits as far as "dating," as he called it, goes, she hoped he might still be persuaded to look at things differently. After all, he was a guy. And guys wanted just one thing, no matter what they said.

She'd checked with Mildred and knew he came to the Drop for lunch around eleven-forty-five. All it had taken was for her to wait for him to get there and go in a couple of minutes later. She'd acted surprised to see him, then gone on about how sorry she was that they'd gotten off on the wrong foot yesterday and that she'd thought about what he said. She'd settled in the booth across from him, knowing she'd blow it if she sat beside him like she really wanted. She had told him she needed someone to talk to about how messed up her life had gotten, and he was hers, simple as that — at least for lunch.

Everything was going great — until Leigh walked in. Will couldn't seem to keep his mind on their conversation after she left the café. He pretended to listen, but she could tell he was thinking about something, or someone, else. Brittany even cranked up the tears for a while, but that didn't pull him over to her side of the booth as she'd hoped. He just sat there looking sympathetic and said he understood why she was so hurt and confused.

Confused, hell. She knew what she wanted. And it didn't have anything to do with sitting around this stupid town watching her dad make a fool of himself.

There's something to be said for a new dress. Just slipping the spaghetti-strapped plum-colored knit over her head seemed to transform Leigh's mood. She looked in the full-length mirror. The bodice was scooped low and just tight enough to make her barely adequate bustline appear sexy. The straight cut showed the firm curve of her hip, and the slit up the side said all the right things. If Mike missed this signal, she was just going to have to give up and shoot herself.

She took extra time on her hair, pinning it up in the back and then strategically picking a few spiraling tendrils to fall loose. When she'd first gotten home, she'd pampered herself with the facial treatment kit that her sister-in-law Kate had given her last Christmas. Now she carefully applied makeup that she'd forgotten she even owned — soft plum eyeshadow, pencil to accentuate the arch of her brow, tinted gloss in her lips, a hint of blush on her cheeks. She hadn't gone to this much trouble in months, settling for no more than a quick swipe of neutral shadow and lick of mascara in her daily routine. But, she supposed it was like riding a bike because it all seemed to be falling into place nicely.

Before she walked out of her bedroom, she slipped her feet into a pair of strappy high-heeled sandals that Kate had forced her to buy on sale last summer. Even though Leigh had sworn she would never wear them, Kate had pushed and persuaded, saying there might be a time when she'd need something dressy and not be able to find something this cheap.

Kate had known what she was doing; it had been the dollars that had finally won Leigh over.

As she posed in front of the mirror one last time, Leigh had to admit, those sandals did make her legs look pretty damn good.

She left the house with hope singing in her heart. She didn't anticipate romance — but a little stunned male gawking would certainly be nice.

Planning her arrival to be just late enough that Mike should already be there, Leigh was glad to see his truck parked in the lot. She got out of the Blazer and immediately turned her ankle when her spike heel slid off a large chunk of crushed stone. The incident caused her to dip and weave to keep from toppling over. Once she had firm footing, she glanced around and was relieved to see she was alone in the lot.

"All right, now," she whispered, "slow and easy." Her first steps were as tentative as a toddler's. By the time she'd reached the door of the tavern, she'd gained a measure of confidence in her step.

It wasn't dark yet, so when she entered the doorway, it took a moment to adjust to the dim lighting. Mike waved to her from a booth in the back. Leigh smiled and took deliberate care to move across the space between them as sinuously as her limited practice could muster — holding in mind a sexy TV commercial she'd once seen as example. About halfway there, she had to stutter-step to keep from being plowed over by a waitress dashing past with a tray full of longnecks.

When she looked back at Mike, he was picking at a bowl of peanuts, not looking at her at all. So much for an entrance.

"Hi," she said, waiting for him to look up before she took a seat.

"Hi, Leigh." He seemed to notice the dress for the first time. "Going out after dinner?"

No, actually I was going out for *dinner.* She wanted to smack him upside the head and scream the words. Then she realized it wasn't Mike's fault she had no sex appeal. Deciding not to bother answering at all, she simply slid into the booth.

"I already ordered you a beer. That okay?"

A far cry from champagne and candlelight. "Sure."

"And the onion rings should be here any minute."

Goody.

The beer and onion rings arrived and Mike began describing the difficult foaling he'd assisted today. He gave full details, making the subject gory enough to make certain that if this had been a date, it would have been the last. But Leigh found herself leaning forward, taking in every detail.

Watching him as he spoke she realized there was no way she could ever consider him anything but the friend he was. It just wasn't going to happen, now or ever.

As soon as Leigh released any hope of making this an actual date, she began to have a good time. They chatted and laughed as they had for years and Leigh slowly came to terms with the cold fact that there would never be more between she and any of her meager prospects here in Glens Crossing. She was what she was. To change that, she would have to change everything about her life.

The idea had actually begun to wear into something near contentment, when Will Scott walked in the door.

Leigh's blood pressure shot up, her heartbeat accelerated and her extremities tingled as he held her gaze and walked past. Those sharp blue eyes nearly left scratch marks as he took in her hair, her neck, her breasts. He wasn't blatant about it, but didn't conceal his interest either. Oh, God, *this* is what she wanted — to feel desired, devoured by a glance, set aflame by mere possibilities.

Why, oh why, did it have to be the one man she couldn't have?

She had to remind herself that just hours ago, he'd been sharing lunch with a mere child. Instead of dousing her thirst for his touch, it made her want to force him into a corner and make him explain. Explain why he would take advantage of a wild-eyed child, why he risked condemnation by courting her in public — why he preferred a giddy teenager over her.

Mike's beeper went off, making Leigh jump as if she'd been shocked. She returned her attention to him; in her peripheral vision she saw Will take a seat at the bar.

"Aw, man. I'm sorry, Leigh, but I've gotta go. That foal must be in trouble."

She grabbed her purse and started to get up.

"No, no." He motioned for her to stay put. "Finish dinner. I'll have them box mine up to go."

She stole a glance toward the bar. The last thing she wanted to do was sit here and eat alone while Will was close enough to tempt her to force him to do that explaining. Instead of making a scene, she'd just wait until Mike was out the door, then leave.

Benny had been bowled over when he'd seen Leigh come through the door. Even more surprised when she sat down with Mike Nichols. Maybe he'd jumped the gun by telling Brian his sister looked like she was gonna elope with the dancer-fella from the other night. His instincts were normally reliable. But maybe Leigh had flipped her lid completely and was turning into one of those girls from that *Sex and the City* TV show.

He didn't like this one bit. He pressed his lips together in contemplation as he drew a couple of drafts and placed them on the tray for the waitress who was waiting with one hand on her hip, blowing big pink gum bubbles. He was gonna have to talk to her about that damn bubble gum — made her look underage, not good for business. He wiped his hands on his apron and he looked over at Leigh again. Change was always bad, and it looked like their little Leigh Mitchell was going through a world of change.

He kept a steady eye on her, even as he went through his normal routine. If there was one thing he could do, it was serve up drinks and still know what was going on even in the farthest, darkest corners of his bar. Like now, he knew if he walked past the jukebox, back into the hall that led to the restrooms, he'd find Jesse Frank making out with that trashy wife of Denny Taylor, who owned the junkyard. He'd told Denny marrying that gal was a mistake. He was pretty sure that Denny knew his wife was sucking the tonsils out of Jesse every chance she got, but pretended everything was hunky-dory.

Uh-oh. What have we here? Benny watched Brownie's new mechanic come through the door. The guy didn't say anything to Leigh as he passed, but he didn't have to. There it was, plain as day — that look he'd seen pass between them the other night, the one that had sent splinters of worry through him. Secretly, deep inside, Benny felt a shimmer of satisfaction. He knew he'd been right about those two. There was definitely something going on between them, he'd stake his Barcalounger on it.

Leigh waited uncomfortably until she was certain Mike had had time to leave the parking lot. It took all of her willpower not to turn and look at the bar, all of her strength not to, with a single crook of her finger, call trouble right to her table. Finally, she grabbed her purse and slid out of the booth. As she exited the Crossing House, she could swear she felt the heat of Will's stare on the back of her neck.

Once in the lot, she pulled off the shoes that felt even more ridiculous than when she'd bought them. Who on earth was she trying to kid? Tomorrow they were going in the Goodwill bag. She slipped a finger through the back straps and picked her way barefooted across the stone lot. The night air moved across her skin and the rough melody of the tree frogs lulled her. It was only eight o'clock. She didn't feel like getting in her car and driving home just yet, so she walked to the bridge and took the path that led down to the creek.

The dusty path felt like cool powder under her feet; the dry weeds on either side whispered as the light breeze moved them. The dark sky above winked with early evening stars. As she moved toward the creek, a sense of melancholy inched over her. It was the same feeling she'd been trying to find her way around, over or through for weeks. She fought its coming. But each time she drove it away with logic, it only found another angle of attack.

After a while, she simply allowed it to settle on her shoulders, thinking the sooner it overtook her, the sooner it would be gone. Better here than at home. Somehow gloominess seemed more manageable outdoors than in the confines of the walls of her house. She could feel part of a bigger universe, look at her problems in the perspective of the realm of nature.

She sat on a fallen log near the water and listened to the soothing night noises. As she focused on the slow-moving water nearby, she concentrated on the sound. Slowly, the rhythm of the song Will had played on the jukebox in the bar the night they danced crept into her mind. It swelled and intensified until it was the only sound in her head. For a long moment she resisted the urge to move to that remembered beat. Then she got to her feet and took a few tentative steps. They came easily and felt oddly sensual in her bare feet.

Closing her eyes, she recalled the fullness of the melody and imagined Will's warmth against her as she moved. By holding her eyes closed she could fully immerse herself in the memory, letting her body flow to the imaginary music. The steps came as if he was leading her. Her body took on the same liquid heat she'd experienced that night. Her bare thighs rubbed against the soft fabric of her dress, a caress she wished could have been delivered by Will's masculine hands. A longing bloomed in her chest and she turned, as she had that night in his arms. She felt his chest against her back, his hands on her waist as her hips rolled with the rhythm. It took nearly the space of two musical beats before she realized he was real.

Jerking away with a gasp, she spun around.

"Don't stop," he said quietly. "I love the way you dance."

She simply stared at him for a moment while her heart settled back into her chest. "What are you doing here?"

He shrugged. "Following you."

"How long have you been spying on me?"

"Not spying. Watching over." He put a hand on her cheek. "Long enough to need a fire extinguisher."

The same burning intensity she'd seen while they danced radiated from his eyes. She could almost allow herself to believe it was solely for her. For the briefest moment she leaned her cheek into his caress. Then her senses returned. "Listen, I don't know what kind of games you're playing, but I don't think I like them."

His brows drew together in what appeared to be genuine confusion, the passion in his eyes only muted slightly. "Games? Where do you get that?"

Leigh took a step back, the better to clear her senses of his sexual magnetism. "I know Brittany Wilson is of age, but that doesn't mean the term 'jailbait' doesn't apply. She's going through a tough time." She raised a hand, palm up, as if to lay reality out before him. "Young and insecure —"

He took a single step, closing the space she'd just created between them. "That's exactly right. *Dangerously* insecure." There seemed to be a power to his statement that made her re-evaluate her earlier assessment of his intentions. He added, "More people around here need to take note of that fact."

The gap widened between where her thoughts had been headed and the direction Will seemed to be taking. For a moment, she just stood there and waited to see what would come next.

"That girl is headed for trouble. For all she knows I'm a child molester, kidnapper, rapist, serial killer." He raised his fingers to innumerate each possibility, then clenched his hand into a fist. "And yet at every turn, there she is, opening the door, laying on the sexual innuendo — and I don't think it's just my charisma that's made me a target. She wants an older man to take the place Daddy's vacated — and she's not being too picky about who does it." The protective passion in his voice sounded much more like a father than a lover.

"So you thought you'd fix things by dating her?" As much as it now seemed he wasn't interested in the girl sexually, Leigh couldn't ignore the fact that she'd seen him with Brittany on three different occasions in as many days.

"What are you talking about?" His tone rose to match hers.

"Lunch?"

His posture relaxed and he ran a hand through his hair, yet the edge remained in his voice. "You think I asked her out to lunch? Then what? Maybe I'll take her to the football game on Friday and the drive-in movies next Saturday night?"

"You two *were* having lunch."

"*I* was having lunch. Brittany showed up about five minutes after I got there and just sat down."

She tipped her head and cast a disbelieving look. "So you say."

"Ask Millie."

"Millie?"

"You know, pink polyester, granny glasses — at the Dew Drop."

"Her name is Mildred; has been for sixty years. Can't imagine she'd change it today."

122

"Well, I asked if I could call her Millie. It suits her better. She said she liked it."

"She . . ." Leigh waved a hand in the air and shook her head. "Stop trying to get me off track."

"I wasn't. You asked."

"All right. All right. So Brit sat with you. You didn't have to let her. And what about yesterday? She was at Brownie's garage talking to you. If you're not planning on dating her, there's no sense in encouraging her. You're handling dynamite here."

"You're telling me. She's looking for attention in all of the wrong places."

"So you're saying she's coming on to you?"

He shrugged. "She's a confused kid, trying to hide behind a mask of false worldly experience and bravado. Inside she's just a frightened little girl looking for somebody to show they care."

Leigh crossed her arms over her chest and eyed him carefully. "Pretty insightful for a newcomer."

"Let's just say I've had experience with someone similar in the past. It's much easier to spot the second time around. Unfortunately the first time . . ."

He didn't finish, so Leigh did for him. "You weren't so lucky?"

His shoulders slumped slightly and he shook his head, a gesture of complete defeat. Leigh saw such intense sadness in his eyes that she had no doubt that this person in the past had meant a lot to him.

When Will spoke again, it was with quiet longing. "I thought if I could get Brittany to talk, to trust me, maybe I could get her to re-evaluate her game plan, find a healthier and safer way to get what she wants."

Leigh saw it like a flash of brilliant light. They were alike, she and Will. The driving need to hold things together, to fix the problem, to save someone — even if it was only from themselves. It caught her unaware and grabbed her heart in a way she'd never expected.

For a brief second, the need to share this insight with him almost made her speak. Then she caught herself. Nothing good would come of attaching herself more deeply to this man. Nothing at all. She mentally repeated it to herself enough times that she almost believed it.

After a moment, she said, "Well, you'd better be careful. People are getting the wrong idea."

He looked her in the eye. "By *people*, you mean you? I know we just met, but Christ Almighty, I figured you at least understood that I could never be involved with a child! To take advantage of —" He broke off, as if to even voice the rest was too repugnant.

She started to say she did understand, did know. But it would have been a lie. The real truth was, she *had* doubted. Doubted seriously enough that she had nearly done a little celebratory two-step when she found out the true nature of the relationship. Unable to deny it, she ignored the statement altogether. Instead she changed the focus away from the murky waters of her personal feelings.

"Listen, the town is already talking. Brittany has been rumored to have an older boyfriend she's been keeping hidden under the radar. Your attention can only lead to certain conclusions — logic and facts be damned." She touched Will's arm to emphasize her warning. "Brittany's father is a powerful man around here; he could make things very . . . *uncomfortable* for you."

"Jesus! Do you think the man's paying *any* attention?" Will flung a hand in the air, showing no concern for his own situation, locked in on Brittany's problem. Then he added in a more quiet tone, "That's all she wants, you know."

Leigh sat back down on the log she vacated when memories of rhythm had called her feet to dance. "I know." Suddenly this whole conversation seemed too burdensome to continue. Will wasn't chasing Brittany. Other than that, nothing could be resolved here and now.

Will sat next to her, the warmth from his shoulder reaching hers. They remained silent for a few moments, their previous companionability seeming to take new root. He appeared as content as she to simply sit in silence and allow the high emotion generated by their conversation to leach away into the night.

Leigh leaned slightly toward him, until their shoulders were just barely touching. Immediately her body jumped to conclusions, the recollection of the way he'd looked at her when he entered the bar only reinforcing it. She tried to ignore the heat that spread from where their shoulders touched to the far reaches of her being.

He said, quietly, apparently still unable to just allow Brittany to flounder on her own, "When there's a simple answer to a difficult problem, why can't people see it? It took me all of five minutes to realize she just wants to be the center of Daddy's universe again. That's it. Nothing complicated. He could take away her pain so easily. . . ." He shook his head, his hair falling slightly forward, blocking his eyes from Leigh.

"Do you really think she's that close to the brink?"

He sighed, moving his shoulder against hers. "I really can't tell, but that's why it scares me — it feels like she's hiding something. There's something playing at the edge of our conversations. I feel it there, like an electric charge that draws the hair on your arm to attention. But I can't bring it into focus. It's the things they don't talk about that pose the real danger."

Leigh pondered that for a moment. Quickly her mind turned his statement around and directed it back at him. There was plenty Will wasn't talking about. The day before yesterday he'd said he understood the need to be someone else. It had pricked her curiosity then, but he'd left before she'd had the chance to question him.

"What about you, Will? I think you have a secret, too. What things are you not talking about?"

He faced her, held her gaze steady with his. "Believe me, there are plenty of things about me you don't want to know."

"Oh, I think you're wrong." Her voice came out barely more than a whisper, raw with unspoken longing.

As she sat there, barefooted on a dirty log, having lived through the most devastating evening her sexuality had seen in months, Will Scott drew every ounce of heated energy to the surface of her skin, made her feel desired, fanned sexual fires that had been banked for her entire life. All this, without ever laying a hand on her. It was in his eyes, his posture, his every exhaled breath.

The moonlight silvered his skin, sparked jet diamonds in his hair. She reached over and pushed the hair away from his forehead.

He leaned closer. His hand rested on the side of her neck, igniting a shower of sparks that drifted down over her body. Instead of kissing her, he pressed his forehead against hers. He whispered so softly she almost didn't hear. "I shouldn't have come here."

Whether he meant here to the creek, or here

to Glens Crossing, she didn't know — didn't care as his lips sought hers. It was a gentle brush at first. Then he settled more firmly against her mouth, his fingers sliding into her upswept hair. It didn't escalate into breathless passion, but spoke of something quieter, deeper. A kiss of tenderness and timelessness. It seemed to go on forever, yet wane quickly. Leigh's entire sense of time and space were temporarily swept away.

When he released her, possibly hours or only a moment later, the chill of the night quickly stole the heat of him from her lips. He continued to hold her with his gaze for a long while, looking like he wanted to say something. But his eyes said much more than his words ever could. Leigh saw the sensitivity, the sadness, the inner conflict. He had reasons for saying he shouldn't have come here — serious reasons.

Sliding his hand over her bare shoulder and down over the goosebumps that had risen on her arm, he said, "You're cold."

Unable to summon her voice, she simply shook her head.

He pulled her against his side, wrapping his arm tightly around her. Her head rested perfectly in the crook of his neck.

He said there were things about him she didn't want to know. But he couldn't be more wrong. She wanted to know everything about him, was desperate to quiet the longing in her soul that his mere presence stirred. Maybe it was only curiosity, the thrill of discovery. Only by knowing him completely would she be able to tell the difference.

It was nine-thirty when Will walked Leigh back to her truck. She offered him a ride home, but he declined, saying he needed to walk, to think. She knew exactly what he meant. Although she and Will shared only a kiss, Leigh felt a sense of betrayal toward her brother. Just last night Brian had asked that she behave sensibly, like a mature adult. At the time it seemed no great sacrifice. But now, after the way this evening had played out, she understood a measure of what she would be giving up by staying away from Will.

Half of her almost wished Will would pick up and move on in the night. Then the decision would be out of her hands. But, oh that other half . . . .

Although she wasn't asleep — had been staring at her bedroom ceiling for hours, thinking about *not* thinking about Will Scott — the shrill of the telephone jerked every muscle in Leigh's body to full attention. Glancing at the clock as she answered, she saw it was one forty-five.

"Hello?" She scooted up on one elbow.

"Sheriff, I think you'd better get out here," Calvin said in a strained voice. "I ain't sure what to do about this."

"About what, Calvin?" She had deliberately put him on the night shift, simply because nothing ever happened at night in Henderson County.

"It's that Wilson girl's car. It's the damndest thing. Sittin' here running with the door wide open, but she ain't nowhere to be found."

Leigh swung her legs over the side of the bed and pushed the hair away from her face. "Did you look for her? Maybe she's in the bushes puking up beer."

"No, ma'am. I hollered and beat the bushes already. She ain't here."

"Where are you?"

"Quarry Road. Just south of the lane to Grissom's farm. And Sheriff" — his pause was heavy and dread coiled in Leigh's stomach — "driver's window's broken — like somebody busted it from the outside."

"Don't touch anything. I'll be right there."

As Leigh threw on some clothes and strapped on her holster, she mumbled, "My God, Brittany, what have you gotten yourself into now?"

Somehow she knew this was going to be bad.

Chapter 7

Leigh went cold as she slowed to a stop behind Brittany's red Camaro. There was no mistaking it; Leigh saw the familiar license plate that read 2SPOILD. Calvin's cruiser was parked just ahead, red and blue lights twirling into the darkness that pressed close from fields bordered by dense woods. The Camaro's dome light shone dimly through the tinted rear window; ghostly illumination spilled from the open driver's door onto the sun-bleached asphalt.

When she opened her door, she heard the bass rumble of Brittany's CD player. Heavy metal. Angry music.

Calvin hurried her way. "You want me to shut it off?"

"No. Did you touch anything?" Leigh asked, her gaze fixed on the empty car as she aimed the Blazer's spotlight, then reached back inside for her flashlight.

Calvin took off his hat and rubbed his head. "Don't think so." He paused and looked nervously at the car. "Umm, I might have when I first came up to it." His face twisted with embarrassment. "I had no idea it was going to be like this. I thought she was around here someplace — you know how she is."

"Yes. Yes, I do." She put a hand on Calvin's shoulder as he shifted his weight from foot to foot, obviously fearing condemnation. "Why don't you get your camera out of the trunk. I want some pictures." Then she called as he walked away, "And call Brownie for a tow. Tell him to bring the flatbed."

"How about her parents?"

She hesitated. "No. Not yet."

Maybe Brittany had loaned the car to someone. In any case, Leigh should be the one to call Kurt and Emma Wilson, see if they know where Brittany is, and where her car is supposed to be.

She approached the Camaro, circling wide, trying to take in the big picture.

Leaning in the door slightly, she was careful not to touch anything. Shattered glass sprayed across the car's interior. Brittany carried one of those little backpack-like purses, which sat on the passenger seat, still buckled, bits of glass glistening like rhinestones on and around it. She didn't see anything that could have been used, either inside or outside the car, to break the glass. Other than the broken window, there was no sign of a struggle. The gearshift was in Drive but the vehicle remained stationary, even with the engine running. Odd.

Leigh knelt and shone her flashlight under the car. The paving was old and porous, but she could see a small wet spot under the center of the vehicle, between the front tires.

Transmission fluid?

She traced her flashlight along the pavement in a line behind the car, but the surface was so worn, spotted and absorbent, she couldn't tell if the car leaked while it was still moving. The puddle under the car was small; it would have to have been leaking a while as she drove for the fluid to be so low the gears disengaged.

Had she started to walk? Brittany had a temper; could she have broken the window in frustration? Leigh looked up and down the length of flat road. If Brittany had headed toward town, as was logical since it was much closer than her house, Leigh should have passed her on the way out here. Besides, would she have left her purse?

Maybe a pissed-off car thief broke the glass when the Camaro broke down. *And buckled up the purse after taking the money and credit cards?* That seemed a stretch.

Calvin came back with the camera.

She looked at the lane to the farmhouse. "Did you check the Grissoms? Maybe she went there to call for help."

"Yes, ma'am. Mister said he didn't see any girl. Then started his UFO talk; said if the girl was missing, we'd better plan a memorial service for her, 'cause she ain't coming back. He said —" Calvin stopped, as if hesitant to tell the rest.

"He said what?"

"He said the aliens are taking the young gals

for . . . for" — he bit his lip and looked at his shoes — "breeding." He said the word so quietly she almost didn't hear it.

"For God's sake, Calvin, 'breeding' is not a dirty word!" How had this kid made it through the police academy? His ears must have been continually red. She sighed. "Did you talk to Mrs. Grissom?"

"Didn't see any need to. They're both crazy as loons."

Leigh didn't point out that there was absolutely no way anyone could assess Mrs. Grissom's mental stability, as no one had publicly heard more than a stray word from her mouth in years. However, she couldn't disagree that Mr. Grissom did have a very faint grasp on reality. Guilt by association.

"All right, I'll speak with her later. Right now, we need some photos."

Leigh slipped on latex gloves and turned off the ignition. She couldn't stand the CD player's frantic, driving beat one more second. Then she directed Calvin and his camera in a thorough examination of not only the car inside and out, but the few yards surrounding it in each direction. It was dark and hard to examine the entire area, but she could hardly leave the car here until morning. Film was cheap; she'd rather have too many pictures of the scene than too few.

As the camera flashed, Leigh saw a small, white rectangular object just under the car, just behind the rear wheel on the driver's side. She leaned over and picked it up. When she turned it over she realized this was no usual bit of country road litter. Racing flags arced over a golden tire with wings — the Indianapolis Motor Speedway logo. It was a ticket stub from the racing museum — dated six days ago.

What were the chances of anyone around here taking a day in mid-week during harvest season to go to a museum open all year round? She swallowed. The chances were much greater that someone traveling through dropped this.

With a dry mouth, she placed the stub in an evidence bag and put it in her car.

The yellow flashers on Brownie's rig appeared in the darkness as it rounded the bend. Calvin pulled his cruiser farther ahead, out of the way. Brownie drove past Leigh's Blazer and maneuvered in front of the Camaro. He climbed out, bristly hair standing every-which-way from sleep, and examined the distance between the vehicles. Apparently satisfied, he started the hydraulics that tipped and lowered the big flatbed.

Leigh winced as the whine stabbed at ears just growing accustomed to this quiet stretch of road. It seemed almost obscene to disrupt nature's quiet lullaby with such a harsh mechanical sound. It went on for what felt like an eternity before the lip settled on the pavement.

Brownie walked over to Leigh. "Brittany just

brought this by the garage as I was leaving today."

"She did? Was she having problems?"

"Said it was makin' a noise — couldn't quite describe it. You know women."

There it was again. Brownie spoke to Leigh as if she didn't belong to the female gender. In this county, she was an androgynous being. Normally, Brownie caught himself, stopping in mid-sentence and blushing beet red; but the realization never seemed to stick from one conversation to another. He didn't seem to notice his faux pas this time.

"Did you find anything wrong?" she asked.

He shrugged. "Will said he'd take a look-see. I went on home — tonight was poker night, you know. But I doubt he found anything, car sounded fine to me."

"Did Will tell you what he found?" Will hadn't mentioned he'd looked at Brittany's car. They'd spent enough of their time together last night discussing her. Why wouldn't he bring it up?

"Nope. He came through the house 'bout forty-five minutes later. Showered, turned down my offer to join the game and left. I'd forgotten about the Camaro." He started toward the car. "Better get this baby loaded."

She stopped him before he reached inside. "Here, put these on." She handed him a pair of latex gloves.

"What's this?"

"Precaution. We don't know where Brittany is."

Brownie's eyes widened. "You think somebody snatched her? I know her old man's got money, but who around here —"

"She's probably just walking home. But," she added, "take the car and have Calvin lock it up in the pole barn behind the jail."

With a shake of his head, Brownie closed the driver's door of the Camaro. She stopped him before he returned to the truck. "Was Will back home when you left to come out here?"

"Couldn't say. Didn't check his bed before I left." He winked. "Asking for personal or professional reasons?"

"Get that car out of here." She waved him off.

He gave her a mischievous grin as he crawled under the front bumper and hooked the wench to the axle.

The ear-splitting whine started again as the cable tightened, setting Leigh's stretched nerves to screaming. Personal or professional? She thought of the ticket stub. God, she hoped it remained personal.

The car groaned slightly and began to inch onto the flatbed. Calvin walked up and handed Leigh a roll of film. "Took all thirty-six."

"Good. I want you to follow Brownie and lock this car in the barn. Put the key in the safe in my office. I don't want *anyone* allowed access 'til I say so."

Calvin looked serious as he nodded, then started back to his cruiser. Leigh thought she saw a glint of satisfaction in his eyes; for once, his cautious approach seemed validated. He was young, but she knew he had the makings of a good officer. His test results at the academy had confirmed it.

"Calvin," she called over the noise of the wench.

He turned.

"You did a good job here tonight."

He touched the brim of his hat and nodded. He nearly managed to suppress his grin until he was turned fully away from her.

She had a sinking feeling that this small affirmation would be the high point of the next few days for both of them.

Kurt Wilson's face contorted with fury as he advanced on his ex-wife. "I told you you had no business staying out here! It's no place for two women alone. If you'd let me keep this house —"

"Oh, right! If you'd been the one sitting here with your little sweetie, Brit would never have had car trouble!" Emma Wilson stood in her nightgown before the massive stone fireplace, spitefully jabbing her finger at her ex-husband's chest.

This argument had been raging for five minutes. The offensive had ping-ponged between the two several times. They'd each in turn managed to parry repeated onslaughts and regain the upper hand. Emma was back on top.

Leigh wasn't sure she should have brought Kurt to Emma's house, but she'd opted for expediency. The Wilsons' had been a particularly ugly divorce. In addition to the usual break-up stress, there was a large sum of money involved and enough injured pride to choke an elephant. Kurt had moved in with a woman only four years older than his daughter. And for months he and Emma had been playing a game of who could hurt who the most. Now throw in a missing child and the ensuing explosion was deafening.

Leigh had remained silent as they yelled and blamed, allowing their initial anger and frustrations to run their course. Now it was time to get down to the business of finding their daughter.

Leigh held up a hand. "Okay, okay. I think everyone's said enough. We need to work together to find Brittany."

Emma crossed her arms over her chest and looked to Leigh with a quivering chin and unshed tears in her eyes. Leigh heard Emma's teeth chattering.

Kurt visibly swallowed the words he had ready to hurl at his ex. He turned his back to the two women, his shoulders slumped slightly. His hands clenched and opened at his sides. After a couple of deep breaths, he straightened his back and turned to face them again.

"What do you want us to do?" he asked.

Leigh made both of them sit down before Emma fell down. "Do either of you know what her plans were this evening?"

Two heads shook in unison, as if pulled on the same string. Then two pair of eyes narrowed as they looked at one another. Leigh spoke before they could voice the fresh accusations she saw written clearly on their faces. "When did you see her last, Emma?"

"This morning. I was out when she came home. She'd changed clothes; her old ones are on her bed. She left a note, said she had plans and would be late."

Kurt mumbled, "A senior in high school with no curfew."

Leigh pressed on before Emma could react. "No idea what those plans were?"

Emma slowly shook her head, the tears now slipping down her cheeks. "Things have been" — she closed her eyes as if searching for the word written on the inside of her lids — "*difficult* with Brittany these last months. I want her to know someone still trusts her." With that, she shot a condemning look at Kurt.

He stiffened. "I trust her! But a girl needs rules —"

"Afraid she'll run off with someone old enough to be her father?" Emma interrupted. Then she stopped, pressed her lips together, appearing to rethink her attack. "She needs *you*. She thinks you've deserted her. You only want to act as a jailer —"

"That's bullshit!"

Leigh stepped in between them. "We're getting off track." Quietly, she asked, "Kurt, when did you see Brit last?"

His ears turned red. His lips tightened and he seemed to have to force the words between them. His voice was barely audible. "Last week."

Emma *humphed,* but held her tongue.

Kurt appeared to shrink right before Leigh's eyes. He was Brian's business partner, twelve years her brother's senior. She had never really noticed the age difference between them, had always sort of thought of them as having played on the same football team. But now she saw the gray in Kurt's thick hair, the deep grooves beside his mouth, and an uncharacteristic defeated set to his broad shoulders.

"No contact since then?" she forced herself to ask. She felt like someone picking at another person's festering scab.

He blew out a long breath as he ran his hands through his hair, leaving it standing on end like an orangutan's. "Ruby said Brit stopped by the real estate office today while I was on a conference call — sometime after four. I didn't talk to her, but I think Brian did."

"I know you've already called her close friends," Leigh said. "But I'd like for you to check further — some of her other acquaintances — just to make certain she's not staying with someone. I'll talk to Brian, see what he knows."

Emma nodded, started to stand up and faltered. Kurt jumped up and grabbed her arm, steadying her. The instant she had her balance, she jerked away from his touch and headed toward the phone.

He said to Leigh, quietly, as if he didn't want Emma to hear, "What if we don't find her anywhere?"

"Then we start searching the area tomorrow morning."

"Why can't we start now?" He nearly shouted. "She could be hurt!" He glanced toward Emma and lowered his voice, whispering through his teeth. "You know she's not at a friend's. She never lets anyone drive that car."

Leigh left the standard reassurances behind. She felt like he deserved the truth, would take it without cracking up. "I agree. She's probably not at a friend's." She paused. "But I've driven the roads five miles in every direction from where her car was. I rousted my deputies out of bed; they're out covering every road in the county. I've notified the state police that we're looking for her. There isn't much more we can do until daylight." She shot a glance at Emma. "Calling her friends is better than sitting here doing nothing."

Kurt picked up his jacket. "Then I'll go look for her myself."

Leigh grabbed his arm. "It's too dangerous in

the dark." She waved a hand at the outdoors. "Ravines, caves, sink holes. I don't have enough manpower to search the woods for you too. Please, you can help more by staying with Emma. Brittany might call."

She felt the muscles in his arm quiver as he held the jacket in a tight fist. After a moment, he said tightly, "First light, I'm out there."

"I'll be in touch before then."

Leigh left the Wilsons and headed to Brian's house.

Chapter 8

Will was awakened by his own screaming. His heart thundered; it felt like a throbbing, over-filled basketball in his chest. He slowly raised his slick palms in front of his face. Something squelchy was mashed between his fingers. His breath came in quivering bursts as he squinted in the dim light. Finally his eyes focused, then closed in relief as he sagged forward, his elbows on the ground. His hands weren't covered with rotting flesh and writhing maggots, only the slimy clay-mud from the creek bank.

He leaned over, rinsed his shaking hands in the sluggish water, then splashed his face.

The nightmare hadn't come for weeks. It varied slightly in its torment. Sometimes he was an unwilling participant. Sometimes he acted only as an observer. Tonight he had been both in the scene and viewing it. He watched himself as he knelt beside a mass grave filled with bodies thrown there like filthy rag dolls. He looked into his own blue eyes as they pleaded for help. At the same time, he felt the rocky ground under his knees, the bite of the rope binding his wrists behind his back, and the pistol pressed to the back of his head.

A millisecond after that he watched, horrified, as the gun bucked in the gunman's hand.

He heard the sharp crack of the shot. And he was once again the victim. He felt his body jerk with the bullet's impact, felt himself hurled down into the pile of decomposing flesh. But he wasn't dead. He gagged on the smell of putrefaction, heard the buzz of the flies, felt the liquefying tissues squish between his fingers as he clawed his way across the bodies toward the edge of the pit.

That's when he awakened. In his sleep he'd crawled five feet from where he'd laid down, digging his fingers into the mud by the creek. After he doused his face once again with cool water, he flopped onto his back and covered his eyes with his hands. He forced his breathing to slow and listened as his rapid pulse receded from his ears. Once again, his subconscious was punishing him. It would replay like this in his head until the day he died. The only way he could gain absolution was to see this through to the end — whatever awaited him.

After being on the move for so long, he'd been too restless to spend another night cooped up in that stuffy little back-porch room at Hank Brown's house. He'd returned here, to the log he'd shared with Leigh, seeking the solace he normally found under the stars. He'd stretched out near the creek and laid his head on his folded jacket, watching the slowly moving heavens, considering what he should do about his growing fascination with the county sheriff. An interest that could be very dangerous in his particular situation.

Will had hoped his visit with Leigh would show her to be just like every other woman — sexually interesting, but easy enough to leave behind. He'd been sorely disappointed. She was deeper, more reflective, and so honest about herself. He could have stayed on that porch, not touching, and soaked in her company for months on end without tiring.

Tonight's encounter had only served to reinforce each and every emotion he'd been trying to deny. There was much more than physical attraction at work. The damnable thing was the sexual current was equally strong between them. The vulnerable, yet inviting look in her eyes as he'd forced himself to release her from that kiss almost drew him into something he had no business doing. Yes, he'd wanted her — so much his body throbbed with it. But he knew, once he made that connection with this woman, there would be no breaking it. She'd already crawled much too deeply beneath his skin.

He knew his wisest course of action was to move on. Collect his pay and hit the road. He simply couldn't afford to be caught now with three dead bodies in his wake. Too much had been sacrificed to get this far. He had always been the hunter, the one holding all the secrets. It had taken weeks for him to adjust to the role of hunted. He had to mind those lessons.

If he could only will this to an end. He imagined he might stay right here in the heartland, call this home and these people his friends. This would be a good place. He could easily see himself dancing with Leigh Mitchell in that ratty little bar every Thursday night for the rest of his days.

But it was out of his hands. All he could do was wait — and try to stay alive.

Yes, tomorrow he had to leave.

Leigh called Brian from her mobile phone before she reached his house. Nothing so disturbing as being awakened in the middle of the night by someone pounding on your door. She knew she should just let him sleep, handle this one on her own — at least until morning. But it was reflexive, instinctive to go to him with troubles. He'd helped her work through every crisis in her life thus far. Although she'd certainly grown past needing him for trivia, it still helped to have him along for the big stuff. And this was big with a capital B.

After five rings, his answering machine picked up and Leigh disconnected the call and tossed her phone onto the passenger seat. It landed next to the plastic bag with the ticket stub from the racing museum. She looked at it for a moment. Evidence? Or just litter? Her gut answered clearly, but at the moment she wasn't inclined to listen.

Although the night had cooled considerably,

she drove with the window of her Blazer open. A hint of burning leaves hung in the air. Although she loved the smell, it made her tense with frustration. Monday she'd have the newspaper run a reminder about the ban on open burning. With no appreciable rain for over thirteen weeks, the entire county was a tinder box.

She rested her elbow on the door, pushing her blowing hair away from her face. Her cheeks were still warm from refereeing the arguments between the Wilsons. The air moving past her face felt like a soothing caress. She concentrated on the sensation, working to quell the panic that kept trying to rear its nasty little head; prayed against hope that Brittany would somehow turn up at one of her friends', that someone had stolen her Camaro in the night.

Of course, it'd been two years since the last car had been reported stolen in Henderson County. And that had turned out not to be a stolen car at all. Leigh had been sheriff for only three weeks. Herbert Calverson had left his pickup parked in a graveled area beside Forrester Lake that served as both parking lot and boat launch. He then walked about a half mile along the wooded shore to his favorite fishing spot.

When he returned about four hours later, the truck was gone. From his description of the vehicle, Leigh couldn't imagine anyone with eyesight adequate enough to drive would take the thing. When she asked if he left his keys in the ignition he'd said, *"Hell, no. You think I'm an idiot? I put 'em above the visor!"* This coupled with his dismissive body language and narrowed looks told Leigh that, in his opinion, a sheriff just couldn't do the job without a full set of male plumbing. But she plodded ahead with her questions and filling out of the proper form, ignoring his occasional snide comment. Finally, when she asked if he'd checked the lake, he'd laughed like a hyena. In fact, she thought he looked a little like a hyena, too — all pointy nose and big ears that sprouted a dozen or so long hairs.

Leigh had taken off her shoes and gun belt, then waded into the cold water. It dropped off quickly, and soon she'd been swimming. About twenty-five feet from shore, she stopped to tread water and felt the hood of the vehicle under her feet. She'd climbed on the top of the truck cab, the water now only up to mid-calf, and waved at Mr. Calverson. The man sputtered and spit, then tromped off down the road, fishing gear in hand.

She'd had Brownie tow the truck to Calverson's farm. The man hadn't spoken to her since, would never even meet her eye when they passed on the street. Wounded male pride, Leigh surmised. The memory still made her smile in satisfaction, her first small step to gaining public respect as an officer. It meant a lot to her, no matter how grudgingly given.

Leigh slowed on the deserted street in front

of Brian's place, then turned into his driveway. Moonlight reflected off the dark windows of the house. She first tried the back door, on the off chance he'd left it unlocked. Not tonight. In going from the back of the house to the front, she passed under a dense maple that blocked out all of the slivery moonlight she'd been navigating by. She didn't see the garden hose coiled on the flagstone path before she stumbled over it. She swore as she bumped against the side of the house. Her flashlight clattered against the stone wall, sounding like breaking glass. Thank goodness Brian was a sound sleeper, otherwise she might just get hit over the head with the baseball bat he kept by the back door.

Once she made it to the front porch, she tried the doorbell — twice. Then she lifted the big black wrought-iron door knocker and hammered it against the metal knob it rested on. Nothing. Granted, he slept like a stone, but that knocker was so loud it echoed down the block. She rapped it once more, putting a little muscle behind it.

She was just about to give up and head down the front steps when the porch light came on and the heavy oak door creaked open.

"Leigh! What's going on?" he asked, sounding not at all sleepy. Well, she guessed she wouldn't be either if she'd been awakened by someone hammering on her front door in the middle of the night. In fact, it happened occasionally. She remembered all too well the adrenaline rush it triggered.

She walked inside. Brian turned on a lamp and stood unselfconsciously, shirtless, in boxers and bare feet.

"Calvin found Brittany Wilson's car out near Grissom's farm. She wasn't with it."

Brian looked at her blankly for a moment. "Stolen?"

"Could be. But we can't locate Brit either. Kurt said she stopped by the office this afternoon."

"Yeah, she did. Kurt was busy. She stuck her head in my office and said hi."

"Did she seem upset? Say where she was going?"

Brian ran a hand over his face. "She said she'd come in to have her dad listen to her car; it was making a noise. I told her to take it over and have Brownie look at it. That was about it. She didn't seem any more moody than usual."

Leigh's gaze sharpened. "What do you mean, more moody than usual?"

"Well, you know, she and Kurt have been at odds. That's all."

"Hmm."

Brian shifted his weight. "You don't think something's happened to her, do you?" Then he thought for a moment. "Maybe she eloped with that boyfriend of hers."

"Kurt already checked. Jared is home, tucked in his bed — alone."

"Poor confused kid. I hope she's okay. Is Kurt with Emma?"

"Yes."

Brian groaned. "They're alone — without a mediator?"

She nodded.

"I'd better get over there. They're liable to tear one another's throats open. It was bad enough before, but if Brit's missing . . ."

"Good idea. When I left there *was* a whole lot of finger pointing going on." She opened the door. "Be at my office by six. I'll call in guys from the volunteer fire department to man the search."

After she closed the door behind her, she felt somewhat more in control, just having Brian aware of what was going on.

Orange brilliance encroached on the dull gray sky as Leigh pulled up to her office at 5:45 A.M. Her eyes felt like someone had dumped a couple of pounds of fiberglass into them, her mouth tasted like an old gym sock, and her head throbbed from lack of sleep. The lure of the toothbrush in her office bathroom called like a siren's song. Not much relief in sight for the other discomforts.

Two men waited outside the door to the low brick building that doubled as the sheriff's office and county jail. One stood still, hands in pockets, leaning one shoulder against the door frame. Instantly she recognized the tall, square-shouldered form topped with longish hair. The other man flitted and hovered around Will Scott — like a moth around a porch light. It took a couple of minutes for the moth's identity to sink in. Hale Grant — the very last person she wanted to deal with this morning.

She hadn't yet set a foot on the ground when the moth flitted her way. He was young for a chief reporter, barely out of college. But there *were* only two others on staff of the *Glens Crossing Recorder*, one of which was ninety-two years old. However small the paper, Hale Grant had made it plain, he took his job seriously.

"Sheriff Mitchell, I understand we have a missing girl."

She cast a glance at Will, still motionless by the door. Then she focused on Hale. "And since *we* have a missing girl, *our* first concern in Henderson County is the welfare of our fellow citizens, not the scavenging of a news story. I assume you're here to volunteer for the search party."

"It's Brittany Wilson, isn't it?"

She ignored him and made her way to the entrance.

"Was there any sign of violence at the scene?"

She stopped and looked squarely at him. "What scene?"

"Her *car*," he said in a tone that said he didn't just fall off the turnip truck.

"Mr. Grant, you'll just have to wait to be briefed with the rest of the party. Excuse me."

Damn those police-band radios. She unlocked the door and went inside without another word to either man.

When she came out of the bathroom, much refreshed from a face washing and tooth brushing, Will Scott was sitting in her office.

"I don't have time for a dance this morning, Mr. Scott," she said as she entered. Might as well start this off on the right foot. She needed to concentrate on what was happening. To do that she had to distance herself from this man who flipped her world upside down each time he came into view.

"I didn't come to dance. I came to help."

She looked at him. He stood and put his hands on his hips. The knees of his jeans were caked with mud, and those new tennis shoes looked like they'd been dragged behind a car. "Bad night?"

He glanced down at himself. Then he brushed at the dirt on his pants. "Slept outside."

She tipped her head inquisitively. "I thought you were staying with Brownie."

"I am. But sometimes four walls are just too confining." His eyes lingered on her, defining his meaning.

Leigh squashed the little thrill that said he'd been as shaken as she by last night's kiss. "How'd you find out about Brittany?"

"I got back about the same time Brownie did. He said you'd called the volunteer fire depart-

154

ment. I figured you could use another hand."

She nearly told him she didn't need the help. No way did she want to spend the entire day with Will Scott within her line of sight, distracting her from her purpose. But she realized how selfish such a thing would be. She needed all of the able bodies she could muster. Brittany's life might depend on it.

"Okay. I appreciate the help."

"Fill me in," he said matter-of-factly as he sat down, leaned back in his chair and propped one ankle on a knee. He appeared just a little too casual to Leigh, too comfortable with such an urgent situation. But then, he was distanced from the emotional aspect the rest of the town had to deal with.

She closed the door to her office. The moth was bothering Steve Clyde, the deputy who just walked in the building.

Settling one hip on the corner of her desk, she said, "Don't know much. We found her car out on Quarry Road."

"Wrecked?"

"No. In the road."

"Breakdown?"

"Maybe."

"Any sign it was stolen — hot wired?"

"Keys in the ignition."

She nearly held her breath as she waited to see if he would admit to looking the car over earlier. To her relief he did so right away.

"Was there anything wrong with it?" she

asked, as if this was the first time she'd heard the news.

"Not that I could tell. She complained of a funny noise, but it sounded fine in the shop. I even drove it around the block." He shook his head. "Nothing."

Will rose and looked out the window for a moment, hands on his hips. "What was left in the car?"

Leigh hesitated. He certainly didn't need to know all this to tromp around the woods looking for a missing girl. "I haven't gone through it yet."

"The cell phone, was it there?" he asked.

She had seen the cell phone, laying on the console. No way would a thief pass on a free phone *and* a purse. But this conversation was getting away from her. She had to remain professional and Will had done nothing yet to gain such a degree of trust that she should share all of the details of an ongoing investigation with him. No matter how astute his questions.

She looked at her watch. "It's six; I need to get this search underway."

Opening the door, she stepped into the outer office. A surprising number of volunteers filled the area. Glens Crossing only had eight volunteer firemen, but there must have been twenty-five men, along with two women, ready to pitch in. The volunteers were in various stages of preparedness: walking sticks, coffee thermoses, water canteens. One man shouldered a rolled blanket and a first-aid kit. A couple of the older men even toted shotguns — one of them was Ed Grissom, the other Herbert Calverson.

The room hushed when she appeared. All eyes looked to her expectantly, then shifted over her shoulder to Will. A couple of whispered comments slid past her ears, undecipherable.

"Thank you for coming," she said in her strongest, take-charge voice, aware of Will slipping past her to stand with the rest of the searchers. Most of them took a step away as he stopped in their midst; only Brownie stood firm. "As you know, Brittany Wilson is missing. Her car was abandoned near the Grissom farm, so our search will radiate from that central point.

"We're going to work in groups. Always stay within eyesight of your other group members. We need to shake every bush, probe every brush pile, check every ditch and ravine. The only way we can be organized about it and not miss anything is to take our time. It'll do no good to rush through an area. We don't want to have to repeat our efforts. Calvin has a map in the break room. If you'll all go in there he'll pass out area assignments and a handheld radio to each group."

As the crowd started toward the break room she added, "I think it best if we leave our firearms here in the office."

Two pair of narrowed eyes turned her way.

She met their stares. "It's rough terrain out there. We're going to have people on top of people. We don't need anyone getting shot by accident."

With obvious reluctance, both shotguns settled on the reception desk.

"I'll lock them away for safekeeping. You can pick them up at the end of the day."

She heard Ed Grissom mutter, "Shotguns don't do no good against aliens anyhow."

Herbert Calverson stepped toward Leigh. This was the first time he'd come close to acknowledging her existence since she pulled his truck out of the lake. He still didn't look at her. His gaze instead flirted with the American flag on the wall over her left shoulder.

"My boy, Corey," he said, now switching his gaze to the window to Leigh's right, "is on his way with his hounds. Best huntin' dogs I ever seen. Reckon if that girl's out there, them dogs'll find her." He looked down his sharp nose at her. His gaze flicked quickly over her face, clearly saying that if she was a man, she'd have had the good sense to call on Corey's dogs herself. Then he headed toward the break room.

"Mr. Calverson?"

He stopped, but didn't turn back around.

"Thank you."

His back straightened and the curved old shoulders squared a bit. Then he walked on, joining the rest of the volunteers to get his assignment.

Will hung back, listening to the deputy handing out maps and radios. It took all of his willpower not to step to the forefront and take control himself. He was used to operating alone, on his own terms, commanding the situation. He told himself he'd remain quiet only until the moment came when he decided this search was taking a wrong turn. So far, Leigh seemed to have things well thought out.

The image of Brittany leaning across the passenger seat of her car kept flashing in his mind. Only this time when she smiled, she became his sister. Jenny had only been nineteen when he left for South America. When she died at twenty-one, a victim of her own insecurities and an overdose of cocaine, it had taken six weeks for him to get the news. Not that it would have mattered. He couldn't go home for her funeral. He could never go home.

Brian and Kurt arrived just as the searchers were piling into vehicles, heading to Grissom's farm. Brian was driving. Kurt jumped out of the car before it even came to a complete stop. He ran directly to Leigh.

"What's the plan?" he said, over the steady barking of Corey Calverson's hounds from a truck bed.

"We're starting with a ground search. I'm going back over the area where we found the car. If nothing turns up, I'll call in the State Police Lab to process the car for forensic evidence."

"Forensic!" Kurt shouted. "You think she's dead?"

She placed her hand on his arm. "Forensic doesn't mean she's dead — it just means it's evidence to be used in the court. We don't have a lab to process fingerprints, hair samples, that sort of thing."

"Why wait? Call now! We can't waste any more time."

"I understand your feeling of urgency, but she hasn't been missing for twenty-four hours yet. She isn't a minor; I'm jumping the legal gun as it is. Let's just see if maybe she took off cross-country as a short cut and got disoriented in the dark. It's the first step. We need to establish she's truly missing."

"If we don't find her?"

Leigh heard the tremor in his voice.

"Then we appeal to the media, get her picture out there and word that she's a missing person. File formal papers and notify all local agencies —"

"That's all? Christ, someone might have my baby —"

"Kurt," she said firmly, "we don't want to waste our efforts. There are certain protocols to follow, proven to be most effective." She looked into his eyes; the panic seemed to be ebbing. She said more softly, "I need to do some footwork. As long as we're standing here arguing, it's not getting done."

He closed his eyes and exhaled. Then he looked to Brian. "What do you want us to do?"

She motioned toward the cars and trucks pulling out of the parking lot. "Go with the search party. Hook up with Calvin at the farm and he'll assign you to a group." She paused. "Kurt, nobody searches alone — including you."

Kurt nodded and started back toward Brian's car. She stopped him with a hand on his arm. "Are you sure you want to do this? Are you prepared for what we might —"

His gaze bore into hers. "You think I haven't already pictured in my head a thousand horrible scenarios?"

"I know, but you could wait with —"

"If it was your child, would you sit and wait?"

She could only imagine the feeling of impotence that must be choking him while the dearest thing in his life might be suffering. "No, no I wouldn't."

He held her gaze for another moment, then climbed into Brian's car.

As Leigh drove behind them toward the Grissom farm, she thought of all the things she hadn't voiced to Kurt. Things she prayed she would never have to. Things that would dump the responsibility for all of this squarely in his own lap. What would his reaction be if it came to pass that Brittany had simply disappeared on her own? Even worse, what if the girl, confused by frustration and naive vulnerability, had made a choice that led her to a place no girl should ever have to go?

For a brief moment, Leigh hoped with all her heart the girl was lost in the woods.

Chapter 9

Clear morning sky shifted so slowly the change was almost unnoticeable — uninterrupted blue to a pale gray blanket overhead. Not that Leigh spent much time looking upward. She paced the pavement, then began combing the ditch. The only things she'd found so far were flattened brown weeds next to the road where Calvin had tromped around the night before. No trail led away into the fields. Even the dogs had come up empty. They'd sniffed enthusiastically in circles around where the Camaro had died, howled a couple of times, then laid down on the road. Corey had said that meant the trail ended here, right where it began.

Leigh straightened and stretched her back. The western horizon darkened with the empty threat of rainfall. The meteorologists all agreed — the sky would drop no rain today. Instead of the usual seasonal blaze of golds and reds in the surrounding hills, dry, yellowish-brown leaves curled on the branch and drifted prematurely to the ground, crumbling underfoot into dust. The woods were as dull as Leigh could ever remember.

She looked around, thankful this field had been harvested. If the corn had still been standing, it would have impeded their progress, although not as much as if it'd been summer and the lush green cornstalks topped a man's head. All of the unharvested fields were filled with dry brown rows — exhausted, withered soldiers after a long campaign.

Her gaze came to the Grissom house. Maybe this would be the best opportunity to have a chat with Mrs. Grissom, while her domineering husband was busy with the search party. Leigh walked up the lane that led to a one-and-a-half-story house covered with gray asbestos shingles. As uninviting as a home could be — no flowers, no landscaping, just a dusty yard covered in bugleweed, dandelion and thistle. A deeply grooved dirt path bisected the weeds, running between the side door of the house and a dilapidated barn with the faint ghost of a *Mail Pouch Tobacco* ad painted on one side.

Dark green roller shades blocked each and every window. It must have been dark as night inside, even on a sunny afternoon. A porch with thick chips of cracked, flaking paint and curling floorboards crossed the front. As Leigh stepped on that porch, she saw the Grissoms had a clear view of the place where the Camaro had stopped last night — if they had happened to peel back the shades long enough to peek out.

A cat, a blah-gray color that matched its surroundings, rubbed against Leigh's leg as she knocked. The glass top-half of the door was also covered by a dark green shade.

She waited and listened, thinking she heard movement inside. No one answered. She knocked again.

"Mrs. Grissom, it's Leigh Mitchell," she called through the closed door.

The shade moved slightly, as if someone had brushed against it. "Mrs. Grissom, please, I need to talk to you. I'll only take a minute."

Surreptitious scratchings echoed beyond the door. Then silence.

Leigh tried once more. "Mrs. Grissom. This is a police matter. I *can* come back with a warrant." She was bluffing. She had no grounds for such a thing, but she thought it might shake up the woman enough to open the door.

The kitty meowed, continuing to use Leigh's legs as back scratchers, but she heard nothing else. After a few moments, she gave up and headed back toward the road.

When she looked over her shoulder, she saw a front window shade drop quickly back to the sill. Calvin was probably right; talking to Mrs. Grissom would be wasted effort. Even so, she'd be damned if she was going to be discouraged this easily. If it took marching up to the door right behind Mr. Grissom tonight, so be it.

As Leigh once again approached the spot where the Camaro had been, she looked over the pavement. Then she got down on her hands and knees and slowly crawled over a ten-foot stretch of road. Not one bit of the broken side window littered the asphalt. The only sign that

165

the car had been there was a little puddle of reddish liquid — transmission fluid from where the car sat for a prolonged period of time.

The radio on her belt crackled. "Sheriff?"

"Go ahead, Calvin."

"You said you wanted to know when the first sweep came back in. They're here."

"And?"

"Not a trace."

"Heard anything from the others?"

"Negative."

Calvin's police academy formality hadn't yet worn into country comfort. "Okay." About a quarter-mile down the road, at the cornfield entrance, she could see where Calvin had set up a field command of sorts: open car trunk, a folding table, maps, radio, and a large cooler. "Hold up before you send them out again. I'll be right there."

The returned group contained Brownie, Brian, Kurt, three firemen, and Will. They all looked worse for the wear: unshaven, clothing nettled with burrs, shoes coated with a heavy film of dust. She nodded to the men, now sitting on the ground downing bottles of water and eating the sandwiches delivered out here by the Wilsons' church auxiliary.

Brian sat with elbows on bent knees and Leigh had to fight the urge to sit down next to him and lay her head on his shoulder, as she had when they were children. Simply with his nearness, Brian had a way of making Leigh's world seem more orderly and safe.

Then her gaze traveled to Will. His gaze held hers with startling boldness, shattering the fragile shell of well-being she'd just created. He didn't make a move to approach her, yet didn't waver in his stare. Now she knew how those poor raccoons felt when headlights bore down on them. How could a man, with one simple look, make her feel so emotionally naked?

He finally got up. Leigh went perfectly still. But he walked right past her, to Calvin's cruiser. There, he rummaged in a big cooler set right behind the rear bumper.

She managed to pull her gaze away, only to see Brian looking at her through narrowed eyes, with serious disapproval on his face.

Someone tapped her on the shoulder. She jerked around, to see a baggie with a turkey sandwich inside dangling in front of her nose.

Will said, "Bet you haven't eaten."

Leigh eyed the sandwich but was unsure she could choke down a single bite. "I'm not —"

"You have to eat. Folks here are depending on you."

After she hesitated a moment longer, she smiled her thanks and accepted the food. He nodded, holding her with his eyes again, then drifted back to the rest of the waiting men. Leigh was silently thankful for his tact. There had been enough suspicion in the townsfolk's eyes when he'd come out of her office with her.

Taking a bite of sandwich that seemed to

grow larger as she chewed, she looked over Calvin's map. She listened as he pointed out the areas where the other three search teams were still working.

Leigh traced a line with her finger. "So we haven't covered this tract — through the hollow and over to the quarry?"

"No. Saved that for last. Rough terrain, and why would she go in that direction? Nothin' out there but a big hole in the ground."

Leigh didn't say what she thought; she wouldn't. The only way Brittany was in the dense woodland between here and the quarry was if someone had dragged her there.

"All right. I'll take this group and head that way now." She looked at her watch. Nearly one. "Wait until five o'clock and send a couple of vehicles over to the quarry to pick us up. I doubt we could cover all that distance and make it back before dark."

He nodded.

She could see the vacillation of emotions in Calvin's eyes. He shifted as if the soles of his feet itched. He was well-versed enough in the logistics of a search to know his was an important job. He'd seemed pleased when she asked him. And yet, he wanted to be out there looking, too.

"Keep me posted," she said to him before she turned to the men sitting on the ground. "Ready for another go at it, gentlemen?"

Kurt paced in a circle off to himself.

Leigh stepped closer to her brother. "How's he holding up?" she asked.

"How do you think? He's like a bear with an arrow in his side. But he's working with us, if that's what you mean. He hasn't tried to take off on his own — or to change the course of the search. I just wish I could ease his mind. . . ."

She grasped his hand. "We all do." She drew in a deep breath and looked at Kurt. Anger and frustration gave his movements a robotic rigidity. She secretly waited for the moment when all that restraint blew, amazed it hadn't happened before now. "Kurt, ready?"

He stopped in mid-orbit and came directly to her. "Ready? This search is a bunch of crap!"

Leigh could almost see the relief valve popping, a breach in the seal on his emotions. She braced herself for the angry torrent she sensed was imminent.

He honed in on Leigh. "What? No argument? No 'We have to follow protocol'? No 'We're doing all we can'?" His cheeks reddened. "*My* daughter is missing! And all we're doing is poking through corn fields and beating bushes! Don't you understand, every minute might count?" His mouth twisted into something truly ugly as he jabbed a finger in the air, pointing toward the tree line. Now he was yelling. "We all know she didn't wander off into the fucking woods. How about getting some real police down here? State boys, FBI, national guard!"

"Think about it," Leigh said. "Those agencies operate on statistics — and those statistics add up to a runaway. Is that the approach you want to take? Even if we convince them otherwise, all we'll have are a bunch of strangers wandering around unfamiliar terrain. Right at this moment what we need are locals — people who know this land, who know and care about Brittany —"

Kurt held up a stiff hand. "Save it. Let's go." He moved off with a rapid, purposeful stride and joined a group already headed out.

Leigh wished she could go forward with such sureness in her step. Instead, she gathered up her group of volunteers and made warily into the woods.

Immediately the grade plunged thirty or so feet toward a creek bed. She took the steepest descent, placing herself between Will and Brian. She set each volunteer's path to zigzag, meeting the one on either side every twenty or so yards. It was going to be slow going.

By the time they reached the tree line, Brian was nearly as edgy as Kurt. He hadn't missed the way Will studied Leigh whenever she was in sight, or the exchange of glances when he handed her that sandwich. He knew it was ridiculous to feel this streak of — not jealousy exactly, perhaps possessiveness described it better. But no matter how old they were, Leigh would always be his little sister. He'd spent most of his life looking out for her and that habit just was not going to die. She was his to protect, now and forever. And he didn't know that he liked the spark he was seeing in her eye at the moment. It was bad timing at best and bad judgment at worst.

Even moving through the rough ups and downs of the woods, Will seemed to have his eye more on Leigh than the ground underfoot. An amazing feat really; twice Brian himself had stumbled when he lost focus as he walked. But Will moved as if his feet had powers of levitation over the dips and holes. Like he'd had experience prowling around rugged terrain.

There could be a whole bevy of reasons for such experience. Unfortunately, only the undesirable ones came to Brian's mind at the moment. Maybe this guy was like that nutcase from Ruby Ridge. Maybe he was a member of a radical militia. Maybe he'd been trained in covert ops and had abandoned the service to use his skills on a more lucrative market. Maybe he spent his time in the woods because people were looking for him out in the open. The problem was, Brian just didn't know — and what he didn't know, he didn't trust. It was an attitude that had served him well thus far, and the only way he knew to protect his sister.

He told himself it wasn't that he didn't want Leigh to find someone. It's that he didn't want her to be hurt by the *wrong* someone. In time, once they'd moved ahead on the political highway, she would be away from this town and able to fish in a bigger sea. Her choices now would carry the weight of her future. She couldn't afford to screw up.

Hopefully, this would blow over before it became a big deal. Leigh would realize her infatuation was exactly that and reign herself in. Didn't somebody say they'd seen her out with Mike Nichols last night? Not Brian's first choice for his sister, but a damn sight better than an unknown drifter who blew into town only days before the one and only missing person disappeared from Glens Crossing.

His nerves felt like he'd been hooked up to a car battery. There was just too much at stake for this to be left up to female hormones and sexual chemistry.

Who knew what this guy was really up to?

Will kept Leigh in his peripheral vision at all times. She had a look of grim determination on her face that he could all too easily identify with. At first he had wondered why she hadn't added to her list of reasons for *not* calling in the FBI the fact that Brittany was eighteen and therefore legally an adult. Although her car had been abandoned, there was no ransom note, no proof of abduction — making this case, at this particular moment, a very low priority on the FBI's to-do list.

If the girl didn't show up in the woods, and if they couldn't unearth further evidence of foul play, Will was going to do a little more digging himself. He had a niggling suspicion that there was much more to this than met the eye. Something told him they were seeing only what they were *supposed* to see.

Not that he could fault Leigh in her handling of the case. So far she had shown nothing but professionalism and skill, level-headed thinking and solid deduction. It was obvious she'd been well educated in criminal investigation.

The only weakness he could see was Leigh's inability to distance herself emotionally. But, he had to admit, she had not allowed that to interfere with her work to this point.

Will glanced beyond Leigh, to Brian, who now appeared to be keeping as close an eye on her as he was himself. Brian's disapproval of even the slightest attention Will paid his sister was evident. It had quickly become apparent that Brian served as her emotional touchstone. Easily understood given the early loss of their parents. But he had to admit, it made him a little jealous to see her rely on her brother. Will could really help her with his experience, yet he couldn't divulge his true identity so she could trust him completely. Leigh was a complex woman and Will sensed her loyalties ran deep — her trust had to be earned. One lingering kiss sitting by a creekbed hardly qualified him.

As they continued to pick their way through the woods, Will noticed Brian steadily reducing the gap between he and his sister. There was a protectiveness there that exceeded common sense — after all, Leigh was the one wearing the gun.

Brownie, Brian, Leigh and Will were all packed into the backseat of Ellis McEntire's 1979 Caprice Classic. Even in his fatigue, Will's focus centered on the heat of Leigh's hip rubbing against his as they bounced along on the Chevy's worn suspension. They traveled back toward Calvin's command post in silence.

They had plunged down ravines, twisted ankles in rabbit holes, scrabbled up embankments, and shouted until they were hoarse, but had not found a single sign of *any* human being between Grissom's farm and the chain-link fence that surrounded the gaping hole of the quarry.

Once they reached it, Will and Brian had stood on either side of Leigh, looking at the sheer limestone wall of the far side of the quarry. For a moment no one spoke. Will had been the first.

"What do you think about divers?" he asked.

Leigh's gaze fixed on the dark water at the bottom of the quarry. A shiver visibly coursed through her. "Let's check the perimeter fence, see if there's a breach."

The fence had been intact, the lock on the gate secure. Leigh had made the decision to hold off a call for divers. She'd said, and Will had to agree, that the possibility of Brittany being in the bottom of the quarry was so remote, their efforts should be concentrated elsewhere first.

Brian offered, "I think we've covered enough ground. If she wasn't within our search area, she's probably not out here." He put a hand on Leigh's shoulder. "It's time to change focus."

Will did not miss the pointed look Brian cast his way, clearly suggesting where he thought that focus belonged. Will held his gaze, unbending under the scrutiny. He had wondered who would be the first to openly cast suspicion toward him, the only unknown factor in this equation. Too bad it was Brian, the one person Leigh respected and trusted above all others.

Leigh didn't seem to notice the exchange between the men. But Will now knew, the battle lines had been drawn. Unfortunately, there would be no contest whose side Leigh would join.

Will studied her for a moment, pointlessly wishing things could be different. He hated the exhausted look in her eyes, knew all too well the frustration of throwing body and soul into something that then fell into a million unmendable pieces. She hadn't said anything since that moment, just trudged to the waiting cars and slid inside.

Over the rugged miles, Will had pondered Brittany's state of mind yesterday when she'd come by the shop. Gone was the flirtatious vamp who'd cornered him for lunch. At first he thought perhaps some of his rebuffing at lunch had produced the desired effect. But there seemed to be an undercurrent flowing around her, no longer sexual, more along the lines of . . . resentful was as close as he could come to naming it.

He decided he'd see what he could discover about Brittany's recent activities. Until then, he'd just try to look innocent and hope Brian's attitude wasn't infectious.

As the Caprice made its way back toward Grissom's farm, Leigh's head bobbed, the need for sleep overriding all else. Brian reached over and pulled her head onto his shoulder, just as Will was contemplating doing the same thing. Her hair had been carelessly swept up and knotted hours earlier. Now corkscrew strands had worked their way loose, framing her face and trailing down her neck. Will had to ball his fists to keep from reaching over and wrapping the long sun-streaked spiral falling across the side of her neck around his finger. With her leaning slightly toward Brian, her hip pressed even more intimately against Will's. There was absolutely no danger of Will falling asleep. Each and every cell of his body was electrified by her nearness.

He closed his eyes briefly, trying to diminish the growing ache in his chest.

He should have left yesterday.

Once all of the searchers were back and ac-

176

counted for, Leigh noticed one missing.

"Calvin, which group was Hale Grant assigned to?" she asked, stepping up beside him as he packed his table and maps back inside his car.

"Grant? He made some excuse — newspaper deadline or something. Didn't come out to the farm."

"Lousy worm." That reporter would leave his own mother's funeral if he thought he could scoop a breaking story. She headed to her Blazer counting the ways she'd like to skin Hale Grant alive.

Her already creative list expanded explosively when she pulled up to her office to find a news van from the ABC affiliate from Indianapolis parked outside. The satellite antenna extended high above the truck. Daylight was fading. The spotlight that shone from the camera onto Hale Grant and the field reporter for Channel 6 clearly illuminated HENDERSON COUNTY SHERIFF on the building behind them.

"Goddamn him," she said under her breath as she threw open the driver's door.

When Leigh walked up beside Hale, well within camera frame, the reporter stopped in mid-sentence, then quickly recovered her poise. "Are you Sheriff Mitchell?"

"Yes. And although I'm not prepared with a statement" — she shot a killing glance at Hale — "I appreciate your being here. A young woman is missing. Brittany Wilson: eighteen, dark brown shoulder-length hair, green eyes, about five-six, one hundred eighteen pounds. I should have a picture to you before the end of your broadcast."

The reporter stepped closer to Leigh, right in front of Hale, blocking him from camera view. Leigh noticed him shifting in order to remain in the frame.

The TV reporter's voice held the heartbroken sympathy of a family friend. "Do you suspect foul play?"

"It's too early to tell. We're just hoping someone sees her and calls in, or" — Leigh looked directly into the camera for the first time — "if you're out there, Brittany, please call home."

"Are there any leads? Any suspects?" the reporter asked, then stuck the microphone in Leigh's face.

"That's all I have for now. I'll send someone out to the van with a picture and the number where we'll be taking calls. Thank you for your assistance." She felt the heat of the intense video light on the back of her neck as she turned and walked to the building. The reporter and Hale Grant then fell back into their interview. Just hearing their overly sympathetic voices made Leigh want to pull hair — Hale's. Instead, she settled for slamming the door behind her loud enough to disrupt the sound feed.

Brian followed her inside five minutes later.

"They've wrapped up the interview. Want me to take a picture out to them?"

"I don't have one." Leigh grabbed her address book off her desk. "I'll have to call Emma."

"No need to upset her further. I have one," Brian said.

Leigh's gaze snapped to her brother's face. "You do?"

"Yeah." He pulled out his wallet. "Ruby and I get a school picture every year. We're just like family."

Poor Brian, didn't have any kiddie pictures of his own to tote around.

"Okay, take it out, and tell them to broadcast this number." She handed him a business card with her name and the office number. "We'll get someone to man the phone twenty-four hours."

"Right." He took the card and walked out.

Within minutes, he was back, holding a photo of a seductively smiling Brittany out to her. "Grant had already given them a picture. You might want to hang on to this one."

"Where'd he get it?"

Brian shrugged.

"I'll keep this one. I need something to fax to the newspapers and the other stations, Indy and Louisville. I'd hoped to wait until I had an organized statement, but . . ." She turned on her computer.

"I think I'll shower and change, then go to Kurt and Emma's. No telling what state Kurt's in at the moment. No need for you to deal with this on all fronts by yourself."

Dear Brian, always trying to ease her burden. "Thanks. I'd appreciate it. I can get these faxed and call state police headquarters to arrange for someone to process the car."

He kissed her on the cheek and left.

Leigh had finished typing the information and was just feeding it into the fax machine when she heard someone clear his throat behind her. She turned.

"Will, what are you doing here?"

"I saw your Blazer still out front, wondered if I might have a look at Brittany's car."

"Why?"

"I'm pretty good at putting puzzles together. Maybe I'll see something that'll be of help."

"Unless you've got a fingerprint kit and fiber analysis lab in your hip pocket, I think we'll have to leave it to the state guys. They should be here tomorrow afternoon."

"I'm not talking about *evidence*, I'm talking about *clues*."

Leigh thought of the ticket stub in the evidence baggie on the front seat of her car. Clues.

"What makes you think you'll see anything I won't?" she asked.

"You said the car was running when you found it."

"Yes."

"In park or in gear?"

"In gear."

"Which means something was wrong with the transmission. Otherwise, it'd idle forward until something stopped it."

Leigh studied him. She decided not to tell him about the fluid under the car just yet.

"I gave that car a once-over yesterday afternoon. I recorded the mileage; I can check it against the odometer reading — see how far she traveled last night. That'll help when you retrace her steps yesterday. And maybe I can tell if something mechanical has been damaged."

Leigh wondered at the way his mind worked. He asked all the right questions. It might be quite telling to see how he went about this.

"Tell me, Will, do you have any experience in police work?"

His startled gaze snapped to her face. He laughed, but the sound seemed manufactured. "Why would you ask that?"

She simply held his gaze.

Finally, he said, "I've done lots of things. And let's just say I have an inquisitive mind."

Narrowing her eyes she said, "Me too." She quickly assembled the possibilities: experience in special forces in the military; disenchanted cop, chucking his career and hitting the road; crooked cop, booted from his job — even as secretive as Will was, that didn't seem to ring true; not a cop at all, just a guy with good deductive reasoning. She suddenly realized none of her scenarios involved criminal activity. He just didn't *feel* like a criminal to her.

After another moment's hesitation, she said, "Can't let you handle the car. But you can go out to the barn with me to make sure it's locked up properly. Then I'll run you home." She really wanted to see how he approached it, what he *saw* when he looked at the Camaro. She picked up the copy of the fax and took it back into her office and left it on the desk. "Remember, don't touch anything."

He laughed. "I've seen enough cop shows to know that much."

Leigh seriously doubted his expertise came from watching TV, but she held her tongue. She took the pole barn key out of her safe and reassured Ellis, who'd volunteered for the first phone-minding shift, that someone would relieve him around midnight.

As they walked along the crushed stone drive to the outbuilding, Will said, "You know, when they process the car, they're going to find *my* hair and *my* fingerprints."

She stopped and looked sharply at him.

He was a full step ahead of her when he stopped and looked back at her. "She did give me a ride. And I drove the car yesterday, remember?"

Leigh nodded, keeping her gaze on the ground.

He took a half-step closer to her. "What did you think I meant?"

"Nothing. I just hadn't thought that far." She

fastened her gaze on his chest. *Liar. You were jumping to conclusions — the conclusions you've been avoiding since you picked up that ticket stub.*

"Look at me, Leigh," he said, tipping her face up with a finger under her chin. "I can help you. But I'll tell you right now, it'll probably raise questions about me in your mind. It's asking a lot, but you *can* trust me."

She held his gaze and remained silent. Every fiber of her being said she *could* trust him. But doing so blindly would be a dereliction of duty. Her instincts were normally trustworthy. But infallible? Hardly. Until they found Brittany, she was going to have to keep her personal feelings and interpretations out of this.

Jangling the keys in her hand, she said, "Let's check on this car."

Disappointment flashed in Will's eyes. She ignored it and walked toward the building sheltering the Camaro and its evidence.

Chapter 10

Leigh switched on the lights in the barn. The overhead fluorescents flickered, then lit, washing the large, mostly empty space with unnatural blue-white light. She was momentarily stopped by what stood before her. In the center of the barn sat Brittany's red Camaro, a forlorn reminder of a carefree youth cruelly interrupted. Leigh had resisted the thought, but she had to presume, until she had evidence to the contrary, that Brittany had been yanked from her car, and her life, by an unknown predator.

Her jaw tightened and she closed her eyes. *I will find you, Brit. I swear.* She gave a mental pause, nearly shamed by what she was currently thinking. *Whether you want me to or not.*

Will brushed her shoulder as he stepped past. Leigh's eyes opened, but she stayed where she was. He circled the car in much the same manner she had when she'd first seen it on Quarry Road. She lingered near the barn door, watching him, trying to read his expression.

He moved slowly, sharp blue gaze raking the vehicle, seemingly taking in every detail. He stopped when he reached the driver's door. A crease formed in his brow as he examined it. Moving with both confidence and obvious care not to touch the door, he leaned his head just inside the broken window and made some unrevealing noise deep in his throat.

"Wallet still inside the purse?" he asked.

"Yes. Money, license, credit cards — all there."

"Cell phone's here, too. Certainly not robbery." He straightened and rubbed a hand over his face, as if reevaluating something. "I doubt she'd leave with nothing if she took off on her own." He seemed to be speaking as much to himself as her. He also sounded like he didn't quite buy the idea.

Leigh had had that same nagging feeling — that things were contrary to what was presented at the scene. Funny Will would come up with the same gut reaction. Her mind again sifted through the possibilities of his past experience. He certainly thought more like an investigator than a mechanic.

He stared at the glass on the driver's seat, most of which had vibrated toward the back during the car's transport to the garage. Then he asked, "Glass on the road?"

"No." She stepped closer, stopping mere inches from him, and looked around his shoulder at the car's interior.

He seemed lost in concentration, running his hands through his hair. Standing just behind him, she momentarily became transfixed on his long fingers as they laced together and settled on the back of his neck. He had very strong hands. The memory of the solid feel of them holding hers as they danced made her curl her free hand into a fist, as if to hold the sensation . . .

Will surprised her by spinning around to face her.

She blinked, shooing away her ridiculously fanciful thoughts and tried to keep her mind on what she was supposed to be doing. Her fatigue seemed to be short-circuiting her concentration. She shushed the little voice in her head that said it was the man, not the fatigue, disrupting her ability to hold a coherent thought.

"I can't tell without looking under the car, but I'm guessing there was a transmission fluid leak. That's the only way the gears would disengage while the shifter was still in drive." He looked Leigh in the eye. "It was in drive, right?"

"Yes."

"The fluids were all fine when I checked it yesterday afternoon."

"You're certain?"

"Yep. It wasn't even low. And I put the car on the lift; no telltale signs of leakage."

"How long would it take to lose enough fluid to disengage the gears?"

"Hard to say, too many variables. I can get the mileage we recorded at the shop yesterday, then you can have an idea of how much driving she did after she left there."

"There's something else you're thinking and not telling me."

He bit his lip. "Can't say yet. Something just isn't adding up to me."

Frustration wormed in her belly. Leigh felt it too. But it remained as elusive as the end of the rainbow — it seemed nearly within reach, yet she was never able to maneuver herself any closer to it.

And Kurt was right, every minute might count, and so far she'd come up completely empty handed. If she thought it'd help, she would call the FBI first thing tomorrow. But she knew how it worked. With so little to go on, until the case turned into a bona fide kidnapping complete with ransom note, little would be done. They'd treat this like a run-of-the-mill missing person. The thing that made it even lower on the priority list for the Feds was that Brittany was eighteen, the age of legal emancipation.

She sighed and rubbed her eyes with her fingertips. "I'll give you a lift back to Brownie's house. Tomorrow morning will be soon enough to check the mileage."

He nodded, then put a hand on her shoulder. "You'd better get some sleep. You look beat."

Leigh looked up into his eyes. Worry weighed heavy in his gaze. She couldn't stand the intensity, so she turned away and tried to make a joke. "Flatterer." She flipped her hand in the air between them.

He didn't laugh, or even so much as crack a smile. He gripped her shoulder more tightly and forced her to look at him by lifting her chin with his other hand. "I mean it, Leigh. You could be in for a long haul. You won't do Brittany any good if you drive yourself until you collapse."

Touched by his concern, she held his gaze, but couldn't manage to get a word out. Finally, she settled for nodding. He looked at her for a long moment, then he drew her against his chest and wrapped his arms around her.

Leigh burrowed her face against his shoulder, the worn softness of his T-shirt against her cheek bringing memories of easier times. Days filled with childhood dramas, when a warm hug and a promise of better to come would set the world back to right. As she lingered there, smelling the scent of him, feeling his strength surround her, she wished she could remain there forever, never face the grim realities of the world of adulthood again. She felt the rise and fall of his chest as he breathed, the soft caress of his hand stroking her tired back. God, she'd never felt so drained.

He pressed his cheek against her hair. "You're doing all that is humanly possible. Don't expect more of yourself than that."

She drew in a long breath, keeping her face pressed against him. "It's not enough."

"Maybe not. But it's all any of us can do."

Leigh heard a heaviness in his voice that said more than his words. Suddenly she knew, wherever he'd been, whatever he'd done, his back too had been against the wall. He'd experienced the helplessness, had been trapped in the careening vehicle with no one behind the wheel. With a sinking heart she knew he spoke the truth, but that didn't make it any easier to bear. The weight of another person's life was just too much to carry right now and she was thankful for his support.

Suddenly she noticed his hands had stilled. She felt him press his lips against her hair. Fatigue fuzzed her thinking. Her body responded on its own, her heart picking up an extra beat, tingling warmth spreading from her core. This was foolish. She had no business being in his arms right now. No business at all . . .

Tipping her face up, she waited, lips parted and moist in anticipation. He looked in her eyes for a long while, seeming to make a serious decision. One hand came up to cradle her head. But he still didn't kiss her.

Finally she whispered, "Aren't you going to kiss me?"

He moaned and lifted his eyes heavenward. "No."

"No?" She blinked and furrowed her brow. He'd started this, now suddenly he was unwilling to finish it. But he didn't release her. She could feel his hardness against her belly. Nothing was making sense.

He blew out a deep breath. "No." He let her go and stepped back. "You deserve better."

Stunned, she didn't know what to say. She'd

never seen a man turn down a willing woman before. Had their kiss last night been so unsatisfactory that he couldn't face another? Had she only imagined the gleam of attraction in his eyes? She brushed her hands on the thighs of her jeans and looked away. "I see."

"No, you don't. You can't . . ."

Her ears burned with humiliation. She fished the key out of her pocket and moved toward the door. "Let's lock this place up and get out of here."

She flipped out the lights and waited in the open doorway. Will just stood where she'd left him, in a shaft of light from the outside mercury vapor lamp angling through the door.

"Coming?"

He ran his hands through his hair, then walked out the door. He paused and gave her a long hard look as he passed. After a moment, she nudged him out of the way and closed up the barn.

Fortunately, she reached the Blazer before he did. She'd forgotten about the evidence baggie sitting on the passenger seat. She snatched it up and stuffed it in the map pocket of her door before Will got in. She didn't know why doing the right thing made her feel sneaky and ashamed.

They didn't speak during the drive to Brownie's. A couple of times she stole a glance at Will. He sat looking straight ahead with his elbow on the door, rubbing his forehead with his fingers, as if puzzling over something.

He opened the door as soon as she pulled to a stop. "I'll call you with that mileage first thing tomorrow."

"Good."

He stood there for a moment, leaning in the open door, looking like he was going to say something else.

Leigh found herself leaning toward him, as if the gravitational pull of her nearness could draw the words out. Was he pondering the case, or were his thoughts more intimate? She'd made a fool of herself once tonight; she wasn't about to do it again. So she waited.

He bit his lip and looked down the street. Then he turned back to her and said, "Good night."

She took off as soon as he'd closed the door, her embarrassment rising like bile. How could she have been so stupid? There was no doubt she was attracted to Will. But she was a grown woman; she should have had more self-control than to allow herself to act on it. And now of all times. With some effort, she forced thoughts of Will Scott from her mind and tried to concentrate on the problem of finding Brittany.

She mulled over the facts, vague as they were. She couldn't get past the feeling that she was missing something — something fundamental. It felt like it was inches from her nose, staring her in the face and she was oblivious to its presence. The photos of the scene should be ready tomorrow morning. Maybe reviewing them would shake something loose. Right now nothing seemed to be coming together in her mind.

All through her shower, fragmented thoughts nagged. She tried to formulate a plan of attack for tomorrow. First she'd talk to Jared, Brittany's boyfriend. Then her girlfriends. From there . . . well, she just wasn't sure.

She towel dried her hair and let it curl as it would as she slapped together a peanut-butter sandwich. She rifled through her mail as she ate. The usual barrage of credit-card offers. A chance to win a million dollars, no purchase necessary. An Oil of Olay sample guaranteeing to keep her skin youthful. Her water bill. What came next took her breath away — a card with the picture of a missing child along with the pertinent statistics and a computer age-progression photo. Missing since 1989. Her sandwich stuck in her throat.

Dear God, she prayed, *don't let it come to that.*

She dumped all but the water bill in the trash. Before she walked away, she looked again at the face of the eleven-year-old boy who left home for baseball practice in Cincinnati in 1989 and never came back. She fished it out of the trash and stuck it under a refrigerator magnet, right in front, where she'd have to look at it every day.

As she fell into bed, discouraged and exhausted, she kept seeing the glittering bits of glass fall from Brittany's purse as she picked it up from the passenger seat of the Camaro. Over and over in slow motion they hit the seat and bounced to the floor, reflecting sparks of light as they tumbled.

Hadn't Will asked something about the broken glass? Try as she might, she couldn't gather another coherent thought as the comforting arms of sleep drew her into oblivion.

The minute Leigh's Blazer was out of sight, Will started walking from Hank Brown's house to the Shell gas station near the fairgrounds. Thoughts of another lost girl plagued his memory. At least there was a glimmer of hope that Brittany could be saved. He'd give his all to see that that happened. As for Jenny, his sister had been lost months before he even knew there was a threat.

The irony of it tormented him each and every day of his life. While he'd been chasing bad guys three thousand miles from home, the real danger lurked in his own backyard. He'd been so stupid, so foolish to think Jenny was safe from the human pollution that corrupted this world. Just because she was a good kid and had stayed out of trouble for nineteen years he thought she was home free. But it was that sweet innocence, that inexperience in dealing with temptation, that had been her Achilles' heel. Once her trust was given, she'd been an easy target.

His gut tightened. How frightened she must have been. How she had needed him.

As always, he whispered a prayer asking her forgiveness. As always, he received no sense of absolution.

He hunched his shoulders and walked on, forcing such selfish thoughts out of his mind. He had to keep his eye on the prize, the big picture, the payoff. Otherwise it would all be for naught. It wasn't just for him, although he wanted it so much he could taste the bitterness of it on the back of his tongue. He had to do it for the others — the dead, the lost, the innocent. He owed them. And if there was one thing this world had taught him, it was that you always had to pay your debts. One way or another. He preferred to do it straightforwardly, with the respect dictated by the sacrifices of others.

It was late enough that the only light in the Shell station was the Coca-Cola clock on the far wall of the office. Will walked around the corner of the building to where the pay phone hung between the doors to the men's and ladies' bathrooms.

As was his habit, he scanned the area before he picked up the receiver. It seemed silly in this sleepy little burg; he hadn't seen a car on the road since he left Brownie's. The only sounds to reach his ears were the steady thrum and chirps of crickets and tree frogs. But circumstance had taught him never to let down his guard. Let down your guard and you die.

He punched in eleven digits. A recording told him to deposit two dollars and ninety-five cents for the first three minutes. Ameritech highway robbery — he couldn't risk being on line nearly that long. He pushed the change through the slot. The line clicked and began to ring. On the fourth ring, a sleepy voice picked up.

"Hello?"

"It's me."

"Jesus!" All shreds of sleepiness vanished from the man's voice. "I thought you were dead."

"Nearly was."

"Why didn't you come in? We could set up some protection —"

"Forget it. When's the date?"

"October thirty-first."

"I'll be there."

"How —"

Will hung up the phone. October thirty-first. Halloween. Someone must have a sense of humor. Thirty-six days. Thirty-six days and he would know if he would ever have his life back.

Chapter 11

By the time Leigh reached her office, Will had already called and left a message. Disappointment turned the latch and peeked out of the closet. She quickly slammed the door on it. However, it rattled around behind that closed door until she could no longer ignore the racket. If only he hadn't left the mileage from the service record on Brittany's Camaro, she'd have an excuse to call him back.

She looked at the phone. Did she *need* an excuse?

Jesus, girl, get those priorities straight.

She tucked the pink phone message slip in her pocket and embarked on her investigation. First stop was Glens Crossing High School. She hated to conduct questioning this way, would rather catch the kids at home or at the arcade downtown. The principal's office just didn't do much to loosen tongues. Even as mouthy as today's teenagers seemed to be, inhibition reigned when jerked from class and put in the hot seat. She didn't have time to pussyfoot around; she needed honest answers. Sex, drugs and delinquent behavior tended to remain behind sealed lips when the atmosphere smacked of the Spanish Inquisition. However, she had to keep moving on this and three o'clock was just too far away.

As she opened the battered glass-and-metal doors of her old high school, she was overcome by a sense of déjà vu. The walls had been painted a different color, but overall the school remained as it had since the building opened in 1950. The smell of used books and old sneakers, too much perfume and teenage hormones; the quiet uniqueness to school halls during class periods; the gritty feel of the terrazzo floor underfoot. Of course, Leigh was here often, still came to all of the basketball games, but entering the building in the middle of a school day was entirely different.

As she walked into the principal's office, she even experienced that sickening dread in the pit of her stomach. If she, after eleven years, hadn't shaken it, how were these kids going to react to questioning in here?

She was relieved when the principal, Mrs. Beaver — Leigh pitied the woman with that name in this place — agreed to allow her to interview the students in the outside commons area. She gave Mrs. Beaver the list and asked for her to call the students down one at a time.

Mrs. Beaver stopped as she headed to the PA microphone. "I don't know if this has any bearing, but Brittany's social studies teacher, Mr. Pennington, said something interesting the other day." She stopped, as if trying to decide whether or not to continue.

"Go on; I need all the information about

Brittany's frame of mind I can get right now. You can trust my confidentiality."

"Well, it's just that he commented on the drastic change he's seen in Brittany's interest in her schoolwork."

"She's really slacked off, then?" Leigh expected as much.

"No, on the contrary. She's never been much of an academic, more interested in the social aspect, you know. But suddenly, he said she'd really buckled down and had started producing surprisingly good work. That's why he mentioned it — Brittany is a very bright girl; he thinks she should be pushed harder."

"What did her other teachers think of that idea?"

Mrs. Beaver raised her palms to the heavens. "None of them had seen much change. Maybe it was just the subject matter that turned her on."

"Thanks for sharing that with me. Everything I can reassemble of her past few weeks will be a help."

The principal nodded and looked at the list. "I'll start calling the students down."

Leigh thanked her again and headed out to the commons.

Five minutes later, Jared Clark pushed open the door. His baggy pants swished on the concrete as he moved toward the picnic table where Leigh had settled. He was a tall kid, broad-shouldered and nice-looking. He obviously spent considerable time in the weight room. He didn't look delighted to be there, but he didn't have the manufactured and well-maintained bored facade she'd seen on so many kids. He sat down, put his hands on the table and began twisting the silver ring he wore on the middle finger of his right hand.

"This is about Brittany, right?" He studied the ring as he spoke.

"Yes. I need you to be completely honest with me, difficult as it might be. This is serious, Jared. The things you share with me could help her. And I do believe that she needs our help."

He raised his eyes and Leigh was surprised to see not mistrust, not reticence, but cold, brittle fear. He quickly looked away again. "I can't help. She wouldn't tell me anything."

"What do you mean, wouldn't tell you anything?"

"It's like, one day we were okay, the next I was invisible. I don't know." He lifted a shoulder. "She just changed."

"When did she change?"

He shifted in his seat and looked away. "After school started."

"Okay. I want you to be frank with me. What you say will go no further than this conversation. Do you know if Brittany had any habits — drugs, alcohol?"

After a long pause he said, "She drank some — but no more than anybody else. Beer mostly, at parties, you know. No drugs."

"You and she aren't still dating?"

His downturned cheeks reddened. "Hardly."

"But you and Brittany had dated for a long time, right?"

"Two years."

"Jared, is there any possibility that she was pregnant and ran away?"

Leigh thought the boy would swallow his tongue. His body tensed and his face bloomed deeper red. After a few seconds he seemed to recover somewhat from the shock of her bluntness. He heaved a sigh and shook his head, still not looking at her. "Brit was on the pill." He was quick to add, "She's eighteen; it's legal."

"I appreciate your candor. It could mean a world of difference to Brittany. But, Jared, you know the pill isn't foolproof. Did she give any indication —"

"No!" Then he lowered his voice. "We never did it without, you know, extra protection." Rolling his lips inward, he bit them nervously for a moment. "You aren't going to say anything about this to our parents, are you?"

Leigh decided to stow the lectures. This wasn't the time. "No, I'm not. You're man enough to do the right thing and help Brittany. It's up to you to decide what to discuss with your parents."

Jared's body sagged with relief. He went back to fiddling with the ring.

"So you two didn't have a fight?"

"Can't fight with someone who won't talk to you."

"Did you try to talk to her?"

"Yeah, I wanted to know why she was blowing me off."

"And?" Jesus, she hated to prod each and every word from his mouth.

"Said she didn't know what I was talking about and walked away."

"Did that make you angry?"

His gaze cut from the ring to Leigh's face. "Yeah, it made me mad."

"When did you see Brittany last?"

He jumped to his feet and spread his arms wide. "What the hell is this? You think I did something to her?"

"Sit down, Jared. All I asked is when you saw her last. I'm trying to figure out how she spent last Saturday. That's all." Leigh already knew Jared had gone with his parents to visit his sister at Purdue University on Saturday. The Clarks had been home about fifteen minutes when Kurt had called to see if Brittany was with Jared. But if he was holding something back in order to protect someone else, she wanted to shake it loose.

"I saw her at school on Friday." He plopped back on the bench and cradled his forehead in his hand. "Didn't talk to her."

"Was she dating anyone else?"

"Not that I know. But she stopped coming to school stuff, so it's hard to say."

The bell rang, signaling the change of classes. He looked back at the building.

Leigh said, "You can go. If anything comes to mind" — she handed him a business card — "please call me."

He stood, but didn't walk away. Shoving his hands in his pockets he said, so softly Leigh nearly didn't hear, "I hope she's okay. I miss —" He broke off and walked away, but not before Leigh saw the collection of tears in his eyes.

According to Emma, Rebecca Lewis was Brittany's best friend; had been since they were in first grade. She was the next on Leigh's list. She showed up shortly after Jared disappeared back inside the building.

Rebecca's interview went almost as fruitlessly as Jared's. With one exception. Leigh asked, "Was Brittany seeing anyone — dating?"

Rebecca looked over her shoulder, as if she expected someone to be eavesdropping, then said, "She didn't want anyone to know." The girl leaned closer to Leigh. "But I think she was seeing someone older."

"What makes you think that?"

"Some of the stuff she said. You know, like suddenly she was *soooo* much more mature than the rest of us. And she'd disappear sometimes — which was weird," Rebecca said, as if it had just occurred to her, "because Brit always loved lots of people around. When I asked her about it, she got a real funny look on her face, you know, sorta dreamy, and said she'd been with

202

someone special. But she never coughed up who it was. I know it wasn't anyone in school."

"Do you think she could have run away?"

Rebecca looked thoughtful for a minute. "Can't see it. She didn't have a big stash of money. And to leave her car like that . . . Brit was never one for doing without, you know what I mean?"

Leigh stood. "Thanks for the help, Rebecca. Let me know if you hear from Brit, or think of something else."

Rebecca remained seated. She looked up at Leigh with worried eyes. "Do you think something bad happened to her?"

"I don't know. Whatever happened, I do know she needs our help."

All threads of suspicion that Rebecca was holding something back vanished when Leigh saw the look in the girl's eyes as she got up and returned to school — loss, fear and confusion. The combination that always comes when a person realizes, "My God, that could have been me." It's the moment when sickness swells in the stomach as the situation stops being a vague set of circumstances pertaining to someone else and becomes a personal threat.

As Leigh watched Rebecca go back into the building, pity for all of the teenagers in Glens Crossing grew in her heart. Their comfortable illusion of security and immortality was being eroded away, replaced by an uncertain future filled with indefinable threats.

Leigh plowed through the rest of the interviews, knowing they'd probably turn up nothing. She was right.

On her way to the parking lot, her wireless phone rang. She pulled it out of her shoulder bag. "Hello?"

"It's me. Any news?" Brian said.

"Nothing. How's Kurt? I haven't checked in with them yet."

"He's out cruising the roads this morning. Just can't sit still."

"Can't blame him," she said as she buckled her seat belt.

"What's on your agenda?"

"Going back out to the Grissom farm to try and talk to the Mrs. again."

"Keep me posted."

"Will do."

"And Leigh, take care of yourself. You know I'll do whatever you need."

"Yeah. Thanks." Leigh ended the call and started the Blazer, thankful to her core that she had Brian.

She closed her eyes and allowed the memory to come. Seldom did she let herself revisit that night, but her frustration and helplessness coupled with the need for her brother's support weakened the wall she'd built around it.

The blare of the train's horn echoed in her ears. The white dot of its headlight grew larger as Leigh sat frozen in the backseat of their family's station wagon.

Her father cursed, "Ice! Dammit, ice! I can't stop!"

Her mother shrieked as she dove toward the backseat, arms outstretched to her children.

Brian had already jumped over the seat back into the rear of the wagon. Leigh pulled against his grip, trying to grab her mother's hand. But Brian was much stronger. He'd yanked her halfway over the back of the seat when it happened.

The sounds of that night fell layer upon layer, like the pages of a thumbed book, until the simple remembrance of the horrible cacophony threatened to split Leigh's skull.

First came the scream of the train's locked wheels grinding against the rails. Then what sounded like an explosion, followed by someone tearing aluminum pie pans apart. Leigh's memory had preserved each and every sound, amplifying it over the years. She remembered the rush of cold air and enveloping darkness as her head slammed against something hard. When they stopped moving, she and Brian were tangled together against the back gate of the station wagon.

As soon as Leigh could move, she'd crawled toward the front, crying frantically for her mother. When she pulled herself up and looked over the backseat, she stared into a dark field covered with silvery frost. She was still trying to make sense of it when Brian pushed her from behind, urging her over the seat.

"Out! Get out! I smell gas!"

Leigh tumbled across the remains of the backseat. Something sharp bit into the palm of her hand. She had trouble keeping her footing as she struggled out of the wreckage. Brian pulled her up by the arm and forced her to run. He ignored her cries to slow down, not stopping until they were a good distance from the car. They sank down onto the cold ground, chests heaving for breath.

The train cars sat motionless upon the tracks, up an embankment on their right, the low rumble of its idling engine far down the tracks the only sound.

She stared at the car. The back wheels sat at an angle to the tracks, the bench of the backseat was shredded, there was nothing in front of that.

Starting to get up, she screamed, "Mommy!"

Brian pulled her back down. She cried and kicked at him, struggling to get away, calling for her mother. But he wrapped his arms around her and held her against him.

"Stop! Stop it!" he yelled as he squeezed her harder. When she quit screaming he spoke in her ear. "If they're okay, they'll find us. We have to stay here so they can. It's dark; we have to stay here."

Suddenly a soft *whoosh* pushed past them. Leigh jerked her gaze to the car. Yellow flames licked from underneath. Before she could say anything, the gas tank exploded, sending a ball of fire into the night sky.

She tried not to be scared. Brian wasn't acting scared. She didn't want him to think she was a baby, so she bit down on her lips and cried silently. For a long time she lay shaking in his arms, feeling the heat from the fire, listening to the fast beating of her own heart, letting her tears soak his jacket.

Suddenly, a blinding light swept across her eyes, looking like a giant star through her tears. A tall man stood holding a flashlight.

"Daddy!"

Brian let her go.

She jumped up and ran to the man holding the flashlight. As she threw her arms around his legs and a hand came to rest on her shoulder, she felt rough denim against her cheek, not Daddy's soft-scratchy wool suit jacket. She heard Brian getting to his feet behind her.

The man who wasn't Daddy yelled to someone near the train, "I got two kids over here!"

Leigh pulled away. "Where's my Daddy?"

The man knelt in the weeds and tried to pick her up. "Let's take you over to the ambulance and have you checked out."

Leigh jerked away and plastered herself against her brother.

Brian said, "It's okay, mister. We can walk." He took her hand and they followed the train engineer up the embankment.

Leigh had been surprised it was such a long walk to the road. Finally she saw the red bubble-light on top of the ambulance. A man with a stethoscope came forward. He too tried to pick Leigh up, but she clung to Brian all the harder. The man knelt in front of them and said his name was Ben. He talked softly, asking them if they were hurt anywhere. He wrapped a bandage around Leigh's cut hand, then helped them climb into the ambulance.

As it pulled away with a wail of the siren, Leigh asked Brian, "Are Mommy and Daddy in another ambulance?"

Brian had squeezed her good hand. "Probably. They couldn't carry four of us in this one."

That was the last time he ever lied to her.

Leigh opened her eyes and stared at the faint scar across the palm of her hand. Her legs felt as weak as if she'd just lived through the whole ordeal again. After a few minutes, she felt strong enough to put the car in drive and pull out of the lot.

Chapter 12

Will noticed the waitress lingering near his seat at the Dew Drop's counter while he ate his lunch. He wouldn't normally; it was just that she smelled as if she'd taken a long swim in a vat of perfume. It wasn't an unpleasant fragrance, given the right quantity. This gal had missed that mark by a mile. He imagined he could see the vapors hovering around her like a noxious cloud. Every time he opened his mouth to take a bite, the bitter taste of it was on his tongue.

He finished his hamburger and folded his napkin. Just as he was reaching for the check, she stepped closer and leaned her elbows on the counter. Ample cleavage pushed at the open collar of her blouse. Her tag said her name was Sally.

"Don't tell me you're not going to have a slice of our fresh-baked cherry pie?" Something more seductive than dessert lurked in her tone.

He managed a friendly smile. "Sounds tempting, but I gotta get back to work."

"I could pack it up to go. Baked it myself."

Will didn't even like cherry pie. But it was stupid to hurt feelings over something so insignificant, so he agreed.

She grinned broadly and said, "I'll have it in

a jiffy." Then she went through the swinging door into the kitchen.

As he stood and dug cash from his pocket, a man's voice filtered from the kitchen. Will could only catch snatches, but what he heard set off a cascade of worry. There was something about "stranger" then "dangerous . . . grabbed . . ." He couldn't hear the waitress's response beyond a hateful-sounding hiss. Then the swinging door exploded into the dining room and the woman returned with a Styrofoam container in hand and a strained smile on her face.

"Here you go," she said, waggling the box in the air at him.

They traveled to the register near the door along opposite sides of the counter. She leaned close and whispered, "I threw in the pie, no charge."

"That wasn't necessary."

"It's good business. You like it, you come back and see m— ah, us."

He paid. "Well, thanks."

All the way back to the garage, Will considered his options. The cook's words bounced around in his brain. There could be no doubt about the subject of their argument. If there was one person in town whose mind had gone down the road of suspicion, there were bound to be followers. He couldn't afford to be caught up in the case of a disappearing teenager, especially as a suspect. There would be publicity, and then . . .

At the same time, if he left now, they wouldn't need a ton of evidence to put an APB out on him. After all, who else would be a more logical suspect? He *could* manage if he had to go to ground for the next few weeks; it'd be a hell of a lot harder with the hounds of every law agency in the country on his heels.

He guessed if he had to choose between suspicion of the locals and legal action, he'd take his chances here among the whispers.

His tension upped another notch when he got to the garage and saw who was talking to Brownie out in front.

Brownie said, "Here's the man himself. Why don't you ask him?"

Will looked at the young newspaper reporter next to Brownie. The sandy-haired kid was tall and athletically built, and seemed quite aware of his good looks. He held himself with a cocky self-assurance that made Will want to grab him by the collar and shake a little humility into him. "Ask me what?"

"As I understand it, you checked out the Wilson girl's car on Saturday?"

"That's right."

"This was *after* Brownie left?"

"Yep." Will knew exactly where this was going but couldn't see a way to stop it without creating a bigger mess.

"Find anything?"

"Mr. . . . Grant, is it?"

"Sorry. Should have introduced myself yesterday." He stuck out his hand and squared his shoulders. "Hale Grant, *Glens Crossing Recorder.*"

As Will shook his hand, it was all he could do to keep from rolling his eyes at the pretense in the introduction.

"Okay, Mr. Grant, it's like this. I'm not sure what the sheriff wants made public record at this time, so I'm going to have to pass on answering that question."

The young man just stared at him for a moment. "I don't see how this could be —"

"I don't mean to be uncooperative." If lying hadn't become second nature to him, Will would have been ashamed at such an outrageous fib. He knew an ambitious journalist when he saw one — and Hale Grant had "big city reporter wannabe" written all over his face. This kid was dying for an important story. It was probably torture every day he had to expound upon who raised the prize 4-H calf and the scores of the local ladies' bridge club. "You'll have to get your details from Sheriff Mitchell."

Will could see the gears shift in the newsman's head.

"I'll do that. Speaking of our sheriff, how did you know to show up at her office before the sun came up yesterday?"

"Brownie told me about what was going on when he got back from towing the car."

"Ahh, yes, he was just telling me how you

and he arrived home about the same time — in the wee hours of Sunday morning."

Will held Grant's gaze, but didn't offer any explanation.

"Where had you been, if I may ask?"

"Out."

Hale looked Will up and down. "As I recall, you looked a trifle — disheveled — yesterday morning."

"I'm sorry to cut this short, but I have six cars to do this afternoon," Will said, as he walked in the open overhead door and deposited the container with the cherry pie on the workbench. "You're welcome to keep on talking while I work."

"No, no, I don't want to bother you. Maybe we could meet for a beer later?"

Now comes the *be-my-buddy* approach. Will sighed at the tediousness of it all. "I'll be at the Crossing House for dinner around seven."

"Maybe I'll stop by."

"That'd be just dandy," Will said under his breath as Grant walked away in pursuit of a more promising angle.

About an hour later, as Will fiddled with a carburetor adjustment, he felt a weighty gaze upon him. He straightened and looked around. There, in the open overhead door sat a broad-chested yellow dog. Slowly, Will moved closer and saw no collar. He knelt and the dog inched nearer until they were almost nose to nose. Only after the dog had had a good, long sniff did Will put up a hand and stroke the yellow head.

"Well, now, where do you belong?" he said softly as he scratched behind the floppy ears.

"That mutt back here again?" Brownie called through the office door.

"You know him?"

"Stray. Somehow manages to keep from getting picked up and hauled to the pound."

"He looks healthy. Somebody must be feeding him."

The dog licked Will's face.

Brownie said, "There's probably some bleeding heart around here keeps meat on his bones."

Will gave him a final pat and went back to work. A few minutes later he looked up and saw the dog had moved inside and had his nose raised high, sniffing the workbench. The yellow tail cut merrily back and forth through the air.

"Like cherry pie, do you?"

The tail wagged faster.

"Well, I do have to appreciate a dog with manners," Will said. "A less refined pooch would have snatched and run."

The dog sat and stared hopefully at the pie container.

Picking up the pie, Will said, "You must be a clever guy to avoid the dogcatcher."

Now the dog's gaze was riveted to Will's hand, but he sat perfectly still, except for the tail that swished back and forth across the dirty concrete floor.

"Come on, better not do this right under the boss's nose." He walked outside, the clickity-click of dog nails right at his heels. "With those claws, maybe you oughta try tap dancing for your supper. Bet the carnival out at the fairgrounds would be happy to pick up a talented fella like you."

It surprised him to hear a little whine come from the dog's throat.

He turned and looked into round brown eyes that seemed to hold a degree of injury. Shaking his head, he thought, *I'm having a two-way conversation with a dog.* Definitely too much isolation.

Once at the corner of the building, Will knelt and opened the Styrofoam box. The dog sat in front of him, but didn't move to eat the pie.

"What? Worried about your figure?"

The dog cocked his head. A long thread of drool dripped from his lip.

Will held out the box. "It's okay. I don't really like cherry pie. It's all yours."

The dog's front paws fairly danced with impatience. His nose twitched and his tongue lolled. But he stayed where he was.

"Eat, for crying out loud!"

The instant Will said "eat," the dog buried his face in the container. Well-trained for a stray. Will thought of Leigh and her oversized stuffed mutt. She seemed to like dogs. Maybe he'd take this one to her if it was still hanging around after work. Then a thought struck him.

What if she didn't want a real live dog? She was the sheriff. Would she be duty bound to turn the guy in? It seemed a shame; he'd evaded capture this long, had managed to survive on his wits.

"Guess we got a lot in common, fella." Will watched as the dog scarfed down the pie.

"Well! I never!"

Will jerked his gaze away from the dog. Not two feet from him stood the waitress from the Dew Drop, hands on rounded hips, Reeboks planted in a battle stance.

"I was just letting him lick up the crumbs," Will said, standing. "The pie was great."

"Crumbs, huh?" She pointed a purple-polished nail at the dog.

Will glanced down. The dog was looking right at her. Bright red rimmed his mouth and a blob of filling sat on the end of his nose. The damned beast wasn't even trying to lick it off! In fact, he seemed to be smiling.

Frantically searching for an apology that wouldn't sound ridiculously lame, Will watched her spin on her heel and head off down the street. Just before she got into a car parked a half-block away, she turned and gave him the finger.

"Guess I deserved that," Will said, then looked back to the dog. "You certainly weren't any help."

The dog licked the sticky goo from his face with a long pink tongue.

"Too little, too late."

He went back inside and threw away the now spotless pie container. As he picked up his screwdriver again, he noticed the dog had laid down in the sun just outside the garage door. After a couple of feeble attempts to keep his eyes open, the furry lids fell closed.

"Traitor."

The Grissom farmhouse looked as battened down as it had the day before. Although the weather was beautiful and there was a refreshing breeze that spoke of autumn, the windows remained closed and covered. Leigh hesitated before she got out of her car, looking for a sign of Mr. Grissom. His pickup truck sat just outside the barn, but she couldn't see him anywhere. She glanced at her watch. One o'clock. Hopefully he'd had his lunch and was back at work on the unharvested acreage down the road. She really wanted to speak to the wife alone.

Leigh's knock brought footsteps heading toward the door immediately. Not a good sign. She was disappointed but not surprised when the door opened and Mr. Grissom stood in a white undershirt, denim coveralls and a red bandanna tied around his neck.

"Sheriff." He nodded as he pushed open the screen door for her to enter. "Found that girl yet?"

They stood in a narrow hallway with a

scarred hardwood floor. A steep staircase ascended the wall on the right. A threadbare red oriental runner covered the steps. The atmosphere was filled with oppressive stuffiness. He didn't invite her further into the house.

"No, that's why I'm here. I was hoping maybe you or your wife remembered something from Saturday night that might help."

"Didn't see nothing. Went to bed at nine o'clock, like always. Up again at five. By then Brownie'd hauled her car off."

"Could I talk to your wife?"

"She didn't see nothing either."

"I'm sure you're right, but it's my job to speak to anyone who could be a potential witness myself."

He didn't appear moved.

She added, "You know, government red tape, forms and papers . . ."

That brought a knowing light to his eye. "Reckon I've had 'nough of them gov'mnt folk to know that. Always got some report to fill out before they can do anything about those damned flying saucers." He motioned for her to follow him. "Won't leave my cows alone, you know."

"Who won't?" She could hardly imagine that the air force investigators who Mr. Grissom had finally convinced to come check out his UFO claims had any interest in his cows.

"Martians. Always plucking one up to study it."

"You've been missing cattle?"

"Naw. Clever bastards always put 'em back. 'Course I don't let Hattie near the windows at night; they don't put humans back. Too hard to get. That's why you ain't gonna find that little gal."

They'd reached the kitchen. Here as in the rest of the house, dark shades covered the windows. Leigh's eyes had grown accustomed to the dimness. A single bulb dangled over the kitchen table, throwing off meager light. Mrs. Grissom's eyes grew wide when she saw Leigh. Her lip trembled slightly before she turned back to her dishes in the sink.

"Hattie, Sheriff Mitchell needs you to tell her you didn't see nothing Saturday night."

The woman turned around, wiping her hands on a towel. She wouldn't look at Leigh beyond one skittering glance.

"Well," Mr. Grissom said in a sharp voice that made the woman flinch, "tell her."

Hattie concentrated on her dishtowel and licked her wrinkled lips. "No." It was hardly more than a breathy consonant.

"There. Now you can write your report."

Leigh ignored Mr. Grissom's terse comment and stepped closer to his wife. She placed her hand over Hattie's as they twisted in the towel, and said very softly, "Mrs. Grissom, you know a girl is missing."

The gray head bobbed, but she still didn't meet Leigh's gaze.

"Did you notice any lights, any unusual sounds Saturday night?"

Instead of looking at Leigh, the woman's gaze cut to her husband. Her lip trembled slightly. Leigh sensed Mrs. Grissom wanted to say something.

"She was asleep. Now we both told you." Mr. Grissom sounded like his patience had been sorely tested.

Leigh turned a smile to him. "All right, then. I appreciate your help. Before I go, I was hoping to buy a dozen fresh eggs. Yours are so much better than the supermarket's." If she could just get him out of here for a couple of minutes, she felt Mrs. Grissom might talk.

"Better 'n cheaper, too," he said with pride. "Hattie, get the sheriff her eggs."

So much for that plan.

Then he said to Leigh, "We got a cooler right in the hen house."

"How nice. Say, in that case, I might as well walk out with you, Mrs. Grissom. Then I'll go straight to my car." She fell in behind the silent woman. "Thank you, Mr. Grissom, for your time."

Leigh made a point of pulling the door closed behind her. Squinting against the bright sunshine, she nearly stumbled down the back step.

Mrs. Grissom appeared to be having no trouble adapting to the change in light. She took rapid little steps directly toward the hen

220

house without a single indication she even noticed Leigh followed.

The older woman unlatched the gate in the fence surrounding the chicken yard. Leigh put her hand on it to keep her from closing it behind her. "Could I see the inside of the hen house? It's been a long time. . . ."

Mrs. Grissom nodded once and walked on across the yard. Leigh latched the gate and followed, glancing over her shoulder to make certain Mr. Grissom wasn't on their heels.

Once inside she watched as Mrs. Grissom's gnarled hands worked smoothly, filling a cardboard egg carton from the cooler. Closing the lid, she turned and handed the carton to Leigh.

"How much do I owe you?"

"Dollar'll be fine." Mrs. Grissom looked at Leigh only briefly.

Leigh pulled a one from her pocket and handed it to Mrs. Grissom. She took it, stuffing it in the pocket of her skirt. She looked so frightened and frail, standing there in a baggy blouse and worn Keds, it broke Leigh's heart. What a lonely existence this woman endured. Had anyone ever reached out a hand in friendship to her?

"Mrs. Grissom — Hattie, I hope if you remember anything out of the ordinary about Saturday night, you'll tell me. Even the most insignificant thing might help — a car door slamming, voices . . ."

The older woman's moss green gaze rose to

meet Leigh's, steadily this time. Then she glanced toward the door. Hesitating another second she swallowed hard. Just as her lips parted to speak, Mr. Grissom's voice boomed through the closed door.

"What's takin' so long out here?"

The door opened wide and Hattie jumped.

"If you got the eggs for the sheriff, you'd best be gettin' back to them dishes."

Leigh wanted to throttle him. But she forced herself to smile sweetly and said, "Mrs. Grissom was just letting me reacquaint myself with farm life. It's been a long time since I was in a hen house. You remember my Uncle Worth and Aunt Belinda?" Leigh continued without waiting for a response. "When I lived with them, I used to help Aunt Belinda collect the eggs every morning." Leigh left out the fact that she'd detested every second of it.

She looked back to Mrs. Grissom. "Thank you for taking the time."

Hattie lowered her lashes, then hurried past her husband and on toward the house.

"Good-bye, Mr. Grissom," Leigh said. It was all she could do to keep from giving him a sharp elbow in the gut as she passed. How many years had it taken for him to completely break his wife's spirit?

Leigh pulled out of the farm lane. She'd been so close. She didn't know if Hattie wanted to tell her something about Brittany, or simply longed for human contact. Whichever, Leigh didn't intend to let this pass. The woman deserved to be heard. It wouldn't be happening with her husband around though.

Passing the harvested corn field on her left, Leigh approached the little copse of woods that marked the edge of the Grissom farm. Nestled against the tree line was a small family cemetery surrounded by a rusty wire fence that was supported by grayed and splintered wooden posts. She'd passed it a million times, always curious about the old monuments, but had never stopped. This time she pulled off the road and walked into the graveyard.

The oldest markers were white arches, lettering worn from a hundred seasons of rain and wind. Lichen clung in darkened blotches to the stones. Leigh knelt beside one and ran her fingers over the faint carving. *Hobart Grissom, died January 11, 1873, aged 56 y. 3 m. 17 d.* Next to him: *Caroline, wife of Hobart Grissom, died April 2, 1845, aged 20 y. 6 m. 30 d.* And on the same stone: *Infant boy, died April 2, 1845.* Leigh shivered as she thought of life on what was then the frontier. Maybe the current Mrs. Grissom's life was a bed of roses compared to her predecessors'.

Moving to an area of newer stones, these low granite rectangles, she saw seven identical markers in a line. Elizabeth Grissom, Robert Grissom, Floyd Grissom, Dorothy Grissom, Samuel Grissom, Helen Grissom, Margaret Grissom. All born between 1939 and 1951. All of the death dates were the same or within a week of the birth dates. Helen lived the longest — six days.

Oh, Hattie, how your heart must have broken. No wonder the woman was so withdrawn. Leigh couldn't imagine Mr. Grissom had been much in the way of healing emotional wounds.

She now had a key, but, she asked herself, did she have the heart to use it?

Leigh waited for nearly an hour, watching for Mr. Grissom to leave the house. Finally, she gave up and decided to try again the next morning.

As Leigh pulled into her driveway, the six-o'clock news was playing on the radio. When they reached the segment about Brittany's disappearance, she clicked it off. She needed no reminder that she hadn't made any headway in finding the girl. The phone hotline had availed nothing but crackpots — she knew because she'd spent the entire afternoon following up each and every call.

The lab technician from the state police had arrived at her office shortly after she'd returned from the Grissom farm. He'd gone over the car, searching for traces of blood, collecting samples and taking fingerprints. Since he wasn't a trained mechanic, he could offer no opinion on whether or not the car had been tampered with. Leigh had to call Indianapolis again to have them send someone qualified to render a judgment on that aspect. He couldn't be in Glens Crossing until late Friday — about the same time she could expect the preliminary reports from the forensics tech.

Her deputy, Steve Clyde, had been assigned to question the carnival workers. They were due to leave town and she wanted information on every one of them. Unfortunately, as far as leads go, that was a dead end. Seems Saturday had been the manager's fiftieth birthday. After the carnival closed at eleven, they all boarded a charter bus and spent the rest of the night at one of the riverboat casinos down on the Ohio. Everyone went. Bus didn't return until nine the next morning.

Kurt Wilson had called seven times during the day. The dispatcher said he was increasingly angry with each call. Leigh telephoned him back and listened for a full ten minutes while he railed and ranted about her incompetence and lack of concern over his missing child.

Leigh had to bite her tongue to keep from voicing something that was, at the moment, based solely on intuition. She had growing confidence that Brittany had finally gone off the deep end and done something foolish. Maybe she had decided to give her old man a taste of his own medicine and left town to punish him. Or maybe she'd put herself in a situation that had a very bad end. Those were the only two theories that made any sense, considering her cell phone, money and credit cards were left in the car. Leigh didn't think a kidnapper would have left such valuable commodities behind.

But she would need, at the very least, some testimony from Hattie Grissom to give either of those a leg to stand on — and give Leigh a direction in which to point her investigation. She was determined to get it. It was just a matter of timing.

When Kurt paused for breath, Leigh patiently went over the ground she'd covered throughout the day, including the clearing of the carnival folk and the visit by the state technicians. Kurt's diatribe immediately veered to the new man in town — the only other variable in the local equation over the past few days.

Knowing that defending Will against accusations would only lead to speculation that she was ignoring him as a factor in the situation, she simply assured Kurt that as soon as she had *any* evidence of foul play against *any* suspect she would be making an arrest.

He didn't seem to notice her careful selection of words, which made Leigh both relax and feel like a heel at the same time. What would Kurt's reaction be if it came to suggesting that Brittany herself was responsible for this whole thing?

Until she had something solid in any direction, she was keeping her mouth shut.

This entire day was taking its toll. She slowly dragged herself out of her car and into the house.

Tossing the mail, the newspaper and the developed photos of Brittany's car on the dining-room table, Leigh headed for a bottle of Advil and a hot shower. Her muscles thrummed with fatigue. Her joints ached; she felt as if she'd run a gauntlet.

She switched the showerhead to massage and allowed the hot blast to knead her neck and shoulders. No matter how she tried to direct her thoughts elsewhere, those seven little tombstones kept creeping into her mind. Tomorrow she'd have to steel herself and go back to the Grissom farm. She'd decided to go in the mid-morning when Mr. Grissom would most likely be out. She hadn't decided what she'd do if Mrs. Grissom refused to open the door. Maybe it wouldn't be so difficult. Leigh felt like she'd made a small dent in the woman's protective armor today. Her shame crept over her as she thought of what she was going to do with that advantage.

By the time she got out of the shower she felt weak and limp. She wrapped herself in a terry robe and fell backward onto her bed.

As she drifted somewhere between waking and sleep, she mentally reviewed the photos again. Will had been right, something didn't add up. She inched back toward the waking world, trying to imagine the possible scenarios that led to Brittany's removal from the car.

Brittany's car stops. Someone, who has been following, comes up to the door on the pretense of helping. Leigh wondered why, then, did Brittany keep the window up and the door locked? And why hadn't she used her mobile phone to call for help? Maybe she didn't have time. Maybe he was on her before she had a chance.

She let the scene play, step by step, in her mind.

If the attacker had broken the window to reach in and open the door, then pulled Brittany out of the car, there should have been glass on the road. The window would have shattered, spraying Brittany with glass. When he pulled her out some of the glass should have fallen off of her and onto the pavement. It didn't make any sense. Unless . . .

Unless the window had been broken *after* Brittany was out of the car.

Leigh's eyes opened and she sat up — too quickly. The room spun and she cradled her head in her hands for a moment. She went into the dining room and retrieved the pictures. Flipping quickly through, she stopped at the close-up of the open driver's door and the pavement under it.

It made sense. The glass covered the entire driver's seat. Not a single shard on the road. And if Brittany was out of the car, was it because she had gotten out willingly? Or had she been forced out and the window broken in some kind of struggle that followed?

Leigh wandered into the living room, tapping

the stack of glossy prints against her other hand. She had to get Mrs. Grissom to tell what she saw that night. Now that she had more definite questions to answer, restlessness stirred deep inside. She prowled the dark house, arranging and rearranging the possibilities in her mind.

Could Brittany have been outside the car when her abductor arrived? That still made no sense. She left the mobile phone inside the car. Surely she would have called one of her parents for help at once when the car quit. The car was left as if she'd been taken abruptly, engine running, lights and radio still on. Was that a fact? Or was it deliberately made to *appear* that way?

Mrs. Grissom held the key.

Tomorrow seemed impossibly far away. But she knew it'd do no good to go back tonight, not with the husband there. Leigh dropped the photos on the coffee table and went into the kitchen.

More to take her mind off of things than out of hunger, she microwaved a bowl of soup — the gourmet kind, from the little glass jar instead of a can. Nobody could say Leigh Mitchell didn't know how to live it up. Then she called Brian to keep her company while she ate. After the seventh ring, she hung up. She tried his mobile.

"Yes." Brian's tone was businesslike.

"It's me." The line crackled with static. "Where are you?"

"On my way to take care of some business down near the Ohio River. What do you need, Sis?"

"I was just frustrated and needed someone to vent to."

"Vent away." The line crackled more. "Sorry, I'm going to lose you. Meet me for break— —rrow morning?"

"Okay. Dew Drop. Seven?"

"S— you —en." And he disconnected.

Leigh took her bowl of soup, which for some reason seemed much more lonely than when she'd pulled it from the microwave, and wandered out to the porch swing. The night was quiet, except for the rise and fall of a chorus of insect song. She pushed herself slowly back and forth with one bare foot as she ate.

As she fished around in the broth for her favorite vegetables — which she always ate first — she tried to deal with the prospect that she was destined to spend the rest of her life in the same rut. When she'd first returned to Glens Crossing, she'd had a few dates. However, the instant she was elected sheriff those came to a screeching halt. Life since the election had been pretty much a solo gig. She sighed and set her half-eaten soup on the porch floor.

The crunch of a footfall on the gravel drive made her sit up straighter and look toward the road. She hadn't heard a car. Her skin prickled with apprehension.

"Who's there?" she called into the darkness.

"Only a wandering soul, seeking a little companionship along his journey."

She recognized Will's voice immediately. Funny, she felt as if she'd known him much longer than a few days. Already his small mannerisms and the timbre of his voice were ingrained in her mind.

He climbed the porch steps. "Hope I'm not intruding."

"Not at all." That was the understatement of the year. She'd just been moping over her solitary bowl of soup — the pitiful symbol of a woman without a single soul with which to share her life. Will's presence spun her mood one-hundred-eighty degrees. "Let's go inside; the mosquitoes have more than their fair share of my blood already."

She tightened the belt on her robe. Suddenly her nakedness underneath seemed — well, naughty. She became intensely aware of the rub of the terry cloth on her nipples as she led him into the house. Why did she respond like this to him? His rejection, albeit clothed in concern for *her* and what *she* deserved, had left a stinging impression. She should be a big girl, do the mature thing and move away from such thoughts concerning Will Scott. But as he followed her through the door, she just couldn't get her body to cooperate.

Motioning for him to take a seat, she wondered why in the hell he kept coming around if he wasn't interested in her. She managed to say in a casual tone, "Can I get you something to drink?"

"Still offering wine?"

"Sure. I could use a glass myself." She headed to the kitchen. "Merlot okay?"

"Great."

As she returned, she stopped in the doorway and studied him for a moment. He was so different from anyone she had ever known. There were plenty of "nice guys" in Glens Crossing — nice and *bland*. There just didn't seem to be any kind of a spark in them. Not to mention the fact that they were as comfortable around her as a hen in a fox's den. But Will . . . he had passion; he'd shown her a glimpse of that fire when they'd danced. As well as tenderness, which she'd felt with his sweet kiss. And there was an undeniable mysteriousness about him; something powerful and intense coiled just beneath the surface. He kept it well concealed. She probably wouldn't have noticed it at all, if it hadn't been for that moment by the creek when he'd held a knife to her throat. As she thought back on it, that incident didn't rouse fear and caution in her. Her reaction went in quite the opposite direction.

Suddenly his comment about understanding the need to be someone else came crashing back into her mind, as it had repeatedly since he said it. The look in his eyes had been so distant, so longing. There were only so many possibilities for a person to need to be someone else. Many of them had to do with breaking the law — others with *enforcing* it. If he was a law-breaker, why in the hell would he be hanging around the local sheriff?

She was mulling that thought over as she stood there. Will had picked up the photographs and was flipping through them. He finally looked up at her with those piercing eyes. Leigh moved from the doorway, her knees suddenly rubbery.

"Hope it's okay that I see these," he said.

Leigh hadn't intended to share the photos with anyone just yet. There were things better kept under wraps until she had this case solved. Things only she, Brittany, and the criminal — if there was one — knew.

Too late now.

"Go ahead. Tell me what you think." She handed him his wine and sat next to him on the sofa.

He took a single sip, then set the glass down and concentrated once again on the pictures. He studied each one with the intensity of an investigator, not the morbid curiosity of a voyeur. Once he'd made it through the stack, he started again. He stopped at the photo of the open door and tapped it with his finger.

"This one. What's it say to you?" he asked.

She looked at him, not the photo. "I was going to ask you the same question."

He gazed at the picture again and spoke slowly. "It tells me the window wasn't smashed while Brittany was in the car."

She marveled that they could be so alike in their thought process — she'd seen it again and again — yet so different in their personalities. She was methodical and dull; he was a razor's edge.

"Look at the way the glass covers the driver's seat, but even here" — he switched to a close-up of the pavement — "you can't see any glass on the road."

Well, Leigh thought with the relief of confirmation, he certainly wouldn't be bringing up such a detail if he'd been the kidnapper, ruining his own setup.

"So what do you think happened?" she asked, trying not to think of how close her naked knee was to his jean-clad leg as they sat side by side.

"Need more input. What about the people on the farm there — Grissoms?"

"I spoke to them yesterday. He says they didn't see anything, but I think *she* has something to tell me. Her husband keeps the poor woman like a prisoner." Leigh thought back to the nervous way Mrs. Grissom had slipped the egg money into her skirt pocket. *Probably handed it over to the old bastard as soon as I left.*

"Think he had something to do with Brittany's disappearance? He does have the UFO thing going."

She shook her head. "Doesn't fit. He might be crazy, but crazies don't organize their crimes. They react, no premeditation. Ed

Grissom is waaaay down on my list of possibilities."

"Good girl."

She was going to question his odd statement, but he looked so deep in thought she held her tongue.

He looked pensive for a moment. Grooves bracketed his mouth as he pressed his lips together in concentration. "Okay. Could be a couple of things. The window could have been broken during a struggle of some sort outside of the car. But then" — he rubbed his chin — "why would the door have been opened again? Certainly not to retrieve anything from the vehicle; the mobile phone and her purse were still there. On the other hand, there's the possibility that it was broken just to accentuate the fact that someone had taken her by force."

Now Leigh's next question had to be, was the disabling of the car a coincidence, or part of the plan? If the entire scene had been set up for effect — the broken window, the radio playing, the open door — transmission trouble would fit right in with that entire scenario. Poor Brit, stranded on a dark country road, falls prey to a kidnapper — simply the wrong place at the wrong time. This was beginning to take shape — and Will was helping.

Leigh stared at him, trying to decipher where he learned his investigative reasoning.

His brow creased. "What are you thinking?"

"I'm thinking you have experience at this sort of thing."

"Kidnapping?"

"You know that's not what I meant. Why don't you stop being so evasive with me?"

He looked away. "Because I don't want to lie to you."

Something in his voice made her heart shift in her chest. Why did this have to be happening to her now? Why him? She had no answer, except the one in her soul that said this was her chance and she had to take it. As much as she'd tried to deny it, she had to admit she'd been hot for him since he led her on the dance floor. She knew they had no future — which should have made it perfect. But she heard a voice down deep inside calling, *Don't you want to know he'll be around in the long run?*

Maybe she had let Will get more deeply into her emotions than she'd intended. But she wasn't calling the plays in this life. And she'd be damned if she was going to grow old and gray regretting not having the courage to, for once, follow her heart. As Will had made it plain he was just passing through, no one would be hurt except herself.

He dropped the pictures back on the table and turned those vivid blue eyes on her once again. Leaning closer, he touched her cheek with his fingertips. "I won't lie to you. I *can* promise what I do tell you will be the truth. Can you be satisfied with that?"

Now or never. Old Leigh or new? She swallowed dryly and slowly raised her hand to his cheek. Holding his gaze, feeling with all her heart that she could trust him, she said, "Maybe not forever — but for right now . . ."

She kissed him, a sweet brush of the lips. "Yes," she whispered against his mouth. To her relief, he didn't pull away.

Please, please, don't tell me you don't want me.

Her heart leapt when he slid one hand into her hair and moved slightly closer. When she leaned into the kiss, pressing firmly against his mouth, a deep and primal sound came from the back of his throat.

A riot of sensations broke out in Leigh's body. The wonder of the crush of his lips, the solid connection of flesh to flesh she'd been longing for. The skin on her neck snapped alive under his lightest touch. The warmth as she buried her fingers in his hair. The tingling in her breasts. The seductive feel of his tongue dancing along the outline of her mouth before gently gaining entry.

By the time he eased away from the kiss, her breath had been snatched away. He looked into her eyes for a long moment. She listened to the heavy rasp of his breathing. His hand lingered on her neck, hers rested on the top of his shoulders.

She waited for him to kiss her again, holding his gaze, trying to read what was going on in his mind. It was obvious what was going on in the rest of his body.

Finally she could stand it no longer. "Touch me." She guided the hand on her neck down her throat and under the rolled collar of her robe. She thought she'd explode with anticipation as his palm rested just above her breast.

He groaned and closed his eyes briefly; a single moment of reprieve from the intensity Leigh was nearly squirming under. His hand remained still. Then he looked into her eyes again and leaned his forehead against hers.

"You know I can't stay."

She swallowed hard and closed her eyes. "I know."

"You still want — ?"

In answer, New Leigh kissed him, pulling him with her as she laid back on the couch.

His hand finally moved, cupping her breast under the soft terry of her robe and Leigh felt like she'd been shot into space. Her body seemed weightless, her limbs as if they belonged to another person. And yet every inch of her was buzzing, electrically charged.

Nips and kisses trailed down her neck as he widened the opening of her robe. The instant his tongue found her nipple, Leigh gasped and arched into him.

He teased her until she hovered on the brink, then returned his mouth to hers in a possessive kiss.

Leigh jerked his shirt from the waistband of his jeans and ran her hands underneath, over his back and sides, feeling tight muscle over solid ribs.

Suddenly he rose to his knees, straddling one of her legs, and yanked the T-shirt over his head. It landed on the table, knocking the photos onto the floor.

Leigh rose to a sitting position, her face inches from his stomach. She undid his belt and unzipped his jeans. She heard his sharp intake of breath as her lips took a provocative stroll around his navel. Her hands explored his sides, sliding under the fabric to caress his hips. He trembled under her ministrations. His body was new and foreign to her, yet startlingly familiar under her touch. It was as if she'd been anticipating this moment for her entire life. Every day had existed only to lead her to this point, to this man.

The mere feel of her breath on his skin made Will frantic to have her. The trust he'd seen in her eyes when she'd asked him to touch her filled the hollow ache in his soul he'd been ignoring for far too long. He'd survived for years by telling himself that he didn't need anyone; emotional entanglement would only drag him down. In that one brief second, Leigh forced him to face the lie.

He shouldn't have come out here. Not tonight. Not when he'd been feeling so lonely. Not when Leigh had played on his mind every waking moment since he'd met her. He knew he should stop, get up and walk out that door.

He had nothing to offer except danger and pain.

His head fell back and he gritted his teeth, praying for the strength to stop. At that moment, it became blindingly clear. She'd reached that part of him he thought he'd effectively destroyed. He knew he was in trouble. There was no doubt in his mind, he would crawl on his naked belly across broken glass for her. He also knew any connection to him was dangerous. But the satin of her lips on his stomach, her gentle stroking of his nipples, all sent his blood rushing toward completion. He'd never had to concentrate so hard to keep himself in check. Given his inclinations, he'd have ravaged her after that first kiss, thrust himself home and possessed her absolutely.

"Leigh." He put a hand on either side of her face and forced her to look up at him. "This is wrong. You deserve so much more than I can give."

Her brow creased. Then she said, with near pleading in her eyes, "I'm not asking for anything more. Just tonight."

She pushed his jeans down from his hips and all thoughts of leaving flew from his mind. He allowed himself the brief fantasy that there would be nights like this without end. Nights and days spent with this remarkable woman. She'd made him see so clearly how he wanted his life to change. Lies that flowed effortlessly off his tongue for so long that he actually had started to believe some of them himself now lodged in his throat, a bitter mass of deception that threatened to cut off life-giving air. Lies that had distorted his perception of himself, his world.

She, with the gentle breath of a kiss, freed him to become himself.

Opening her robe completely, Leigh drew him back with her. The rest of the world ceased to hold a single measure of significance. His past, the unalterable course of his future and even the dead man who haunted his dreams meant nothing. And for a moment, he allowed it to be so.

The instant their bodies joined, Leigh struggled to keep from tumbling over the precipice. She didn't want it to end quickly — or ever. The fact that she knew their time was limited made it all the more important that she revel in each and every sensation, every intimate detail.

At the same instant her world burst into a blazing white light, she heard Will call her name. Her heart clung to that cry, wishing it was for more than the moment alone.

Chapter 13

Sometime during the night Will had carried Leigh into the bedroom. They'd made love again. She yearned to knock down that thin barrier he seemed to retain, locking away his innermost soul. And, at times, she could see he wanted that too. But every time she managed to open that door a crack, he slammed it closed again. As much as she wanted to deny it, it wasn't just sex to her. She'd told him that tonight was enough, and she'd meant it at that moment. But now she knew she wouldn't rest until she knew him wholly and absolutely.

He touched her with what seemed near reverence; always mindful of her desires, always there with a murmured endearment. He loved her with an intensity that seemed far beyond the physical act. Which only made it that much harder for her to believe he'd so soon be gone.

The last time Leigh looked at the clock, as she snuggled her back against Will's chest and he wrapped an arm around her waist, it was four A.M.

When her five-thirty alarm went off, Leigh flung an arm in its direction, smacking it so hard it fell from the bedside table. It clattered to the hardwood floor with the snap of breaking plastic, but the damned radio played on.

She put her pillow over her head and wriggled in Will's direction. But she scooted to the far edge of the bed without coming into contact with him. Raising up on one elbow, she looked around the dim room with bleary eyes.

No Will.

She reached between the mattress and the wall, pulling the plug on the radio. She didn't hear water running in the bathroom.

Last night Will's clothes had remained where they'd landed, scattered on the floor of the living room. She couldn't see from her bed if they were still there.

Her first attempt at speech came out in a froggy croak. She cleared her throat and called, "Will?"

Reluctantly sliding out of bed, she peeked through the doorway into the living room. Her terry robe was flung across the back of the couch. No sign of Will. She grabbed the robe and walked around the sofa.

His shoes, socks and T-shirt lay in various spots around the coffee table. At least he hadn't slipped away like a cheap one-night stand. Which in fact had been the fear in her heart from the moment she found him gone. She didn't know if she could bear it if he treated her in such a manner — not that she could imagine such a thing after his sweet mix of unrestrained passion and thoughtfulness throughout their night together.

The front door was open. When she listened

carefully she heard the quiet creak of the swing moving back and forth. Slowly she pushed open the screen door.

The picture Will created — wearing only his jeans, black hair mussed and falling over his forehead, bare chested with one foot on the floor, the other resting on the swing seat with his arm resting on bent knee — set off a fluttering in her chest. She watched him for a moment, thinking he didn't know she was there.

"Come. Sit with me," he said, reaching out a hand.

He moved so his back was against the arm of the swing, and snuggled her between his legs so her back reclined on his chest. Then he enveloped her in his arms. Even in the early morning cool, he gave off heat. She was glad of it, for goosebumps had broken out on her bare legs.

"Do you always know what's going on around you? You seemed so absorbed in thought. . . ."

"No," he said, in a sad tone, "sometimes I don't see things at all — until it's too late."

She twisted so she could look into his face. Did he mean he regretted sleeping with her? As she studied, she decided the look in his eyes was far too distant — as if he was peering into the past. "Can you tell me?"

He kissed her lightly on the forehead and brushed her hair away from her face. "It won't make a difference. What's done is done." He paused and bit his lip. "But thanks for asking.

It's been a long time since anyone cared enough to."

Leigh didn't know why his words cut her to the quick. They were sweetly delivered, the sentiment grateful. But it felt like a slap in the face. Last night they'd shared intimacies heretofore unknown to her, on a level that probed deep into her soul. Now, he refused to share his pain.

"Maybe it won't change anything," she said. "But sometimes it helps to let it out."

He pushed her head down against his shoulder and stroked her hair. He let loose a long breath. "Honestly, if I was going to tell anyone, it would be you. Some things are just better left alone."

She decided to go out on a limb. He'd given her one and only one crumb in all of their conversations together. It was time to use it.

Rubbing her hand along the arm wrapped around her, ready to latch on if he tried to pull away, she said, "How did your sister die?"

Along the length of her body, she felt him stiffen. She held deathly still and waited.

After a long moment, he took a deep breath, the rise of his chest the only assurance Leigh had that he hadn't turned to stone behind her.

"Drug overdose." He paused and Leigh could feel his breath catch. "She was only twenty-one."

Leigh resisted the urge to turn around and look him in the eye. This revelation was difficult enough for him; she felt the need to leave him a shred of privacy. "Was she older or younger than you?"

"Nine years younger."

"It must have been awful."

"I wasn't there."

She waited for him to say more, but he remained silent. When she leaned her head back on his shoulder, she felt a drop of moisture hit the top of her head. He held her tightly against his chest, assuring that she could not turn to him. For a long while they just rocked back and forth on the swing in silence.

Leigh weighed his words and denied her need to comfort, to ask for more. For the first time she noticed the big yellow dog sleeping in the corner. She raised up and Will's arms finally loosened.

"Who's this?"

Will's laugh carried relief. "My new shadow. Can't seem to shake him."

"No collar or tags."

"Brownie says he's a stray."

"Well," she said as she slid onto the porch floor and crept closer to the dog, "he can't just run around loose. We have leash laws."

"I'll be sure and tell him when he wakes up."

She cast a disparaging look over her shoulder. "Smart ass." Laying a hand on the dog's head, she said, "He is cute."

With apparent effort, the doggie lids opened

and brown eyes peeked out. Then his eyes closed again.

"You wanna keep him?" Will asked. "I'll take him to the vet for his shots."

"No way. I don't have time to take care of a dog."

"He seems to be pretty good at that himself."

"How's he managed to dodge animal control?" She got up off the porch floor and dusted off her hands.

"He's obviously a clever fella — at least more clever than the dog catcher." Will laughed.

"Hey, it's a nasty job, but somebody's gotta do it."

"You aren't going to turn the poor guy in, are you?" Will's eyes narrowed. " 'Cause if you are, I don't think you and I can be *friends* anymore."

She looked innocent and leaned close for a kiss. "What dog?"

He pulled her onto his lap and kissed her thoroughly. "I love an officer of the law with good common sense."

"Well, I won't be able to help him if he's caught, so just hope he stays on his doggie toes." She headed into the house. "Why don't you put on some coffee. I have to shower and meet Brian for breakfast."

"Yes, ma'am."

Brian. Leigh considered how much to tell. She decided she'd just have to set things straight right off. Surely he would see reason. People would get used to the idea she was dating someone — no one had to know the dirty details. It was all perfectly acceptable in this day and age anyway.

That little voice in the back of her mind, the one Brian had cultivated for so long, said, "Acceptable for a man. A woman can't be so careless."

She stepped under the shower stream, trying to drown it out. Couldn't she have one moment, just for herself, without worrying what the rest of the world would think?

By the time Leigh came into the kitchen, she'd decided she *was not* going to feel guilty. Will handed her a steaming mug of coffee and kissed her on the cheek. God, how could something that made a person feel this good be wrong?

She smiled at him, sat down and sifted through yesterday's mail. As she sipped her coffee, he put the milk back in the refrigerator.

"Leigh." Will's serious tone drew her attention immediately. "What are you doing to yourself here?" He pointed to the missing child mailer on the refrigerator door.

"Nothing. It's just a reminder."

"It's self-punishment. Take it down."

She stood and faced him. "Until I find out what happened to Brittany, that stays where it is."

He put his hands on her shoulders and said softly, "And what if you can't?"

"I will. She couldn't have vanished into thin

248

air. There's a trail somewhere, and I'm going to find it."

He looked as if he was going to argue further, then shrugged and hugged her to his chest. "God help you."

Leigh didn't know if he was wishing for God to help her in her quest, or simply that she was going to need saving herself.

"Finish your coffee before it gets cold," he said as he let her go.

Leigh sat back down at the table, repeating to herself over and over that she *would* find Brittany. She flipped open yesterday afternoon's edition of the *Glens Crossing Recorder* and her coffee stuck in her throat.

The bold headline read: WHAT EVIL HAS COME TO OUR COMMUNITY? The story elaborated, in the worst purple prose Leigh had ever set eyes on, how Glens Crossing had enjoyed a world untouched by the crime and hatred that seemed so rampant in the rest of today's society. While children elsewhere shot each other with handguns, this community basked in the wholesome security reminiscent of the 1950s. Then the article launched into several paragraphs of gory speculation about the fate of Brittany Wilson. It ended by calling upon the people of this community to ask themselves what has changed, what new element has been introduced into our midst in this last week?

She knew exactly where Hale Grant was headed with this. He couldn't have been more specific in his finger-pointing if he'd mentioned Will Scott by name.

"That son of a bitch."

Will looked over her shoulder at the paper. "What's wrong?"

"Our local paper has decided to stir the emotional pot." She pointed to the headline.

Will picked the paper up and read the article. As he read, his lips tightened and a furrow appeared in his brow. "That's why the little bastard cozied up to me last night. I knew he was up to something." He slapped the paper against his leg.

"Last night?"

"Yeah. He was pumping Brownie for information when I got back from lunch yesterday. Then he started on me. Stopped to have a beer with me at the Crossing House after dinner — very curious young man."

"What did he ask you?"

"Nothing and everything. He was fishing." Will grinned. "He left very frustrated."

Leigh looked at Will. "Do you think he followed you here?"

From the look in his eyes, Will grasped the implication. He put a hand on her shoulder. "No. I'm certain he didn't.

"Listen, I'll just leave the back way, hike through the woods and follow the creek back into town."

"Don't be ridiculous. I'm a grown woman; I don't need to sneak around."

"You don't know how difficult he can make this investigation. A few allusions here, an off-handed remark there and suddenly *you're* the one under suspicion. You can't conduct a thorough investigation if you have to spend your time defending yourself against prejudicial selection of suspects. Believe me, I know."

Her gaze sharpened and a little trill of victory shot through her. "I *knew* you were a cop."

"Not exactly. Forget it. That's not the problem at the moment. I'll slip out, then you and I had better keep a low profile."

"Not see one another." It seemed impossible that their limited future together had abruptly become altogether nonexistent.

"If I didn't think it'd do more harm than good, I'd pack up and leave town today."

"I see." He seemed mighty comfortable with casting her aside.

"No, you don't see. I can tell by the tone in your voice. Being with me right now could be damaging to your position. It's not worth the compromise."

She tightened her jaw. "It's not your job to decide what's best for me."

He touched her cheek, relaxing the tense muscles of her face immediately. "All I'm saying is that we shouldn't be seen as an item, at least not for the next few days."

"I'm going to have a little chat with Mr. Grant."

"He wants a story, Leigh. And I think he'll

do almost anything to get it. Be careful."

"I will."

He kissed her and left by the kitchen door so quickly she hardly registered it. She leaned against the jamb and watched him through the screen. He hadn't gotten ten feet from the back steps when the yellow dog bounded around the corner of the house and fell in beside him, tail wagging and balls swinging with each step.

Just when Leigh was ready to call Brian and wake his lazy ass up, he slid into the booth across from her and said, "Well, well, you certainly look rosy this morning."

Thankfully, the waitress appeared with coffee before Leigh could reply. Brian ordered pancakes. Leigh ordered an English muffin. After all, she hadn't run today. Her cheeks warmed. She'd certainly burned off a few calories during the night though.

He leaned across the table and peered at her closely. "You're blushing!"

"Don't be ridiculous."

"That guy from the bar . . . Leigh you didn't —"

"What I did or did not do with 'that guy from the bar,' or any guy for that matter, is none of your business."

Damn him, he always could read her uncannily well.

He grabbed her hand as she reached for the cream. "I'm not kidding around here, Leigh.

That guy is bad news. For all we know *he* grabbed Brittany."

"Not you, too. There isn't a shred of definitive evidence that points in his direction."

Brian licked his lips and lowered his voice. "There are things you don't know about Brittany. She *likes* older guys. It's just possible that they were out there in her car together, something happened . . . Maybe he buried her in the woods and walked back to town. We don't *know* this guy!"

Leigh grabbed onto what she wanted from his comments. "What do you mean, 'she likes older guys'? Are you one of those guys?"

"Of course not!" His right eye twitched at the corner as he said it. He reined in his emotions and said, "You're missing the point. That guy blew into town and a couple of days later someone *disappeared* from this county for the *very first* time." He tapped his index finger against the tabletop to emphasize his statement. "Stuff like that doesn't happen here. You're the sheriff —"

Leigh slapped her palm against the table. "Damn right, I'm the sheriff." She looked around at the stares she'd just attracted and lowered her voice. "Just listen to yourself! Use simple logical thinking. Why on earth would he hang around town if he'd abducted or killed her? And if he buried her in the woods, why didn't we find some trace when we lifted every milkweed leaf between here and the county line?"

He pressed his lips together for a moment, as if sealing off words too hurtful to allow to pass. Then he said, in a tone so dark Leigh hardly believed it was coming from her brother, "Mark my words, Will Scott is trouble. I don't want to see you dragged down just because you need a roll in the hay."

"You bastard." If that came out, what was he holding back?

Brian leaned back and blew out a long breath. "I'm sorry. I didn't mean that. It's just that I'm worried about you. Things are getting crazy. . . . Until we find Brittany, it's going to get worse."

"Which leads me back to my original question, what about Brit and older guys?"

He closed his eyes for a moment. "She's been testing the waters, trying to hook up with a couple of men."

Leigh looked him square in the eye. "And I say again, are you one of them?"

Brian looked away. "She's just trying to get back at Kurt. She's not going to do anything really stupid."

"I think she already has."

Judge Barton paused as he passed their table on his way to the door. "Brian! Just the man I needed to see. We need to get that paperwork together for the congressional run. I know the primary isn't until spring, but we need to set these wheels in motion. As election chairperson, I can't have our candidate lagging behind."

Brian smiled and raised a palm. "I'll get with you later this week. I promise."

The judge looked at Leigh. "You make sure he keeps his word. It's time for a change in this district."

Leigh forced a smile and fought back all of the conflicting emotions this morning seemed to be brewing. "Will do."

Brian had been Glens Crossing's golden boy since junior high. Charming, popular, athletic. When he'd gotten the football scholarship to the University of Michigan, there had been no doubt in anyone's mind that he'd be quarterbacking in the pros. He'd have made it too, if he hadn't blown out his knee in his final collegiate game. Instead he'd returned home, married his high-school sweetheart and started a real estate company without so much as a whimper of disappointment.

When Leigh finished college, Brian had talked her into not taking the FBI job she'd been offered and returning to Glens Crossing. He'd promised she wouldn't be sorry. She'd worked local law for five years, then he'd fallen in behind her and managed the impossible: getting her elected sheriff at twenty-eight.

He had explained her election had been step one in the plan for the budding Mitchell family political dynasty. Step two, his election to U.S. Congress, was already in motion. Leigh knew he had everything it took to win — looks, intelligence, dedication, ambition, and now the backing of the party.

The judge walked away and Brian surprised Leigh by standing up and dropping money on the table to pay for the breakfast that hadn't even arrived yet. He looked down at Leigh with disapproval in his eyes. It was almost more than she could stand.

"Like I said, you're the sheriff. But just remember who put you there. Everything *you* do reflects on *me*."

He left the café without looking back.

Leigh forced herself to sit there long enough to finish her coffee. She couldn't begin to choke down the muffin.

Leigh tried to put Brian out of her mind for now. There was nothing she could do at the moment to reassure him she had no intention of screwing up his chances at a political future. She knew what she owed him, and it was a damned sight more than behaving herself in public. She knew her job, and no matter what the personal cost, she'd do it.

She decided to visit the newspaper office before heading out to dig around in Hattie Grissom's old wounds. *You're just putting it off.* She shook off the thought. But somehow she didn't feel her ethics were much above Hale Grant's and his sensationalism for personal gain.

As she was reaching for the door to the *Recorder*'s office, it swung out and almost hit her in the face. Hale Grant's gaze slid quickly past as he apologized and side-stepped her.

"Wait a minute," she called as he hurried down the brick sidewalk. "Hale."

"I'm already late. Can it wait, Sheriff?" He continued to move away.

Following, she said, "No, it can't."

He slowed and allowed her to catch up.

She fell into step beside him. "I suppose you have a good explanation for your leading story in yesterday afternoon's paper."

"Explanation?"

Leigh wanted to smack the look of mock confusion off his face. "You know we have no leads regarding Brittany Wilson's disappearance. In the future I'd appreciate you limiting your articles to the *facts*."

He stopped and turned to face her. "Those were the facts, Sheriff."

"I suppose buried under all of the innuendo and insinuation there were the bones of a few facts. Listen, it's my job to protect this community and the path you've started down —"

Poking a finger in the air between them, he said sharply, "If it's your job to protect this community, why are you ignoring the evidence?"

"What are you talking about? What evidence?"

He laid a finger on his cheek and looked to the sky. "Let me see . . . . maybe the fact that Will Scott is new in town, nobody knows a thing about him, he's secretive as a mummy, he was out all night when she went missing, he worked on Brittany's car just before it broke down out in the middle of nowhere — and oh, yes, there's the matter of the ticket stub."

She started to say something, but he raised a hand with an air of infuriating superiority.

"Don't blow a gasket. I saw the evidence baggie through the window, sitting on the seat of your car. I don't suppose you've asked Mr. Scott if he'd visited the Speedway Museum before he blew into our fair city? Maybe you were too busy dancing —"

She leaned close and pointed a finger at his chest. "Listen, mister, this is *my* investigation and what I have and have not asked is none of your concern. Any more inflammatory stories like the one I read yesterday and —"

"And what? You gonna try to censor the press?" He actually looked down his nose at her, the cocky little bastard.

"My job is to find Brittany. Just stay out of my way." She turned around, then headed to her car before she balled her fist and decked him. As she got into the Blazer, she admonished herself. She'd done just what Will had warned her against. She'd lost control of her tongue and probably done more damage than good.

She could hardly wait to see what tonight's paper would deliver.

Leigh was in no mood to do what she must at

258

the Grissom's. But it was now or wait another day. She had to catch Hattie while the lord and master was out in the fields. From what she'd deduced of the man's schedule, that was now.

On the way to the farm Leigh replayed the little scene she'd just had with Hale Grant, tormenting herself with all of the things she *should* have said, all the words she wished she could recall. As much as she hated to admit it, she'd played directly into his hand — had even fueled the fire. Now Will would probably pay the price.

She knew what the odds said. She knew what logic dictated. But, dammit, she didn't need to have that smug little twerp throw it in her face. In her heart she knew Will Scott had nothing to do with Brittany's disappearance. How could she defend her stand publicly and not look the fool? What kind of credibility would she have if it became public knowledge that she'd slept with Will? If Grant got wind of it, how would that impact Brian's congressional run? The media could be relentless. No doubt, she was handling dynamite.

Hale argued facts, as much as she hated to admit it. Prejudiced in their presentation, but facts just the same. Anyone who hadn't looked into the passionate vulnerability of Will's vibrant blue gaze and felt the tenderness in his caress would have come to the same conclusion. There had been a naked yearning to be touched, to be *connected* in his eyes. Leigh knew

259

the psychological profile of a man prone to violence against women. Even in the most desperate throes of passion, the moment when all control shattered and there was nothing left but driving need, he was — well, not gentle, she thought as she recalled the force of that need — considerate. There was nothing in his intimacies to indicate he harbored a single violent thought when it came to women. Just the opposite. He seemed much more the type to defend than attack. Yes, he was new in town. Yes, he was mysterious. But that didn't make him a criminal.

That thought sparked a new avenue of attack. If Will wouldn't help himself, she'd have to do it for him. As sheriff she had plenty of tools at her disposal. She'd just have to use a few of them to fill in the blanks Will seemed determined to leave unscripted.

She tried to reel in her racing thoughts; she was jumping ahead.

Forcing her thoughts away from things already done and things yet to do, she tried to formulate a specific plan of attack for her immediate task. What if Hattie wouldn't even open the door?

Turning onto the farm lane, she saw Hattie out in back, hanging sheets on the clothesline. Leigh thanked her lucky stars and thought just perhaps the winds of fate were changing and things were going to start moving in her favor. She had to force herself not to run around the house, fearing Hattie would return inside before she made it to the backyard.

"Good morning," Leigh called, as she rounded the corner of the house.

Hattie jumped and clutched her chest. For a moment Leigh feared she'd given the woman a coronary. Then the unnaturally wide eyes relaxed to normal and Hattie appeared to finally draw a breath.

"I'm sorry. I didn't mean to startle you."

Hattie lowered her gaze to the ground. "Just not used to morning callers."

I'll bet not, Leigh thought. She doubted a single solitary soul in this town had extended the hand of friendship in Hattie's direction for decades. Why hadn't she taken notice before now and done something herself? Too wrapped up in her own life, she shamefully admitted.

Leigh bent down, picked up the clothespin Hattie had dropped and handed it to her. The woman took it with obvious reluctance, as if Leigh were handing her something forbidden instead of a simple clothespin. Leigh felt the sting of neglected kindness and vowed to make a better effort in the future.

Hattie finished pinning the sheet to the line. As she did, she said, so softly Leigh had to strain to hear, "Ed'll be home directly."

"Mrs. Grissom," Leigh said as gently as she could, "I wanted to talk to you, not your husband."

She saw the way Hattie's shoulders tensed

261

and her gaze slipped sideways, looking at Leigh without turning her head.

"I promise I'll be gone by the time your husband comes home for lunch."

Picking up the empty laundry basket, Hattie said, "Didn't see nothin'."

"May we sit on the back step here?" Leigh asked even as she moved in that direction. She sat down and Hattie perched on the corner of the step, her body tensed, a nervous bird ready to fly at the slightest provocation.

"Mrs. Grissom, I understand if you don't want your husband to know you spoke to me. I promise to keep our conversation confidential. But I have to tell you, if you tell me something that later proves to be pertinent in this case, I may have to call you to testify in a courtroom."

With what she was about to do, she felt the least she owed Hattie was fair warning. It shamed Leigh to see the naked fear in the older woman's eyes. She'd never seen such a broken spirit. Before she allowed pity to take over, Leigh plunged on.

"You know Emma Wilson's daughter is missing."

Hattie nodded.

"Did you see something that night — the night Brittany's car was left on the road?"

Hattie's lips rolled inward and she looked away.

"I think you wanted to tell me something yesterday. Something that could help this girl."

The gray head shook in a quick motion, nearly a twitch. "No."

Leigh got up and knelt in front of her. She grasped both of the thin, age-spotted hands. "I'm asking you for Emma. I'm asking you, as a mother."

Hattie's startled gaze cut to Leigh's face.

"Think about it. What if it was your Dorothy or Helen?"

Rocking slightly back and forth, Hattie shook her head and looked to the sky.

Feeling like a heel using the woman's dead children as leverage, Leigh nevertheless pressed on. "Remember your precious daughters. What if Helen was someplace cold and dark, alone and frightened — and someone, just by saying a few words, could bring her home, make her safe again?"

A thin cry came from deep in Hattie's throat. She squeezed her eyes closed and covered her ears with her hands.

Gently, Leigh pried the hands from the sides of the woman's head. She held them firmly. "Look at me, Hattie." The lids opened and tears slipped from her eyes. After a second she focused on Leigh's face. "Don't let Emma face the same devastation you have. Don't let her lose her daughter. Help her, Hattie. You can do it." She squeezed the frail hands a little tighter. "Please."

Hattie's lips trembled. She licked them and her gaze darted around like an escaped criminal's. Her voice was a whisper as dry as cornhusks. "A car."

"Brittany's red car?"

She nodded. "And another."

"Did you see anyone around the other car?"

"A man." Then her words seemed to come more easily, as if she just needed a little priming of the pump to start the flow. "Sometimes I get up after Ed's gone to bed. Like to sit on the porch and be near the babies." She motioned toward the nearby cemetery. "Ed don't like me to talk about them. But I still feel them." She put a hand over her heart. "Here."

Leigh swallowed her pity. "So you'd come to the porch. Tell me what you saw."

"The red car stopped. That girl got out. Then the other car pulled up behind. A man got out. Then I heard a sound, like somethin' bein' broke. Then they went away in the man's car."

Leigh's heart picked up speed. "Did he force Brittany into his car?"

"Oh, no. She got right in, by her ownself."

"Can you describe the man's car?"

Hattie thought for a minute. "Don't know cars much, 'specially new ones."

"That's fine. Do you remember what color it was? How many doors did it have?"

"Light — white or yellow, maybe. Four doors."

"Was it small, or full sized?"

"Middlin', I'd say."

"Mid-sized, light colored, four door. Can you remember anything else? Anything about the man?"

"Couldn't see faces. He was taller 'n the girl."

Leigh forced herself to ask another question. "Did the man have longish hair?"

Hattie shook her head. " 'Twas dark, but I'd say just reg'lar man-hair. Short like." She held her thumb and first finger about an inch apart.

After she released her held breath, Leigh asked, "Did they turn around, or drive on when they left?"

"Just pulled around the red car and went on down the road like nothin'." She flipped her thin hand in the air to emphasize the insignificance it appeared to hold at the time.

"Can you remember about what time it was?"

" 'Round ten."

"Oh, Hattie, thank you. You've done the right thing."

A faraway smile crossed her face as tears left wet tracks on her powdery cheeks. "Helen would have wanted me to."

Leigh replied in an emotionally choked whisper, "Yes. Yes, she would."

Chapter 14

A white, four-door, mid-sized car. Such a general description fit a couple hundred vehicles in Glens Crossing city limits alone. Not quite a needle in a haystack, but near enough. It would be a task beyond imagining to attack this through BMV records. Leigh decided to check with the man who serviced at least half of the vehicles in the county. She headed toward Brown's Garage.

She had a feeling she'd find her suspect in the local population. It appeared Brittany left willingly — Hattie had given solid ground to Leigh's original suspicion. If the girl had gone with a stranger, it seemed like she would have taken her purse and cell phone. Then again, why leave them at all? And, if she'd left voluntarily, why was the car still running?

Only one answer made any sense. Brittany *wanted* it to look like she'd been abducted. Once that thought settled, it quickly began to take root. Had she run away with someone? None of the local high school boys had gone missing. But Brittany's friend Rebecca speculated she was seeing someone older. College student? Leigh's mind took a new turn as she pulled to a stop in front of the garage. Could he have been someone even more mature? Married?

Something else Rebecca said rang particularly true. Brittany wasn't one to do without. She'd been spoiled since the day she was born, and didn't quibble about the details. Life had been an easy ride, at least in the physical sense. The emotional side had been quite the opposite. Which might just be what led her into this mess in the first place — what better way to get Daddy's attention than to make it appear something dreadful had befallen her?

Brittany was used to creature comforts. And since she didn't take her own money and credit cards, it only stood to reason that whoever picked her up could supply the cash. College kid hardly fit. But an older man . . .

Leigh quickly shifted mental gears when she saw the big yellow dog sleeping just outside the open overhead door of the garage. He'd sprawled on his back, paws crossed on his chest, ears flopped out on the pavement on each side of his head. Will definitely seemed to have a steadfast follower.

With the possibility of seeing him again, she was torn between exhilaration and dread. Just hours ago, they'd sworn off each other. Still, her stomach did a little tightwire dance just knowing he was nearby.

Taking a deep breath, she vowed that if she saw him she'd keep a professional attitude. Tempted as she was to torture herself with a glimpse of Will, she chose to avoid the overhead door. Instead she went to the entrance to the office where Brownie's elderly Aunt Rose usually manned the phone and typed invoices. The office wasn't air conditioned, so the window beside the desk and the door between office and garage were both open. Clipped to the plywood "in" and "out" bins was a little pink fan that blew Rose's scant white hair like dandelion fuzz on the wind. Her brown gaze darted to Leigh the instant she stepped in the door.

"Hello, Sheriff." A perfect set of snow-white dentures appeared with her smile.

"Good morning, Rose. Brownie in?"

"Should be back any minute. Ran to pick up a part. Can I help you with anything?"

A loud clang, followed by a mouthful of swearing drew Leigh's attention toward the garage.

"That's Will." Rose leaned across her desk as she shared her appraisal. "Such a nice boy."

Leigh choked back a chuckle. "Sounds like it."

Waving a hand in the air, Rose said, "Oh, pish! You know how men are. Least little thing goes wrong and they have to let off steam. My Carson can cuss a blue streak. You'd think the world was coming to an end. Next thing you know he's sweet as apple pie." Her eyes narrowed. "Say, maybe I can get the two of you hooked up for a little date. . . ."

"Generous of you to offer to share, but I

don't date married men." Leigh gave a mischievous wink and smile.

Rose pursed her lips and shook her head. "No wonder you're still a single gal."

"Son of a bitch!" Will's words were punctuated by the sound of a heavy metal tool hitting the concrete floor. Within seconds he stuck his head in the office door. "Rose, do we have any Band-Aids?" He held one hand wrapped in a dirty shop rag.

He didn't, even for a millisecond, appear startled to find Leigh there. The guy didn't give so much as the flicker of an eyelash. He simply nodded a greeting and looked back to Rose. What a poker face. Fortunately, Rose was looking at Will, not Leigh, whose cheeks warmed considerably as her body ignored her mental declaration to remain detached and professional. The poor, misguided woman wanted to fix her up for a date with Will, having no idea that just hours before he'd been settled neatly between her legs, igniting a most phenomenal display of carnal fireworks.

Rose got up from her chair with amazing agility for an eighty-three-year-old. "Let me see that."

He unwrapped the rag to expose a bloody gash across the back of his hand.

Rose made a *tsk-tsk* noise. "Why that's filthy! You need that flushed out right away. We'd better use the peroxide." As she started to hustle him toward the restroom at the back of the garage, the phone rang. "Sheriff, you take him back there and make sure that's cleaned out proper. All of the stuff is in the medicine cabinet."

Leigh hesitated, but Will headed toward the bathroom. As Rose picked up the phone, she used her other hand to shoo Leigh after him.

Will had his hand under running water when she slipped into the tiny bathroom behind him. The old board door was attached to a spring that kept it from hanging open into the garage area. It thudded closed.

With them both inside, there was barely enough room to turn around. Leigh pressed against Will's back as she reached to open the medicine cabinet, trying to ignore the tingling in her breasts as they made contact with solid male muscle. She set the peroxide and the box of bandages on the sink ledge and concentrated on the matter at hand, hoping the sight of a little blood would quell her rising desire. She peered around his shoulder to supervise the cleansing of the wound.

"More soap," she ordered.

He obeyed. But the suds kept foaming gray.

"You've got too much grease on your hands. Here, let me." She guided his hands under the water to rinse them. Then she put some liquid anti-bacterial soap on the back of his injured hand and carefully massaged it in and around the cut. It wasn't long before the slow slick feel turned from functional to sensual. When she glanced up, his gaze was on her face. Her heart did a little hot-peppers-skip-rope before it settled back into normal rhythm.

Tearing her gaze away, she concentrated on doctoring his hand. He didn't flinch when she poured on the peroxide and watched it bubble. As she dabbed his hand dry and ripped open the widest Band-Aid from the supply, she felt his breath on the side of her neck. She bit the inside of her lip to counter the delightful tickle.

When she placed the bandage over the cut, he nuzzled her hair aside and feathered his lips along the side of her throat.

Leigh closed her eyes and willed her pulse to slow. Surely he could feel its rapid beat under his lips. She heard him slip the slide-bolt into place.

"I thought we were going to cool it." Leigh couldn't keep the trembling out of her voice.

"We are. Right after this." He slid his hand between her legs.

Even through layers of clothing, it took no more than the slight pressure of his touch for banked embers to burst into brilliant flame. "What about Rose . . . ?"

"She'll have to go home and get hers from Carson."

She stifled a laugh and wedged herself between him and the sink. What was it about him that made her cast reason to the wind? She wasn't this kind of girl; she always behaved in a proper fashion, always careful of her reputation. Never had she —

His tongue flicked her ear, robbing her of both thought and breath. A chill rippled down her spine and the heated flesh between her legs was bathed in a flood of moisture.

What the hell. There was no sense in pretending she had any intention of stopping him. She wanted him too much. After this, intimate contact would be forbidden. That thought alone made her frantic to feel him inside her. She threw her head back, buried her fingers in his hair and guided his nuzzling lips toward the open collar of her blouse. He hadn't shaved this morning and the rasp of his beard intensified all sensation.

As his busy fingers unbuttoned her blouse, his left elbow banged loudly against the bathroom wall.

"Shhhh." Leigh's admonition was lost in a gasp as he pushed the cup of her bra down and away, clearing the path for his mouth.

Her nipples tingled and drew taut as he teased them with teeth and tongue. She realized she was groaning loudly when his mouth covered hers and he swallowed the sound.

As he kissed her, she slid the zipper down on his coveralls and shoved them off his shoulders. His lips mimicked their urgency, intoxicating and demanding. With rough hands, he freed her from her jeans and panties and lifted her slightly, until she was sitting on the cool edge of the sink.

Leigh thanked God he only wore a T-shirt and boxers under the coveralls. She didn't think she had the patience to deal with jeans and a belt. With insistent fingers, she slid her hands down his belly and felt he was more than ready.

Kissing, their tongues parried and explored. She wanted more. She wanted him completely inside of her — wanted to absorb him, heart, body and soul. It was more than the breathless excitement of sex — much more. It was an emotion totally foreign to her, and it scared her witless.

Suddenly, he pulled away, leaving her lips craving his. Did she say her thoughts out loud? The intensity in his eyes said she had — but that was impossible, his mouth had been covering hers. Then, holding her gaze with his, he slid two fingers inside her.

Her head fell back and hit the mirror. He put his other hand behind her head to shield her from bumping it again.

She said in a ragged gasp, "I'm ready already." She spread her legs wider and rotated her hips in invitation.

Grasping her backside with one hand, still cradling her skull with the other, he drove himself home. She slid her arms around him, under his T-shirt, feeling the coiled strength of his muscles. She came almost immediately. Digging her fingers into his back, she rode on waves of pleasure as he moved against her.

It took no more than three or four strokes before he groaned and his sweat-slicked muscles jerked tight under her hands.

They clung together for a moment, his breathing ragged in her ear. The sensitive skin of her nipples rubbed against his damp shirt with every rise and fall of his chest.

He kissed her once more, deeply, tenderly. "God, I'm going to miss you," he whispered against her lips.

She clutched at him more tightly, burying her face in the crook of his neck. Feeling the press of his lips on her hair, she breathed in his scent, wishing with all her heart that circumstances were different. She wasn't the sheriff. Brittany hadn't disappeared. Hale Grant hadn't stirred up a hornet's nest. Everything *except* that she'd never met Will Scott.

As she began to come down from her sexual high, she realized the tiny bathroom was like a sauna. The air smelled heavily of sex. Beads of perspiration covered Will's body. The hair on his forehead was damp and clinging. She felt slick with her own sweat. How in the hell were they going to walk out of here?

Will seemed to read her mind. "Rose is probably still in the office; she doesn't like coming back in 'the dirty part' of the business. Won't use the bathroom the entire time she's here. So I'll go out and get to work. You can powder your nose or something, then go back to the office."

"It'll never work. Look at me," she said.

A devilish smile crossed his face as he zipped up his coveralls. "Can't help but."

Leigh gave an exasperated grumble as he slipped out of the bathroom. She locked the door and began to set her clothes back to order, hoping Brownie hadn't returned. That hope evaporated when she heard his booming voice talking to Will.

"Oh, God," she moaned, then splashed cold water on her flushed cheeks. After a quick glance in the mirror to assure herself she didn't have "I just had sex" written all over her face, she steeled herself and opened the bathroom door.

"There you are. Saw your truck out front. Got a problem with it, Sheriff?" Brownie asked.

Will didn't raise his head from his work.

"No." The word came out as a squeak. Leigh cleared her throat and tried again. "It's fine. I need your help with something else." She glanced at Will. "Can we talk in the office?"

"Sure. It's time for Rose's break anyhow."

Leigh followed him into the office.

"Aunt Rose, I'll watch the desk for a bit. Go on over to the Dew Drop and get yourself a coffee."

Rose opened a desk drawer and pulled out her purse. As she passed Leigh on her way out, she paused and narrowed her eyes. A knowing smile curled her lips and she waggled her index finger at Leigh. Then she went on her way.

"What was that about?" Brownie asked.

"Nothing. I think she's trying to fix me up with Will."

Brownie sighed. "Ever the matchmaker. She found Marianne for me you know. My brother's wife, too," he added, in a way that sounded as if the thought had just occurred to him after twenty-five years. "Got a real sense about these things."

Leigh decided to just drop the subject before it got her into trouble. "I'm trying to come up with a list of owners of as many light-colored, four-door, mid-sized cars as I can. Do you keep any kind of list?"

He got up, peered out the front door, then returned to the desk. Pulling out his keys, he unlocked a file cabinet drawer. "Rose gets in a snit when I even talk about putting all this on a database — hates computers, thinks they're out to make humans obsolete." He pulled out a laptop and sat it on the desk. "Gotta do this when she's not around. You know, the old gal is in her eighties. But Rose'll have a job here as long as she wants. Once she's retired, I'll be able to switch over to a computerized system like that." He snapped his fingers. "And see here." He pointed to the screen divided into long columns. "I can keep track of each vehicle's service history. All the national chains are doing it.

"I'll just call up white, silver and tan sedans. Can't help you with weeding out the size.

You'll have to do that by make and model." He watched the screen with a satisfied look on his face. Then he reached back inside the file cabinet and got a disk. "Don't have a printer here, no place to hide it. Have to do all my printing at home. If I copy to a disk, you should be able to open it on your computer."

Leigh looked over his shoulder as he opened the program. Good, it was compatible with her office computer.

Once the file was copied, he handed the disk to her. "Names and addresses all there. Don't suppose you can tell me what this is about?"

"Sorry."

"Figured."

"You'll keep this just between you and me?"

"Course, Sheriff. Long as you keep this" — he smiled as he nodded toward the drawer he was locking — "between you and me."

"Deal."

As she returned to her car, she saw someone had stapled a missing person flier on the telephone pole on the corner. When she drove by she deliberately avoided looking at the half-page photograph of Brittany Wilson. She needed no reminder of the beaming vitality and cheerful smile of the girl whose life had been interrupted — either spurred by emotional trauma or true misfortune. Whichever, Leigh had to get to the bottom of it before Will paid the price.

★ ★ ★

As Leigh looked at it, it seemed an impossible spiraling line of dominos, each falling, crashing another life into disarray, the entire thing coming full circle before starting all over again. Kurt Wilson gets midlife wanderlust and leaves Brittany and her mother for a girl not much older than his own daughter. Brittany angry, displaced, acts out, disappearing and, by simple bad timing, Will Scott falls under suspicion. Leigh herself happens to be chafing under the mantle of quiet responsibility at just that same moment, dreading a milestone birthday, making Will an irresistible commodity. Meanwhile, Brian is trying to launch a political career, which will bring Leigh's actions as elected sheriff under close scrutiny. Kurt Wilson is a man of power and wealth, and mad as hell that Leigh hasn't found his only child.

Brian's worry about his image wasn't just some vain pretense. It was a small congressional district — a small county for that matter with the hungry media forever snapping at political heels. The mere suggestion of professional impropriety on her part will bring the whole thing crashing down on all three of them — Will, Brian and Leigh. It seemed a never-ending circle of potential disaster.

Once back in her office, Leigh opened the file Brownie had given her. She began to scroll through the data. There were fifty-six cars listed. She deleted ten right off, being older, what she and Brian called "land yachts" — much too large to be considered midsized by anyone, no matter how unfamiliar they were with automobiles.

As she looked at the remaining owners' names, there were several people she knew well. Three were elderly women who shouldn't even be driving, hardly fitting suspects in an abduction — staged or legit. Five she recognized as high school students. She wrote those down. Then an interesting name popped up. Hale Grant owned a champagne beige 1998 Honda Accord.

Now there was something to chew on.

By the time she'd finished her eliminations, she had a list of thirty-three cars. She divided the list in half and gave them to deputies Steve Clyde and Calvin Walker to do the leg work. She held out Hale Grant's name from those lists. She wanted to talk to him herself.

Glancing at her watch, she decided to check the FBI and state databases before lunch. Best to arm herself with as much information about Will Scott's life as she could before Hale pulled another stunt like the one yesterday. If Will wasn't going to help himself, she'd just have to do it for him. She knew the nature of this town. Once an idea took root, it spread like chickweed — and was just as hard to kill.

She closed the door to her office and logged on. Once she'd entered all of the necessary passwords and identification numbers, she was allowed access to the restricted VICAP — Violent Criminal Apprehension Program. First she searched for Will Scott's name in various forms: William Scott, Wilbur Scott, Wilson Scott. Then she tried flipping it around into logical aliases: Scott Williams, Scott Williamson, Scott Wilson, Scott Willet. When nothing matched, she entered his physical description and an age range. She blew out a breath of relief when she didn't find anyone that could even remotely be Will in the database.

Had she really worried that she would? Somehow the very thought seemed a betrayal — even though it was her job and she had every obligation to investigate all possible avenues.

Her own lack of ethics settled like a lead cloak about her shoulders. She'd crossed the line. She'd become personally involved with a man who, by circumstance alone, should be under suspicion for the abduction of a girl under her protection. How could she begin to argue that Will had nothing to do with Brittany's disappearance when she'd allowed herself to become emotionally entangled with him?

Shaking her head, she forced herself to forget what couldn't be undone and get back to things she *could* control. Maybe she'd delve a bit deeper into Will Scott's identity. She tried to tell herself it was just to prepare herself in a professional sense, eliminate the niggling conscience that said she was shirking her duty. But the ugly truth was, she needed to know to settle her own curiosity.

She dug out her credit card and logged onto *AutoTrackXP*. Since this was a database open to any and all who cared to pay, she decided to keep this personal and pay for it herself. Also, this search entailed much more than criminal history; this got down and dirty with your personal life — all of it. It took longer because she had so little to go on and had to use different combinations of names. She searched for some trace of Will's past — birth record, high school transcript, previous address, but came up empty. Nothing that matched the particulars she *did* have. No trace of the man she'd passed the night with, or the boy he used to be.

If he *were* a cop, a theory that seemed more and more right every time she saw him, perhaps there was a good reason he was using an assumed name. He certainly thought like a detective. Maybe he was in some form of federal law enforcement. But the little devil on her shoulder whispered in her ear, "Or maybe he's skipping out on child support, or running from the mob, or any one of a million other less noble reasons." And, if he were using another identity for police reasons, he should be carrying full documentation of that identity. So far, Leigh hadn't even seen a wallet. Then there was the fact that an undercover operation would have all identity information logged into traceable sources.

God, her reasoning was clouded, hazed by hormones and loneliness.

Focus on this like you were taught. Remove yourself. But that was a great deal easier when she sat in a classroom and dissected crimes committed on people who existed only in paper and ink, with equally imaginary suspects.

As much as she wanted to keep her search totally to herself, she picked up the phone and called Brownie.

Rose answered, stuck in another not-so-subtle plug for Will Scott's romantic potential, then got Brownie on the line.

"Trouble with the item I gave you?" he asked immediately.

Leigh had to smile at his cryptic description of the disk. Poor Brownie, that was sure to get Rose's antenna quivering. "No. Got what I needed. But I have another question."

"Shoot."

"Did Will Scott fill out any employment forms when you hired him?"

Brownie hesitated. "You working for the IRS now?"

His teasing tone didn't do anything to settle the fear welling in Leigh's belly. "This is *off* the government record."

"Well, since he's only temporary, I didn't see any problem when he asked if I'd just pay him in cash. You know, save him a little, save me a little."

"So you don't have a social security number, record of past employment?"

"Now you're making me feel like a lousy businessman as well as a tax evader. But no, what we got is a real informal agreement. He's only here 'til Skeeter gets back."

"All right. Thanks."

Before she could hang up, Brownie said, "You're not believing all that baloney Hale Grant put in yesterday's paper, are you? I'm a pretty good judge of character, you know. I wouldn't keep Will around for one minute, let alone allow him to live under my roof if I even suspected he was capable of such a thing."

"Hey, I'm just gathering information, not accusing anyone." Far, far from it. Her questions begged to be led in the other direction.

"Well, it wasn't him."

As much as she wanted to throw herself wholeheartedly into believing Brownie's infallible character assessment, she forced the next words from her lips. "Are you sure? You're the one who saw him arrive home in the wee hours on the night Brittany disappeared. And when I saw him at six A.M. he was a mess — looked like he'd been dragged through a pigsty."

"If he'd done anything to that girl, would he have shown up on your office doorstep looking like he did? And why in the hell would he be sticking around?"

Leigh's tense shoulders relaxed. Those were some of her own mental arguments. They sounded so much less like grasping at straws when she heard someone who hadn't had sex with Will say it. She tried to keep her voice even and professional. "Like I said, I have to ask the questions."

"Fine. Just be careful who you ask. This is a mighty small town. Panic travels fast."

She caught the meaning of his warning, even though he needn't have issued it. She had no intention of discussing Will Scott with Hale Grant. She had another topic altogether in mind for that particular newspaperman.

Chapter 15

Will couldn't keep his mind on what he was doing. Twice now he'd lost the spring to the carburetor he was working on. As he crawled around on the floor of the garage looking for the missing part, he cursed himself. He couldn't get the smell of Leigh out of his nose, or the feel of her off his skin. She was providing much too big of a distraction. Experience told him he couldn't afford to let emotional entanglements cloud his judgment, dull his senses — not yet. And he couldn't deny this was more than just sexual attraction. She drew out protective instincts he'd long ago counted as one of many casualties of the brutal course his life had taken, the pitiless things he himself had done.

Suddenly, beseeching brown eyes flashed in his mind, begging for rescue. Will sat back on his haunches, the hard concrete garage floor biting into his knees, and closed his eyes, waiting for the inevitable gunshot that followed, then the sickening muffled thud as the body fell into a gruesome pile of like-fated souls. Will's nightmares had recently begun invading the previously safe territory of daylight hours. He'd never find peace. He had survived only by making painful choices — and was forever damned by them.

Forcing the bile back down his throat, he located the errant spring and returned to the carburetor. His thoughts turned to the crux of his current problem. What, in the whole kidnapping scenario, had he overlooked? That missing child poster on Leigh's refrigerator kept gnawing at him. She was going to pursue this case until her dying breath, he could see it as clear as day.

He had to help her figure this out. And his time was running short.

Muddying up the waters even further was that newspaper ass. Grant seemed hell-bent on casting suspicion Will's way. He knew it would be easy enough to get away — vanish into thin air. He'd done it often enough before. But if he fled now, it would solve one problem, but create another — and Leigh would be the one to suffer. As long as no one knew who he was, it was better that he stick around. But if things heated up much more . . .

A fire truck raced past the garage, siren wailing. Will stepped outside and watched it head out of town. The yellow dog got slowly to his feet and stood beside him, looking in the same direction.

"Curious to a fault too, huh, boy?" Will ruffled the top of the dog's head.

Two pickup trucks with blue flashing lights on their dashboards shot down the street after the fire truck.

Brownie hurried out the door, fireman's

helmet tucked under his arm. As he got in his truck, he called, "Got a brush fire. Watch the shop for me, Will."

Will gave an affirmative wave. Then he looked to the sky, but saw no tell-tale smoke. Couldn't be too big of a fire. He patted the dog again before he returned to his work. "We'll get you a collar at the hardware store during lunch. Might as well make you legal — then at least one of us will be."

In about an hour, he'd wrangled the carburetor into submission. As he wiped his hands, Rose appeared in the doorway between office and garage. Will could feel her watching him for a few moments before she spoke.

"Better get yourself some lunch, Will."

"Thought I'd wait for Brownie to get back. Hate to leave you here alone."

"How do you think we managed before you came?" She shoved her hands on her thin hips and looked most peeved. "I'm quite capable of handling the place for an hour. All you young people are alike. I'm not so old and useless —"

"Whoa!" Will put up his palms. "I wasn't insinuating anything of the sort."

"Well" — she huffed and pursed her lips, making her mouth look like a pink prune — "I don't like being treated like a doddering old fart. The packaging may be worn, but the merchandise is still in prime shape. Now you get along to lunch." She pointed toward the street.

"Yes, ma'am." Saying anything more would

only serve to inflame.

On his way to the Dew Drop he noticed the addition of yellow ribbons tied on the utility poles and the trees of the courthouse square. Symbols of a town with hope that one of their own will return safely. In ordinary circumstances, he'd say that was blissfully wishful thinking. But in this instance, he thought that maybe, just maybe, Brittany was out there, having left on her own, the abduction scenario completely fabricated. Until he found something to substantiate it, however, it only sounded like someone trying to maneuver attention away from himself by casting blame upon the victim.

He could feel time and opportunity slipping away from him. And there was nothing he could do about it. He shook off the sensation and entered the Dew Drop.

Sally, the normally friendly waitress, obviously hadn't forgiven him for serving her prized cherry pie to Dog. She flung the plate with his tuna sandwich like a Frisbee and it clattered to a stop on the counter just short of sliding into his lap. Then she turned, ignoring his nod of thanks, and stalked back toward the kitchen.

As he ate, he became aware that the voices surrounding him had diminished to hushed, hissing whispers. He could feel the cold chill of stares on the back of his neck. Slowly, he rotated on his stool. As his gaze traveled over the other patrons, their heads snapped back to their plates and they went after their lunches with focused concentration. He could almost see the screws turning in their brains, asking themselves if a kidnapper sat coolly eating a tuna sandwich right under their noses. Hale Grant's suggestive poison had spread fast.

He looked at each one of them long enough to insure they understood he wasn't hiding, then finished his lunch. On the way back to the garage, he stopped to pick up a collar and leash for Dog — he couldn't bring himself to actually name the beast. That seemed much too permanent.

Duckwall Hardware was a narrow storefront halfway between the Dew Drop and Brownie's Auto Repair. Will entered and saw a wall of paint cans on his left whose shelves climbed so high a ladder was needed to reach the upper ones. Two aisles crammed with assorted merchandise, ranging from kitchen appliances to socket wrenches to garden hoses, were to the right. He didn't see anyone around, so he wandered to the rear of the store and found the pet supplies.

By the time he made his way back toward the front, the clerk had appeared at the cash register, which was fifteen feet from the front display window, just beyond the shelves of paint. He was a short man of about twenty with a military brush cut and a smug attitude that radiated like body heat.

"So," the clerk said as he took the leash and

collar from Will and punched the numbers into the cash register, "surprised to see you still around here."

Taken aback by the frontal assault, but having been warmed up by the surreptitious whispers and sidelong glances during lunch, Will looked him in the eye. "Why would anyone want to leave this charming little town? Everybody's so warm and friendly."

"Yeah, well, you don't fool me, asshole," he said from behind the safety of the counter that separated them. "I'm in the Reserves and I know a fuckin' criminal when I see one." It was obvious junior had been rehearsing this little line, just waiting for the opportunity to use it. Didn't matter that it made absolutely no sense. "Gonna run for sheriff pretty soon. Get this county back on track. That cunt don't have a clue what she's doing."

"How much?" Will reached for his money, holding his breath to keep himself in check.

"What?"

"The bill."

He told him and Will paid.

As he was handing Will the change, he said, "Everybody knows that Wilson girl was sneaking around with you, you pervert. You got some balls to be hanging around here."

Will grabbed the guy's wrist before he withdrew his hand. He leaned across the counter and got right in the clerk's face. Looking into startled eyes he said, "That's right kid, I got balls of steel. Don't make me give you a demonstration." He knew it was a calculated risk. Bravado or bravery? Either the guy would piss in a puddle or grab Will by the throat. Will was betting on pissing. "Besides," he said, when the kid stood there looking like he'd just stumbled into a nest of water moccasins, "I heard *you* were banging Brittany. Funny how things get around."

Will let him go, picked up the leash and collar and started to walk away.

"Little Miss Pussy Sheriff should have locked you up on Sunday."

Will stopped; a red cloud enveloped him. After a second, he picked up a can of bug spray sitting on the shelf next to the check-out. He made a show of looking at the can, as if he couldn't figure out how it worked. Then he "accidentally" hit the button. A plume of spray went directly toward the clerk's face.

The man screamed and jumped backward.

Will dropped the can. "Oh, my gosh! How did that happen? I'm so sorry! Are you all right?"

"Get out of here!" The man wiped at his eyes with his shirt sleeve.

"Let me help." Will touched the kid's arm and was immediately swatted away.

"Get out!"

Will stepped back. "Better get some water on that face." Then he started to walk away. "And as for 'Little Miss Pussy,' that's *Sheriff Mitchell*,

291

or Ma'am — next time your eyes are unswollen enough to see her."

Once out the door, Will balled his hand into a fist and slammed it into the parking meter out front. It wasn't as satisfying as breaking the kid's nose, but a damn sight less dangerous. After a moment, the red haze began to leave his vision and control inched back within his grasp. It came slowly, but when it did, his own foolishness nearly choked him.

Goddammit! One more stupid stunt like that and he *would* have to leave town — risk of APB or not. He knew his attachment to Leigh could be dangerous — quite possibly the death of him. Now he had confirmation.

He'd been lucky the kid didn't have the guts to back up that mouth of his.

He started down the sidewalk, assuring himself the kid wouldn't call the city police. No way would a guy like that admit he'd come out on the short end of a pissing match. There hadn't been anyone else in the store. If the story came out at all, it would be vastly different than the way it actually went down. Somehow he thought people around here probably already had this guy's number. There wouldn't be so much as a ripple in the pond over this one.

He hoped.

Will had walked half a block before he realized Dog was hurrying along the hot concrete beside him.

"Next time I go down that road, do me a favor and bite my hand off."

Dog looked up with happy brown eyes and his tongue hanging out of his mouth.

"Somehow you just don't seem the snap and snarl type. Gonna have to get me a pit bull."

Before they got to the garage, Will stopped. Dog immediately sat beside him with a look of expectation on his face. Will leaned over, snapped and adjusted the collar around the thick neck.

"I know it's not much, but it's all I've got to offer at the moment."

Dog wagged his tail. By God, if it didn't look like he was smiling at him. Will knelt down and ruffled the fur on either side of the big head, feeling a strange kind of mutual understanding. Maybe this nomadic maverick suffered the same longing to be attached that he found in himself since arriving in Glens Crossing.

The dog's rough tongue swiped across Will's face.

"All right, all right. I'm sorry about the shit about the pit bull. It's you and me."

He took out his pocket knife and modified the leash to suit him, clipped it on the collar, then the two of them headed back to the garage.

Rose was out in front as he approached, emptying the mailbox. She pointed to Will's sidekick. "What's that?"

Will's brow creased with concern. "A dog."

The woman had seemed fully in charge of her mental faculties when he'd left; maybe she'd had some sort of stroke while he was gone.

"For heaven's sake! I know it's a dog! What's that hanging from his neck?"

"His leash."

Rose cocked her head and scrunched her already wrinkly face. "A little short isn't it?" She pointed to the scrap of leather. "That's not even long enough to grab onto and stand up straight."

"The law says he has to wear a leash. I don't think it says how *long* that leash has to be."

"Ahhhh, I see." She smiled and nodded. "Trying to raise an issue with our lovely sheriff? There're easier ways to get to know her, you know."

Actually, he was just thinking how he was going to have to stay away from her — completely. "Really, I'm just trying to keep this guy out of the pound."

"Wish someone had done as much for Leigh."

Will started to give a snappy comeback about Leigh in the dog pound, but saw in Rose's face that she was serious.

She sighed and shook her head. "How that poor girl avoided growing into a bitter, resentful woman I'll never know. She's as positive and outgoing as anyone I know, but the hurt she's suffered . . ."

Will's stomach turned in on itself at the mere

thought of Leigh in pain. He knew he should just leave this conversation right here, not get pulled in any deeper with a woman he was going to have to leave. He should drop it and pretend he didn't hear the heartfelt sympathy in the old woman's voice. But he couldn't. He leaned against the door frame and asked for more. "Hurt?"

Rose shook her head slightly. "I guess it's really none of my business. Forget I said anything."

Will could see that was the last thing she really wanted. Her mouth said "forget it," but her eyes said "come on, beg me just a little, then I won't be a gossipy old woman." It had been more than obvious she'd been working toward kindling a romance between he and Leigh. Whatever she had to say, she was going to say it, but wanted to make him dig for it first. Two could play at this game.

"So she had a rough time." He shrugged. "Happens to lots of folks." He started toward the garage.

Rose raised her voice slightly, so he wouldn't miss a word. "Well, I wouldn't be one to speak ill of the dead . . ."

He kept walking, albeit slowly.

"If I had known how that aunt and uncle were going to treat her, I'd have taken her in myself."

That stopped him. Cold.

He turned. "She was abused?" He had to

force the last word from his lips.

She didn't answer him directly. It almost seemed as if she enjoyed drawing him back and making him wait. Maybe this was all part of her plan to get him and Leigh together. Well, she'd won this round. He returned to the bait and faced her.

"That girl certainly could have done better than coming back to this two-bit town," Rose said. "No telling what she would have become if someone had thrown her a scrap of encouragement." Then she looked sharply at him, as if he'd been responsible for Leigh's lost possibilities. "Not that I'm not happy she's back with us. But she had potential for so much more than serving our backward little community." Rose's gaze took on the glaze of remembering. "You know her folks were killed when she was a little girl?"

Will worked very hard not to shake the old woman as he repeated his question. "Was she abused?"

Rose rolled her lips between her teeth until they disappeared and shook her head. "Not in the physical sense." She paused a minute, seeming to organize her thoughts. "It's like my roses. If I dug one of them up from its warm and sunny spot in the garden and carried it deep into the woods and planted it where it was blanketed in constant deep shadow, it would survive, but it would never be what it could have been in good soil and bright light."

"Why did they take her and Brian in then?"

"Oh, Brian they wanted. A son — that's all Belinda talked about. She'd finally gotten a son. But Brian refused to be separated from Leigh. So she grew up unloved and unseen, a shade in her own home."

Will wondered at Leigh's hidden strength. He'd sensed it was there, but had no idea it was made of tempered steel. "She told me she lived with relatives. She didn't say a single derogatory thing about them."

"Oh, no. She wouldn't ever. Once I said something to her about Worth and Belinda being unfair and negligent. You know what she said?"

He shook his head.

"She said, 'They did the best they knew how. Besides, I wasn't the greatest prize to have thrown on their doorstep — so shy and awkward.' My God." Rose's mouth drew into a puckered frown. "I didn't have to live in that house and it makes my blood boil to think of it. How can she be so forgiving?"

The best they knew how. Leigh had said those same words to him. *Best they knew how, my ass.* It made Will's blood boil, too, anyone having made Leigh view herself in such a way. "What about Brian? The two of them seem close."

"Brian loves her, no doubt about that. I think *now* he sees the partiality, the unfairness, but then . . . When you're treated like royalty,

297

you're not so apt to notice the slights dealt to the peasants.

"You see, Brian was always in the spotlight, showered in confetti. While Leigh cleaned up the trash after the parade. She lived in his shadow, but always seemed happy for his good fortune, never petty or jealous. Brian was a star athlete, too busy with practice for a job — got a football scholarship; Leigh had to work in her Uncle Worth's drugstore after school and pay for her own education. They bought Brian a car; Leigh rode a bicycle." She waved a hand in an all-encompassing gesture. "You get the idea.

"Now, don't get me wrong, I don't blame Brian. He was just a kid, too. But I think that's why he worked so hard to get her back here after college. To make it up to her."

Will realized his hands were balled into tight fists when his nails bit into his palms. He didn't release the pressure, as if by taking pain himself he could spare Leigh hers. He wanted to take her deep inside himself, protect her, make her see herself through his eyes. How could he think of leaving now? It would only reinforce her view that she wasn't worthy of being loved. He knew she'd said now was enough. But if it wasn't enough for him, emotionally insulated as he'd worked to make himself, how could it be for her?

Then again, maybe she just didn't feel as much for him as he suspected. Maybe he'd misread the intensity in her eyes. As much as it would be better for her if that was so, he self-ishly prayed it wasn't.

Rose started talking again. "If you ask me, I think he goes a bit too far. Wants to run her life so it's just what he thinks it should be."

Will had to draw himself away from visions of wrapping Leigh in the protective cocoon of his own body. "Who?"

"Brian. Thinks he knows what's best for Leigh."

"And you don't think he does?"

Rose seemed to have snapped out of her mood for reminiscence and introspection. She waved the subject away with a blue-veined hand, then pointed at Dog. "There's a vet gives free shots at the farm store out on the highway every other Saturday. Should be there this weekend. You'll maybe want to take Rover by if you're going to keep him."

"Oh, I'm not keeping him."

"Don't look that way to me." She pointed at the dog sleeping on Will's shoe tops and walked back inside her office.

"And can you just imagine, there I was, help-less as a newborn kitten?" Alma Lynn White's voice drifted over the shelves from the next aisle.

Leigh picked up the bottle of aspirin, the reason she'd come into Hayman's Drug — which had changed names when Uncle Worth sold it, but still cast the spell of childhood memories every time she walked in the door. She listened carefully as she eavesdropped, waiting to hear the belle's accolades of Will's "rescue."

"Well, how could I have known then that he was a kidnapper! It just makes me breathless to think about it. I could have been his victim — he could have done *unspeakable* things to me. Why, a lady just isn't safe these days."

Damn that woman! Two days ago, Will was her knight in shining armor.

This malignancy was going to stop here and now, before it spread into a fatal disease.

She rounded the end of the aisle and saw Alma Lynn talking to Sally from the Dew Drop. Alma Lynn fluttered her wrinkled hands near her throat and chattered on about the horrible danger she'd faced. Sally stood with her white server's apron tied around her waist, leaning into Alma Lynn's words with her arms crossed over her chest and her cherry red lips turned down into a fearful frown. It was the growing acknowledgement in Sally's eyes that pushed Leigh over the edge.

"Excuse me!" Leigh said as she strode toward them.

Both women turned startled gazes toward her. Alma Lynn said, "Leigh." Alma Lynn never called her Sheriff, explaining shortly after the election that such a thing just didn't suit a lady.

"I couldn't help overhearing, and I think you

should be ashamed of yourself." Alma Lynn's normally mobile mouth instantly closed, as if to shut out a bothersome bee. Leigh went on, "Here you are, after just two days ago telling the world what a *gentleman* Will Scott was when he 'rescued' you, now spreading vicious lies about him. Why you were in no more danger from Will Scott than you are from Ed Grissom's UFOs —"

Leigh's mouth snapped shut when someone grabbed her by the arm and spun her around. "Little sister! I thought I saw you come in here." Brian threw an arm around her like he hadn't seen her in a month.

He put on his most charming politician's smile and said, "Alma Lynn, did you just come from Hildie's?"

"Why, yes. Nice of you to notice." Alma Lynn actually blushed.

Leigh wanted to box Brian's ears.

"You ladies will excuse me if I steal my sister away, won't you?" Brian led Leigh toward the front of the store, telling Sally over his shoulder that he'd be by the Dew Drop for a big slice of cherry pie in a bit — would she save him one?

He took the bottle of aspirin from Leigh's hand and deposited it on the counter as they passed the register. Then he pulled her out the front door and halfway down the block before he stopped just inside the alley. He spun her to face him.

"What in the hell was that?" he asked,

leaning over her like an angry father.

"I was just going to ask you the same thing!"

"As if we don't have enough trouble right now, you have to go around picking on gossipy old women."

"Exactly, she's a gossip — and she's fostering dangerous and unsubstantiated rumors. This has to stop before —"

"Yes, it does have to stop! Here and now! My God, Leigh, don't you see what you're doing?" Brian's eyes flashed with an anger Leigh had never seen there.

"I'm doing my job." She poked him in the chest, a little anger of her own taking control. "I can't allow public speculation to get out of hand. I have to find Brittany, but I can't do that while I'm fighting lynch mobs and witch hunts."

"Jesus Christ, how can you be so short-sighted? Maybe he did do it — did you ever consider that?"

"Of course I considered it — and ruled it out. He didn't." She couldn't help the defensive lifting of her chin.

Brian ran a hand through his hair and looked into the street to see if anyone was nearby. Then he leaned close and said in a very sarcastic voice, "He didn't do it just 'cause you're sleeping with him?"

Leigh flashed hot. "Goddamn you! You have no right to accuse me —"

"Don't I? You've *never* acted like this —

never been so irresponsible. I don't even know you anymore. How could you let him do this to you?"

"Brian, there are things you don't know —"

"I think there are a few things *you* don't know either. There's talk — damaging talk. Seems Will Scott has been asking questions about Brittany — and not just since she disappeared. He's been seen with her on several occasions. No one knows a thing about him. *He's* the most logical suspect in this case, and you act like he's innocent as the new-fallen snow! People see, Leigh; they see plenty."

"What are you talking about?"

"You've changed. Everyone's talking about it. First there was that dirty little dance at Crossing House. People might have forgotten that. But then you show up at the bar dressed up like New Year's Eve." He paused, as if the next thing was too horrific to mention. "And someone saw you."

"Saw me what?"

"Come out of the woods with him, Saturday night. People know you're sleeping with him."

"I wasn't having sex with him in the woods — *people* have it wrong."

Brian backed her up against the brick wall. "Leigh, I'm not trying to come down on you. I'm worried sick about you. What if he is dangerous? You could get hurt." He paused. "Remember, you and I are on the same team. Even if he's harmless, we can't take any chances of something like this getting out of hand."

"What do you want me to do, Brian? Arrest Will Scott just to keep the gossip down? And what about Brittany? What about the truth?"

"All I'm saying is that you're not doing yourself, me, or that Scott guy any good behaving like this. Now is not the time for change. Now is the time for you to show these people just what they're paying for — a capable, competent sheriff who they can trust. They elected the Leigh Mitchell of a few days ago, not some barfly shacking up with the most likely suspect."

"No one is going to bully me into doing something unconscionable just so it satisfies the public. It won't do Brittany any good for me to spend time traipsing down the wrong path — and Will Scott *is* the wrong path, I'm certain of it." She leaned closer and pointed in the direction of Brian and Kurt's office. "You see, I don't think any of us *really* know that girl. I intend to find out the truth — no matter if it's palatable for the folks around here or not."

Brian's eyes narrowed. "I don't think I like where you're going with this."

She crossed her arms over her chest and took a satisfied step back to show him how confident she was of her course.

Brian looked at her long and hard. "Be careful Leigh. Kurt is a powerful man — don't make accusations you can't back up with facts."

"I don't intend to. But I can't find those facts

while I'm dodging pot shots and trying to keep Will's neck out of a noose."

"Yeah, well, just don't put mine in there instead." He spun around and stalked out of the alley, not looking back.

Brian stopped once out of Leigh's line of sight. His hands trembled as he rubbed his face. Goddammit! He hated the things he'd just said, the way he'd sounded. But he had to do something to get Leigh's attention. She was in a vulnerable and dangerous position, not only professionally, but he'd bet emotionally as well. Scott was a stranger, passing through. Even if he didn't have anything to do with Brittany, he couldn't bring Leigh anything but heartache. There was no reason for her to sacrifice her future for a guy who'd be a hundred miles down the road this time next month. If she wouldn't watch out for herself, maybe she'd change her course to protect him.

He drew in a deep, steadying breath and headed back to his office, trying to block the hurt and anger in her eyes from his memory.

Although mad enough to break bricks, Leigh had to face it, there were things in what Brian said that made sense. She wouldn't do Will any good by acting in a way that made people less than confident that she was doing her job. She had to find the middle ground, supportive of his innocence, yet not blindly stupid. Secondly, she did have to be careful. Kurt was one of

Brian's main financial backers in his quest for a congressional seat. She had to have evidence to back up her suspicions before she risked alienating him by besmirching his daughter's name.

Meanwhile, she had to find a way to arrest the growing community feeling that Will was guilty of plucking Brittany from the safety of her home and family. To do that, she decided, she couldn't distance herself from him as they had earlier agreed.

The best way to keep Will safe would be an open show of support.

Or so she thought at that moment.

Leigh decided to finish a dreadful afternoon with a distasteful task. It was going to take all of her restraint not to go for the jugular when she caught up with Hale Grant.

She found him leaning on the fence at the football field, tape recorder in hand and camera around his neck.

"Doing a story on the team?"

He jumped as if he'd been unexpectedly smacked on the backside with a wet towel.

"No." He turned back to the field. "Just doing some background stuff for a piece I'm working on."

Leigh cast her gaze toward the boys charging the blocking sled. A collective *hummmph* whiffed through the air as they made brutal contact. "Does that 'piece' have anything to do with Jared Clark and Brittany Wilson?"

He lifted a shoulder carelessly, keeping his eyes on the players, but Leigh sensed his tension. "Homecoming is next week," he finally said. "They were nominated for king and queen. Thought it might make a good run, especially since —"

"Don't suppose you wanted to pump Jared for information?" Leigh leaned her elbow in the fence, inching just a bit closer to Hale.

"Hey, it's a free country." He remained in his relaxed pose, but turned his head to face Leigh squarely. "If the kid wants to talk to me, I'm willing to listen."

"Oh, I'm sorry," Leigh said with mock contrition, putting her hand over her heart, "I didn't realize Jared had called you with an invitation."

"I don't need this shit." He straightened and lifted his elbows off the chain-link fence. A muscle twitched in his eyelid. "I'm just trying to find out what the kid knows. I know Brit dumped him. Maybe he 'acted out.' Maybe he just needs someone close to his age who'd understand."

"And you'd be just the one — always so confidential and all." She ignored his sour look. "I thought you already had a suspect all picked out."

"Can't hurt to keep looking. Don't see that you've arrested anyone yet."

She decided not to rise to that particular bait. "Back to the subject of youthful confessions, is there anything you've forgotten to tell me about your acquaintance with our missing girl?"

"Like what?" Now he was leaning slightly toward her. Perhaps she'd hit a nerve?

"I'm just thinking, if Brit broke up with Jared, maybe there was a reason. Maybe there was — someone else."

"Now wait just a minute! How in the hell did you jump to such a conclusion?" That eyelid twitched double time. "I didn't have anything to do with her."

"Oh, come on," Leigh said in a conspiratal tone, "you've been hanging around high school events for the past couple of years now. Brittany is a good-looking girl, looking for something a little on the wild side —"

"Goddammit, I'm just doing my job, not trolling for chicks."

"I have a witness who saw a car like yours at the scene when Brittany disappeared —"

"There are thousands of cars like mine —"

"Where were you last Friday evening, between nine P.M. and one A.M.?"

"Home. Alone. You've got no reason —"

"I'll be careful of where I voice my suspicions" — she leaned closer and smiled, speaking between her teeth — "if you'll get your head out of your ass and report the *truth* instead of going off half-cocked, spouting a lot of foolish innuendo and circumstantial hoo-ha just to get a lead story."

"Are you threatening me? I knew you had

a thing for that guy."

"Who I have a 'thing' for is not the issue here." She moved just a bit closer and was satisfied when he leaned away. "You let me do my job and stop trying to frighten the people of this town. We have a missing girl and damn few clues. But now I have a witness who places another car at the scene — one that fits the description of *your* vehicle. I'm beginning to think you're blowing smoke just to make sure nobody looks too closely at you."

Leigh spun around and walked away, listening to Hale spit and sputter behind her.

She cursed herself for losing her restraint; something she rarely did — at least until Will Scott entered her life. She hadn't meant to tell Grant about the witness, just shake him up enough to think before he publicized his opinions to the world. But Goddamn him, he pissed the hell out of her.

Instead of telephoning Kurt, Leigh decided to make a couple of house calls on her way home that evening. Her purpose was double-edged: she wanted to assure herself that the Wilsons were coping, and she wanted to take a little nose around Brittany's room. First she drove to Kurt's house in town. When his wife answered the door, Leigh momentarily mistook her for a friend of Brittany's. Rail thin, blonde hair in an odd combination of knots and tufts that reminded Leigh of an exotic bird, dressed in a midi top and Capri pants, silver hoops in one pierced eyebrow and her navel, she looked like she was ready for a rock concert. It took a moment for Leigh to once again mentally adjust to the extreme age difference between husband and wife.

"Yeah?" the young woman said, blowing on her drying nail polish.

"Is Kurt in? I'd like to speak to him."

"Nah. He's out at his house."

Leigh didn't comment on the fact that *this* was his house and the property outside of town now belonged to Emma. Somehow she didn't think the point would soak in.

"All right. If I happen to miss him there, will you have him call me when he gets back?"

"Sure." The door closed before Leigh had a chance to say anything else.

As she got back into her car, she empathized with Brittany. It was one thing to have your family torn apart by a cruel circumstance like her own had been, but to have it destroyed purposefully by a male midlife crisis and an over-sexed postadolescent had to be even more shattering.

That thought set off another trail of thinking. How would an eighteen-year-old only child react to such an event? All of the bits and pieces began to collect into a clear picture. Brittany was prone to walk on the wild side. Doing something drastic to punish her father would follow suit. But would she go so far as to abandon her comfortable life to do it? The answer rang clear — only if there was another comfortable life waiting for her. Leigh had to find some clue that confirmed Brittany had taken up with someone older — then the next task would be to find out just who that was.

Once she'd figured that out, what then? If Brit left willingly, as an adult, it was no longer an issue for the law. It would be between Brittany and her parents. God, was that too much to hope for? She felt a flash of selfishness, but quickly pushed it away. So what if she hoped for an outcome that, although it might hurt Brittany's parents, would mean the girl was safe — and would at the same time disentangle Leigh and Will from the whole mess. While Old Leigh might feel duty bound to solve all of the problems of the people involved, mending both family and community wounds, New Leigh would definitely vote for release from involvement.

All thoughts and suppositions evaporated when she saw Will and the yellow dog half a block ahead. Will's hair was wet and combed back and he wore a sleeveless undershirt that showed the movement of solidly muscled shoulders. Just a glimpse of him made her flash hot all over. She wanted to yank him into the car and ravage him right here. *Why not? What's the difference between here and the bathroom at the garage?*

"God, you're becoming depraved," she whispered as she pulled to the curb and rolled down the passenger side window.

Smiling when he noticed her, he walked over to the car and leaned in. The fresh smell of soap and toothpaste came with him. Leigh held on to the steering wheel tightly to keep from reaching out and yanking him in through the window.

"Hi." He smiled and touched off another spark of indecent thought.

"Hi." Why was she suddenly backward? There was nothing she'd concealed from him; he knew her better than anyone on earth — at least in the physical sense. She swallowed dryly. When he just stood there smiling at her, she finally said, "Where are you headed?"

"I felt like a steak, and when I mentioned it to Dog, he said he had a hankerin' for a steak bone. So we're headed to the Crossing House."

Leigh leaned over to look at the dog, sitting right behind Will on the parkway grass. "A steak bone, huh?"

The dog's tongue lolled out and she heard his tail swishing in the dry, brittle grass.

"I see you got him a collar."

Will stepped back and reached for the dog. He held up an eight-inch length of leather, knotted at the end. "Got him a leash, too. Now he's legal."

Leigh burst out laughing. "I hardly think that qualifies as a leash."

"Why not? It's hooked onto the collar around

his neck. I can hang on to it if I want. What more does the law require?"

"Hmm. Guess I'll have to find that particular ordinance and read it for specifics. But I'm sure this doesn't get it."

Will dropped the leash and leaned inside the car once again. His face was deadly serious when he said in a voice lowered as if he didn't want the dog to hear, "Filthy, murdering criminals go free by manipulating the word of the law. I can't see any reason why this poor, well-behaved dog deserves any less."

Leigh couldn't believe the vehemence in his tone. He was actually trembling and his knuckles were white where he gripped the door.

"Jesus, Will," Leigh said softly and put a hand over his. It felt as if it was made of stone. "This isn't about the dog."

He stepped back, leaving her hand to slide free and rest on the door. She felt the moist heat left on the vinyl from his touch. Watching him closely, she saw the tense muscle in his jaw work furiously for a moment, then begin to relax. He hung his thumbs in the empty belt loops of his jeans and looked into the hazy sky. His chest rose with a deep breath, which he held for a moment. As he exhaled, all of the tension seemed to leave his body. The change was as rapid and complete as it had been after he'd attacked her on the creek bank that first night.

"Yes, it is. It's *all* about this dog." Then he added, still looking away from her, "It has to be."

Before Leigh could gather her thoughts enough for a reply, he slapped the side of his leg, calling the dog to his side, and the two of them headed off down the sidewalk.

She felt like she'd just seen the inner workings of his mind, his soul — something he kept deeply buried and was obviously sorry he'd let see the light of day. She now knew he harbored a ruthless sense of justice and a compassion beyond comprehension. She suspected he'd been wronged.

And she knew without a doubt, he was a cop.

Chapter 16

Leigh drove the twisting road following the wooded hollow to Emma Wilson's house. She watched the scenery pass with silent worry. She'd never seen things this dry. The few leaves that still tenaciously held their green color were masked by a heavy layer of dust. The whole county wore it. Every color, natural and man-made, sat muted under a gritty, gray film. She only prayed that the brush fire this afternoon wasn't the first of many. Their volunteers had managed to get this one out in short order — but what if it had spread into the woods? They had enough experience and manpower to stomp out burning grass and douse the occasional garage fire, but a full-blown forest fire would tax their little squad far beyond its limits.

Of course, with the Hoosier National Forest as their next-door neighbor there would be plenty of outside help. She only hoped it'd never come to that. She'd seen woodlands ravaged by fire, blackened ground punctuated only by a dusting of white ash and the occasional branchless, bare tree trunks, like toothpicks in tar. It'd be several lifetimes before a forest would be fully restored.

She sighed and mentally scolded herself. No

sense in creating worries that may never happen — that was the Old Leigh. New Leigh dealt with each thing as it arose, planning ahead, yet not drowning in what ifs. She had enough on her plate at the moment with finding Brittany — and figuring how to keep Will out of hot water while still protecting his identity.

She'd been shaken, yet somehow reassured, by Will's quiet outburst at the curb. He was a cop — one of her own. That explained why he didn't transform into a standoffish goober every time the two of them were alone. She'd only had three dates since becoming sheriff, two of which were with born-and-bred locals that she'd been friends with in high school. Neither could stop stepping all over themselves; it was as if she'd changed into a creature from another planet when she'd donned her badge and they feared the violent wrath of her alien culture. The third was a lawyer who, for reasons unknown, had come to open his first practice in Glens Crossing. It only took Leigh an hour to realize that her main attraction was her handcuffs. And then, of course, there had been the fiasco the other night with Mike.

Now that she was convinced Will was a cop, she had to wonder, why was he hiding? Anyone who worked so hard to watch over a stray dog had to have a good heart, so she felt justified in concentrating on the more decent reasons he could be operating undercover. FBI? ATF? Perhaps, but what would he be doing in Glens Crossing? Anytime federal law was working in your district, notification was to be made. And she certainly hadn't received any such notification. That particular possibility opened all sorts of unwelcome doors. If he was here investigating something or someone, it had to be so closely associated with her personally that she was being kept out of the loop. Would he be so callous as to use her that way? It just didn't wash — and yet if it was the case, she was the most inept, gullible creature on God's green earth.

She immediately searched for other, less personally painful possibilities. Immigration? There was the perpetual talk that some of the migrant farm workers who passed through here every year were without papers. Leigh hated to admit it, but she didn't delve too deeply into the possibility. If she discovered an illegal, she'd have to do something about it. And, with Indiana's incredibly low unemployment, that'd put some of the larger farms around here in a world of hurt. So she sat like the "see-no-evil" monkey and let things proceed as they had for decades.

Hoping Immigration wasn't Will's bag, she considered other possibilities. Maybe he was hiding from someone he testified against — maybe a cop gone bad . . .

This was ridiculous. She'd just have to ask Will face to face. Tell him she'd figured him out and give him the opportunity to confide. He had no reason to keep his identity from her; she was absolutely no threat to him. And yet, he had the air of someone used to not trusting. Just because she'd let him into her heart — a serious Old Leigh problem — didn't mean she'd penetrated his. Did he view her as someone he could trust with his innermost secrets, or just as a quick and easy tumble before he moved out of town and out of her life forever? He couldn't have made it more clear; he was moving on. Which, according to her New Leigh plan, was just what she was looking for. Still, maybe he really liked Glens Crossing — maybe he'd stay.

Forcibly closing her heart to such speculation, she turned onto the gravel lane at Emma Wilson's property. The house itself was around a broad curve and up the hill, still not within sight. Noticing the large plume of dust the Blazer kicked up, Leigh slowed nearly to a crawl. She pulled up next to Kurt's BMW, parked in front of the steps that led to the broad wooden porch.

She grabbed her shoulder bag and hesitated as she got out of the car. All of the blinds on this side of the house were closed. A breeze moved the rush-seated rockers slightly back and forth, making an odd muffled click on the uneven planks of the porch floor. Leigh felt as if she was entering a ghost town as she slowly climbed the limestone steps.

Pausing before she rang the doorbell, she heard movement within. Not deserted, yet she still couldn't shake that feeling of a place forsaken.

A long moment after she rang, Kurt peeked through the door's sidelight, then unlocked and opened the door. His haggard face momentarily registered what Leigh interpreted as a look of panic. It looked as if he'd faint dead at her feet. Then he yelled into the interior of the house, "Emma! Sheriff's here."

Leigh stepped closer and put a hand on his arm. "It's all right. There's no news. Sorry, I didn't mean to frighten you." She hadn't considered what her unannounced presence must have indicated to a couple whose child had gone missing. "I just felt it was time for something other than a phone call."

Emma slipped up behind her ex-husband, remaining half-hidden, looking around his shoulder at Leigh with one worried eye. Silently, she clasped his right hand with her own. His fingers curled around hers in unspoken response.

Leigh momentarily wondered if this tragedy had shaken some sense loose in Kurt. Maybe, too late, he realized what he'd thrown away.

"Can I come in?" she finally asked when there appeared to be a stalemate at the threshold.

"Oh." Kurt glanced back at Emma, who nodded. "Sure. Excuse our manners; we're just worn out." He stepped back and motioned Leigh inside.

"I won't stay long. I just wanted to have a look at Brittany's room, if I may."

"Emma." Kurt's voice, though soft spoken, seemed to make her flinch.

"What?" she said in a high squeaky tone.

"Show Leigh to Brittany's room."

Emma seemed to recover a bit, then turned and started up the stairs.

"Brittany's room is at the end of the hall." Emma pointed toward a closed double door, her hand holding a well-wrung tissue. "I think I'm going to lie down. Kurt'll see you out when you're finished."

"That's fine. Thank you."

Leigh started toward the doors, but stopped and turned when Emma said, "Please, leave everything where you find it. That way Brit won't think I've been snooping while she was gone. She gets so upset when someone invades her privacy."

"I understand." Leigh kept her assessment that if somebody *had* done a little snooping, maybe they'd have a better idea where the girl had gone and who took her there.

Stepping inside the room, Leigh had a hard time finding a clear spot of carpeting to walk on. Clothes, shoes, CDs, makeup, loose change, headphones, magazines, diet-soda cans and snack wrappers covered most of the floor. *How in the hell would Brittany know if a cyclone moved through here, let alone if anyone nosed around a little?*

The screen saver bounced around the monitor sitting on her desk. Leigh moved the mouse to see if any program was open.

Nothing. Just the Windows main menu. *What had you been hoping — she'd left a long letter, "Why My Life Sucks.doc," elaborating the details of her life and who happened to be in it at the moment?* Leigh grimaced; that was very close to what she'd been hoping. Much too easy.

Leigh tried to open Brittany's e-mail files, but they were password protected. She took a blind stab at coming up with the password, but, not surprisingly, had no luck. She'd have to load up the computer and send it to the state lab to have one of their computer nerds get inside.

In such disorderliness, it was difficult to ascertain what, if anything, had gone wrong in Brittany's life. For all of the junk everywhere else, the walls were inordinately bare. As Leigh looked more closely, she saw dozens of tack holes in the blue paint. She stood and moved to the bureau mirror, running her index finger over the glass. It slid, then dragged tackily in several places where Scotch tape had recently held something. It appeared that Brittany had stripped her room bare of memorabilia and photos. The bulletin board hanging on the outside of the closet door sported a forest of push pins but nothing else.

Leigh searched the room for a trash can. She found it under a bath towel. Staring back at her from the can were Brittany and Jared, her high school boyfriend, in a mix of wacky poses on a strip of pictures taken at a photo booth. The carefree playfulness of it momentarily stopped Leigh cold. How quickly things are snatched away — things we never appreciate until they're reduced to longing memories.

Her mind made an immediate and unexpected jump to Will. A cold lump settled in the center of her chest. She closed her eyes and fought the urge to cry. Longing memories — in a few weeks that would be all she had of him. Oh, how quickly someone can slip right into your soul, threatening to take a piece of you when they leave.

Drawing in a deep breath, Leigh exhaled and blew away that unintentional wash of self-pity. She opened her eyes, sharpened her attention and shook the wastebasket to see what else she could see without dumping or touching the contents.

Without being able to discern the total picture, Leigh saw several snapshots, the tack-punctured corner of a folded poster, a dried flower, several movie ticket stubs, and what appeared to be a Valentine card. Everything was loosely layered, unbent and uncrushed. This was not the work of fury.

Leigh reached down and plucked out the Valentine. It carried the same sappy sentimental message as any. When she opened it, she saw Jared's scratchy handwriting: *Love forever, Jared.*

Well, sometimes *forever* just doesn't cut it, even in teenage love.

On the floor of the closet sat an open cardboard box. Carefully packed inside, each wrapped in tissue paper, were a collection of dolls: some expensive china-faced, some American Girl collector series, some worn and well-loved discount store plastic with hair matted from years of affection.

Rebecca Lewis's words at the high school commons came crashing back: ". . . like suddenly she was *soooo* much more mature than the rest of us."

Brittany had carefully and unmaliciously tossed away her childhood. Not with angry rebellion, but with what appeared to be calm and dispassionate disposal. She was moving on.

What had brought her to such an emotional turning point? The older man? Who was he? Glens Crossing was a small town; secrets were extremely difficult to keep. Someone always saw, or heard, or suspected. Just look how quickly her own reputation had taken a nosedive — all because she wore a dress in public one night and shared a single innocent dance with a stranger.

Leigh's ears burned. Well, maybe not so innocent.

Brittany's romance, if there was one, had to

be extremely well-guarded. Why? The disapproval of her parents couldn't be enough; the girl constantly pushed those boundaries. Quite often since the Wilsons' divorce Brittany had gone for the shock factor with her father: sent home from school for breaking the dress code — actually, it was more like smashing it to smithereens; dying her hair orange and accenting it with black lipstick and eyeshadow; dancing like a wild woman at the Memorial Day street dance; a rash of speeding tickets. But all of that had seemed to have died down in the past month or so.

It had to be for another reason. Leigh decided the guy was most likely married. Her soul ached anew for this troubled girl. In an effort to find love and acceptance, Brittany had only set herself up for more heartbreak.

Leigh finished looking through the room, noting the things that supported her theory and not finding anything that led her in another direction.

Gathering up the computer tower, she headed back downstairs. She found Kurt in the kitchen with a scummy-looking cup of coffee untouched in front of him.

She set the computer on the kitchen table and sat down.

"I'm sending Brit's computer to the lab to access her e-mail files."

Vacant eyes turned her way.

"Maybe she's been corresponding with

someone . . ." Leigh prompted, hoping her statement would jog some forgotten memory of his daughter's conversations.

Kurt nodded absently.

She stood. "I saw the television ad you put together. It's quite compelling. I'm sure if anyone knows anything we'll be getting a call."

"Hope so." He rubbed his palms together. "I'm staying with Emma until we . . ."

Putting a hand on his shoulder, she offered all she had — empty words. "We'll find her." What she didn't say was that he might not like the results when they did, not because Brittany had met with ill fate, but because she was responsible for this entire mess herself. That bridge would have to be crossed after Leigh found her way to it.

Kurt's eyes closed and his mouth tightened as he nodded. Leigh saw his throat working and decided to leave the man his dignity. She picked up the computer and left the kitchen before he broke down completely. As she loaded the tower in the back of her Blazer, she saw him pass the sidelight at the front door. Leigh felt a lump rise in her own throat. He was headed upstairs to Emma, the only person who could begin to understand his pain.

Leigh passed the Crossing House Tavern on her way home. She'd intended to confront Will about his past tomorrow, but now, as she passed within yards of where he sat eating dinner, she decided to use the excuse to stop. Braking quickly enough to squeal her tires, Leigh made a sharp turn into the parking lot.

There was plenty of space; it was early yet for the evening crowd. The sun had set, but the blush of day still clung to the horizon. She put the Blazer in park and sat for a moment staring at the cotton candy swirls in the western sky. Once she opened this subject there was no turning back, no pretending she didn't know, no more fanaticizing about heroic reasons for Will Scott to be skulking about under an unregistered alias. It was going to be on the table. Then she'd have to deal with it, good, bad, or unbearable.

Her stomach fluttered with nerves, like she was an eighth grader heading to her first dance.

What if he refused to talk to her?

What if her questions drove him away from Glens Crossing forever?

What if he did confide in her and the truth was much uglier than she could stand?

Enough. She got out of the SUV and went inside before she talked herself out of it. She passed the sleeping yellow dog just outside the door. He opened one eye and watched her pass. She paused and studied him for a moment. "Bet you know more about him than I do."

The puppy's eye closed and Leigh went inside, possibly to destroy a relationship she'd only begun to explore, a bond with the potential to be deeper than any other she'd experienced in her life.

The bar wasn't exactly deserted — two of the booths were occupied, as well as four of the stools at the bar. A couple of guys were shooting pool in the back.

Will looked up the instant she walked in the door, as if he'd been expecting her — or had a special radar tuned just to her. He sat at the booth in the farthest corner from the door, facing front. He didn't show any sign of welcome, or wave her to his table.

In that first instant she'd felt a flash of disappointment. Was he unhappy to see her? Still in a pissy mood from their curbside conversation? Then she realized that his guarded features couldn't disguise the spark in his eyes. He was letting her take the lead, allowing her to decide if anyone would see them together.

She walked toward him, saying a hello to Benny as she passed. Without waiting for an invitation, she slid into the booth across from Will.

"Unless you're here to arrest me," Will said, casting a glance around the bar, "I don't think this is a good idea."

Leigh looked around. The two guys playing pool had stopped and were looking her way, pool cues planted on the floor beside them like pitchforks. *The angry mob.* As she moved her steady gaze to the bar, all but one of the men seated there reluctantly turned back to their drinks.

She said, loud enough that her voice broadcast throughout the bar, "I'm not here to arrest you. I came for dinner." Then she stared hard at the pool players until they finally broke under her gaze and returned to their game.

Feeling righteous and justified because she knew Will was a cop, not a criminal, she ordered a salad and a beer when the waitress crept warily over to the table. When she left with only a curt nod, Leigh turned to Will.

"We need to have a nice, *honest* chat. It's time to stop bullshitting me."

She saw the resignation in his eyes and knew he wasn't going to shut her out. A moment of panic flared in her chest. She was about to take a step through the looking glass — what if she only found the angry Queen of Hearts shouting, "Off with her head!"?

"What do you want to know?" His tone sounded bone weary.

Leigh drew a deep breath. "Are you a cop?"

He turned his beer bottle by the neck, leaving a spiral pattern of wetness on the table. His gaze stayed on the trail of water. "I was."

"Are you now?"

"Remember when I told you that I would never lie to you?" Missing from his voice was the warm gentleness she'd grown used to.

"Yes." Her stomach tightened.

He looked at her with a directness that made her heart take a stutter-step. That same intensity that had captured her at the carnival held her motionless. After a moment, he said, "I meant it."

"And . . . my question?"

"I can't tell you." It was a simple statement — no hidden anger, no tinge of remorse. It was as if she'd not spent a single intimate moment with him. It really pissed her off.

"Why are you here? Why did you come to Glens Crossing?" She leaned closer and lowered her voice, trying to force a hard edge into her question. If he wanted to play cop and suspect, she would just put on her sheriff's badge.

He settled back in the booth and rubbed his forehead, as if to massage his thoughts into place. "I've had a hellacious couple of years. I just needed to find a place of peace for a few days."

Leigh tried to ignore the clear emphasis he'd put on *a few days.* "That doesn't tell me why you're here."

"It's not all that complicated. I spent a couple of weeks here with relatives when I was a kid. It was a great time, like those old Kodak commercials — puppies, lemonade, swimming holes, fresh baked cookies. Quite a change from the chaotic days of my *normal* life."

Her resolve to sound as detached as he was acting faltered. It broke her heart to hear him speak of a childhood with so little joy — she could identify all too well. But she'd had Brian — if Will's sister was nine years younger, she doubted she shared much of the burden.

"Sounds like your life hasn't changed much, then." A softness crept in her voice without her permission.

Leigh had hit the nail on the head. Will looked into her eyes and saw so much empathy that pain and frustration erupted anew. Not pain from his childhood; he'd long since come to terms with that. Pain from hers; a child unwanted and unloved, forging her way in this world with only the support of a brother who couldn't begin to understand what it was like to walk in her shoes. Will understood — and the mere thought of it stole into his heart and clawed like an untamed tiger. He wanted to reach out and touch her face, to say so much that was bottled up inside. But he kept his hands still and only said, "I guess you're right."

"Tell me about this 'normal' life." She wasn't just making conversation; she looked like she really wanted to know.

He pushed his half-eaten dinner away and settled his elbows on the table in front of him. "Nothing terrible. It was just . . . unsettled. My dad couldn't stand to let the grass grow. He'd have a job for a few months, a year, then" — he snapped his fingers — "up and quit. Time to move on. He liked cities, not quiet towns like this. Spent my life elbowing my way in as the new kid."

"And your sister?"

"She came along eight years before my dad died. Mom stayed put for her — no new schools. I'd thought she had it made. . . ."

Leigh reached across and put her hand atop his.

He snatched it away and tucked it under the table. "Let's not buy trouble."

After a long, awkward pause, he decided to venture into less personal territory before emotions got the upper hand and ruled them both. "Anything new with Brittany?"

He watched her struggle for a moment, fearing she wouldn't follow his lead. He meant what he'd said; he wouldn't lie to her. But, dammit, it was just too dangerous for her to have an inkling of his past identity — or his current situation. Finally, he saw her let go.

"Yes," she said. "No. Ahhh, shit, I just can't get a handle on it."

"Maybe I can help."

She narrowed her eyes, and for a moment he feared she was sliding back to her original purpose. "Okay," she said, "I'm not opposed to outside *law enforcement* help."

He didn't respond, just nodded and waited.

"I just can't shake the feeling that I'm only seeing what I'm *intended* to see."

"And that is?"

"That someone yanked Brit out of that car and stole her away in the night. But — there's the glass thing. None on the road, an even spray on the driver's seat. Brit couldn't have been inside the car when the window was shattered."

He nodded again, remaining silent, allowing her to follow her own thoughts. He understood the value of simply stating the facts out loud. It had a way of crystallizing and focusing where your instincts were leading. Again, he admired her sharp insight and reasoning skills. If he simply acknowledged and followed, he knew she would end up right where his mind had led him.

She continued: "It's all just a little too convenient, her taking her car by Brownie's with a complaint that apparently didn't exist. Then there's Hattie Grissom's account. When I finally questioned her alone, she confessed that she did see Brittany that night. There were two cars. Brit got in with a man, apparently willingly, and drove away."

"Any description?"

"Only of the car. She was too far away to see the man's features."

"Have anyone in mind?"

"None that are making sense. I'm suspecting it's someone older that she'd taken up with fairly recently. Someone who could provide for her — I can't imagine Brittany forgoing creature comforts just to get back at her father."

Bingo. "So you think that's what this is about?"

"Don't you?" Her gaze sharpened on him. "I've heard how you've been poking around town, asking questions — about *lots* of things."

God, he thought he'd been discreet and

vague in his inquiries. He'd underestimated the power of the small-town rumor mill — simple questions that passed without notice in a larger venue drew sharp interest in a tight-knit community such as Glens Crossing.

Instead of addressing her question, he asked one of his own. "If this was to get back at Kurt, what about Emma? How does Brittany feel about her mother?"

Will could see that this question had hit its mark. He liked the way Leigh's brow pulled together when she concentrated. It made him want to smooth it out with kisses that would rob her of conscious thought altogether. *All the more reason to stay away from her. He was getting far too close and could bring her nothing but pain.*

"That's what doesn't make sense to me. Emma treated Brit more like a friend than a daughter — which might have exacerbated the whole situation to begin with. A lot of Brittany's anger toward her father is on her mother's behalf. Sure she's pissed about his defection from the family, hurt by Daddy's transference of affection away from her, embarrassed about his choice for a second wife, but I'd always gotten a distinct impression it was the damage to Emma that bothered her the most. I can't see Brittany letting her mother suffer like this."

Will thought Leigh had scored a bull's eye. Why would Brittany allow her mother to endure such heartbreak? That only left two alternatives: 1) Brit *was* kidnapped, 2) Brit did set it up — and Emma knew.

"So where does that leave you?" he asked.

"I have to think if she'd been kidnapped, there would have been some form of ransom demand — Kurt is a wealthy man. So far, nothing. I'm banking on her running off with someone with the wherewithal to take care of her."

"What about Emma?"

The second Will asked the question Leigh's mind slammed into overdrive. Impressions and images from the past few days tumbled and turned, creating an entirely different picture than the one she'd been trying to construct. The scene that brought an immediate halt to the rolling collage was Emma standing behind Kurt at the front door, their hands clasped as she leaned into him for support.

Once again, Will had worked on her thoughts as a magnifying glass in the sun, taking seemingly insignificant fragments and bending them, focusing them into one sharp pinpoint of meaning. She should have trusted her own instincts more, followed where they led, but it had taken Will's simple confidence to make her see clearly.

"I think maybe Emma knows more than she's telling." And first thing tomorrow, she'd find out just what that was.

Will's prideful smile warmed her to the center of her soul. She felt like a student basking in the approval of a beloved mentor. Within seconds that smile disappeared, as if he'd caught himself doing something he wasn't supposed to. Leigh felt the absence of it as she would the warmth of the sun.

The waitress who had tried to pick Will up the first night in the bar delivered Leigh's salad and beer. This time there were no flirting looks or hip-flipping, just a cold hard glare.

She said, "Thought you had better taste, Sheriff."

Leigh knew she wasn't talking about the food, but followed right along with the double meaning. "Well, sometimes I like something a little different — it expands my horizons. You'd be surprised what you can discover with an open mind."

"And sometimes you can get bit by a snake just walking around in the grass." She snapped around and walked back to the bar.

Will said, "Guess she told you."

Leigh flipped her hand. "Don't worry about it." She dug into her salad, with more appetite than she'd had for days. There was something about discovering the direction to the truth that truly did set you free. By this time tomorrow, she'd have some idea where Brittany was and Will's name in the clear; she felt sure of it. Then they could go on from there. Where, she didn't know, but at the moment she felt as light as a feather on the wind.

Then Will shattered her sense of peace.

"This isn't over, Leigh. The waitress is right; I'm still the snake. Finding Brittany won't change that." He got up. Pointing a finger at her, he raised his voice so it resonated in the small bar, "Unless you have a warrant, stay away from me."

Leigh's salad stuck in her throat as she watched him grab his dinner plate and move it to the bar. He sat near the end, far from the other patrons. Leigh realized the entire room, with the exception of Will, was staring her way. With a great deal of effort, she returned to her salad. She managed to sit there and push the lettuce and tomatoes around, rearranging them into various designs long enough for the attention to fade away. Then she got up and walked out of the bar without looking at Will Scott.

Damn him! She didn't need protecting. Tomorrow, after she had talked to Emma and had proof that Brittany was safe, she would take great pleasure in dealing with Will.

There was still so much that he wasn't telling her. She had to ask, why? Why, if she was close to having proof that Brittany was safe, would he still distance himself from her? The old question reared its head. Was he here on official business, investigating something in Glens Crossing? That would answer why he was still so evasive about telling her anything about his current situation.

There were only so many reasons he could be working in her jurisdiction without her knowledge, only so many reasons why he couldn't disclose to her why he was here. It had to be an investigation that was closely tied to her, perhaps the city police or her own department. Try as she might, she couldn't come up with a single reason why either department could be under suspicion of wrongdoing.

Perhaps the link to her was personal, not professional.

Brian was gearing up for a congressional run; could it have something to do with him? He and Kurt had been involved in some pretty big deals in the past. Could that be the focus?

There was more than one way to skin a cat. Right then, Leigh made a decision. She'd been toying with the idea for a day or so. She'd done the right thing and given Will the chance to come clean — and he'd fudged. A sense of betrayal inched its way into Leigh's heart. She knew it was unfair; he was just doing his job, yet she couldn't help but be hurt by his secretiveness.

During the initial evidence gathering, Deputy Clyde had filed the fingerprint and hair samples taken from Will and anyone else known to have been in Brittany's car. It was time to put them to use.

Instead of driving home, she went to headquarters. It would be so much easier to do this tonight without other people buzzing around asking questions. She gathered what she needed and, with her heart hammering in her ears, she scanned Will's prints. Then she composed a cover letter and made three copies. She sealed three identical sets of information in three next-day delivery FedEx envelopes and dropped them in the "out" box. By tomorrow Will Scott's prints would be on their way to the FBI, ATF and DEA.

Now all she could do was wait. It wouldn't be long.

Will left the Crossing House a good hour after Leigh. He'd hung around, sipping a single after-dinner beer, ignoring the curious stares of the other patrons. No sense in allowing speculation that he and Leigh were secretly meeting up after that unfriendly parting. He wanted no hint that the scene in the bar was staged.

Even if they got lucky and their speculation about Brittany was right, he still had no business dragging Leigh into his turbulent and uncertain life. This was a good time to break it off. He couldn't leave until he was certain Brittany had taken herself away from Glens Crossing — but once that was confirmed . . .

He hated the way his gut twisted at the thought of leaving. He felt himself weakening, his longing to be near Leigh warring with his common sense. Maybe he would stay a while longer. He promised himself he'd keep his distance from Leigh, not ruin her life out of selfishness. But he had to wait until Halloween somewhere. Why not here?

He headed into the darkness, carrying a Styrofoam container with not only his steak bone, but a couple others the kitchen help had thrown in. Apparently his notoriety hadn't spread to include his new buddy; the townsfolk weren't casting stones at the canine. Dog trotted by his side, patient but trailing a string of saliva from his chops. Anxious brown eyes kept a bead on the box.

"Just a little longer."

Will needed to walk, think, consider his options, or he'd never get to sleep. His mind was occupied with Benny Boudreau's false "buddy-buddy" reception after Will moved his dinner to the bar. The bartender most likely had Leigh's best interest at heart; Will had seen the protective way he looked at her. But instinctive defensiveness made Will balk at the callow inquisition. He had to contain himself to keep from grabbing the man by those bushy black eyebrows and telling him to mind his own damn business.

Of course, the reason for his own extreme reaction was obvious. Benny had been dead right in his innuendo; Will had it bad for their sheriff — and it wasn't good for either of them. He was a man buried in lies. He wondered how Benny would react if he realized just how dangerous Will was. Just half of what Will kept hidden would make the man's hair fall out.

Who would have thought the chameleon-like skills he learned moving from school to school would come to play so prominently in his adult life? He'd hated it then, arriving in a new situation, sizing up the lay of the social landscape. Each place had been slightly different from the last — what was cool changed, so he changed to accommodate it. During his high school days, although he attended six different schools in four years, he'd managed to remain afloat at all but one. In fact, he'd usually been so adept at integrating that he fell in with the popular kids. But that didn't mean he liked it. It was a matter of survival, not happiness.

The single exception had been Don Diego High in southern California. It had been his sophomore year, and he'd transferred in November — after everyone had already fallen into their social niches for the duration of the year. Will usually spent the first day or two scoping things out, keeping himself distanced from most everyone until he had the troublemakers, the scholars, and the jocks all pegged.

But that first lunch break he'd come out of the boys' restroom, smack dab in the middle of a real hazing. Three broad-shouldered, pea-brained Neanderthals (who Will later discovered made up the bulk of the defensive line on the football team) had a kid pinned against the concrete block wall. In a normal situation, this kid looked like he could hold his own — the glare in his eyes said he was no stranger to a fight. But against three guys, the smallest of

340

which probably weighed in at two fifty, he was a goner.

Without a thought, Will took a running start and rammed his head into one of the big guys' kidneys. It went rapidly downhill from there. There was never any doubt who would emerge the victors. Will had known the outcome going in, but the red-eyed fury that overtook him when he saw the lopsided odds made him ignore logic.

Once his bleeding had been sufficiently staunched and the school nurse had put a splint on the other kid's dislocated finger, the five of them were marched into the principal's office. Police were called. That's when Will learned the victim's name was John Ingalls.

John Ingalls. Probably the smartest person Will had ever met. Only problem was, he'd been ridiculed for so long, that he carried a chip on his shoulder that made it impossible for him to accept friendship. He always acted as if Will had an ulterior motive for helping him. A shame; normally an event like that bonds two people together. But John never opened himself up enough to take that chance.

Of course, the hazing didn't stop; it just included Will now. Even that didn't make him regret his actions. He spent the rest of his sophomore year looking over his shoulder every time he heard three hundred pound footsteps. Eventually, he fell in with a small group of friends, but John Ingalls remained an island unto himself.

Right at the moment, Will felt a little like John Ingalls — forever isolated, untouchable, with no way to reconnect.

Walking as he had been without conscious thought about his direction, he was surprised to find himself on the road to Leigh's house.

Wouldn't a psychologist have a heyday with that one?

A quarter mile from her drive, he cut into the woods. He moved deeper into the cover, coming upon Leigh's bungalow from the back. He was tempted to knock on her kitchen door, draw all of the curtains and lose himself in her innate decency. It'd been a long while since he'd thought of such things. Decency was just another principle obliterated from his ideology, along with honesty and compassion. She alone seemed to have the power to make the rest of the world and all of its ugliness go away.

When he neared the edge of the clearing that served as her backyard, he saw her moving around in the kitchen.

She stopped in front of the sink and stared out the window. For a moment he stopped breathing, thinking she'd seen him. Then she filled the glass in her hand from the tap and moved to the refrigerator. With her hand on the freezer door, she stopped in mid-motion.

"Just get the ice, drop it in your glass, and move on," Will said under his breath. "Don't do it, baby, don't do it. . . ."

If he could have telepathically imposed his will upon her, he would have. But no such powers were within his grasp and he had to watch with a tightness in his chest as she stared at the missing child mailer, the only scrap of paper affixed to her refrigerator. He should have ripped the thing to shreds and run it down the garbage disposal when he'd had the chance.

Her finger moved to the photo and lingered there. He knew what she was doing: asking herself what if she was wrong? Where would she turn then to find the girl? Of course, the picture wasn't of Brittany Wilson, but it didn't matter. He'd felt the same gut-wrenching helplessness himself a time or two. It served no earthly purpose but to torment the soul.

If he didn't know better, he would have thought she received his psychic missive for she did just as he'd mentally ordered: got her ice and sat down at the kitchen table. His breath caught as she ran her fingers through that curly hair. He could go to her; no one would know. He could take the pain away — at least for a minute.

Then what? He was a man without a past and most likely with no future. All he could bring her was heartache — and risk. It was a bad idea before this missing girl focused attention on him. Now it was impossible. He could not, would not, allow himself to be a threat to Leigh's safety, or her career.

Having had a moment to overcome his urge

to go inside, the rest of the world be damned, he sat down on a fallen tree trunk and opened the box of steak bones. He gave one to Dog and reclosed the box. Dog flumped happily at Will's feet and gnawed on the bone he'd waited so long for.

"I know how you feel, buddy. I've waited a long time for her, too."

A breeze moved through the woods, sounding like a thousand whispering voices. He knew what those quietly rasping voices said as they tumbled over one another in the tree tops. It had been the same condemnation for months, the same torment as in his dreams. And it sickened him because he knew he deserved every bit of it.

Thunder rumbled off in the west. Will cast his gaze skyward but was no better informed of its state than he had been when he looked at the ground. The stars had been blocked out for the past two nights by the heavy haze. He couldn't tell if it was simply that, or if thunderheads had finally built out of the heat and humidity.

The air now moved in a steady breeze. He'd seen this type of front move through drought-plagued areas before, tempting and teasing with electrical theatricals, but offering little or nothing in the way of moisture.

Will watched as the kitchen curtains fluttered inward. The gentle wind moved a curl across Leigh's cheek. She remained still. Unconsciously, he reached out to brush it away. His hand lingered in the darkness, close enough to feel, too far away to touch. A great pressing emptiness ballooned in his soul.

Leigh got up and turned out the light.

After her bedroom light followed suit, Will slid to the ground and rested his back on the fallen log. He'd wait until Dog finished his feast, then make the trek back to Brownie's.

A cool, fat droplet of water landed on Will's forehead. As it slid a ticklish path toward his hairline, his eyes opened. His neck muscles protested as he raised his head off the log behind him. How long he'd been asleep, he didn't know. It was still dark, the breeze was strong and the sky brightened intermittently with lightning. Slowly he rotated his head side to side until the muscles began to unbunch.

Dog lay sleeping with his head on his paws. The Styrofoam container sat open and empty beside him.

"Little bugger, helped yourself, did you?"

Another drop of water plopped on the back of Will's neck. He heard the occasional splat of large raindrops hitting foliage.

"Come on." He slapped his leg as he stood up. "We'd better beat it back to Brownie's before it storms."

As if to emphasize the urgency, a lightning bolt zigged across the heavens. A heartbeat later the ear-splitting crack brought Dog to his paws. They hurried through the woods, protected from most of the rainfall by the dense foliage. By the time they reached the road, the patter of drops the size of robin's eggs had slowed and soon stopped. The chip-and-seal pavement was dotted with dark water spots. There hadn't even been enough rain to completely wet the surface.

He decided to keep to the edge of the woods. Unlikely as it was, someone might drive along this road and get the idea that he'd been at Leigh's deep into the night. She didn't need any more talk and speculation at the moment.

Glad for the dry walk, yet sorry for the parched land, Will was halfway to town when Leigh's Blazer shot past, lights flashing.

Chapter 17

By the time Will walked into the downtown area, it was obvious something big was brewing. Normally, Glens Crossing rolled up the sidewalks about nine P.M., with only the Crossing House Tavern remaining open. But tonight the streets hummed with activity. Lights blazed in the fire station at the rear of the tiny city hall building. Even the Dew Drop's dining room bustled with commotion.

Will walked into the garage bay for Glens Crossing's single fire engine. The engine itself was gone. He stuck his head through the door leading to the city offices, where the dispatcher was speaking to what was obviously another fire department.

"Yes. Everything you can spare. Smith Farm Road, near the turnoff for the old Kaleidoscope Caverns. The sky's on fire; you can't miss it."

The woman disconnected, leaned back in her seat and blew out a long breath that ruffled her bangs.

"Excuse me," Will said.

The dispatcher jerked straight up in her seat and clutched her hand over her heart. After a long second, she appeared to breathe again and smiled thinly. "You startled me."

"Sorry." Will thought the start didn't just

come from being surprised, but by who did the surprising — kidnapper of young girls. "What's going on?"

"We're rounding up all the help we can get. Got a wildfire. Trying to keep it out of the national forest."

"Maybe I can catch a ride out there and lend a hand." He didn't know much about firefighting, but in a situation like this, every hand found purpose.

A call crackled over the radio. Will's heart seized when he heard Leigh's voice through the static. He hadn't thought, but of course she'd be involved. "Central dispatch. Sheriff Mitchell here."

As the dispatcher turned to pick up the radio, she said, "I'm sure they can use you.

"Dispatch, Sheriff. Go ahead."

Will took a step back, but hung near the doorway and listened.

"Better call the Forestry Service; we've got a wild one on our hands. Barring a wind shift or a miracle, the national forest is directly in its path."

Leigh's voice sounded stressed, thin and breathless. He had to get out there. When he returned to the main drag, he saw Brownie's pickup in front of Duckwall's Hardware with the driver's door open. As Will trotted over, Brownie emerged from the store, lugging a hand-held engine-driven brush trimmer. He set it in the truck bed and hurried to the driver's door.

"Hey!" Will called and ran faster.

Brownie paused with one foot up in the truck.

"Will! Climb in, man. We need you."

By the time Will had the passenger door open, Brownie had started the truck and put it into gear. Will's backside had barely touched the bench seat when Brownie hit the gas.

"Bad?" Will could see the man's skin was already covered with black soot made greasy by sweat.

"Real bad. I got all of the Husquevarnas out of the hardware; a couple of guys went home to get their own brush cutters. We gotta clear as much underbrush ahead of the fire as we can."

Long before they reached the roadblock, Will got a good whiff of smoke in the air. At this distance, it smelled like a boy scout camp. But when he saw the light of the fire reflected off the low-hanging clouds, he grasped the breadth and intensity of the blaze.

They stopped next to Deputy Clyde, who was manning the barricade on Smith Farm Road.

Clyde held a clipboard and a pen. "Brownie." He tipped his head. The deputy leaned over further and peered inside the truck cab. "Who's with you?"

"Will Scott. Works for me."

Will spoke up. "Here to help."

Deputy Clyde gave Will a long, hard look before he scribbled on the clipboard. "Gotta keep

349

track of everybody going in. Be sure and check in with fire command." His eyes narrowed on Will. "And nobody works alone. Teams of three and four."

"Right." Brownie got the truck rolling again.

About a half mile further down the road, a field full of corn stubble served as a parking lot. Will saw Leigh's Blazer right away.

"Where's the sheriff?" he asked Brownie.

"Over at the command truck — you know, radio equipment, maps and all."

Will must have made an unconscious sound of relief, because Brownie looked his way before he got out of the truck. "We gotta check in there. You'll see her."

When he did, he wasn't comforted in the least. She wore thick leather gloves, her T-shirt was sweat soaked and her face reddened under a scarred hard hat; obviously she hadn't been spending all of her time at the command vehicle. Even from where he stood he could sense the desperation in her motions. He forced himself to stand on the fringes and let Brownie get their radio and instructions. What he wanted to do was rush in, grab Leigh, fling that damned yellow hard hat into the brush, wipe the sweaty soot from her face and take her far away from here, somewhere safe — if he only knew of such a place. Will Scott hadn't seen *safe* this side of twenty-five.

Leigh stood by a man who must have been the fire chief and pointed to a map. They exchanged a couple of words, then she nodded and headed toward her Blazer. As she walked past, she saw Will for the first time.

"What are you doing here?"

"Whatever I can."

Her furrowed brow said she didn't like it one bit. "Well, we're certainly not going to turn away good help —"

"Hey, Sheriff! Better get a move on. Crew just radioed and we've only got a half-mile before it's gonna be too hot to get in there."

She raised her hand. "Right." She turned to Will. "Stick with Brownie; he knows the terrain. It's easy to become disoriented in the smoke."

"Where are you going?" Could he possibly hope she'd say home for a bubble bath?

"One of the guys thinks there are some migrant workers staying in an abandoned shanty up in Delaware Hollow. I'm going to get them."

"Alone?"

"Yes. Can't spare manpower just so I can have company."

"I'll come."

"No." Trotting toward her vehicle, she called over her shoulder, "Go with Brownie."

"Wait!"

She slowed and looked back at him, but didn't stop. "Will, please."

"You speak Spanish?"

She stopped.

"They're going to be really spooked when

you show up in the middle of the night."

Leigh eyed him speculatively and wondered if he was INS. She sure as hell didn't have time to stand around and try to force particulars from the lips of a man who'd managed to get into her bed and not share one iota of personal information.

In the end it didn't matter. He was already in the Blazer.

"We'll have to go around; the fire's between us and them." Leigh swung the Blazer onto the road.

As they slowed to a stop before circumventing the barricade, a brilliant white light arced across the road just in front of them. Leigh leaned forward and looked toward the origin of the beam — a helicopter.

"News media." Leigh leaned out the window as Deputy Clyde approached. She kept the truck rolling as she yelled, "Keep those people out of here. It's only a matter of time before the ground crews show up. We don't want any toasted reporters."

The deputy touched the brim of his hat and nodded.

Leigh accelerated, renewed urgency tugging at her senses. She could actually feel the heat of the flames inch closer to an innocent and unsuspecting family.

It took twenty minutes to drive around the fire zone and approach it from the other side. She had traveled as fast as she dared, lights flashing and siren blaring. Will had remained silent the whole way. Occasionally she stole a glance at him. His features were unreadable in the darkness.

Turning onto the old logging road that snaked into Delaware Hollow, she locked on four-wheel-drive, turned off the lights and siren. The smoke was thick enough here that her headlights were more of a liability than a help — like driving in dense fog. Coughing, she closed the windows, switched the fog lamps on and turned off her headlights. Some improvement, but not much. She slowed to a near crawl as they rocked and bounced down the neglected road.

"We may not be able to drive all the way; no one's cleared this ro—"

"Watch out!" Will shouted and pointed dead ahead.

She slammed on the brakes, seeing the fallen tree across the road at that same moment. Even at their low speed, the Blazer thunked loudly and Leigh's shoulder harness jerked across her chest when they hit.

Will put a hand on her shoulder. "You okay?"

"Yeah." She turned off the ignition, thankful they hadn't hit hard enough to deploy the air bag. "Guess we walk from here."

They quickly grabbed flashlights and climbed out.

The thick-trunked tree had obviously gone down quite some time ago. Most of its bark had fallen away and the branches had become brittle and broken. A few spear points remained and Leigh was careful not to catch her clothing on them as she climbed over. Limbs crunched and snapped underfoot as they crossed the debris.

"This lane leads right past the shanty," Leigh said as she hurried forward.

"Good thing. Hard to keep your bearings in this smoke. Be pretty humiliating to have rescuers rescue the rescuers."

Leigh gave a bark of laughter that drew smoke into her lungs and sent her into a coughing fit, but she kept moving. She looked up but the sky was completely masked. "I'd feel better with a compass."

"If wishes were horses . . ."

"Yeah, yeah. And if your aunt had balls she'd be your uncle. I know 'em all."

Now Will laughed. It irked her that he managed it without so much as a wheeze.

The lane got narrower and more overgrown. Leigh could barely keep her stinging eyes open beyond slits. She stopped a moment to orient herself. It seemed like they should have reached the shack by now. Could they have passed it? It was only about ten yards off the road, but in this smoke . . .

"There!" Will said. "Is that it?"

A fuzzy dot of light barely penetrated the haze.

Leigh hurried in that direction. Wild rose

thorns tugged at her pant legs and scratched her arms. She heard Will curse behind her and knew he was getting slashed, too.

A warped piece of plywood was propped against the opening in the front of the lean-to. A dim light filtered through a broken board. It went out.

"They know we're here," she said. "Call to them in Spanish. Do you speak it well enough to explain the fire?"

Will took a couple of steps closer, raised his voice and said something. The only word Leigh understood was *hola*. Could he speak Spanish? It rolled off his tongue as if he'd been born to it.

Rustling came from inside. Then someone whispered, "Shhhhh!"

Will kept talking. Leigh wondered what he was saying. It certainly didn't have the sound of barked orders; it flowed soft and soothing. She almost reminded him of the urgency, then realized that the quickest way to get these people to the car was with calm assurance, not bullying panic.

He paused and said something that sounded like a question.

A tiny voice squeaked in response. *"Sí."*

As Will slid the plywood aside, Leigh shone her flashlight inside and caught her breath. There, huddled in the corner like a stack of kittens, were five wide-eyed children. The littlest looked to be around four, the oldest maybe twelve. The eldest stepped in front of the other children, shielding them with his body, and addressed Will. His voice didn't waver, yet Leigh could see he was frightened.

Will's back stiffened. He looked over his shoulder into the darkness, then asked the boy something else.

The youngster pointed to the west; his speech picked up speed.

Will turned to Leigh. "His father went to see where the smoke was coming from. He told them to wait here."

"Shit, that means we have someone wandering around in the fire zone."

"You take the kids. I'll go after the father and meet you at the truck."

Then he turned to the children and spoke in a reassuring tone. At first the oldest boy shook his head. Then Will pulled him aside and spoke to him out of earshot of the others. When he was finished, the boy walked with proud shoulders to his siblings and herded them out the door. Leigh and Will followed.

Will put a hand on the eldest's shoulder. "This is Esteban." Then he pointed to Leigh. "*Esta es* Leigh."

She smiled and nodded, then said to Will, "I should go after the father, it's not your job."

"No. I can call to him, make sure I don't spook him. Besides, I've tracked through undergrowth at night before," he smiled, flashing white teeth in the darkness. "In fact,

I'm real good at it."

She eyed him seriously. "All part of the mysterious package?"

He grabbed her shoulders and kissed her quickly on the mouth. "Now get moving. If I'm not back at the truck in fifteen minutes, head out."

Leigh started to shake her head.

"Yes. If he's further away than that, it'll be faster to cut across country than come back this way. You're stuck with roads. Just get those kids out of here, and I'll meet you back at fire command."

Leigh looked briefly at the children. "All right."

Will moved into the hazy darkness, heading into the fire. Leigh stood and watched until she couldn't see his silhouette any longer. Just as she turned away, she heard Will call, "Fifteen minutes. After that I'm going another way."

Her insides twisted; she wanted to argue, but she yelled, "Got it."

Chapter 18

"Okay, guess we're ready," Leigh said, gathering the children. She started toward the truck with feet that wanted desperately to move in the opposite direction. She hated to be forced into inaction while Will took the risk. But she'd known he was right; he had a much better chance of coming back with these children's father than she.

The truck seemed much further away than she remembered. After helping the children over the fallen tree, Leigh buckled the little ones in the back seat and she and Esteban climbed in the front. She fished around in her memory for anything she could recover from high school Spanish. Name, how do you say, name? *Llymma?* No. *Llamo?* Close enough.

She pointed to the youngsters in the back seat. Not even attempting to create a sentence, she simply asked, *"Llamo?"* She felt like an idiot.

The boy rotated in his seat and pointed to the girl on the passenger side. "Adriana." Then he moved across the seat. "Dolores, Lucita, Leandro."

Leigh repeated each name, smiling at the child to whom it belonged. Adriana looked shyly at her hands in her lap. Dolores just stared back at her without registering any change in her wary expression. Lucita giggled; she was missing her two front baby teeth. Little Leandro stuck his thumb in his mouth.

Then Leigh put her hand on her chest and said her own name. She got no response beyond Lucita's continued giggling. When she looked back to Esteban, he shrugged and smiled at her.

After that they sat in silence only broken by an occasional cough. The smoke was getting thicker. She looked at her watch. Sixteen minutes.

"Come on, Will."

She knew waiting longer wouldn't serve any purpose. Will made certain of that with his promise to exit the woods by another direction. Slick bastard.

She reached for the key in the ignition, but couldn't bring herself to turn it. Motioning for Esteban to stay put, she climbed out of the truck.

Standing on the fallen tree, she strained against the darkness and her burning eyes to see a hint of Will's flashlight beam through the murk. Nothing. She turned on her own light and arced it wide, but the thickening smoke made a solid curtain of gray; it might as well have been an impenetrable brick wall.

She tucked the flashlight under her arm and cupped her hands around her mouth. "Will!

Can you hear me?" That was when she saw the first flames.

She scanned full circle around her. The burning seemed to be a small, isolated patch at the moment. But she knew that would quickly change.

"Will! Dammit, answer me!"

She waited a precious second, then turned back to the truck with fear prickling every nerve ending. Hesitating with her hand on the door handle, she wondered briefly if Esteban could drive.

My God, Leigh Mitchell, what are you thinking? She opened the door.

As she got in, Adriana screamed shrilly, *"Inciendto! Senorita! Inciendto!"*

Leigh flashed a reassuring smile over her shoulder as she started the engine. "It's okay. We're going." Going — and Will was out there somewhere, doing *her* job.

Putting the Blazer in reverse, she decided it would be faster to turn around, even though the lane was very narrow. There were a couple of curves she didn't want to negotiate with all of the smoke.

Adriana kept crying, "Papa! Papa!"

Leigh shouted over her shoulder. "Quiet! Your papa'll be fine!"

The little girl cringed, pressing herself back in the seat, as far away from Leigh as possible. Have to make up later; right now they needed to get out of here.

She had the truck more than halfway turned around. Backing up one more time should have done it. The rear passenger tire rolled into a hole of some sort — maybe a groundhog burrow, because it was big enough and deep enough to cause the truck to sit completely cockeyed, its fog lamps hitting high in the tree branches.

Leigh put the gearshift in low and tried to pull forward. The chassis groaned and she felt the slightest movement, then the front tires slipped in the thick carpet of fallen leaves. If she gave it more gas, chances were they'd slam into the tree on the other side of the lane. She tried backing, then rocking forward with no more luck. She tried again. And again.

There had to be a way to get more traction. She jumped out and went to the front. Falling to her hands and knees, she clawed a path in front of the driver's side tire, flinging matted leaves and twigs wildly to the side. A cough beside her made her heart leap, thinking Will had returned. But when she looked up, it was Esteban, squatting in front of the passenger side, clearing a path for the other tire.

A cinder floated in front of her face. Looking up, she saw a line of light high in the trees overhead. One by one, the high branches were catching fire.

"Okay, that's it. Get in!" she yelled and pointed back to front seat.

Esteban scrambled into the passenger side.

Leigh tried rocking the truck free. "Come on, now. Not too much gas," she coached herself. It was difficult not to push her foot to the floor; glowing embers drifted in the smoke around them like fireflies. Here and there tiny flames would lick up, waver, then either go out from lack of fuel, or, worse, catch fully.

She rocked once, twice. The children behind her made a crazy chorus of squeals, cries and whimpers. Esteban shushed them. The noise was tempered to near nothing. Leigh mentally commended their bravery. Her own heart was hammering like a cornered rabbit's; she could only imagine the terror they felt.

On the third try the Blazer lurched forward. She cranked the steering wheel and stepped on the gas, slinging dirt and gravel against the floorboards.

She looked at Esteban. He was grinning widely as he jostled next to her, grasping the handle on the dash to keep from sliding completely off his seat. "Hey. Buckle up." She pointed to his seat belt. "Don't need a bloody nose."

The children remained quiet in the back seat. Leigh noticed an occasional sniffle from Adriana's side of the car.

A new breeze lifted, helping with the smoke, but pushing the flames faster. At least the woods weren't burning around them. They were ahead of it — for now.

As soon as Leigh cleared the hollow and had

a radio signal, she called fire control.

"I have five children with me. All fine. Will Scott is looking for their father. He's west of Delaware Hollow, in the fire zone. Get someone out there to look for them, now!"

"Roger, that," Fire Chief Jeffers said.

"Stan, this is moving much faster than we thought. It chased us out of the hollow."

"Confirmed. We're on it."

"See you in twenty."

As she drove, Leigh kept an eye on the woodlands bordering the road, hoping against hope to see Will's flashlight waving her down. It wouldn't penetrate far in the smoke, but if he was close enough . . .

Glancing at Esteban, she wondered what she would do with these children if their father didn't materialize soon. With blinding clarity, she realized her mistake. They hadn't asked about papers. If they didn't find the father, and if the shack burned . . . Why hadn't she been thinking? She would just have to find some way to keep these kids out of the system until she had things sorted out.

She slowed as she approached the road block. Not by choice; there was an absolute traffic jam as Deputy Clyde tried to separate the television vehicles from fire equipment and volunteers. Along the narrow berm on both sides, vans with satellite dishes and tall antennas sat with cargo doors open, equipment glowing green inside. One reporter had situated himself in front of the flashing barricade, right in Steve Clyde's way. Leigh inched forward, then angled across the width of the road, nudging the reporter and his cameraman away from the barricade.

She got out of the truck and hurried to Steve. "Has it been like this long?"

"It was like they were all dropped out of the sky from the same mother ship. One minute nobody, the next" — he pointed at the congestion — "this."

"Can you manage? I don't want any of these reporters to get through. There's enough confusion up there as it is."

"No problem. Most of them are behaving."

Just as he said that, Leigh noticed someone leaning in the open window of her Blazer, a cameraman ready right behind him.

"Hey!" She ran back to her truck. "Get away from there!"

He turned on her in an instant. "Are these the illegals caught in the fire?"

Leigh wanted to shove him away, knock him down and kick him once he was on the ground, but settled for putting her hand over the camera lens. "These are minors. No one gave you permission to photograph them."

The reporter said, "Come on, now. We're just doing our job." He made a show of looking at the emblem on her car. "You the sheriff's wife? Taking care of these kiddies?"

She swung around to him. "I *am* the sheriff.

And I'm going to be taking care of *you*, if you don't back away from this vehicle and leave these children alone."

Putting both hands in front of his chest, palms out, he took one step away. "Okay, okay. No offense . . ."

Leigh opened the back of her Blazer and dug around in a box. Pulling out a roll of yellow police tape, she marched over to a fence post about ten yards down the road from the barricade. She tied it there and attached the other end to a cone in the center of the road.

She pointed to the other side of the tape and said to the reporters milling close by, "No one crosses this police line without arrest." She looked pointedly at the reporter she'd just shooed away from her truck. "I can't spare the manpower to baby-sit you. Am I clear?"

The man looked perturbed, but nudged his cameraman across the line. Then he made a show of stepping over it himself.

"Thank you." Leigh got back in her truck and slammed the door.

She had considered leaving the children here with Steve, but he had his hands full.

Parking her Blazer in the field, she gathered the children, taking Lucita and Leandro by the hand, and headed to the control truck. As they approached, Leigh saw there had been a new addition to their setup. A long table stretched at a right angle to the driver's door of the command vehicle, covered with thermoses, large galvanized wash tubs filled with ice and bottled water, plates of wrapped sandwiches and fruit. Unloading additional food from the back of a minivan, were Mildred and Sally from the Dew Drop.

Leigh would have to have been both blind and deaf not to register the hungry reaction of her wards. Ten eyes were glued to the piles of food and Leandro said something that must have been deemed impolite by his older brother, judging by Esteban's stern reaction.

"Mildred," Leigh called. "Think you could fix my friends up with a snack?"

"Sure." She motioned for them to come closer. "We can set up a regular picnic."

"Mind if I leave them with you for a few minutes? I need to check in."

"I'm going to be here, so don't worry about a thing."

"Well, they don't speak English —"

Mildred grinned. "I think this food will do all the talking we need." She waved Leigh away. "We'll be fine."

"Thanks."

Leigh patted Esteban on the shoulder, then turned him to face the waitress. "Mildred." Then she turned him to herself once again and looked him in the eye. "I'll be back for you."

She didn't think he understood her words, but he nodded. His gaze settled palpably on the back of her neck as she walked away and she felt like she was abandoning a basket of helpless puppies at the humane society. She knew they'd be well cared for, and yet . . .

She sent a silent prayer for their father.

The first light of day pushed from the east, making the smoky sky glow a dull, muted orange. Chief Jeffers was sending out fresh firefighters to relieve those on the front line as Leigh approached.

"How are we doing?" she asked as soon as he was free.

" 'Bout like you'd expect. That breeze cost us at least a hundred acres." Stan looked as tired as Leigh felt.

"Anyone radio in about the missing man?"

He shook his head. "Nothing about your friend either."

She turned away, trying to look like she was checking out the flames in the distance. She didn't want Stan to see the naked fear she couldn't conceal.

She drew in a breath and asked, "Where do you want me?"

"I'm going out to see things firsthand. You stay here and direct incoming help." He leaned over the map and pointed. "I've got crews here, here, and here. I've just sent one unit coming from the other side to Delaware Hollow. We're getting help from the bigger departments — Evansville, Bloomington and Jeffersonville. When they arrive, I want them to concentrate here." He pointed to a spot near the edge of the fire zone. "If we can get this wet and cleared, I think we can keep out of the national forest."

"Okay."

"If the road's still passable, send them through the center." He stuck his fireman's hat on his head and walked toward his truck.

Leigh looked at the map. Her eyes blurred. She didn't see the pinpoints where the crews were placed, nor the line marking the advancing edge of fire. She saw only a vast, dangerous wasteland of flame, smoke and falling debris, and she wondered where Will was.

Chapter 19

Gnawing worry threatened to explode into full-blown panic as the noon hour passed with no sign of Will and the missing man. Radio calls repeatedly cracked, alerting every cell in Leigh's body, sending nerve endings into quivering fits, only to be followed with the hot rush of disappointment when she queried about the missing men. She'd gone through the drill enough times that she was certain the next time the radio sprang to life she'd be immune. She was wrong. Calls continued to come in. Her body grew exhausted from the repeated adrenaline rush.

The reality of the situation gnawed and poked at her. Smoke could easily take both men down before the heat and flames actually reached them. If they were somewhere unconscious, the fire could literally sweep over them where they lay. Leigh shuddered. The coffee someone had pressed into her hand a few minutes ago soured in her stomach. She barely made it behind a scrubby evergreen before it came back up.

Chief Jeffers finally returned from his scouting tour, looking not at all like the man who'd left six hours before. Grime streaked his face where he'd swiped sweat away from his eyes, his hair was soaked, his clothing had several places where hot embers had left their mark. When he got close enough, Leigh saw his irises were nothing but two dots of blue in a blood-red sea.

"Took longer than I expected," he said to Leigh as he accepted a bottle of water and a towel from Mildred, who although clearly exhausted herself, refused to leave while there were volunteers to feed. "Got into a hot spot, out near the hollow, couldn't leave those boys high and dry."

Leigh swallowed, the sound of her own dehydrated tissues rasping against one another loud in her ears. *The hollow.* "And now?"

"Contained. That shanty where them kids were hole up is toast." He held her gaze, the redness of his eyes making her own smart in sympathy. "You did the right thing, getting those kids out."

"No word about the missing men?"

A heavy hand landed on her shoulder. "Sorry. It was bad, but that doesn't mean they didn't get clear. It's a lot of ground to cover."

Good God, Leigh thought, terror rising in her throat, *he couldn't even make his voice sound like he believed it.* And the chances were getting slimmer by the second. Why had she let Will manipulate her into letting him go?

Her stomach threatened another upheaval. She breathed deeply and waited for the nausea to pass. "I want to go out."

Stan shook his head in a distracted way as he took a swig of water. "Sorry." He wiped his lips with the back of his dirty hand. "You've been at this as long as I have. Can't send you out without a few hours' downtime."

"Goddammit, Stan! Send me out!"

He jerked his gaze to her face and she immediately regretted her outburst. It only confirmed that she had no business out there right now. She tried to backpedal. "I'm fine. I can't sleep anyway. Downtime won't do me a bit of good." Holding his gaze steadily, she added, "Use me."

She didn't think she could tolerate one more hour of standing around, wondering if Will was trapped by smoke, downed by a broken leg, or burnt to a crisp. At least if she was out there, she could hack at a few logs to rid herself of the tension.

Stan pressed his lips together, making little black soot creases that looked like stitches around his mouth. Before he answered, a commotion erupted near the entrance to the field where her Blazer was parked.

Leigh looked up to see Hale Grant hurrying across the corn stubble, tripping, then regaining footing. Following him were a man in a shirt and tie and one holding a camera.

"How in the hell did he get through?" she said as her gaze moved quickly ahead of them. There, emerging from the tangled undergrowth

371

of goldenrod and cocklebur were two figures, one leaning heavily on the other.

Immediately, Leigh's feet were flying in that direction, her heart thundering in her ears. She was vaguely aware of Stan running right behind her. His footfalls quickly fell far behind. Instead of running the extra fifteen yards to the open gate, Leigh vaulted over the wire fence, barely touching a fence post with one hand. Hale Grant and his crew reached the far side of the field first. They stopped a few feet away, apparently unwilling to risk the scraping sting of thorny weeds for the sake of a story that would eventually walk right to them. They had what they wanted — they were *first.*

Leigh shoved past them, leaping over the small drainage ditch at the edge of the field, landing just in front of the two faltering men. An incredible lightness overtook her body when she recognized Will. Safe! Will was safe.

He stumbled under the weight of the shorter man, whose feet were now dragging uselessly in the dirt. The innocent faces of the children flashed in her mind. *Let him be unconscious. Don't let him be dead.*

Tucking herself under the man's other arm and wrapping her arms around his middle, Leigh shored up some of the dead weight dragging on Will and they managed to clear the ditch. Once in the cornfield, Will's knees buckled and all three of them went down. His chest heaved with heavy breaths. The other man lay unmoving where he dropped, showing no signs of life.

Leigh ran her hands over Will's body, searching for injury. He brushed her away, coughing and pointing toward the other man. He noticed the camera for the first time. He rolled away, giving the cameraman his back and shielding the man prone on the ground.

"Get" — he coughed, then continued in the voice of a two-pack-a-day smoker — "away!"

Leigh leaned closer to him. "What?"

He jerked his thumb behind him.

Looking at the news people, she saw the red "record" light on the camera. "Stan, clear that news crew out of here! Hold them over by the command center. I'll deal with them later."

She ignored Hale's protests about freedom of the press as he and his crew were led away. Placing the tip of her index finger on the unconscious man's neck, she felt for a pulse. Strong and steady. She'd wait for the paramedics to move him for fear of worsening his injuries. Looking up, she saw them hurrying across the field with medical cases in hand. It took all of her willpower not to abandon the man before they got to his side. As soon as they knelt down, she crawled over to Will, cornstalk stubble poking through her pants as she did.

The rattle and rasp of his breathing frightened her. Placing a hand on his back, it rode on his inhalations, which were often interrupted by coughing. She leaned around to get a better look at his face, still averted from the camera.

She called over her shoulder to the medics, "I think one of you needs to look at him."

Even before the words were out of her mouth, she saw Will's head shaking. He pushed her roughly away from him, got to his feet and staggered toward the ditch where he stood with his back to them. He seemed thoroughly pissed off. For a moment she just watched as his shoulders slowly took on a natural rise and fall with the rhythmic return of his breathing. Then she turned to the paramedics and asked about the other man.

"How is he?"

"Probably gonna make it." Then the paramedic paused and jerked his head toward Will. "Better get him to the hospital and have his lungs checked out. Could be some delayed symptoms."

"All right." She watched as they loaded the man into the waiting ambulance. Then she approached Will. She started to touch him, but stopped. His rejection radiated in waves.

"What is it, Will?"

For a long moment, she thought he was going to ignore her. Then he turned. His gaze swept quickly beyond her, then settled on her face. "Nothing."

"The camera, was that it?"

His gaze narrowed. "How do you do it?" His anger seemed to have disappeared. Now he just sounded exhausted.

"Do what?"

"Read my mind."

In her dreams! "It was your face, not your mind."

He looked away again. "You need to confiscate that film footage and destroy it."

"Will, if the man's an illegal, I hardly think they'll set up a manhunt from a local television station's video report. If we keep him away from interviews, he should be able to disappear right back into the woodwork. There's no need —"

He grabbed her by the shoulders, fingers digging in hard, and drew her a half-step closer. "It's not him, Leigh." Pausing, he cast his eyes briefly to the heavens and bit his lip. "It's me."

His gaze returned to hers and held it unflinchingly. She sought reason, understanding, but found nothing but a wall of confusion. A thousand questions whirled in her mind. But she was afraid to voice even one.

Quietly, he spoke again, his voice filled with something that sounded like shame. "It's me."

Chapter 20

"It was a live feed." Leigh climbed in the Blazer, where Will had waited while she'd used all of her legal authority and no small amount of bluffing to try and confiscate the footage.

He didn't say anything, just scrubbed his palms fiercely over his face and breathed deeply.

They sat in silence. The hazy late afternoon sunshine was muted further by the smoke and ash in the air. The unusual light gave a surreal quality to the atmosphere. That, blended with her fatigue, made Leigh feel like she was experiencing something happening to someone else. The world around her no longer seemed three dimensional. All that existed at the moment was inside this vehicle — and even from that she was detached. She knew she couldn't depend on her logic; her emotions had been flattened by the past hours. Unable to deal with Will's disturbing admission at the moment, she started the truck and put it in gear.

"Where are we going?" he asked, sounding more drained than she felt.

"I'm taking you to the hospital."

"No." It sounded lifeless. It sounded final.

"Will, there could be damage to your lungs —"

"Enough, Leigh!" Nothing flat about his tone

now. "I'm not going."

"Why not, for God's sake?" She released the steering wheel and let her hands fall into her lap.

"I — don't — need — a reason." His tone exploded with exasperation as he separated the words as if she couldn't understand English. Stiffness overtook his body.

"Listen!" She matched his intensity and frustration. "I've had about as much of this evasiveness as I can stand." Swiveling in her seat, she faced him squarely. "I'm law enforcement, too." She poked a finger at her own chest. "And, undercover or not, you understand the chain of command. You're in my jurisdiction. I can help you. It's time you tell me exactly what's going on."

He remained silent, his rigid posture unbending, his gaze locked on something beyond the windshield.

She sat staring at his profile with all of those potentially devastating questions begging to be let out. Maybe she was wrong. Maybe he wasn't still a cop. How could this man, who'd risked his life to save a stranger, be the same one who came after her like a commando with a knife? The man by the creek could have slit her throat; how could that same man be such a tender lover? If he was a cop, then what was he digging for? It had to do with her, or she wouldn't be kept out of the loop. Either way, she was damned. Don't ask. Don't tell. Biting her tongue, she put the car in gear.

As the Blazer bounced back onto the paved road, Will said again, "I'm not going to the hospital." His voice sounded dull and flat, not at all combative like before.

"Fine." She wanted to add, "I hope your lungs seize up and suffocate you in your sleep." But such pettiness seemed out of place considering what had just transpired. He had a secret. And it hurt that he wouldn't trust her with it. "I'm taking you to Brownie's for some sleep." Suddenly she was frazzled beyond fatigue. Not from battling the fire, but from trying to make sense out of Will Scott. And, at this point, she wasn't sure she wanted to.

"And you?" he asked.

Leigh could feel his gaze boring into her, so she kept her eyes firmly on the road. "I've been ordered downtime, too." She didn't say anything else as she drove toward town.

Before she'd left the command center she'd seen that the children were taken to the hospital with their father, Beto. From there the youngsters were going to stay with the minister of the Presbyterian Church until Dad was released. There had been no questions concerning legal papers or insurance claims. It seemed everyone was turning a blind eye to this one.

Leigh stole a glance at Will and thought that her own blindness just might lead straight to ruin. Something tugged deep within her each and every time she laid eyes on him, making her throw her common sense into the basement, latch the door and turn out the light. Occasionally she heard it down there, under the floor, calling to get out. She always created her own mental noise to drown out the cries.

Will sat with his elbow on the door, forehead held in his hand. And he looked so, so . . . *defeated* was the only word she could think of. She tried to tell herself she was doing the right thing. He'd asked her to trust him, yet given her little reason to do so. And still she'd done it. She had no concrete reason why the possibility of his image broadcast on television brought so much distress.

Right now, her own lack of ethics sickened her. Yet, she couldn't turn her back on him.

Finally, they arrived at Brownie's house. Will stopped with his hand on the door handle. "Leigh . . ."

She kept her gaze fixed on the speed limit sign posted on the parkway. "Just get out."

He hesitated only a fraction of a second, then climbed out of the car. The ache in her chest swelled as she watched his normally straight shoulders bow ever so slightly under whatever burden he carried.

Once home, Leigh showered, filling her mind with the details of the day: the impact of saving those children, what the aftermath of this fire would bring — everything except Will. She then fell onto her bed in utter exhaustion, hair wet, body wrapped in a towel. As long as conscious thought was in her power, she managed to keep Will away. But soon that control began to slip. As sleep slowly pulled her into its embrace, thoughts of Will began to torment her — the fact that he risked his life to save a man he'd never even met, the defeated look in his eyes when he realized the camera had captured his image and sent it irretrievably into space. Those eyes were truly the windows to his soul, if only she could see through them clearly. A cascade of images pressed her memory — the playfulness in those eyes at the carnival, the heat that radiated from them as they'd danced, the cold detachment after he'd attacked her by the creek.

Then he suddenly disappeared. She heard him calling to her through a pall of smoke, pleading for help. Turning full circle, more and more rapidly, Leigh couldn't discern which direction his voice was coming from. Her last conscious thought was of spinning helplessly out of control, into a dark, bottomless shaft.

"All right, all right," Leigh muttered as she pulled her nose out of the pillow. Without removing the hair from her face, she maneuvered the telephone receiver under the tangled mass to her ear. "Hello."

She hadn't fully come back to this world, but when she heard Stan Jeffers's voice, reality came crashing through like a wave of icy water.

"How we faring, Stan?"

"That's why I called. It's contained. Just waiting to douse the final few hot spots, but it's over. I've dismissed all of the civilian volunteers and notified your deputy to take down that road block. Time to get things headed back to normal around here." There was a touch of giddiness in his voice. He'd waged war and won.

"Great. Need anything else from me?"

"No, ma'am. Just get yourself rested up."

"Sounds like a plan. Thanks."

"Bye."

"Stan?"

"Yeah?"

"Good work."

"Coulda been really ugly. We got lucky."

The line went dead. Leigh looked out the window and saw it was fully dark. She was asleep again before she could focus on the clock to see what time it was.

A feeling of déjà vu washed over her when her alarm rang, once again interrupting her sleep. Rolling onto her back, she groped blindly to shut it off, realizing she'd now lost the towel wrapped around her body. Slowly the events of the past days floated back into consciousness. A new sense of gladness sprang in her heart. Today she'd finally be able to question Emma. Once she had confirmed that Brittany had run off on her own, the cloud of suspicion would be gone from over Will's head and they could stop playing these games.

Maybe, her conscience whispered. *You still don't know why he's in Glens Crossing.* Could she dare hope it was as innocent as he explained — he'd had a bad time and needed a break?

Then why did he panic when he realized he'd been on camera?

One step at a time, she cautioned herself. First confirm, then deal with Will.

Kurt opened the door when Leigh rang the bell at Emma's house. First thing in the morning and Kurt was here, not at home with his young wife? From the looks of him, he'd been in the same clothes for a couple of days. His eyes appeared sunken and dark and the way he moved — it was as if someone had sucked all of the life out of him. He held himself like a man losing a battle with a long illness — posture stooped, eyes dull, skin lifeless.

"Kurt. I didn't expect you to be here," Leigh said as she entered.

"Been staying with Emma."

"I'm sure she appreciates it."

He nodded and pointed toward the living room. "We're in there. Coffee?"

"That would be nice. I just have a couple of questions for Emma."

He walked toward the kitchen. Leigh hoped he took his time. What she had to ask Emma was better done alone.

Entering the living room, Leigh set her eyes

on Emma and stopped dead in her tracks. Kurt looked like the life had been wrung from him, but Emma looked almost radiant, better than Leigh had seen her since the divorce. Gone was the strained expression of the first days after Brittany disappeared that had made her appear as if the slightest tap would cause her to shatter like spun sugar.

The gears clicked in Leigh's head. There was only one logical explanation for Emma's apparent well-being.

Leigh nearly grinned in anticipation as she entered the room.

There wasn't time to waste, not with Kurt in the house. She sat on the sofa next to Emma. "It's so nice of Kurt to stay out here with you."

Emma smiled. "Yes. It's been a big help. I don't know what I'd do . . ." She fished a tissue out of her pocket and dabbed at a nose that didn't appear to be running.

Leigh leaned closer and lowered her voice. "Have you heard from Brittany since she disappeared?"

Emma's startled gaze skittered toward the kitchen. "Of course not. If I had I'd have called you."

Putting a hand on Emma's arm, Leigh said softly, "You're certain?"

Emma jumped to her feet and wrung her tissue. "Of course I'm certain! Why would you ask such a thing?"

"There are things about Brittany's disappearance that just aren't adding up. I think she may have decided to leave on her own."

"That's ridiculous!" Kurt's voice thundered from the doorway. "My baby was yanked from her car on a dark country road, and you're trying to make it sound like she ran away! Where in the hell do you get off? You and I both know who did it. Now you've concocted this fantastic story to get your boyfriend off the hook. Well, it's not going to work. I'm going to call the FBI."

Leigh caught the surprise in Emma's eyes. For the briefest moment it looked like she was going to say something. Then she just folded in on herself and collapsed on the sofa.

Kurt pointed toward the door. "Get out of here! I don't want to see your face again."

"Kurt, the FBI can't create evidence that isn't there. I truly believe that Brittany left Glens Crossing of her own free will. Neither Will Scott, nor anyone else for that matter, snatched her. Just let me explain why —"

"Get out!" His face had flooded with so much color, Leigh worried he'd give himself a heart attack.

"All right." She let herself out the door, leaving Emma right where Leigh suspected she wanted to be, wrapped securely in Kurt's arms.

As Leigh drove to her office, she still smelled smoke in the air, even though all reports confirmed that the fire was out. She closed the window and cranked up the air conditioning, trying to alleviate the onset of a blinding headache mixing with a sour stomach.

Could it have been just last Thursday that she'd awakened overcome with a heavy spirit because her life was so boring?

Now she had to find a way to convince a woman with a secret — one that happened to be bringing her exactly what she wanted — to give that secret up. It was going to take a catalyst, but Leigh had no idea what it might be. She'd been lucky to find the motivation for Hattie Grissom in her dead babies. What would be the button to push for Emma Wilson?

Without saying a word to anyone, Leigh went into her office and closed the door. She had to find an angle of attack.

Right away there was a knock and Francine, the dispatcher, stuck her head in. "Coffee?"

Leigh moaned. "You're a godsend."

Francine returned with the coffee. Before she left she said, "Saw you on television last night."

Leigh looked up. "What?"

"On the news; you and that fella who saved the Mexican."

"Oh. Local news?" They were replaying the footage. Nothing to be done about it now. Even though she was currently pissed as hell at Will Scott, she couldn't fight her instincts that he was a decent man who needed to be protected.

"Yeah, channel six, I think."

Good. Maybe it would die here and now, in

their own local viewing area. Today would bring more news and the fire and those pictures would fade into distant media memory. "Thanks for the coffee."

"You bet." Francine headed back to her dispatch desk, closing Leigh's door behind her.

Before Leigh could organize her thoughts on how to sneak in the back door of Emma's mind, the door to her office burst open.

Brian stood there, anger snapping in his eyes. "Goddammit, Leigh. You've gone too far!"

"Slow down." Leigh held up a hand. "What are you talking about?"

He slammed the door shut behind him and stood before her desk. Leaning forward, bracing his palms on her desktop, he said through clenched teeth, "Kurt pulled out. He's not backing my congressional run."

"Why?" She asked the question, but knew all too well what must have transpired.

"You know good and well why. You've blown it. You can't find his daughter and now it seems you've come up with some fucking fiction about Brittany running off on her own." He slammed his fist against her desk. "Are you so desperate to clear your boyfriend that you'll sacrifice all we've worked for?"

Leigh shot to her feet. "Wait just a minute!" She pointed a finger at him. "You have absolutely no right to insinuate that I'm not doing my job. I'm getting at the truth — and it's not my fault if Kurt can't handle it. I'm only sorry that he's taking it out on you. I'll talk to him —"

Brian turned the finger of accusation back on her. "Stay away from Kurt. You can only make it worse."

"How can the truth make it worse? Once he sees what's happened —"

"And what is that, Leigh?" He walked around the desk to come directly face to face with her. "What *has* happened?"

Leigh drew a deep breath and put another step's distance between them. "I've worked very hard to maintain my professional focus. And solid evidence just doesn't exist. There *isn't* a case — against Will or anybody else. All we have is a father who doesn't want to face the truth about his daughter and a frustrated and frightened town stirred by the innuendo Grant's sticking in the paper. Sure, without the facts there are plenty of people who think Will Scott is guilty — simply because he doesn't belong."

"It's more that that! First of all, nothing even remotely like this happened before he showed up." He ticked the reasons off on his fingers. "Nobody seems to know anything about him. He worked on Brittany's car; maybe he tampered with it. Maybe he laid in wait. We know he was out the entire night that Brit disappeared. But we *don't know* him; maybe he's got a hidden dark side."

Brian backed off an inch, drawing a deep breath and scrubbing his hands over his face.

"Dammit, Leigh, I'm worried about you! What if you're next?" His voice broke as he said, "What if this guy takes you away from me? You're all I have. . . ." He reached out and pulled her roughly into an embrace.

His words resounded in her head, their stark meaning breaking her heart. She was all he had? That certainly didn't say much for his wife. She wrapped her arms around him. They remained quiet for a few minutes while her anger seeped away and her heart rate slowed back to normal.

Finally she pulled away. "You have to trust me. There are things you don't know. No one else knows." She paused. "I have a witness."

"A witness? Who?" His tone sounded as hopeful as a child asking Santa for a new bike.

"Hattie Grissom saw another car the night Brit disappeared. Said the girl got in willingly. Will doesn't have a car."

"Oh my god." The temporary relief Brian felt with the prospect of something solid to back up Leigh's assertion that Will Scott was harmless evaporated like breath on a cold morning. "You've got to be kidding!" He held his head, turning in a circle, then pointed in the direction of the Grissom farm. "That old woman is nuts and everybody knows it."

The fear that had momentarily calmed in his belly erupted anew. It was worse than he thought; Leigh had lost all sense when it came to this guy. She was leaving herself totally vulnerable.

"I don't think so. I think she's just a frightened and broken soul who nobody cares about."

He worked to keep his voice level. He didn't want a fight; he wanted her to be safe. "Leigh, really. That place is shut up tighter than Miami in a hurricane. How in the hell could she have seen *anything?*"

"She saw it, Brian. I believe her."

He turned away again and wiped a hand over his mouth. He had to make her see. "Okay, let's say she *did* see another car. That doesn't change the facts: Scott was the last person to see Brit. He worked on her car. It would have been easy enough for him to snag the keys to one of the vehicles left at the garage overnight. He could have used a car and returned it before Brownie or Rose knew it was gone.

"Did Mrs. Grissom say what kind of car?"

"White, four-door, mid-sized. There are hundreds that fit the description. Including Hale Grant's."

"Ah, Leigh, don't try to shift the focus to someone else again."

She had spoken the truth, but Brian made her feel small and spiteful. She held her tongue and watched as he paced the room for another moment.

He spun to face her, snapping his fingers. "Kate's car was in the shop the night Brit disappeared! Scott could easily have taken it out."

"And he could have stolen one and returned it before anyone knew it was missing. Or he could have used one of Ed Grissom's UFOs to transport her." This conversation was spiraling out of control. Leigh felt herself sliding down a long, loose-soiled bank. Grabbing wildly for a handhold to get them back on track she said, "Hattie said the man in the car had short hair — Will's is long."

Brian waved a hand in the air. "Will you listen to yourself! Jesus, Leigh, how much clearer does it have to be? You're basing your case on the testimony of a crazy old woman who *allegedly* saw the incident from some fifty yards away in the dark of night and said the man had short hair!"

"He didn't do it." At Brian's groan, she held up a hand. "Hear me out. I know he's hiding something in his past, but I don't believe it's criminal. I actually think he's a cop."

"You're insane."

"There's been plenty to tell me he's law — I'm just not sure in what capacity." She didn't dare voice her concern that Will might be here checking out Brian himself. "There are other factors that tell me Brit took off on her own — besides Hattie's testimony. Here's a girl who's been hurt and abandoned by the father who has spoiled her since the day she was born. She's been looking for a way to get his attention. I think she found a way to do it.

"You see, suddenly she dumps her boyfriend, abandons her friends, folds away all of the things in her room that speak of childhood. Her best friend thinks Brit was involved with an older man — you yourself admitted she liked older guys.

"Corey's hounds found no trace of her scent around the spot where the Camaro had been abandoned, there was no sign of her in the woods or on the roads.

"And the thing that seals the deal for me — I think Emma knows where she is."

"How do you get that?" From the look on his face, Leigh's insanity had been confirmed with her last statement.

"When I first told the Wilsons that Brittany might be missing, she was a wreck and stayed that way for a few days. When I saw her today — Brian, it was like she'd been reborn. She was relaxed, even rested. Sure, she tried to make a show of emotion, but no parent can completely forge that gut-eating panic that sets in when a child goes missing. She hasn't got it."

"You're making this sound like a conspiracy. Don't you want to add some government agency cover-up that's hiding Brittany away on a Caribbean island?"

"Make fun if you must. But that's not going to change the facts. The only foul play involved in this girl's disappearance is the deception she and her mother are perpetrating upon her father and the fact that this entire community is treating an innocent man like a pariah."

Brian shook his head slowly. It was clear he didn't buy a single word of what she'd said. There was a heavy sadness in his voice when he said, "Leigh, you're burying both of us here. And I don't think you even see the danger."

He turned and walked out.

Leigh stood looking at the open door, wondering how, in one week's time, her well-organized and uneventful life had turned into such a shit hole.

After a respectful amount of time, Francine crept into Leigh's office with the afternoon paper. "I know you get the paper at home, but thought you might want to see this right away." She laid a copy on Leigh's desk and left as if expecting the newspaper itself to explode.

Leigh picked it up. Francine had folded the article she wanted Leigh to see so it was on top.

Once again Grant had taken the indirect approach to getting his point across. The headline read: "Sheep's Clothing Doesn't Dull Wolf's Teeth." It was a long meandering article whose essence boiled down to a warning not to be fooled by certain acts of heroism and community service that most likely have been manufactured to create a woolly disguise for a true predator. He discussed the nasty habit some kidnappers and murderers have of becoming intimately involved in the investigation of the crime. That was all part of their high.

Leigh ripped the page from the paper and shoved it into the shredder. There was a childish satisfaction at seeing those hateful words cut into confetti.

There was only one way to change the rushing tide of public opinion — the most powerful force at work at the moment. She picked up the telephone and made the call she'd been considering most of the afternoon.

Chapter 21

Once finished with the calls, Leigh leaned back in her chair and stretched her arms over her head. As much as she knew she was taking the right course, it made her stomach churn just the same. There would be no going back now. This would either work, or she'd lose everything. She did feel badly that Brian was forced to play the same game of Russian roulette, but she had to do what was right, even if it cost her her job, her community, her brother.

If she could just get Emma to roll over, this could all be finished. But she still wasn't sure what tactic to use to get the woman to give up her secret. Leigh doubted her actions today would be enough. But maybe tomorrow it would come to her. For now, she'd done all she could to buy more time.

"Francine," Leigh said as she left her office, "I'm going to be out the rest of the day. Radio'll be on."

Francine looked up and nodded, sympathy in her eyes. *At least I have one ally,* Leigh thought as she left the building.

She drove straight to Brownie's.

Bypassing the office, she entered through the overhead doors. She found Will under a blue Toyota truck. She grabbed his ankles and pulled, the wheels of the creeper he was on squeaking in protest.

He sat up, knees bent, feet straddling the creeper, wiping his hands on a shop rag, looking not at all happy to see her.

"Here to make an arrest?" he asked.

"Of course not." Leigh tried to tell herself that his displeasure didn't bother her. "I came to tell you some news."

"Emma buckled?" For a brief second, the light of hope shone in his eyes.

"No. Not yet, but I'm working on that. I did, however, call the local news stations and tell them to announce that while we're still investigating, all signs point to Brittany having left on her own. I asked that they show her picture and encourage anyone who has seen her to contact us."

He shot to his feet. "Dammit, why? You know it's only a matter of time before either Brittany shows back up or Emma spills her guts. All this does is bring a whole truckful of trouble on your head."

"I had to do something. Things were getting out of hand."

He looked at her hard and long. "Listen to me. I don't need your help. I don't need you taking stupid risks for me. Things would have worked out on their own." He paused and looked angrier than Leigh had ever seen him. "You shouldn't have done it."

Without another word, he threw down the

rag and walked out of the garage, through the back door to the alley. A moment later, when Leigh had tamped down her anger enough to follow, he was nowhere in sight.

Ungrateful son of a bitch.

Leigh cut back through the garage to the front sidewalk. The yellow dog lay sleeping in the sun. He opened one eye.

"When you see him," she said, as she passed, "give him a good bite on the ass for me."

Rose was just leaving for the day through the front office door. Leigh nearly knocked the woman off her feet as she stormed past to reach her Blazer. Rose's purse did fall to the ground with a thump.

"Oh, Rose! I'm so sorry." Leigh bent to pick up the purse. "I wasn't watching where I was going."

"Not to worry. No harm done." She glanced toward the garage. "Here to see Will were you?"

My God, did she just wink at me? "I just had something to tell him."

"You know," Rose said, looking toward the garage herself, but her eyes seemed focused beyond it, "something's been nagging me about that boy since he got here."

Leigh made a noncommittal grumbling in the back of her throat. Something had been nagging her, too — but she doubted she and Rose shared the same troubles.

"I used to play bridge with Salma Beeson —

oh, she was much older than me; been gone nearly twenty years now. She had a great-nephew stay with her one summer shortly before she died. Will reminds me of that boy — the eyes."

That got Leigh's attention. "Was this boy a Beeson?"

Rose scrunched up her face and rolled in her lips. "Hmm. Don't think so. Can't recollect what his name was though — wasn't Scott. Think I'll ask Will next time I see him anyhow."

"You do that." She thought, *Then maybe I'll have something to go on to find out what in the hell he's doing here.*

By the time she pulled into her driveway, Leigh's head was throbbing and her stomach was trying to digest itself. Both ailments she gladly blamed on Will Scott.

Once inside, she downed four aspirin and got herself a bowl of cereal, forcing herself to eat without an appetite. For distraction she turned on the television. The national news was playing. She didn't really tune in to what was being said until she heard Henderson County, Indiana, mentioned.

The anchor said: "More tragedy in the heartland today. Last week eighteen-year-old Brittany Wilson disappeared from this quiet countryside. No leads have been forthcoming. Then, as the community was still frantically searching for the missing girl, a serious wildfire threatened the Hoosier National Forest, drawing all able hands into service." A video of footage of the fire from the air took over the screen, then came the shot of Will stumbling out of the woods with Beto. "One Hispanic migrant worker was lost in the fire zone, miraculously rescued by a single man who refused to give up, risking his own life to save that of another." The camera zoomed in on Will's face just before he turned his back to the camera. "Could the missing girl have been caught up in the wall of fire? Only time will tell."

Shit. Shit. Shit. Leigh's calls had been to local news stations. She hadn't even considered any of this receiving national coverage.

She pushed the cereal away. Goddamn national news. And Will had been spooked by local coverage. She wondered if he'd seen it.

Her telephone rang. She jumped to get it, hoping it was Will.

Kurt didn't even say hello before he started in. "I want this harassment of my wife to stop."

"What harassment?" She assumed he meant Emma, not his real wife.

"You've made public statements that are very damaging to my family. I want them retracted."

"Maybe you'd better check with 'your wife' before you press this further. Don't you find it odd that she's holding together so well — so much better than yourself?"

"Emma is a strong woman; she's being strong

for me." The defensiveness in his voice said he hadn't emotionally walked out on his wife of twenty years after all. "Stop trying to lay blame where it doesn't belong by slandering my family. Why are you doing this to us?"

"Calm down. I'm not targeting you. I don't have enough evidence to arrest *anybody*. Kurt, I really believe Brittany is okay — she took off on her own."

"Bullshit! You'll hear from my lawyer in the morning." He slammed the phone down so hard that Leigh had to pull the receiver away from her ear.

She put down the phone and buried her face in her hands. What if she was wrong? What if Brittany really was being held somewhere and Leigh just couldn't find the clues to lead her there? She would have not only let Brittany down, but ruined her own career and Brian's as well.

How could things get any worse?

Over the next hours, Leigh decided not to let her worry over Will's nasty reaction make her lose any more sleep. It was time to have it out — completely and conclusively. It was very late, but she dialed the phone anyway.

"Hello." Brownie's voice sounded slow and groggy.

"It's Leigh. Sorry to wake you, but I need to speak to Will."

"All right." The sound of rustling bedclothes was followed by bare feet thudding across hardwood floors.

Leigh could hear him knock and call Will's name. A hinge creaked. Then Brownie muttered something she couldn't quite make out. The feet returned.

"He's not here."

Leigh glanced at her watch, even though she was fully aware that it was near two A.M. "What do you mean he's not there? Is he out on the porch?"

"No." A heavy sigh preceded his next words. "He's gone, Leigh. Picked up and cleared out. Been actin' funny all evening — like a caged animal. I shoulda kept an ear open."

"Did he leave a note?"

"Nope. Just a fifty-dollar bill on his pillow."

Leigh thought she heard that bill being crushed in Brownie's big, calloused hand. She felt like her heart was being crumpled, too.

"Dog's gone, too," Brownie added, as if that was the final undeniable proof.

"Okay, thanks."

Gone. Just like that. No good-bye. No explanation.

She'd put everything she held dear on the line for him. Now he was gone.

God, she was such a fool.

Chapter 22

Leigh spent the next several hours vacillating between drowning in broken-hearted humiliation and pacing the floor in roiling anger. It amazed her that she could swing so wildly from moment to moment, easily justifying each mood. She worried for Will's safety. In an alternate moment, she wanted to thrash him within an inch of his life for taking off without a word to her. Didn't he know how this would look to the community? What position he placed her in by taking off?

Leigh sat on her front porch swing and watched the sky lighten with a new day. She dragged herself inside and took a shower, then headed to the office. She wished there was some way to avoid the day. Once word got around that Will had disappeared, all of the advantage she'd hoped to gain by making her public statement would have evaporated. She'd done it for nothing.

Before Leigh even settled in behind her desk, a call came for her from the FBI. Damn, Kurt must have some clout to get a reaction this quickly. Her mind was hurriedly assembling her presentation of the Wilson case, so it took a moment for it to sink in that the agent calling was from the Washington, D.C., office and had nothing to do with Brittany.

"Sheriff Mitchell, you recently queried our department concerning fingerprint identification of a possible member of our organization."

"Yes." Here it was. Her heart hurried its beat. She had just known Will worked for one of the federal organizations.

"As you know, we cannot divulge information concerning our operatives in the field."

She wanted to snap, *So why in the hell are you bothering me!* But she managed to maintain a civil tone. "Are you implying this individual *does* work for your department?"

"No, I wouldn't be permitted to say that. But we do have an interest in this person's whereabouts. Is he still in your jurisdiction?"

Leigh was in no mood to follow this vague, bureaucratic dance: just try to figure out what you need to know by what I'm *not* saying. "No. And I have no idea where he's gone."

"When did he disappear?"

" 'Disappear' is a pretty weighty word to use for a citizen of legal age who's just decided to move on down the road. Is this individual wanted for a crime? I have a right to know; I have a community to protect here." She couldn't keep the edge out of her voice.

"We simply need to locate him. He's no threat to your community."

Maybe not to the community, Leigh thought, but he'd certainly wrought havoc in her personal life. "I don't know when he left or where he was going."

There was a pregnant pause on the other end of the line. "We know he was there two days ago. If he turns up, or contacts you, call my office." It was an order, not a request. He rattled off a number. "And, Sheriff?"

"Yes?"

"This is a high priority case for us. Time is of the essence."

"I have your number."

They signed off. Leigh sat staring into space for several minutes before she could force herself to move again. "What on earth are you into, Will?" Not an FBI agent. Not a criminal. But the FBI wants to know where he is. Will running again. That left a vast realm of unpleasant possibilities. She rubbed the heels of her hands over her scratchy, sleep-deprived eyes and wished for the throbbing in her head to reduce itself to the equivalent of a marching band prancing on her brain.

For the first time she noticed the envelope on her desk. Brian had written her name across the front in his chicken-scratch and sealed it. It held something too bulky to be a simple letter.

She tore it open, pulled out a note: *Take my advice — get out of here and spend the weekend in my cabin. Get some rest. Maybe your mind will clear.*

What he meant was, maybe she'd get her head out of her ass.

Turning the envelope upside down, a key

tumbled out, making a little thud as it hit the blotter on her desktop. It may as well have been a wall crashing down for the way Leigh started at the sound. Maybe she *should* hide out for the weekend — although not for the reasons Brian intended. There were so many questions to be answered. Where did the FBI fit into the mystery of Will Scott? Damn his hide. And how was she going to get Emma Wilson to admit that she knew where her daughter was? Would there be any way to repair the rift she'd caused between Kurt and Brian? Then the ever incessant buzzing in her head that said maybe she was wrong — maybe Brittany was kidnapped. Maybe Leigh had allowed her emotional entanglement with Will to blind her — seeing only what she wanted to see.

How could she have been so stupid?

Perhaps solitude would help her focus, sort out her emotions from the rest of this mess.

Besides, after yesterday evening's news, she feared the next few hours would bring a barrage of complaints from the people of Glens Crossing and the circling of Hale Grant and his legion of media vultures. Hiding out at Brian's cabin was getting more appealing by the second.

Just as she was straightening her desk, a knock sounded on her door. She fully intended to clear the hell out of here before much more of the day passed. She hoped whatever was on the other side of the door wouldn't take too long.

"Come in."

Expecting one of her own, Leigh blinked in surprise to see an unfamiliar man holding a U.S. marshal's badge in front of him step through her door.

"Can I help you?"

The man resembled a large brown bear, deep-chested and broad-shouldered. He extended one huge hand. "Bruce Littlejohn, U.S. Marshal."

Leigh could not have picked a more improbable name for this man had she worked on it all day. Biting her tongue to keep from laughing, she knew she was quickly slipping over the edge. The crumbling cliff of sanity shook under her feet. She needed sleep. She needed distance. Soon each and every event, no matter how sobering, would be met with a wild cackle and a mad rolling of the eyes.

She took a deep breath, keeping her lips pressed tightly together and shook his hand. "Leigh Mitchell."

He nodded and smiled. Each one of the sparkling teeth set in that huge jaw looked as large as a piano key.

"Please, have a seat."

As he sat, he pulled a picture out of his shirt pocket. "I understand this man" — he tossed the photo on her desk in front of Leigh — "has been in Glens Crossing."

Leigh's breath stuck in her lungs. Staring up at her was Will Scott, hair considerably longer, face less lean, but those blue eyes just the same.

She started to tremble and forced herself to become still.

"Who is he?" she asked in a remarkably even tone.

The marshal leaned back in his chair and laced his fingers over his broad middle. "That's not important. What is important is that we find him — and soon."

"For what?"

"I'm not at liberty to say. Just understand he in no way presents a danger to your community."

That seemed to be a recurring theme this morning. "I see." She saw very clearly. Federal law was after Will and, in some capacity, he was one of their own. Now that left two possibilities: 1) they wanted to put him in jail, or 2) they wanted him to testify.

"What can you tell me about him?" Marshal Littlejohn's eyes probed deeply, as if he expected her to be holding something back. Or, Leigh thought, maybe that was just her guilty imagination working.

"Little more than you're telling me. He was here. Now he's gone." She cut her hand through the air, mimicking a vanishing act.

"When did he leave?"

She leaned forward and folded her hands over the picture. "What makes you think I've been keeping such close tabs on the man?"

Marshal Littlejohn ignored her question. "We know he was helping with the fire."

Leigh's gaze sharpened. TV coverage. "I only saw him briefly after that. I don't know when he left." Not a lie.

"Sheriff, this man could be in serious danger if I don't find him."

Funny that Will would hide from someone trying to protect him. There had to be much more. First the FBI, now a U.S. marshal.

"Leave me your card." Leigh extended a palm. "I'll call if he comes back."

Fishing a card from his pocket, the marshal rose and placed it in Leigh's open hand. "We appreciate your assistance in this matter." He paused. "What name is he currently going by?"

She stood and tried to smile confidently, but her insides were writhing like a sack full of snakes. "Scott, I believe." She offered her hand. "I'll be in touch if I learn anything."

He left and closed the door behind him. Leigh collapsed onto her chair and pressed her palms to her temples, countering the threat of an exploding skull. One of those mad thoughts crept into her mind. She could see herself as a cartoon, easing her hands away from her throbbing head, resting them gently in her lap, a smile on her face as her head remained intact — up until the next moment when gray matter splattered her office walls.

"God, I've got to get out of here."

Driving out of town, Leigh felt like someone escaping from one of those grim prisons in a futuristic movie. One of those places where the last of the truly good were unjustly hunted and incarcerated. She actually found herself looking in her rearview mirror as the last stoplight receded from view, half-expecting a crew of leather-and-chain clad, spiky-haired, heavily tattooed minions of the current evil dictator to be fast approaching on dusty, black Harley-Davidsons. After the last few days, the evolution of ever-worsening events had made her own world as strange as any screenwriter's fiction.

She needed distance. Solitude. With each passing mile, the grayness fell away, layer by depressing layer, until her surroundings were once again colored with normal hues, peopled with average citizens.

That lasted until she entered the blackened and charred fire area. Once again she was catapulted into a bleak, ravaged post-Armageddon world where hope bore no fruit. Where quiet towns and true love had been wiped cleanly from the face of the planet.

That thought startled her. Did she want love? She had begun her relationship with Will wanting nothing more than a little adventure. Now adventure seemed greatly overrated. She longed for something more profound, more fulfilling. Something everlasting. Will had given her a glimpse of the woman she wanted to be. Had touched her soul more deeply than any man ever had, awakened passions she had no idea she held. Passions that currently ripped and tore at her heart until it lay open and bleeding in her chest. His heartless departure left her questioning her very essence. Wrong. She'd been so wrong.

All of this emotional confusion was counter-productive, she told herself, as she stretched the tension out of her neck muscles. There were serious decisions to be made, questions that had to be answered. In order to focus she had to clear her mind of thoughts of love and betrayal. She turned on the radio, opened the windows of the Blazer wide and let the wind carry away her thoughts.

The gravel lane that led to Brian's secluded cabin curved through dense woods undisturbed by the fire. As Leigh pulled beside the front porch, the only sign of the recent disaster was a fine dusting of gray ash on the horizontal surfaces of the floor, railing and steps. Unlike many lakeside homes, this one wasn't log or cedar. Built around 1910, it had one-and-a-half stories with deep eaves, a rock foundation, small-paned windows and yellow lapboard siding with white trim. Brian even had the roof shingles replaced with the original color of hunter green. It would have been a real loss if this had burned. The newer homes could be replaced, but this was one of a kind.

Thankful that the cottage had been spared, Leigh carried groceries up the steps and unlocked the front door. The lower level was basically one room, an L-shape that ran across the front and included a kitchen in the back corner. Behind the narrow staircase running parallel to the width of the front room was a small bath and laundry area. The entire interior was covered in white painted bead-board, including the ceilings.

She dragged in her suitcase, locked the door behind her and put the groceries away. Then she walked away from the kitchen, put her hand on the square newel post and climbed the creaking stairs. It wasn't quite five o'clock, but the rose-flowered bedspread in the dormered spare room was calling her. Just a short nap, then she'd prepare herself a nice dinner and treat herself to the Janet Evanovich novel she'd tucked in her suitcase at the last minute. No more contemplating her problems tonight. Tomorrow she'd tackle everything with a fresh outlook.

Opening the window, she collapsed on the bed, certain her thoughts would never allow her to escape into sleep. She'd give herself twenty minutes, then get up.

Time moved on without her. Leigh shivered as cool air moved across her skin. Curling into a tight ball, she thought absently that she should get up and close the window. Then she pushed that thought away and allowed dreams of brisk days, blue skies and fall leaves to once again draw her into their calming fold.

Quivering muscles drew her back to the state

of near consciousness. Through a half-slitted eye, she registered that the room had darkened. Burying her face in her pillow, she relished her last bit of rest. She rubbed her arms and turned over. So cold. She wanted to get up, close the window, crawl under the blanket, but her mind was mired helplessly in a shroud of sleep. As she shivered, the dream drew her deeper; the sun warmed the rock upon which she was lying. It wrapped her in a blanket of pure warmth. Slowly her body relaxed.

A creak from the floor beside her bed shot panic through her veins. The dream evaporated. Gasping, she sat bolt upright on the bed and reached for the light.

A hand locked on her wrist. "Don't."

Her heart did a stutter-step. "Will?" She remembered to breathe. Her heart continued pumping adrenaline to the far reaches of her body. Her mind shuffled wildly through the possibilities his presence could mean.

"Shhhh." He eased her back on the bed and sat beside her. The rocker next to the bed continued to move as if he'd just jumped out of it, the slight gleam of the moon sliding back and forth on the slats of the back.

How long? How long had he been here?

"It's okay," he murmured. A warm hand rested on her brow.

She became cognizant of the fact that she was cocooned in the quilt that normally lay folded on the back of the rocker.

"How did you get in?" The doors had all been dead bolted and the downstairs windows latched. Brian believed in locked doors. And Leigh was much more careful with his property than her own.

There was enough light coming from the three-quarter moon through the east-facing window that she could see his features now. He smiled — an eerily cold sight in the bluish light.

"I'm good with locks. One of my gifts."

There was something in his voice, the way he said "gifts," that reminded her of his steely detachment beside the creek that first night. He'd told her then if he'd meant her harm she'd be carrying her head. It was simple enough to deduce, since her head was still firmly attached, he hadn't come here to harm her. Leigh reminded herself that Will was a man possessing two distinct sides: one passionate and gentle, the other calculating and lethal. She'd managed to focus on what she wanted to see, blocking out the man who'd held a knife to her throat. Powerful. Deadly.

She told herself, Will's darker nature had a reason. She needed to find out just what that reason was.

Although she wanted to lambaste him for sneaking out of town in the dark of night, leaving her holding the bag, she said, "What do you want?"

"I had to see you again." His tone held

nothing of the longing she'd secretly hoped for. If fact, he sounded quite matter-of-fact.

"Why? You didn't see fit to say anything before you crept off in the night — like a criminal." Leigh grabbed onto that spark of anger, shutting out the little voice that said he never led her to believe the end would be anything other that exactly that — gone. She looked away from him, so he couldn't see the tears in her eyes reflect the moonlight. "You shouldn't have come back."

He put a hand on her shoulder. She shrugged it off.

"I had to make sure you understand exactly what kind of person I am — I don't want you living with misbegotten illusions, clinging to something that can never be. I never planned —" He paused and she heard his throat work a dry swallow. "I never wanted . . ."

"What?" she snapped, jerking to a sitting position on the bed. "You never wanted what, Will?" Her patience with this illusive dance was wearing thin.

He drew in a deep breath, held it, then Leigh heard it leave him in a rush. He stood and paced the width of the small bedroom. The ceilings in the second story were uncommonly low; Will appeared oversized for the room. A shaft of silver moonlight glinted off his hair and cast his shadow on the wall. He scrubbed his hands over his face, then ran his fingers into his hair, looking like he was trying to, with the force of his bare hands, keep something from escaping his brain.

"I'm so fucked." He said it so softly and with so much pain that Leigh wasn't sure if he intended for her to hear. So she resisted the urge to get up, wrap her arms around him and lay her head on his chest. Gone was her momentary anger. She wanted to tell him no matter what the circumstances, she would help him through. No matter what had so marked his past, she would be there for him.

Instead, she sat silent on the bed, heart rioting in her chest, unsure what words would make him close up and flee again.

Suddenly, he spun, grabbed her hand and pulled her off the bed. "Let's get out of here. I need some air."

Leigh stumbled along behind him. The only sound was the complaining of the old risers under their weight as they descended the stairs. Will walked out the front door and let go of her hand. He nearly seemed to forget she was there as he slowly walked across the lawn and down the length of the narrow dock extending into the lake.

She followed behind, barefooted, dewy grass cold under her feet. She stopped before she reached the water's edge, near the boat shed, a place built for oars and floatation devices. Suddenly she felt like she needed one of those life vests.

The dock was empty; Brian had yet to purchase a boat. The wooden planks were grayed and worn. A giant sycamore blocked most of the moon's light. In the darkness it nearly appeared that Will walked on water. Leigh shook off the shiver that image created and picked her way along the dock, wary of splinters in her bare feet. Stopping behind him, close enough that she felt the heat from his back, she resisted the urge to slip her hands around his waist. She stood, waiting, until he was ready to talk.

Bull frogs croaked, crickets chirped and whined, a fish jumped in the lake creating a delicate splash, but Will remained silent. The defeated set of his shoulders reminded her of the way he walked into Brownie's house after the ordeal with Beto and the television camera. In her mind, she couldn't shut out the echo of his broken words, *"It's me."*

Leigh's hand hovered in the air, ready to touch his shoulder, when he spoke. "You know I didn't harm Brittany, but it doesn't matter. I have other blood on my hands."

Leigh froze.

He didn't turn to look at her, so she stepped in front of him, inches away from the end of the dock. "I think you're still a cop."

His gaze jerked to her face, the whites of his eyes admitting she had hit the nail on the head.

Putting a hand on his cheek, she said, "Explain to me."

His eyes closed and he breathed deeply. He slowly removed her hand from his face and dropped it at her side.

"I've lived in the sewer so long, there's no getting the stink out of my nose. I won't poison you with what I've done."

This time Leigh tried the opposite approach. He didn't want her to touch him, so she let him know she wanted to be touched. Taking his hand, she placed it over her heart, resting on her breast. He tensed, as if to pull away, but she pressed harder, keeping it in place. "I know you —"

He made a disgusted noise and tried again to remove his hand. She held tight.

"I may not know where you came from, how you've lived — but I know *you*." She choked on the words, swallowed the lump rising in her throat and pushed on. "I've seen deep inside you — when you slept, as you looked out for that dog, when you risked your life in the fire to save those children's father. You knew the risk of exposure, yet you did it anyway."

"You don't know me!" He jerked hard, successfully pulling his hand from her. Cold immediately penetrated her chest where its warmth used to be. "You don't know what I've done. You live here in this cozy burg, among decent people —"

"Goddammit, Will!" She thrust a finger toward shore. "The freaking dog even knows you!" The yellow dog sat at attention, a light blob against the blackness of the grass near the dock. Leigh stopped and pulled herself together. "They say animals know the true nature of a person. I'd say that guy over there is testament of your worth. I'm testament to it. I care about you! Now explain to me what's going on."

"Too many people have died because of me. I have to make those sacrifices mean something." He spun and grabbed her shoulders. "I don't have a life of my own — I probably never will. Don't you understand, Leigh? I don't *want* you to care."

She held his gaze, unflinching. "Too late," she said softly. She wanted to touch his face, but his brutal grip held her arms at her sides. "Too late." This time her voice was no more than a whisper.

"Christ, forgive me!" He crushed her to his chest, wrapping his arms tightly around her and pressed his face into her hair.

Leigh put her arms around his waist. She breathed in the scent of him, absorbed his warmth, willed him never to release her. His chest rose and fell with rapid breaths, his body trembled.

"I love you, Leigh." He said it so quietly that Leigh suspected her own imagination had created the words. Then he repeated it. "I love you." He kissed her forehead. "But it doesn't change anything."

She started to protest, but he silenced her with a kiss. His mouth found hers, roughly at first, then gentling as he slid his hands into her

417

hair. She tasted the bittersweetness of the moment, felt the moisture of the tears on his cheek, and knew nothing would be the same for her ever again. He was kissing her good-bye.

Cradling her face in his hands, he looked at her for a long moment. "I want to remember you like this." His lips feathered a kiss on each brow. "How you're looking at me right now. Because when I tell you what I have to say, that look will be gone."

She covered his hands with her own, turning her head to kiss his palm. "Nothing you could tell me will change how I feel."

He pulled his hands away and turned his back to her again. Sighing, he began: "Just over two years ago I went undercover for the DEA. I've spent the time since living with people who make my skin crawl, doing things that have permanently stained my soul — things I can never repeat to anyone, not even you."

A jolt of recognition ran through her and she finally understood his true sacrifice. "That's why you weren't around when your sister died." It was too horrible to be true. Will had devoted his adult life to thwarting the drug trade, only to have his own sister one of its victims.

He rubbed his face, nearly obscuring his words. "I was out chasing the bad guys in South America while the wolf was in my own backyard." He exhaled, as if he could blow the memories away. "I couldn't go home — couldn't even send flowers for her funeral. Not without endangering the operation — and everyone back home."

Leigh heard him swallow and she felt the sting of tears in her eyes.

He went on: "For years I've lived on false emotion, wearing smiles I didn't feel, being someone I'm not. Burying myself so deeply I never thought I'd truly feel again." He half-turned to look at her. "But you make me feel. I don't know if I can take it. There's so much . . ."

Looking back over the lake, he said through clenched teeth, "I was so close!" He clenched his hand into a fist and raised it halfway. "Within days of having all I needed to completely unravel the cartel. We were still in Colombia, readying a shipment. Miguel Aznar, the head of the cartel, was going to head to Miami via his own jet. I was to accompany the cocaine in a sea plane for a rendezvous with a boat offshore. Then I was to meet Aznar at his Miami home. Once I had him on U.S. soil it was going to be over.

"About eleven o'clock the night before we were to leave, Aznar, two of his other 'trusted' underlings and I were sitting beside his pool, smoking expensive cigars and drinking even more expensive scotch. They were calculating the staggering profits the next day would bring. I couldn't stomach the conversation, so I just sat there doing my own mental calculations — like how many years this dick was going to spend behind bars once I had him in court. I couldn't wait to see his face when I got on the witness stand.

"There was a commotion out in the front drive. I went to inspect. All of the guards hurried toward a military-style truck as it pulled up to a stop. In the back there had to be eight or nine men, bloodied, blindfolded and bound. Aznar's goons had rounded up those they suspected posed a threat to the cartel. I recognized a couple of the kids; they'd been running their own operation on the fringes of Aznar's — cutting out the middleman, so to say. By the time I saw them, they didn't need blindfolds. Their eyes were swollen shut."

Will paused and massaged his forehead between his thumb and forefinger.

"There was nothing I could do to help them. Christ, they couldn't have been over seventeen."

Leigh put a hand on his back. "They were breaking the law, Will. There's nothing for you to feel guilty about."

He rounded on her. Leaning close, he said through gritted teeth, "You think kids get these ideas on their own? They'd been sucked into that cesspool and never had a chance." He straightened and closed his eyes. "Besides, they aren't the issue. There was another man, in his twenties. I'd known his cover was going to be blown the instant I'd seen him a month before. He was working from another angle and somehow had ended up in the same place as me. But he was too green, too unprepared for the assignment. But I didn't warn him — too afraid to compromise my own cover.

"He was the last to be executed. The last to fall into the mass grave."

"My God. I'm so sorry, Will. But it wasn't your fault."

He went on as if he hadn't heard her. "He knelt there, crying like a child. I think he had me made by then — I saw the accusation, the pleading in his gaze as the gun was pressed to the back of his head. I'll have to give him credit, he didn't blow my cover. I think he realized it wouldn't save him anyway. Suddenly his gaze hardened and he nodded. I knew he wanted me to do what he could not. Fry these bastards.

"It's what he said before he died that made me come back here tonight."

Leigh sniffled back her tears and asked in a tight squeak, "What?"

"His last words were, 'Why didn't I tell her?' He was looking straight at me when he said it. 'She'll never know I loved her.' "

Leigh threw herself into his arms and was relieved when they tightened around her. "Oh, Will. I'm so sorry. I'm so very sorry."

"You see," he said in a choked whisper, "he owns my life now. I can't let him down." He made soothing noises and rubbed her back. "I decided those weren't going to be my last words. If I'm going to die, I'm not going to do it with things left unsaid."

Leigh strangled on a sob. "They're after you." Now she understood why Will was so worried about the television coverage. Everyone in that cartel had to be gunning for him. If he didn't make it to court, there'd be no case, no justice.

She remembered the U.S. marshal's visit earlier today. Looking up at him, she sniffed. "There's a marshal looking for you. I've got his number. I'll call him and we can arrange for you to be taken someplace safe."

He brushed away her tears with his thumbs and looked into her eyes. He spoke to her as if he was explaining the cruel facts of life to a child. "There is no safe place. Two marshals died trying to prove there was. I escaped by sliding down the garbage chute. No, Leigh, the only way I can do this is alone. I think I can make it to court in one piece; I've got the date. After that . . ." He shrugged.

"After that, you'll still be a marked man."

"Depends on the outcome of the trial. If we can successfully break up the cartel, then there won't be anyone left to come after me. Those further down on the ladder will move on — other cartels, start up their own."

"God, it sounds so fruitless!" She pounded her fists against his chest.

"It is. You have to start somewhere. If you don't stamp out a few occasionally, they'll overrun the world."

How could he be so complacent about the sacrifice he was making? How could he function with this shadow hanging over his head? Starting somewhere just didn't get it for Leigh. She wanted results — solid, gratifying, irreversible, permanent results.

"You're never coming back, are you?"

A groan came from deep in his chest. "I can't."

This time, Leigh wasn't able to choke back her sob. She cried, blubbered on his shoulder like a baby. He rubbed her back and whispered comforting sounds in her ear, making her feel ashamed and selfish. His was the life forfeited, and here he was consoling her. Her shame made her cry harder.

He pulled her face from his shoulder and kissed her, robbing her of her breath, her strength. When he stopped, she collapsed against his chest. His heart sounded strong and steady, a clear contrast to the frantic beating of her own. He'd come to terms with his fate — the fact that his life had been stolen.

"How will I know you're okay?" she whispered.

"Because I always am. I got myself into this box because I let my heart speak louder than my brain. It won't happen again — I'm leaving my heart here, with you."

Suddenly she pushed him away. "You son of a bitch! This might be all fine and dandy for you — waltzing in here, unloading this on me so you can die — or whatever — with a clear conscience. But what about me?" She jabbed a finger at her breastbone. "What if it's not okay with me for you to tell me all this and just give up on us? What if I want more? You've made all the choices, decided how it's going to be, without a shred of input from me. Maybe I want to take the risk and wait."

He grabbed her shoulders. "Don't you understand? I might *never* have my life back! I won't spend the rest of it thinking of you, sitting here, growing old alone because of me."

"Well, I just don't see how you have any say over it. You might be used to making these monumental decisions and living by them, but you can't make them for me. If I want to spend the rest of my days sitting in my jammies on my fucking porch swing, watching the driveway for your return, there isn't a damn thing you can do about it!"

"God, you're beautiful when you're mad." He reached for her, but she spun away.

"Now I see you're probably not worth it. I won't be waiting. But not because you told me not to. You're just too damn infuriating."

He tried for her again. She stepped out of his reach, and off the end of the dock.

The shock of the cold water smacked some sense into her. Why was she wasting time arguing, when he'd be gone by morning? As she worked toward the surface, she decided to take him straight to bed. That thought vanished when her head bobbed out of the water and her ears were filled with raucous laughter.

That son of a bitch.

Will knelt on the dock, extending a hand to pull her out of the water, laughing so hard he was losing his breath.

She firmly grabbed one of the pilings under the dock with one hand as she reached for him with her other. When he shifted his weight to give her some lift, she jerked him headfirst into the lake.

To her surprise, he didn't release her hand, but pulled her under with him. When they surfaced, he had one arm hooked around her back, pulling her face close to his as they treaded water. "Dirty tricks never go unpunished."

Dog had run to the end of the dock and was carrying on like a mother hen.

"I'm okay!" Will shouted. "Go lay down."

To Leigh's amazement the dog quieted and walked back to shore. "I hope you don't think I'm going to be so obedient."

"I think you've adequately ruined that particular illusion."

"Glad to hear it."

His free hand slid under her shirt and unfastened her bra. "Better get these clothes off before we both drown."

"Wouldn't it be smarter just to get out of the lake?"

"Smarter. Not more fun."

"You're not going to punish me by taking off

with my clothes are you?"

"Hardly do me any good. Not a soul around for miles. So you're naked, big deal."

As she peeled off her saturated clothes she said, "I'll show you it is a big deal." It was a struggle but she managed to flop her wet jeans, shirt and bra onto the dock. She didn't remember it being so damn tiring when she'd had to strip down to her underwear in the water during lifesaving class. Panting like she'd just finished a fifty-meter butterfly she said, "Now you."

To her frustration, he was barely breathing hard when his jeans joined hers.

Will backed her against the dock piling, and grabbed the dock on either side of her so he didn't have to keep treading. Then he found a toe hold on the piling itself, allowing Leigh to straddle his knee and keep her head above water.

Kissing her, he rubbed his leg between her thighs. "You still have your panties on," he said against her mouth. "That'll never do."

She knew by the feel of him against her thigh that his boxers must have landed with the jeans.

He slid a hand inside her panties to cup her backside. "My God, Leigh, this water's freezing and you've got me ready to break out in a sweat."

That admission gave her a spark of satisfaction. Her nipples were ultra-erect from the cold. She grabbed onto the dock and raised herself until her breasts crested right at the surface. It didn't require any explanation. Will's mouth immediately found a nipple. The delicious contrast his warm mouth made to the chill sent heat exploding straight from her core; it felt like those little shoots from Fourth of July sparklers — blue-white, cold-looking, yet hot to touch.

Then he disappeared under the water. He freed her from her panties and his mouth initiated the same hot-cold explosion between her legs. She'd never been so painfully aroused. Then conscious thought penetrated the sensual fog. How long could he hold his breath? She hoped a little longer — unwilling to give up the sensation quite yet.

He brought her dangerously close to climax before he came up for air. When he kissed her, he tasted of lake water and her own arousal.

"I'd love to return the favor." Her voice sounded breathy. "But I'm afraid I'll drown."

"Can't have that." He hoisted himself out of the water, onto the dock. Leigh watched the water run off the length of his back and legs as he did.

Reaching down, he plucked her out of the water. He started to lead her back to the cottage, but she stopped him. It was even chillier out in the night air and would probably offer similar contrast. Kneeling before him, she treated him to the newly discovered wonders of temperature disparity. She knew it did as much for him as it did for her when he buried his hands in her tangled, wet hair and gasped.

Then he pulled her away. "Better get in the house while I can still walk. Much more and I'm going to be no more than a puddle of muscle and skin."

He picked her up and carried her to the house. Leigh smiled in the darkness, unable to express the giddiness in her own heart.

They made love under the rose print comforter, quickly banishing the chill of wet skin and night air. Leigh occasionally caught herself in a morose moment, missing him already, but quickly chased those thoughts off. There would be plenty of time for sadness later — maybe years and years.

When they settled into a sated embrace, Leigh vowed to remain awake all night. She had the rest of her life to sleep, and the only sure thing with Will was this moment. She spent time memorizing his profile, his roguish hair, his dark lashes against his cheek in slumber, the relaxed softness of his lips. Tracing them with her finger, she whispered, "You can't make me not wait for you."

As she unwillingly slipped into sleep, all she could see was his face when he'd said he loved her. She ducked into darkness before she could hear the rest, the part where he said it didn't change anything.

Chapter 23

The riotous chatter of birds brought Leigh awake in the gray hours of the morning. She reached for Will and her hand landed on something cool and wet. Jerking upright, she saw a single dewy rose on his pillow — yellow, from the trellis in the side yard. Picking up the flower, she brushed the moist petals against her lips, then breathed in its sweet scent. She'd thought it too late for roses. And Will had thought it too late for them. This rose proved one thing — anything was possible.

Folded like a tent on the nightstand was a sheet of paper from the legal pad downstairs. If she ignored it, she could pretend Will hadn't left, that he was just out on the dock, waiting for the sunrise. She rolled onto her side so she could look out the window and held the rose to her heart.

By the time she forced herself to pick up the note, the sun streamed brightly through the window. With lead in her stomach, she opened the page. She smiled; Will didn't write in cursive, but had a draftsman's hand at printing — clear and bold.

Leigh,
    I kissed you goodbye before I left. You

wrinkled your nose and swatted me away. I don't take it personally.

There isn't much left to say. You know how I feel. You know my life. Please don't bury yourself in stubbornness and wait for something that, no matter how much I want it, can never be.

I had to put Dog in the boathouse to keep him from following me. I know you'll take care of him. I've had a chat with him; he's promised to look after you.

Wherever I go, I'll carry you with me in my heart.

Be happy.

Will

Leigh wrapped the bed sheet around her, picked up the rose and tucked it behind her ear, then walked outside. Her jeans, shirt and bra were spread on the porch railing to dry. She shivered at the thought of Will dragging on wet clothes and walking off in the pre-dawn darkness.

Dog must have heard her approach because scratching sounded against the inside of the shed door as she neared.

"Okay, boy. Here I come."

Lifting the simple latch, Leigh had to jump back as the door immediately swung outward, a blur of yellow fur flying by. Dog made a circle around her, then explored the yard, sniffing the ground, Leigh supposed in search of Will. That could pose a problem. If the dog was any kind of tracker, he'd catch up with Will in a matter of hours. That was unless Will caught a ride out on the highway. Better not take any chances.

She called the mutt, to no avail. He actually behaved as if he were stone deaf. She clapped her hands and cavorted in a circle, holding up the trailing ends of the sheet. She realized that she must look like a nymph in *A Midsummer Night's Dream* and, although there wasn't a soul for miles, tempered her actions.

Her efforts to draw the dog near enough in play to grab that pitiful excuse for a leash he still wore were wasted. Dog kept his sniffer to the ground. He was slowly working his way toward the drive.

Next she tried creeping up on him, slow and easy, hoping to grab the stubby leash. Settling her foot silently in the grass, which seemed foolish since the dog seemed not to hear anything at the moment, she got closer and closer . . . until she figured she could reach. Her fingers inched nearer to the leather tab. Almost there. Just as she closed in on that final inch and closed her fist, Dog leapt out of reach, leaving Leigh with a handful of air.

For the next few minutes they played a game of like-charged magnets. Every advance she made resulted in an equal retreat by the canine. And he seemed to be enjoying himself immensely.

"Enough of this." She hurried back into the house and emerged with a half-pound of ground chuck she'd intended on grilling. Starting by lobbing a small amount of burger in front of Dog's nose, she managed to lure him closer, until he nudged his nose right in the butcher's paper.

"Don't feel bad. All men are ruled by their stomachs," she said as she ruffled the fur on his neck. "Well, that and another lower body part." She assumed the same applied to unneutered dogs. "Now, let's see . . ." She kept a hold on the "leash" and went back inside the shed. "This oughta do." Taking a length of rope, she threaded it through the collar and led Dog with her to the end of the dock.

She dangled her feet in the water and watched the sun sparkle on the faint ripples in the lake. Dog settled next to her and she absently stroked his head. This was a deep lake whose bottom fell off quickly. The level had dropped with the drought, but not as much as had been predicted. A narrow band of yellow-brown dried mud showed all around the shoreline.

"Do you think we'll ever see him again?" The dull ache that started in her chest when her hand found the rose in her bed had developed into a sharp, gouging pain. *This must be how it feels to have your heart cut out with a spoon.*

Dog inched closer and licked her hand.

"Thanks for the comfort."

Just then, something rubbed against her ankle. Leigh jerked her legs out of the water, sending Dog skittering to his feet, nails clacking on the dock. She looked down fully expecting to see a snake winding through the water.

Laughter bubbled out as she reached down to pluck her pink panties from where they'd caught on the piling. She held the dripping lace in front of her face, her laughter catching in her throat and coming out as tears.

She wasn't sure how long she sat there and cried, wet panties wadded in one hand, yellow rose tucked behind her ear, Dog's head on her lap. But the sound of a bass boat near the far shore brought her back to her senses. She picked up the edges of the sheet so she didn't trip and walked back to shore. She paused to tie the dog to the porch rail, then headed back into the cottage, to her real life and the search for breaking Emma's silence.

As Leigh sat in the cottage's living room sorting through the possibilities for the man who could have helped Brittany set up her disappearing act, Hale Grant again popped into her mind. That slimy little bastard had rubbed her the wrong way from the beginning of this whole ordeal. Could he have been hiding Brittany all this time? Then she had to ask herself, if Grant was the one involved with Brittany, why keep it such a secret? He wasn't married. Brittany was eighteen. Big deal.

Then it hit her. Why hadn't she thought of this before?

Kurt Wilson was one of the major stockholders in their small, local paper. Pissing off Brittany's daddy could well be the death of Grant's illustrious career in Glens Crossing. If he and Brittany cooked up this scenario to gain attention — hers from her father, his from the news media in general — then how did they anticipate this to conclude? There could be no mutually beneficial outcome, as far as Leigh could see. And, as much as she wanted to grab onto this line of thinking, tie Hale Grant into the scheme, something just didn't ring true.

Leigh took a mental step back and looked at it from another angle. Maybe it was no accident that Brittany waited until near quitting time to go and have the only stranger in town check out a complaint on her car. Maybe part of her plan all along was to set Will up. That might explain why the Speedway Museum ticket just happened to be lying on the road. But how did this scheme work with a man without a car? Could she have actually thought that far ahead, that Will would have access to the keys of the automobiles in the shop? A little shiver ran down her spine. Could this girl have been so calculating?

The phone rang. Leigh stared at it, deciding whether or not to pick up. Francine was the only one who knew where she was. Of course,

Brian probably figured it out if he called and she wasn't at home or the office. And she just didn't feel up to sparring with Brian at the moment.

In the end, she answered. To her relief it was Francine, telling her that the computer guy in the state police lab had finished and was faxing a list of Brittany's e-mail addresses and records of activity.

So much for solitude. All in all, she'd spent a total of about three hours alone since she'd gotten here. Although many of her questions had been answered with Will's visit, there still remained the burden of discovering exactly what had happened to Brittany. This could be the break she needed.

She quickly gathered her belongings and locked the cottage door behind her. She untied Dog from the porch rail and put him in the back seat of the Blazer, leaving the back windows down just enough that he could stick his head out the window as she drove back to Glens Crossing.

After she pulled into the lot at her office, she left the rear windows open a little so Dog wouldn't suffocate while she was inside.

"You behave yourself. No peeing, no digging, no chewing. Got it?"

Dog looked at her as if the mere suggestion that he'd do such a thing hurt his feelings. He sat down and turned his head away from her.

"No sense in getting all pissy about it. You

and I are in for a long haul; we'd better get off to the right start."

He continued to ignore her.

"Fine." She got out and closed the door.

The fax was several pages long, listing Brittany's e-mail address book and the first and last date they had been used, as well as the number of times total. She had no idea all of this information lay hidden in the recesses of a computer, but was infinitely glad someone had the skill to access it. At the end, there was a note from the computer guy that said he'd send a list of the content of her temporary files by the end of the day. From those Leigh could see where Brittany had been cruising on the web.

Leigh scanned the list and nothing of value came out of the first names and e-mail addresses at first glance. She needed to go over the list with someone close to Brittany to figure out if anyone was new in the past couple of months.

Since Dog was waiting in the car, she decided to go by home and drop him off, then go to Emma's to go over the fax.

When she got back to the Blazer, she realized Dog must have some rodent blood in him, because he'd managed to flatten his body and slip through the partially open window.

Well, of course, that just worked in nicely with the rest of her screwed-up life. No matter what was asked of her, she just didn't seem to be able to deliver. All Will wanted was Dog to be taken care of and she couldn't even keep track of the mutt. Some guardian she was.

She sighed. "I guess you've gotten along all right on your own before this week." She scanned the lawns and hedges as she pulled out on the highway, just in case the pooch remained nearby. Then she said, out the window, "Be careful, buddy."

She yearned to run away herself. Just pick up and go.

She imagined heading to the banks of the Ohio and just sitting there until she withered and died, an old woman in a young woman's clothes. Never again facing hard truths, never loving, never disappointing anyone again. There seemed a great appeal in that at the moment. Responsibility, passion, love, decisions, could all be damned.

So, why not? Why not just go and sit there on a rock until her ass grew roots?

She'd become embroiled in a mess that she could see no end to. Brian, her family, her rock, was losing his dream, branded by *her* choices. And Will, forever resigned to passionate memory. She didn't think she could ever move past what she felt for him. Deep in her heart, she knew there would never be another who touched her innermost soul as he did.

All she would ever have were the memories of those stolen moments with Will, when her inner self awakened. She'd reveled in his closeness, drank from the well of desire, and ridden on impossible hopes. And that was all gone.

To hell with New Leigh. Old Leigh was looking pretty good right now. But there was no getting her back. The only thing left was Hollow Leigh. And she didn't look forward to living the rest of her days with her.

But there was one thing about Hollow Leigh. She owed Brian. She owed Will. She owed her community. She had to face herself every day in the mirror. And there was only one way to do that. She had to find out what happened to Brittany.

Chapter 24

As Leigh drove through town, she saw Marshal Littlejohn's car parked on the square. What on earth was he still doing here? She swung around the block again, looking for a parking spot.

She found one near the Dew Drop and started to go in and ask if anyone had seen the marshal. Then she saw the yellow dog sniffing around in the side alley. A second chance to fulfill Will's request. She headed down the alley, slowly approaching the dog, talking softly, telling him that a good dog would give up and come along peacefully.

It tugged at her heart when she saw the stubby leash still attached to the collar Will had bought for him. They were more alike, Will and this dog, than she'd imagined. She could see it so clearly now. Both surviving on wits and ingenuity. Both forced to live a solitary life. Both finding a place to belong only to have it ripped from them. No wonder Will had such affection for the animal. Their relationship was based on mutual admiration. As she got closer, she could tell by the defiant gleam in his eye that he held no such admiration for her. She wasn't worthy of his trust.

Creeping along an inch at a time, she closed

the gap between them. She nearly got within arm's reach when he retreated, not quickly and not far, just enough to remain out of her grasp. She stopped. He stopped. She moved. He moved. She'd have sworn she saw "na-na-na-na-na" in his brown eyes.

"I'll bet if you had fingers, you'd be thumbing your little black nose at me right now, you little shit." She used a soft, sing-song cadence. She'd always heard dogs understood the inflection, not the words.

After several minutes of the same fruitless game they'd played at the cabin, Leigh gave up.

"Obviously, you're *not* a good dog." She used a disgusted tone, hoping the dog got her meaning, loud and clear. Then she headed back to her truck.

When she looked over her shoulder, the dog stood watching, as if he couldn't believe she'd given up so easily.

Leigh stopped in her tracks. It wasn't like her to give up. How could she let a dog, of all things, get the best of her?

She considered calling animal control to help catch him. But it seemed much too humiliating — for the dog. Will wouldn't like it. That wasn't at all what he intended when he'd asked her to look after his kindred spirit.

Well, if she couldn't catch the mutt, the least she could do for Will was track down that marshal and see what he was up to. She entered the Dew Drop. Sally was working the counter.

Leigh took a seat and ordered a cup of coffee that she didn't particularly want. When Sally sat it in front of her, Leigh asked, "Had any unfamiliar faces around here this afternoon?"

Sally put a hand on her hip and tipped her head to the side. "Funny you should ask. There was this skinny guy, long hair. Sat right where you are. Had one of them little tape recorders." She made a three-by-four rectangle with her thumbs and index fingers. "Said he worked for a magazine and was lookin' to write an article on the guy who'd saved that Mexican from the fire."

Definitely not Littlejohn. "What did you tell him?"

"That he'd probably be disappointed. That guy was trouble if I've ever seen it. No sense in trying to make a hero out of him. I told him flat out that that Scott guy probably kidnapped the Wilson girl — that's why he ran off."

The tone of the waitress's voice told Leigh that she'd be glad to serve as judge, jury and executioner if Will happened back into town.

"Did this magazine guy tell you his name or who he worked for?"

Sally shook her head. "I didn't like talking to him, even if he was a big magazine writer. He had funny eyes."

"Funny eyes?"

"Yeah" — she leaned her elbows on the counter — "all watery and, like, almost no color to them." She shivered. "Gave me the creeps."

"Did he say where he was headed from here?"

She shrugged. "I told him that Scott worked for Brownie."

Leigh took a sip of the coffee and laid a dollar on the counter. "Thanks, Sally." As she got to the door, Sally spoke again.

"Oh, yeah, there was one other guy, just a while ago. Black guy. Thought he might be a football player, but he was just one of those salesmen. Stopped 'cause this reminded him of the town where he grew up. Real nice fella."

"He ask any questions?"

"Nah. Well, yeah, but just the usual stuff: did I grow up here, is the town as quiet as it looks — stuff like that."

Littlejohn was so slick, Sally didn't even know she'd been pumped. Leigh had to admire skill like that. The question remained, why was he still here?

She went straight to Brownie's garage when she left the café. Brownie said the magazine writer had indeed been there, about an hour before.

"Say who he worked for?" Leigh asked.

Brownie scratched his head. "You know, don't think he did. Got the impression it was one of the big New York deals, though."

"What'd you tell him?"

"Told him that Will was a real good worker, pitched right in when we had the fire. And that he left a couple days ago."

"How'd he take the news of Will's departure?" By now she was beginning to suspect this was no writer, but the hit man from the cartel.

Brownie squinted, as if trying to recall. "Asked if I knew where he went. Other than that, he didn't react to much of nothin'. Kept real even-keel." He moved his hand through the air on a level plane to illustrate.

"Did he interview you about the fire and the ordeal with Beto and his kids?"

"Nope. Just said his thanks and headed off."

Definitely not an investigative writer.

"Drove or walked?"

"Walked."

"Which way?" Not that she had a chance in hell of running across him again.

"Back downtown."

"Call me if he happens by again, will you?"

"Sure enough. Too bad Will won't get written up in a magazine. Maybe that'd stop tongues from waggin' around here."

Leigh nodded and left. If only the people of this town knew the truth about Will, they'd hang their heads in shame. He wasn't one of the bad guys, just the opposite — and that very fact made it impossible for him to defend himself.

She returned to her car and drove around town, on the off-chance that she'd spot the skinny man. After cruising the square and surrounding blocks, Leigh gave up on finding either Littlejohn or the hit man and headed home.

It shook her deeply that the man whose job it was to put a bullet into Will's brain was creeping around her town. But she reassured herself that as long as he was snooping here, Will was safe somewhere else. She thanked God Will had disappeared so quickly. A little shiver ran down her spine, realizing the risk he'd taken to see her one last time. They'd been lucky. She only hoped Will's luck would hold out.

Chapter 25

It was late enough that Leigh decided to wait until the next morning to go see Emma. Since the dinner hour was upon them, she had no doubt Kurt would be there. She wanted to have the time alone with Emma to work with the fax. It would be a good way to ease into pressuring her for the truth.

When Leigh got home, the light on her answering machine was blinking. She pressed the play button and continued on to the kitchen. The first message brought her back to the desk.

When the machine clicked on, there was a long pause. Then Emma's voice came through the speaker. "Leigh, it's Emma . . . I have to hurry; Kurt's in the other room. I need to talk to you. He's —" The phone disconnected with a clatter.

Leigh had little time to wonder what Emma had to say, for the second message launched her into a fury. It had come in an hour after the first. "Sheriff Mitchell, this is County Commissioner Kessler. There's been an emergency meeting of the board called for tomorrow morning at nine-thirty. You are requested to be present. This is an informal meeting — the commissioners, the merit board and the party committee — you don't need to concern yourself with retaining an attorney."

"Attorney my ass!" she shouted as she swiped her hand across the desk, sending the recorder and a stack of bills to the floor. The recorder clattered off the baseboard and ended up replaying the messages again. She grabbed the cord and yanked it from the outlet. Still the voices continued. Damn that battery backup.

It didn't take long to put two and two together. Kurt had been a very busy man.

She spent several minutes circling the room in agitated motion.

How was she going to defend herself and still retain Will's hidden identity? She'd better come up with a way, because if it came to a choice between turning in her resignation and blowing Will's cover, there was no contest. Not after the details of his undercover operation he'd shared with her. Her ruined career weighed against the extreme sacrifices withstood to create a case against a drug cartel? Those scales weren't even close to balanced.

But she wasn't going to roll over. She would face the board, lay out the facts, and hope Kurt's influence hadn't already cast a predetermined outcome.

County sheriff was an elected position in Indiana. So, in reality, there wasn't much that could be done to unseat her — short of arrest by a court order. No way was that going to happen. She hadn't broken a single law — only pissed off the man with the most clout in this part of the state. Would the commissioners listen with an open mind and see there was no justification for Will's arrest? Or had their minds been influenced to the point that her dereliction of duty was a foregone conclusion?

Maybe she should have a talk with the prosecutor beforehand. Henderson County was so sparsely populated that it shared a prosecutor with a neighboring county. She'd only worked with Prosecutor Vandergast on three cases — there also wasn't much crime in Henderson County. He seemed to be a reasonable man, thorough in his job. She couldn't imagine him even requesting a warrant for Will on such circumstantial evidence. They hadn't even proven Brittany had been abducted, for Christ's sake.

Leigh felt like she was juggling balls of fire over a gasoline spill. There was no way to stop. And as long as she kept them moving, not resting in her hand for a prolonged period of time, she had a chance of not getting burned. It was a dangerous and delicate operation.

There was Brittany — whose true fate had not yet been confirmed.

Will — who had a U.S. marshal and a drug cartel hit man skulking about Glens Crossing. Both with equal determination to carry out their goal. He was a man who fate put in her path at her most vulnerable moment. A man she shouldn't care for, but now would willingly lay down her life for.

Kurt — a father crazed by worry for his child

with enough financial and political power to ruin her — and her brother by way of collateral damage.

Brian — who had dreams and political ambitions enough for both of them. Dreams now in danger of evaporating like fog with the rising sun.

Emma — who knew more than she was telling and probably could clear up this entire mess.

And out there somewhere, a yellow dog that she should be caring for, but was at this moment foraging his life on the streets alone.

Suddenly she was so tired, she couldn't hold together a coherent thought. If she was going to meet this head on in the morning, she'd better get some sleep — there had been precious little in the past week and it was beginning to take its toll.

She had to take things one at a time and not allow herself to be dragged down by the overwhelming day ahead.

First things first. A drink. Some crackers. Then bed.

Taking a wine glass out of the kitchen cabinet, she paused. There on the top shelf was a bottle of vodka she kept for Brian. Leigh rarely touched hard liquor herself, but tonight she'd make an exception. She needed to sleep. If she mixed it with orange juice, she could even justify it as being good for her. Vitamin C was very important in times of stress.

She took a sleeve of Club crackers and a short tumbler of vodka laced with orange juice and went onto the porch. She closed her eyes and concentrated on the crickets, who were just breaking into song. Breathing in air that had begun to speak of apples, pumpkins and frost-laced mornings, Leigh closed her eyes. Suddenly, the memory burst forth. There before her, as if she hadn't been separated from that night by over twenty years, was the frost-silvered field beside the railroad track. Briefly, she felt the same grip of panic that she had when she realized the front of the family car was gone.

Opening her eyes, she looked at the patch of sky visible between the trees. It was the same night sky, without the chill of winter. For a long time after the accident she'd been uneasy under a clear, starry sky. She'd actually been glad that Aunt Belinda insisted she go to bed right after supper until she was twelve. That way there was no chance of having to go outside and feel all of that empty space overhead, insidiously creeping under her skin, arousing a dreadful sense of vulnerability.

By the time Leigh reached high school, she'd overcome her aversion for the dark heavens, only giving in to it with the occasional nightmare.

Now, as she gazed at the pinpricks of stars, it struck her that the sky overhead was the only thing left for her and Will to share. That thing she'd at one time most dreaded was her only link to the man she loved.

She sipped her drink and prayed once again for Will's protection. It seemed so little to ask, for someone who had endured so much for such a noble cause.

The drink disappeared much more quickly than the crackers. As unaccustomed as she was to it, Leigh felt the effects quite heavily. It had only been dark for half an hour, but she slogged into her bedroom and threw off her clothes. Crawling into bed and closing her eyes, she felt her body humming slightly with the alcohol. She imagined herself in a black hole, a place void of light, air and warmth. As she floated there, untouched and unfettered, she decided she liked it.

It was a dangerous request. One he hated to make. But Will could see no way around it. The only other person he trusted was Brownie. And he would just be too obvious.

He called Rose from a pay phone.

"Hello?" her voice held a hint of unease. Whose wouldn't receiving a call in the dead of night?

"It's Will. I can't talk long, but I need a favor."

He was relieved when she didn't carry on, asking a thousand logical questions. She simply said, "Name it."

"There's going to be a meeting tomorrow at

the courthouse, nine o'clock."

She nearly snorted. "I know. Saw it on the news. What a bunch of malarkey!"

"I need you to be there. If things don't go well for Leigh, just come out the front door of the courthouse and walk to the Dew Drop."

"Will do. Now, answer one thing for me."

Shit, the questions. "Okay."

"You related to Salma Beeson?"

Will couldn't keep from smiling. The old girl was on the ball. He said, "Yes, ma'am," and then hung up.

Leigh awakened before dawn and ran three miles. When she got back home, the message light was blinking on her answering machine — which thankfully had survived her fit of temper last night. She nearly ignored it. With everything that was happening, it couldn't possibly be anything she wanted to hear.

But it might be Will.

She pushed the play button.

"Leigh." Brian's voice sounded strained. "If you're there, pick up." After a couple of seconds, he continued: "I . . . I just want you to know I tried to stop it — the meeting. Up against Kurt, I . . . Never mind. I hope you get this before you go."

The machine clicked off.

Brian didn't sound like himself. He sounded tired. But he wanted her to know he hadn't abandoned her. That gave her a warm sensation in the center of her chest. He might not be able to save her, but at least he wanted her to know he was on her side.

Blood was still thicker than politics, at least for Brian.

Leigh took what he offered and anchored herself to the strength of family. Then she showered and dressed in her full uniform, complete with standard issue firearm. Once her hair was tamed into a French braid, she was as ready as she'd ever be.

She didn't use the "Reserved for County Sheriff" parking spot next to the courthouse door. Today it just didn't feel right. Instead she parked in front of the Dew Drop.

She decided to soak up some of the acid churning in her stomach with a couple of pieces of toast. When she walked in, she was surprised to find Marshal Littlejohn there, dressed in an open collar and sport coat, sitting in a booth in the rear of the restaurant. He faced the front door. As she approached his table, he looked up.

"Sheriff." He nodded in greeting.

"Marshal. Mind if I join you?"

"That'd just make my morning." With a handsome smile, he motioned for her to take a seat.

The waitress arrived and Leigh ordered orange juice and toast. When she left, Leigh said, "I'm a little surprised to see you're still in town. I thought you were desperate to locate Mr. Scott."

He leaned back in the booth and slung one thick arm over the back of the seat. "I poked around elsewhere, but ended up back here. I just have a hunch he'll surface in your town again." He looked at her from under dark brows. "I understand he has a special interest 'round here."

Leigh cocked her head and tried to look confused. "How so?"

Littlejohn leaned forward and put his elbows on the table. "Now, Sheriff" — he lowered his voice until Leigh had to lean closer to hear — "I think you know very well what I'm talking about. Everyone in town knows. And I can see it in your eyes — Scott is no passing stranger. With all of this going on with your hearing, he'll show. I'd bet my life on it."

"Marshal." Leigh's voice cracked and she cleared her throat and began again. She leaned over the table toward him, until they were nearly nose to nose. Two could play this game. "You're very much mistaken. Scott is gone. He won't be back — for me or any other reason. You're wasting your time."

Mildred returned with the coffee and toast. Littlejohn and Leigh stopped hovering over the table and settled back in their seats.

"Be anything else?" the woman asked, with a curious glance toward the marshal.

Leigh dredged up a smile. "No, thanks, Mildred."

Tennis shoes squeaked on linoleum as the

waitress reluctantly headed back to the kitchen.

Littlejohn smiled. "I suppose it's my time to waste. I'm sticking with my plan. I need that man."

"Care to elaborate on that a bit? What's so important about this guy?" She certainly couldn't *not* press for an answer. It was logical for a sheriff who *didn't* know what was going on with Will.

"Nothin' I'd like better than to fill you in, but it's out of my hands. I just follow orders."

Tired of playing cat and mouse, Leigh picked up a slice of toast and slid out of the booth. "Suit yourself." She started to walk away, then called over her shoulder, "Thanks for the breakfast."

Out of the corner of her eye, she caught Littlejohn's broad grin as he lifted his coffee cup to her and she was sorry she hadn't stuck him with a bigger bill.

When Leigh entered the council meeting room, she was stunned by the crowd. Even in the corridor she'd had to thread through a small group of reporters, fronted, of course by Hale Grant. Due to limited space, there had been a lottery for the single media seat. Thankfully, Grant didn't win it. She wasn't going to name names in this meeting, but there was still the slim possibility that Grant was involved with Brittany's disappearance.

As she moved to her seat at a table facing the

council panel, she was surprised to see Emma seated right behind her, not with her ex-husband across the aisle. Next to Emma, she was even more surprised to see Brian. Well, not surprised exactly. In normal circumstances she would expect him to be by her side. But considering the fall of recent events and their last parting, she hadn't been counting on it — even after this morning's message. His presence gave her a measure of comfort. And yet, she knew, this she had to do on her own.

He smiled at her as she passed and she nodded her appreciation in return.

The council was swift and direct in their questions, which were obviously carefully orchestrated by Kurt Wilson. Leigh answered honestly, explaining in detail the difference between circumstantial, inadmissible and useful evidence. Very quickly she saw there could be only one outcome. They were going to request her resignation.

She knew she wasn't required to give it. She could ignore the request and go about her business. But the council held the purse strings and her department would suffer, which in the end meant the community suffered. Also, if the party chose to make an issue, Brian could lose all backing. Better she go quietly and disappear from the picture.

Well, if she was going down, she was going to do it with dignity. She didn't rise to the bait of cheap shots and nasty remarks. With great determination, she remained unflustered and unoffended — at least on the surface.

The council thanked her for her time and patience and asked for thirty minutes for discussion. Leigh rose and left the room with her head held high. She, as well as every other living and breathing soul in that room, knew it was only a pretense — the charade of unbiased consideration.

Sitting in the back, near the door, was Aunt Rose. Leigh wondered what brought the woman here, curiosity or support? When Rose locked gazes with her and smiled, Leigh had her answer. At least there were a few people left in Glens Crossing who weren't ready to stone her.

Leigh went straight to the ladies' room in the basement of the courthouse and splashed cold water on her face. The roiling acid in her stomach inched up her throat. She couldn't really believe it had come down to this. Her life was about to take a ninety-degree turn at a hundred miles an hour. She could smell the smoke of burning rubber, feel the shudder of the steering wheel in her hands, hear the scream of tires against asphalt, but she refused to close her eyes. She would keep them wide open and her hands on the wheel until she came to a rocking halt — where that would be, she had no idea.

She looked at her dripping face in the mirror. "Well, at least you won't have to wear this ugly uniform ever again."

She'd meant to reassure herself, but the opposite occurred. A sense of defeat and loss settled more heavily on her shoulders. She reminded herself that this sacrifice wasn't without payoff — at least as long as Will managed to get a conviction with his testimony against the drug cartel.

Grabbing a paper towel, Leigh dabbed her face dry. When she looked in the mirror again, she saw Emma standing directly behind her.

She turned. "Emma." She decided not to say more. There was obviously a reason the woman had followed her down here. The less Leigh pried, the more she hoped came tumbling out. There was something about a guilty conscience that loosened a tongue faced with silence.

Emma's gaze cut away; her nervous fingers played with the strap on her purse. Leigh stood like a stone and waited.

After a moment, Emma said, very quietly, "I need your help."

Leigh decided the cold treatment would bring forth more than warm fuzzies. "I'm sorry Emma, but I'm not in the position to be much help to anyone at the moment."

Emma shifted her weight from foot to foot. "Maybe I can help you, too."

When Leigh just looked at her, Emma went on. "It wasn't supposed to be like this . . . those men, they're going to try to fire you . . . Kurt's called the FBI."

"I know." Leigh didn't bother to explain

those men couldn't *fire* her.

"Leigh, you know I never wanted to cause you trouble. I just don't know what to do. . . ."

"Maybe you'd better tell me what's going on."

"I don't want Kurt to hate me . . . I really didn't know — until Wednesday."

"Brittany's okay."

Emma turned surprised eyes in Leigh's direction. "How did you know?"

"I already told you, I think she left of her own free will."

"It's just . . . well, it didn't seem to hurt to keep it to myself. Kurt was so . . . I thought if we spent more time together, we could . . ."

"Where is she, Emma?"

"Florida. She ran off with an associate professor from IU. She wanted her dad to pay for what he did to us — that's why she . . ."

"Made it look like she'd been kidnapped," Leigh finished for her.

Emma nodded.

Associate professor from IU? Leigh had to admit she was a little disappointed that Hale Grant wasn't involved. She quickly sifted through the snippets of information she had gathered over the past days. One simple, unremarkable statement, shifted to the surface. Brittany's social studies teacher said her attitude and grades had improved — and yet her other teachers hadn't seen a change.

Leigh asked, "How did she meet him?"

"He came to school as a guest speaker." She ran a shaky hand through her hair. "You have to help me make Kurt understand. Maybe I could say I just heard from her this morning."

Leigh was torn between wanting to wrap the poor woman in a hug and slapping her silly for being so foolish. But, she had to admit, love did make you foolish sometimes. Look how Will risked seeing her once more.

"And how are you going to explain sitting through that meeting and not saying anything?"

Emma's eyes brightened. "I could say she called my cell phone — just now!" She looked like a woman who'd just found her way out of a dark and cavernous tunnel.

Would it matter? In the end the facts would remain the same. Leigh had been right in her investigation. Will was innocent. Brittany was safe. Kurt could no longer hold Brian in any way responsible. It only pissed her off that slimy little bastard Hale Grant would have a front page story. Of course, his story would be so much more sensationalistic if he had the whole truth.

"All right. Let's go back upstairs and crash their little 'discussion.' "

Will watched from the utility truck he'd borrowed from Brownie's garage. Seconds seemed to be dripping by at the speed of motor oil on a sub-zero day. Even the air felt thick as he sat in his hard hat and coveralls. It was eleven o'clock. Leigh had been in front of that panel for an hour and a half. This couldn't be good.

There were several people milling about the courthouse steps and lawn. Some reporters, some curious townsfolk who couldn't squeeze into the cramped meeting room. Will kept his eye fastened on the door. Several times it had opened, but much to his relief, Rose had not appeared.

Then, at quarter past eleven, she came though the door. She walked straight down the steps, not talking to any of the people gathered there, and turned toward the Dew Drop.

He watched until she traveled the block and a half to the café, silently hoping the woman would walk on by and head to the garage. But she opened the door and entered.

Damn. Damn. Damn.

He felt the past three years turn into sand and fall uncontrollably through his fingers. He started to get out of the truck, half-hoping that U.S. marshal was still around somewhere. He guessed protective custody held better odds than sitting in a Podunk county jail waiting for the hit squad to arrive.

He just couldn't believe it boiled down to this. He recalled standing at that dark intersection, deciding whether or not to come to Glens Crossing. He could have easily made the opposite choice.

Even the way things were, he was glad to his core that he hadn't.

★ ★ ★

The meeting ended quickly, with everyone so embarrassed they closed up their notebooks and fled the room nearly faster than Leigh. She left Brian talking to Kurt in the hall outside the council room.

She stepped out of the courthouse door, glad to be exonerated, yet deeply unsettled. She'd been ready to chuck this town and everyone in it and start over. A part of her was sorry that wasn't going to be happening. Without Will, everything just seemed too dull to imagine.

As she started down the steps, she caught sight of Marshal Littlejohn on the sidewalk across the street. For an instant their gazes locked and he grinned at her. A cold, knowing grin that made the hairs stand up on her arms. Suddenly she felt like a moth caught in a spider's web.

Then, as she reached the bottom of the concrete steps, the little knot of press people moved in on her and she lost sight of anything beyond them. Thank God Will was away from here. The questions that had been formulating for hours came at a rapid rate. Leigh found herself hard pressed to keep up with them.

A man in a light blue utility coverall pushed through the people around Leigh. He was directly in front of her before she realized it was Will. She felt like she'd been punched squarely in the chest. If Littlejohn was here, the hit man might be too. Leigh's stomach felt like she'd swallowed a bunch of grasshoppers.

She grabbed onto his arm and moved away from the reporters.

"You shouldn't be here," she hissed to him, fighting the urge to just throw her arms around him. "The marsha—"

The yellow dog bounded across the court-house lawn, knocking Leigh backward and hit-ting Will square in the chest with his forepaws.

A sharp crack came from near the street.

The dog yelped. Will spun and fell to the ground, face-down.

Leigh drew her gun. Her frantic gaze jerked toward the sound of the shot.

Squeals and shrieks erupted all around her, a flurry of movement as people took cover.

Another shot ripped through the chaos. Leigh crouched, swept her gaze and her gun over the crowd, now laying belly down on the ground.

Near the street curb, Marshal Littlejohn lay sprawled on his back, a bleeding hole in his chest. His semi-automatic lay on the sidewalk five feet from his hand.

The sounds around her bled into one wild mix — the whimpering dog, screams and cries from people on the ground, shouts from inside the courthouse, her own hammering heart, making it impossible for her to use her ears to locate the hit man. She swung from side to side, gun gripped at ready in front of her.

Then the impossible happened. The hit man

stepped from behind a utility truck parked across the street, empty hands held high.

Leigh straightened, keeping her gun aimed at his heart. The noise in her mind had become a chant: "He killed Will . . . killed Will . . . killed Will . . ."

Her hands trembled slightly. Sweat trickled down her body. Her finger flexed over the trigger.

Through her red fog of rage, she realized the man was still walking toward her.

"Stop! Stop right where you are!"

He stopped and held his hands higher. "U.S. Marshal David Dobbs."

"Bullshit!"

"My badge is in my hip pocket."

Leigh fought the compulsion to shoot him. *He killed the marshal. He killed Will. Oh, God, Will's dead. . . .*

Tears blurred her vision. She blinked them away.

She shouted, "Where's your weapon?"

Deep inside she wanted him to make a move, one single move toward that weapon.

Then he did.

Her grip tightened on the trigger.

A hand grabbed her ankle. "No! Leigh, no . . ." Will's voice seared across her brain. For a millisecond she couldn't decide if it came from inside her head or out. "He — is — a marsh . . ."

Chapter 26

It had only taken seconds for Leigh to figure out that she'd been duped. The grin Littlejohn had given her as she descended the steps had instantly taken on clear meaning.

Leigh sat next to Will, holding pressure on his shoulder. There was a clear entrance and exit hole in his sleeve. The bullet had passed through the fabric, piercing Will's flesh, and then hit the dog.

Will ignored his injury, leaning close to Dog's face, urging him to hang on. Sticky blood matted the golden fur on the animal's side. Dog panted in shallow, rapid breaths. Will slipped his hand underneath, feeling for blood on the animal's underside and withdrew a dry hand.

The paramedics arrived, pronouncing Littlejohn dead and moving on to Will. He refused to let them look at his arm until they'd worked on Dog. When he made the demand, they looked to Leigh for help. She didn't like the large amount of blood spreading on Will's sleeve or the paleness of his lips. She suspected his injury was much more grave than it appeared. And it was plain, as long as he held consciousness, he wasn't going to the hospital until Dog was taken care of.

"Do it."

They didn't move in that direction. "Ma'am, we don't treat animals."

A second medical unit rolled up, siren blaring.

"You take the dog. These guys can get Will."

"Our supervisor —"

"I'll take care of your supervisor. Now get this dog to the goddamn vet before I put a bullet in one of you!"

They started moving. From the looks on their faces, they didn't like it one bit.

As they loaded Dog onto the gurney, Leigh called, "That dog is a Henderson County deputy. I want him treated accordingly."

One of the men started to say something, then closed his mouth and nodded. Smart man.

The sleeve of Will's coveralls was darkened with blood all the way to the wrist and a small puddle was forming on the ground. Leigh called for the second medical crew to hurry.

The paramedics crouched beside Will on the ground.

David Dobbs walked up behind Will and spoke to the medics. "Bandage him up and we'll get him in my car."

"You can't be serious! He needs to go to the hospital." Leigh couldn't help sounding like a hysterical mother.

"How safe do you think he'll be in a hospital? Media's been hot for this town for days now. How long do you think it'll take another hit man to follow up once this makes the airways?" He jerked his chin in the direction of Littlejohn's body. "How do you think that guy found him?"

"How did *you* find him?" Leigh asked.

"You told me he was here."

"*I* did?"

"The fingerprints you sent all over the place."

"Oh." She guessed it was a good thing, but the way he said it made her feel like a bumbling fool.

"By the way," he added, "there'll be a crew coming by to debug your house and phone."

Leigh's mouth fell open.

"It wasn't me. Littlejohn had already done the work when I got here."

"That's his real name?" She focused on the facts to keep her skin from crawling at the thought of someone creeping around in her house planting bugs to listen to her every move.

"Yep. Proud man. Arrogant. He never thought we'd catch him."

That's what made him so good, Leigh thought. *That confidence.*

She narrowed her eyes and asked, "You knew Will was gone. What made you think he'd come back?"

"After I got a whiff of what was going on between the two of you, I knew he wouldn't let you weather this storm alone. It's not in him to

466

abandon something just because it's for his own good."

Will groaned. "Shut up, Dobbs."

The medics secured the gauze bandage on Will's arm. Getting to his feet, he wobbled a little unsteadily for a moment. Leigh reached out and supported his good arm.

Once balanced, he nodded to Dobbs, who moved a few feet away. He put his right hand on her cheek and drove a stake into her heart with those blue eyes. "I have to go."

The lump in her throat prevented her words from leaving her body. She wanted to tell him to hurry. She wanted to warn him to stay safe, to beg him to return, to tell him she loved him. But it all remained bottled up inside her chest. All she could do was blink back the tears welling in her eyes.

Wrapping his hand around the back of her neck, he pulled her against him and put a kiss on her forehead. His lips felt cool, sending fear slicing into her heart. Against her ear he said, "God, I wish things could be different."

"I feel so cheated." The words came out in no more than a high, breathy squeak.

"We were, Leigh. We were."

Then he kissed her — a kiss of everlasting farewell.

A wild mix of emotions rioted in Leigh's soul, making her clutch him to her heart. Relief that he was alive. Fury at the cruelties of fate. A hint of the passions they'd shared. An unbelievable lightness born of loving someone more than your very life. Heart-wrenching pain over what had been lost. She knew there would forever be a void deep in her soul. He would take the best of her with him and would not be here to fill the space with his love.

As he released her from the kiss, his gaze firmly held hers, burning the image of those intense blue eyes into her memory for eternity. Abruptly, he let her go and walked away without another word.

Her own arm was bathed in his blood and she felt more adrift than she ever imagined possible. Even standing on the courthouse square in the town where she'd grown up. For the first time in her life, she felt like she didn't belong. And maybe she didn't. Not anymore. She'd wanted change and she'd sure as hell gotten it.

Nothing would ever be the same again.

Epilogue

Thunder rumbled in the distance. Leigh paused in her packing, tilting her head to the side, listening to the bass tone roll over the top of her house. Maybe this time it wasn't an empty promise. Maybe today it would rain. She'd always liked rainy days, especially when she could spend them in this cozy bungalow.

This would be her last chance to hear the restful patter of drops on her roof, her last night in her home. She wasn't sure where she was going, but she knew she couldn't spend the holidays here in Glens Crossing, and Thanksgiving was just two days away. Her things were headed to storage while she interviewed for jobs. She was going for a much larger venue for her future. No more living where everyone knew when you purchased new underwear.

Brian hadn't liked it, had fought her at first. But in the end, she'd convinced him that she needed to grow up, face challenges of her own choosing by herself. It was time to go her own way, time to forge her own agenda and let Brian tend his. Leigh just didn't have the stomach to forge ahead in politics; she was law enforcement and always would be. Brian was beginning to see that.

He came up from the basement with a box and set it beside the front door. Brushing off his hands, he said, "That's the last of the basement junk. I'm really impressed, Sis; you don't keep a lot of crap."

"Thanks — I think."

"Are you sure you don't want me to help with the rest of the house?"

"I really need to do it myself. I have to decide what goes into storage and what goes with me."

He stopped in front of her. "I still can't believe it's come to this. If I promise to keep my nose out of your business, will you stay?"

She laughed and waved a finger in the air at him. They'd had this same conversation at least a dozen times in the past month. Brian respected her decision, even if he couldn't understand it completely. But this was a painful process for both of them. They were closing a long chapter in their lives. He'd apologized for pushing her in a direction she apparently didn't want to go. And she'd told him never to apologize for caring too much.

Of course, they would always support one another. But now they were on different paths. No more Mitchell family political dynasty.

"Okay, I won't ask again." He kissed her forehead. "Call me tomorrow." He headed to the front door.

"Thanks again."

He waved over his shoulder as he left.

Leigh stretched the kinks out of her shoulders and looked at the big stuffed dog sitting on the rocker in her living room, sizing him up for a box. His plastic eyes seemed to beg for a reprieve. She laid a hand on his head and the rush of affection she felt for the furry toy took her by surprise.

"Okay, you win. Where I go, you go." In her mind's eye she saw the comical sight of Leigh Mitchell, ex-county sheriff, driving out of town having an animated conversation with this huge stuffed animal strapped next to her in the front seat. Wouldn't that have tongues wagging.

A knock on the door startled her. Her heart sped up, as it did each time the phone rang or knuckles rapped on her door. She hadn't been able to completely stamp out the hope that Will would somehow return to her. She held that hope close in the long dark hours of the night, knowing she was a fool.

Pushing that ridiculous anticipation away, she opened the door. She couldn't mask her surprise at seeing Hale Grant on her front porch, oversized corduroy jacket drooping on his shoulders.

He looked uncomfortable. "Can I come in?"

She shook off her astonishment and stepped aside, opening the door wider.

He looked around at the stacks of boxes, then back to her. "I've come to ask you to reconsider."

Leigh felt like she was just about a half-step behind in this conversation. "Reconsider?"

"Staying on as sheriff."

She arched a brow and crossed her arms. "Now that surprises me, coming from you."

His spine stiffened. "Hey, I was just doing my job."

She didn't respond, just stared at him and thought how young and idealistic he still was.

He squirmed uncomfortably for a minute then said, "Well, will you stay?"

Leigh sighed. "No. My resignation is final. Steve Clyde will serve as acting sheriff until the new election. He's ready. I'm leaving." She caught herself before she explained in detail why it was impossible for her to stay in Glens Crossing. Stopped before she told him this place held more bad memories than good. Before she spilled the ugly truth about her childhood. Before she broke down and said how she couldn't look at the lights of another carnival on the Henderson County fairgrounds. Those reasons were hers alone.

"I feel responsible." He said it very quietly and Leigh knew the cost of those words.

"Don't."

He stuck his hands in his pockets and nodded as he backed toward the door. "Good luck, Sheriff."

"Thanks."

Leigh stood at the door and watched him get into his Honda and back down the driveway. He hadn't apologized, exactly. But she'd bet her life that was as close as Hale Grant had come to saying "I'm sorry" in a very long time. After his car disappeared onto the road, she closed the door and returned to her boxes.

As she packed the going-away gifts from the people in her department, the sky darkened enough that she had to turn on the lamps in the living room. While taping a box closed she heard a fat raindrop tap against the window, followed by another, then another.

She stepped onto the front porch as the tapping became a steady rustle. Dark blotches marked her concrete front steps. Then the skies let loose and the rain poured like a waterfall.

The ground was so hardened by drought that puddles formed quickly. Leigh happily watched those puddles gather rain.

A pair of headlights swung onto her drive. She looked up, but didn't recognize the mean-looking black Firebird that pulled to a stop. The rain made it impossible to see who sat on the other side of the windshield. Moving to the top of the steps, she waited while the driver's door opened.

Will got out and stood beside the car in the pouring rain. His hair quickly became plastered to his head, his chambray shirt sticking to his chest.

"Oh, my God!" Leigh jumped over the steps, landing on the lawn in a single leap. In two more strides, she reached him, knocking him backward against the car door as she flew into his open arms.

He held her tightly, burying his face in the side of her neck. Then he pulled back enough to kiss her.

She broke off and stepped backward, out of his embrace, pulling on his arm. "Let's get out of this rain."

He tugged her back against his chest. He closed his eyes and raised his face to the falling rain. "Isn't this what you've been waiting for? Enjoy it. Feel it."

Will's hands cradled the back of her head. Tilting her face to the sky, she let the water sluice across her cheeks, felt it trickle down her throat and under her shirt. Penetrating her skin. Rinsing clean her very soul.

After a few minutes she shivered. He braced his hands against the small of her back. "Guess we'd better go inside before you freeze. Maybe I can warm you up."

"No doubt." She took his hand and led him into the house.

He came to an abrupt halt just inside the door. "What's this? You're leaving?"

She turned to face him and heard water droplets hit the floor at her feet. "I resigned. It just seemed the right time to go."

"Go where?" A deep line creased his brow.

"I don't know yet. I'm still looking for a job."

"In law?"

"Can't imagine doing anything else. I'm thinking of a federal agency. Something big — impersonal."

"Oh, Leigh" — he shook his head slightly and pulled her into his embrace — "it's never impersonal. It always hits you in the gut, no matter if you know the people involved or not."

She laid her cheek against his soaked shirt. "I didn't think I'd ever see you again. The coverage of the trial was so sketchy. Are you . . . ?"

She felt his chest expand with a deep breath. "That particular cartel is history. No one left who cares enough to come after me."

The lead weight she'd been carrying in her chest for the past weeks lifted a little. "Thank God. Now what?"

He moved her an arm's length away and pushed the wet hair from her face. His gaze softened and warmed. Tenderness poured over Leigh like warm honey.

After looking into her eyes for a long moment he said, "Once, a long time ago, I got stuck on a Ferris wheel. And, there in front of me was a little girl with a curly ponytail who beat back her own fear to comfort another."

Leigh drew in a breath to say something, but he put his finger against her lips.

"Just weeks ago," he said, "I saw that girl face down the same fears again, only this time she had a choice. Courage like that is hard to find.

"Leigh, I'll remember those moments the rest of my life. There's no way I'm going to let that girl get away."

She held his gaze. Could it be true? Had she been that close to the man who changed her life forever and not known it? She felt so connected to him now, it seemed impossible for her to have passed so closely and not felt something, some shimmer of energy, some awareness, some tingling of her sixth sense.

Unable to corral the words to express what she felt, she simply said, "I'll be damned."

Will leaned close, cradled her face in his hands and kissed her forehead.

There was certainly electricity flowing now — enough to power all of Henderson County. She had thought she'd never be this close to him again, had steeled herself against hoping, against wanting. Now she could face it. She loved him more than she could ever imagine, would choose his love over all else in this world. That realization hit her hard, making her knees go all wobbly.

He whispered against her hair, "I think you're missing my point."

She fought the urge to collapse against him, to allow herself to be absorbed completely into him. She didn't want to talk, she wanted to touch. "And that point is?"

"I've left the DEA. I'm looking for a new life. Will you help me?"

"What, specifically, do you want me to do?" She took his hand from her face and twined her fingers with his, their hands palm to palm. Then she kissed the knuckles of his left hand, her eyes flirting mischievously with his. She'd get him to stop yapping and touch her

— one way or another.

"I want you to be my wife. I want you to marry me."

"Marry you?" She stopped teasing his fingers with her tongue and let go of his hands.

"Isn't that traditionally what people do when they're in love?"

"Well, I guess . . . sometimes. I just never thought . . ." She stepped slightly away from him. She was about to plunge into dangerous waters. Marry him? As much as *she* wanted to wake up beside him every morning, kiss him goodnight every night, she couldn't imagine him living a life of convention and routine. Her heart said grab him — grab him now, before he realizes what he's said. But her good sense put on the brakes. He'd suffered so much, for so long, she didn't want to do something that in the long run would add to his unhappiness.

"Never thought what?" he said.

Her cheeks warmed. "I never thought of you as the marrying kind. I'm afraid the monotony might be too much for a man accustomed to as much excitement as you."

Jerking her to him once again, he kissed her. All of the pent-up passion she'd felt in him during their first encounter on the dance floor exploded once again. The kiss was an act of possession, hot, forceful. When he let her go he was smiling. "Do you actually think that'll get boring?"

Leigh's fingertips went to her lips. She felt

like she'd been branded. And in a way, she guessed she had. "Not in this lifetime."

He reached for her again, but she took a step back. "Not so fast. There's more to a marriage than sex. How do I know next time you get yourself into something dangerous, you won't shut me out again?"

"I told you, I quit the DEA."

"And you're not going to do police work of any kind for the rest of your life?"

"Well, I didn't say that."

"If I say yes, it's yes to everything. None of this withholding for my own protection crap. I want to be a partner in every way, not just for the good stuff."

She could see his mind working. Will Scott wasn't a man to make promises he couldn't keep. She waited. Then it occurred to her there was a question she hadn't yet asked. "*Is* your name Will Scott?"

He grinned and looked good enough to eat with a spoon, with his hair wet and hanging to his shoulders. "It is now." He took her hand. "I know you don't know much about me — my past. But I do think you know we're good together. I want to make it permanent."

"You've dodged my condition."

He blew out a long breath. "It'll be hard. Some things just need to be . . . I'm so used . . ."

She put a hand on his cheek and felt the slight rasp of late afternoon beard. "I know. But if you love me, you have to trust me." She paused and looked into his eyes. "Like I trust you."

"How can I argue with that? You trusted me when I gave you no reason to." He pushed his hair back from his face with one swipe of his hand. "All right. All the way, everything in my life will be yours. Now I have a condition."

"What?" She held her breath.

"Tomorrow. Marry me tomorrow."

"Will! The movers are coming tomorrow. I can't —"

"It's the perfect time. Then we'll go job and house hunting."

"I don't know . . ."

He silenced her with a kiss. As he tugged her wet sweatshirt over her head, he inched her toward the bedroom. His mouth was on hers the instant the shirt passed her lips.

"Tell me yes," he whispered against her mouth.

"I can —"

His tongue darted against hers and his hands slid down to lift her hips against him. Again, he released her mouth just enough to speak. "Tell me yes."

Leigh groaned as she backed up against the closed bedroom door.

A long whine came from behind the door. Will jerked Leigh behind him in one fluid motion and held her there.

"Is someone in there?" he asked in a hushed tone.

"Open the door and see."

Carefully, as if there might be legions from hell behind the door, Will opened it a crack, then fully.

Dog was sprawled across the full width of the bed. His head came up and his tail beat a rhythm against the comforter when he saw Will.

"Hey! He's okay." Will fell to his knees beside the bed and accepted the doggie kisses lavished upon him. "Not much of a watchdog. Jesus, I can't believe he didn't know I was here before now."

"It's the drugs. The vet has me keeping him 'calm.' I'd call it just short of comatose. Had to dose him again; for some reason he was getting absolutely frantic while I was packing."

"I know why." He rubbed the dog's head vigorously. "He didn't want you to leave before I got back. Right boy?"

The heavy lids blinked once, twice, then stayed closed.

Leigh knelt beside Will, damp skin prickled with goosebumps.

He put a hand on her shoulder. "I promised I'd warm you up."

His simple touch had a profound effect; she was warmer already.

"Does he have a doggie bed to go to?"

"He's been sleeping with me."

Will kissed her, leaning her back onto the carpet. "Guess we'll have to make do." He kissed her again. "Say yes."

Leigh's senses were becoming fogged as his fingers worked to unfasten her bra. "Yes."

"Tomorrow," he said against her mouth. "Tomorrow."

"After the wedding, we'll buy a doggie bed."

Leigh chuckled thinking of the standoff that was just around the corner. Dog thought that *was* his bed. And here they were, making love on the floor like a couple of teenagers with no place else to do it.

Will raised up on one elbow. "What's funny?"

"Be quiet and warm me up."

About the Author

In her first career, Susan Crandall was a dental hygienist. However, her love of reading soon expanded to a love for writing, so she left her gentle tools of torture behind and began to pen novels. After spending several years in the big city (Chicago), she returned to the Indiana town where she grew up. There, she and her husband are raising their two children and an eighty-pound "labsky" (half-black lab, half-husky).

Susan loves to hear from her readers. Write to: P.O. Box 1092, Noblesville, IN 46060. Or visit her Web site at: www.SusanCrandall.net.

The employees of Thorndike Press hope you have enjoyed this Large Print book. All our Thorndike and Wheeler Large Print titles are designed for easy reading, and all our books are made to last. Other Thorndike Press Large Print books are available at your library, through selected bookstores, or directly from us.

For information about titles, please call:

(800) 223-1244

or visit our Web site at:

www.gale.com/thorndike
www.gale.com/wheeler

To share your comments, please write:

Publisher
Thorndike Press
295 Kennedy Memorial Drive
Waterville, ME   04901